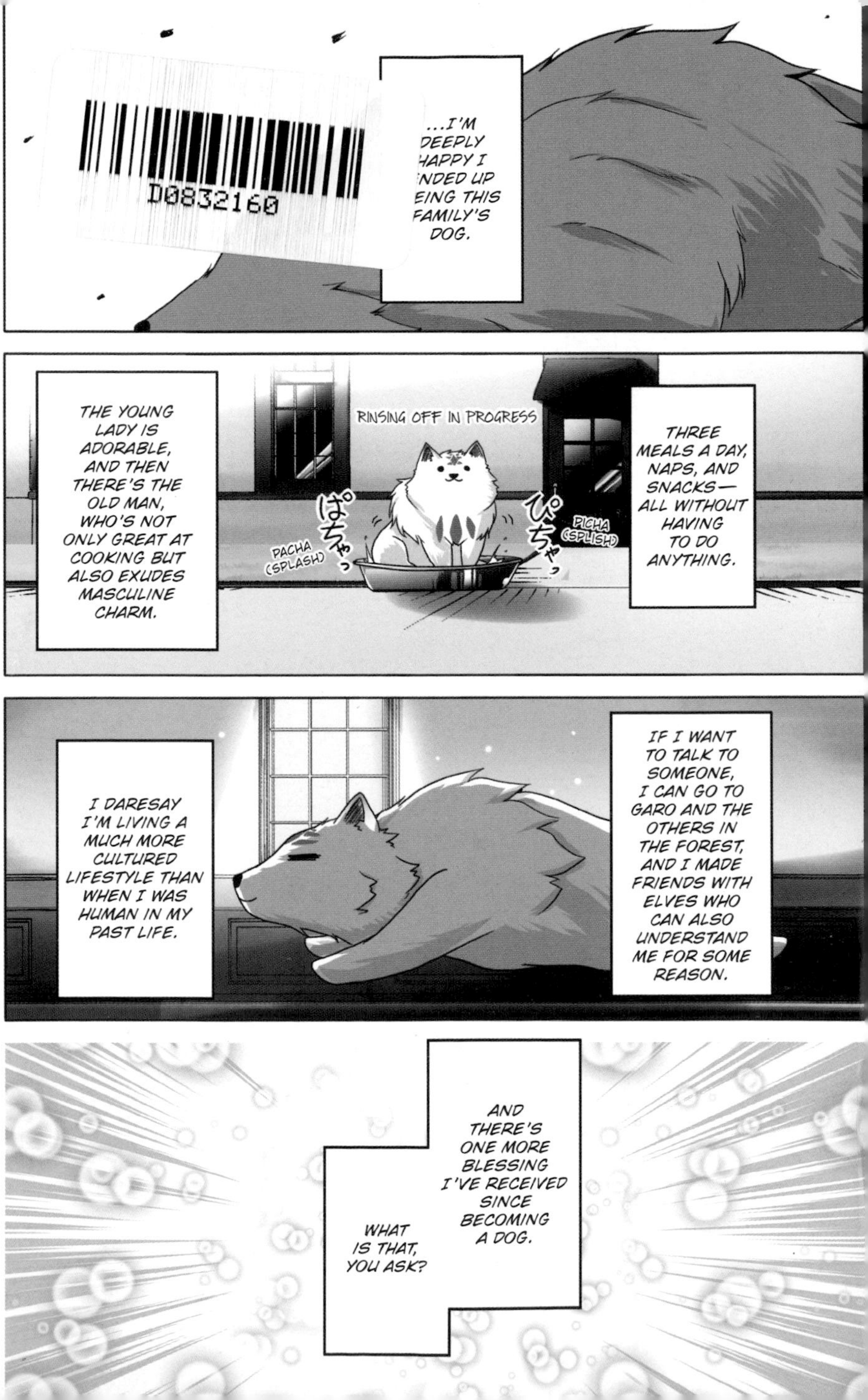
...I'M DEEPLY HAPPY I ENDED UP BEING THIS FAMILY'S DOG.
THREE MEALS A DAY, NAPS, AND SNACKS— ALL WITHOUT HAVING TO DO ANYTHING.
RINSING OFF IN PROGRESS
ぴちゃっ
PICHA (SPLISH)
ぱちゃっ
PACHA (SPLASH)
THE YOUNG LADY IS ADORABLE, AND THEN THERE'S THE OLD MAN, WHO'S NOT ONLY GREAT AT COOKING BUT ALSO EXUDES MASCULINE CHARM.
IF I WANT TO TALK TO SOMEONE, I CAN GO TO GARO AND THE OTHERS IN THE FOREST, AND I MADE FRIENDS WITH ELVES WHO CAN ALSO UNDERSTAND ME FOR SOME REASON.
I DARESAY I'M LIVING A MUCH MORE CULTURED LIFESTYLE THAN WHEN I WAS HUMAN IN MY PAST LIFE.
AND THERE'S ONE MORE BLESSING I'VE RECEIVED SINCE BECOMING A DOG.
WHAT IS THAT, YOU ASK?

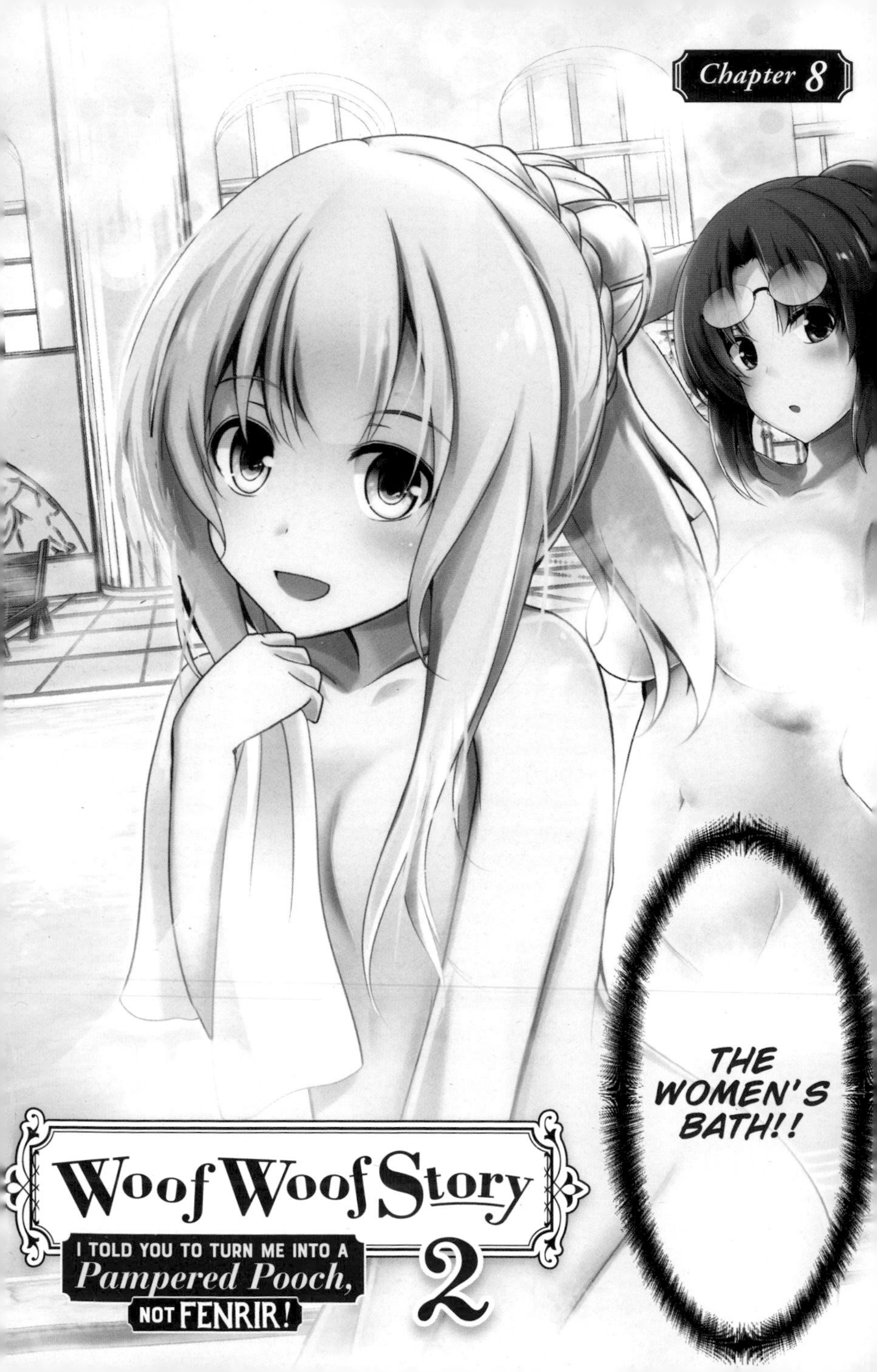
Chapter 8
THE WOMEN'S BATH!!
Woof Woof Story
I TOLD YOU TO TURN ME INTO A Pampered Pooch, NOT FENRIR!
2

ART: **Koikuchi Kiki**

ORIGINAL STORY: **Inumajin**

CHARACTER DESIGN: **Kochimo**

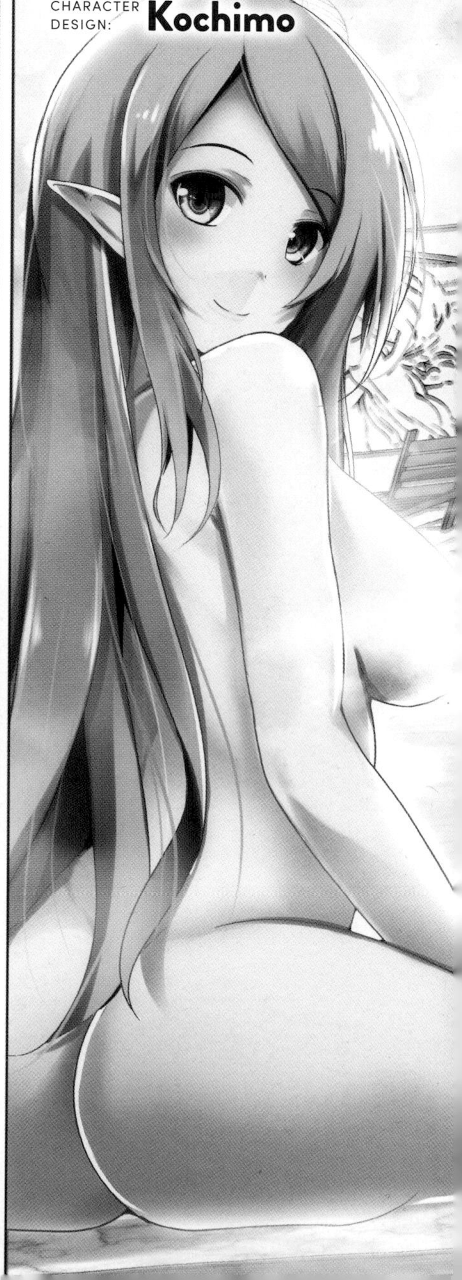

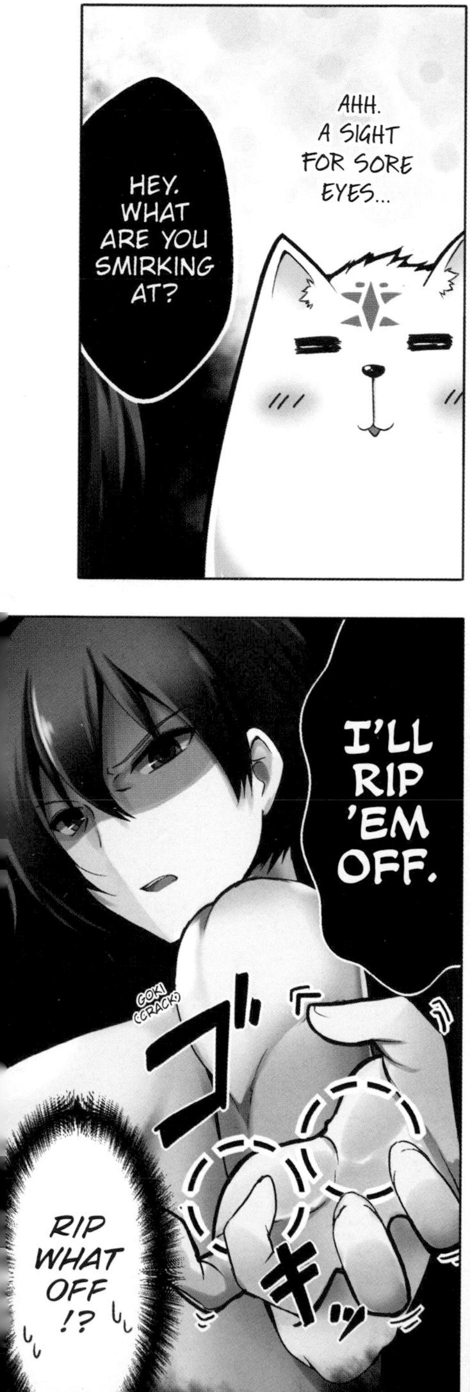
AHH. A SIGHT FOR SORE EYES...
HEY. WHAT ARE YOU SMIRKING AT?
I'LL RIP 'EM OFF.
GOKI (CRACK)
RIP WHAT OFF!?

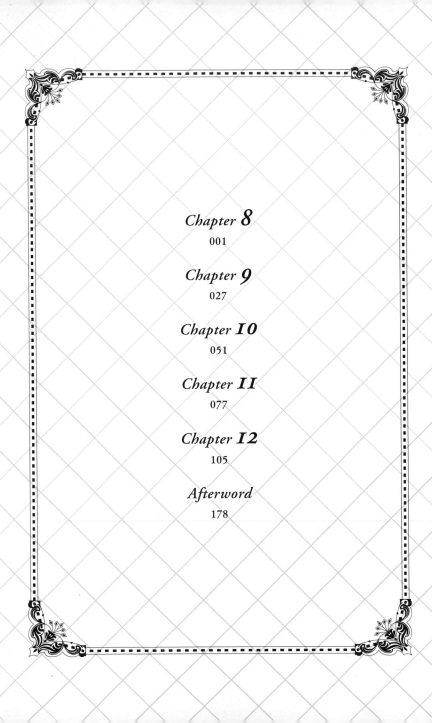

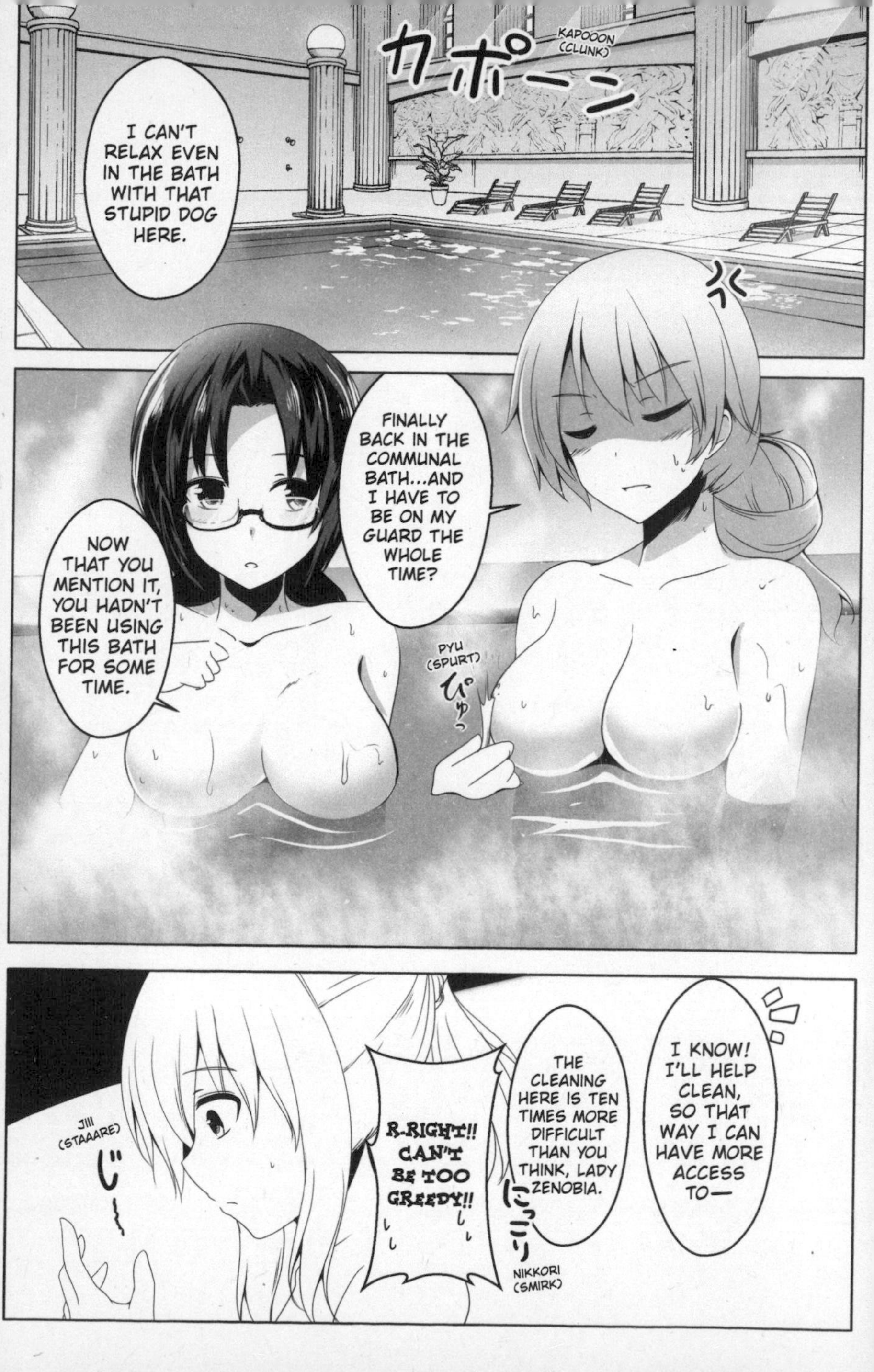
カポーン
KAPOOON (CLUNK)
I CAN'T RELAX EVEN IN THE BATH WITH THAT STUPID DOG HERE.
FINALLY BACK IN THE COMMUNAL BATH...AND I HAVE TO BE ON MY GUARD THE WHOLE TIME?
NOW THAT YOU MENTION IT, YOU HADN'T BEEN USING THIS BATH FOR SOME TIME.
ぴゅっ
PYU (SPURT)
I KNOW! I'LL HELP CLEAN, SO THAT WAY I CAN HAVE MORE ACCESS TO—
THE CLEANING HERE IS TEN TIMES MORE DIFFICULT THAN YOU THINK, LADY ZENOBIA.
にっこり
NIKKORI (SMIRK)
R-RIGHT!! CAN'T BE TOO GREEDY!!
じ〜
JIII (STAAARE)

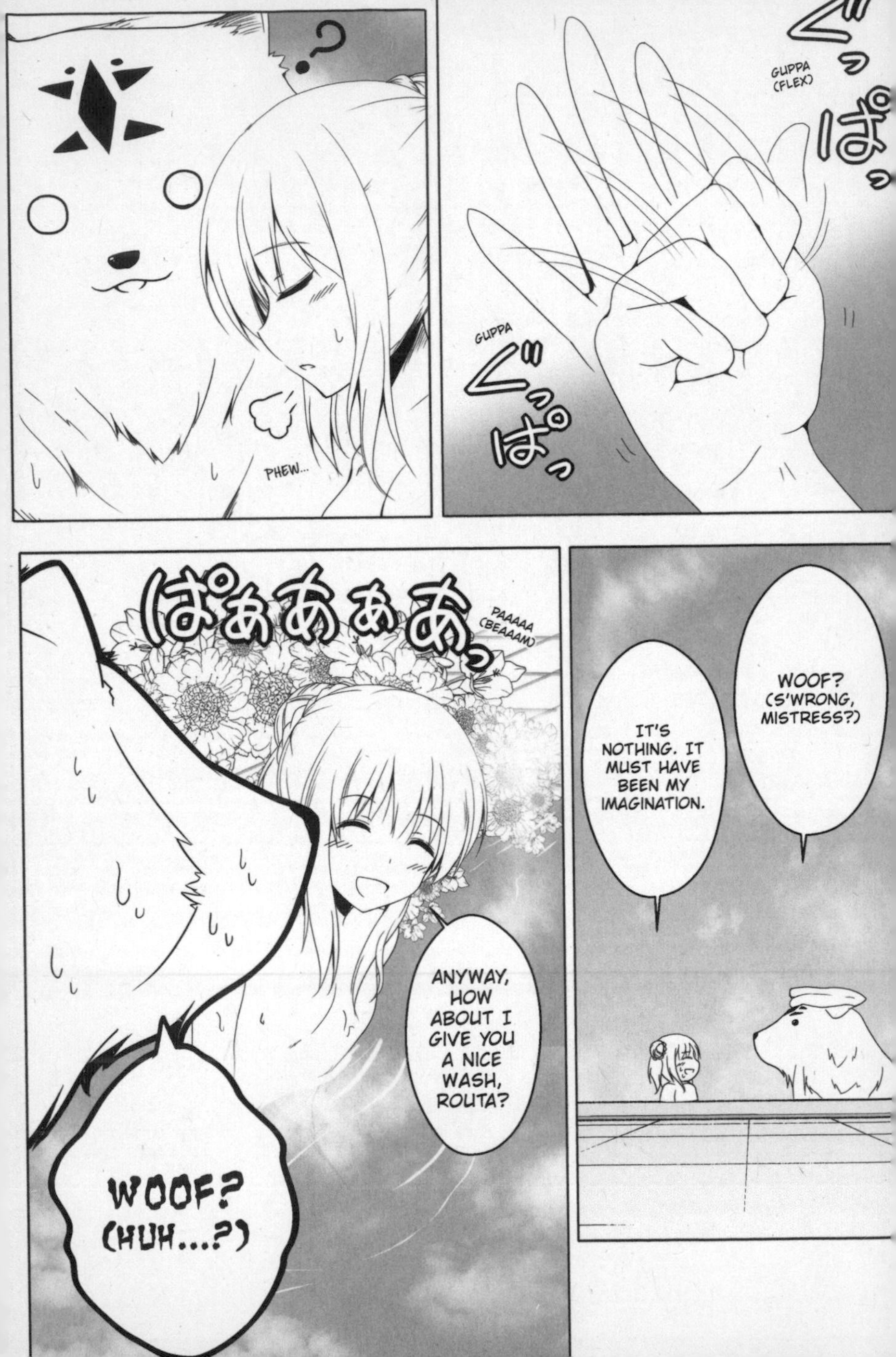
ぐっぱっ
GUPPA (FLEX)
ぐっぱっ
GUPPA
PHEW...
WOOF? (S'WRONG, MISTRESS?)
IT'S NOTHING. IT MUST HAVE BEEN MY IMAGINATION.
ぱぁぁぁあっ
PAAAAA (BEAAAM)
ANYWAY, HOW ABOUT I GIVE YOU A NICE WASH, ROUTA?
WOOF? (HUH...?)

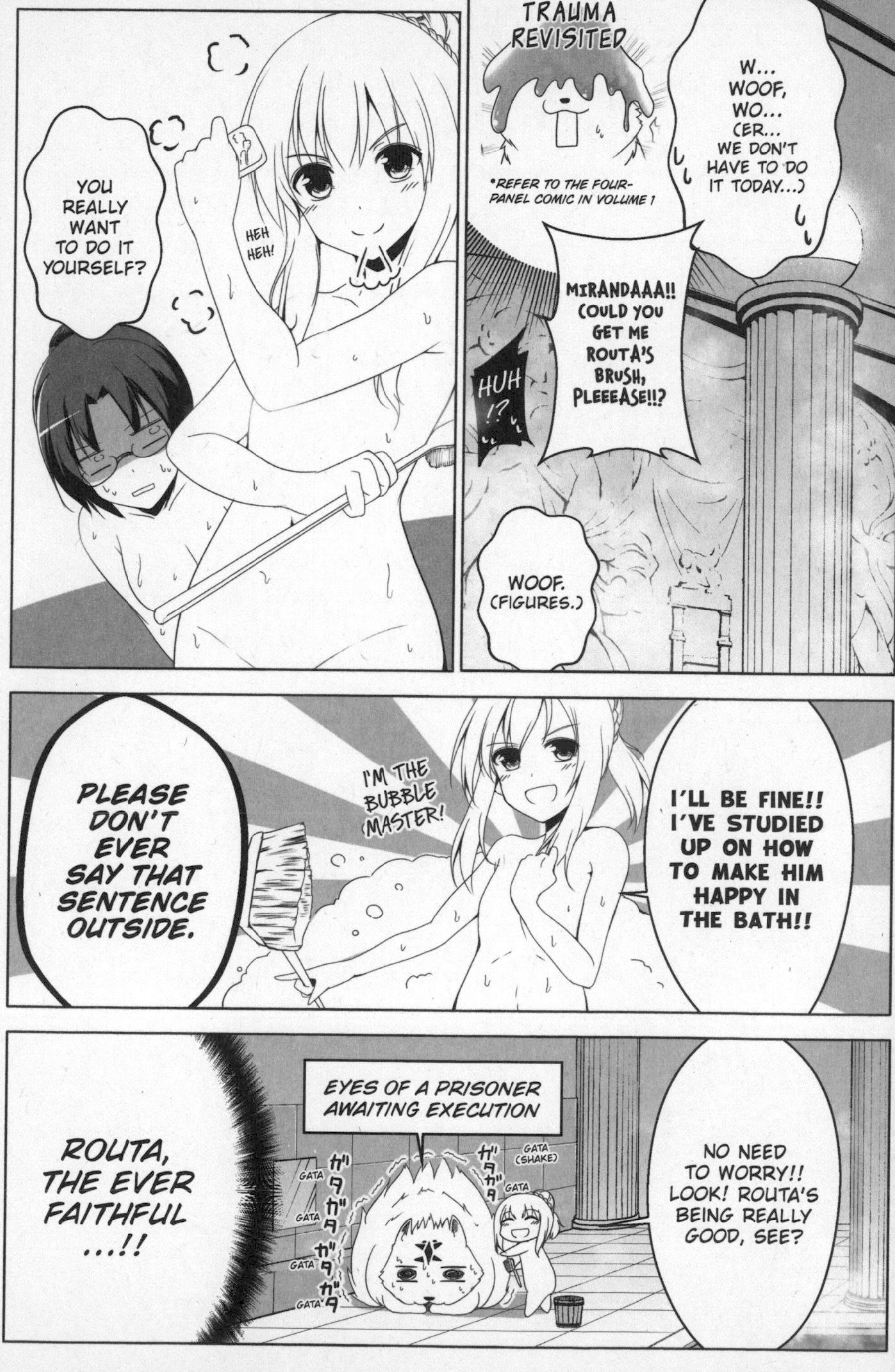
W... WOOF, WO... (ER... WE DON'T HAVE TO DO IT TODAY...)
TRAUMA REVISITED
*REFER TO THE FOUR-PANEL COMIC IN VOLUME 1
MIRANDAAA!! COULD YOU GET ME ROUTA'S BRUSH, PLEEEASE!!?
HUH!?
WOOF. (FIGURES.)
YOU REALLY WANT TO DO IT YOURSELF?
HEH HEH!
I'LL BE FINE!! I'VE STUDIED UP ON HOW TO MAKE HIM HAPPY IN THE BATH!!
I'M THE BUBBLE MASTER!
PLEASE DON'T EVER SAY THAT SENTENCE OUTSIDE.
NO NEED TO WORRY!! LOOK! ROUTA'S BEING REALLY GOOD, SEE?
EYES OF A PRISONER AWAITING EXECUTION
ガタガタ GATA GATA (SHAKE)
ガタガタガタガタ GATA GATA GATA GATA
ROUTA, THE EVER FAITHFUL ...!!

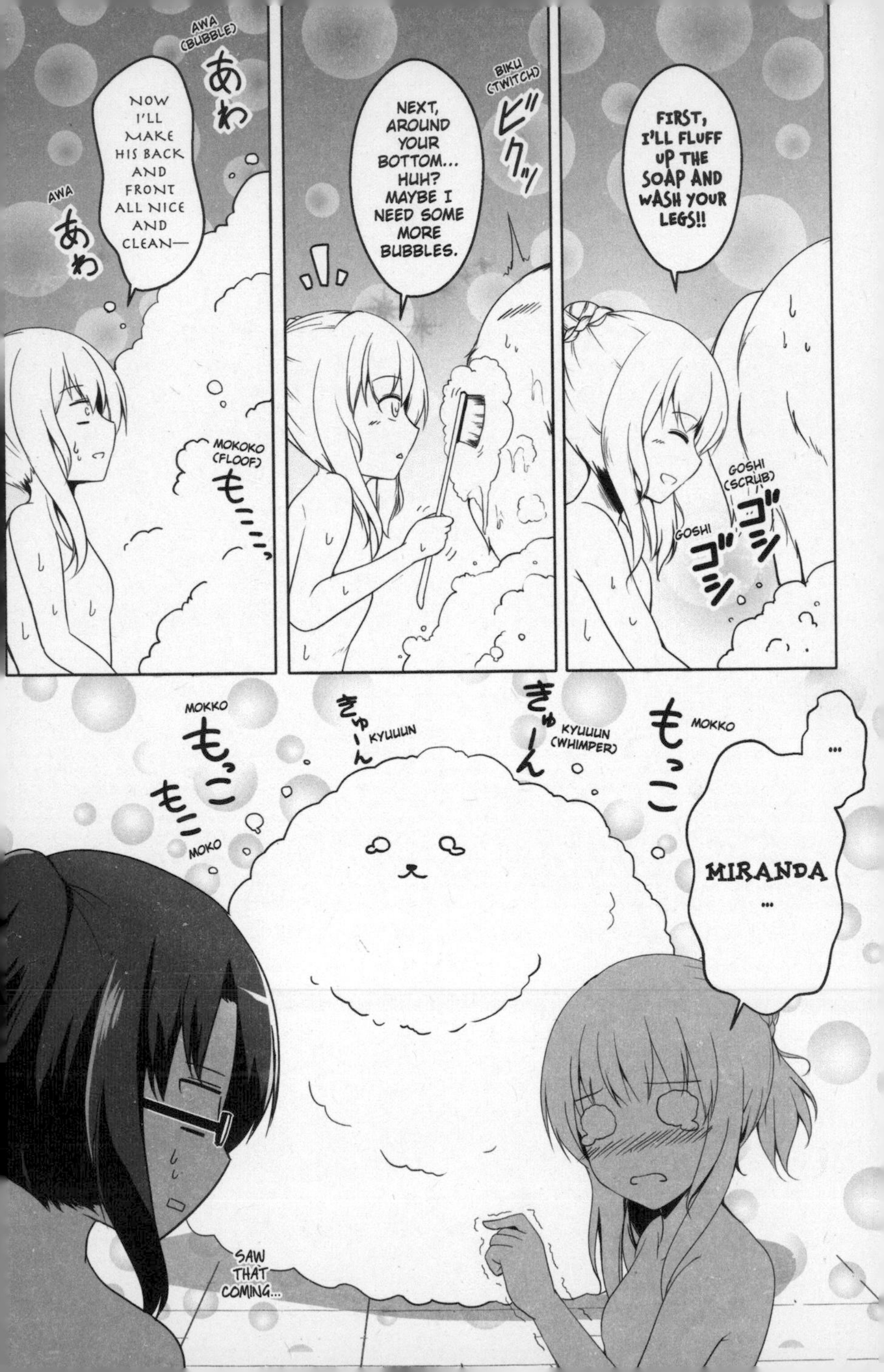
FIRST, I'LL FLUFF UP THE SOAP AND WASH YOUR LEGS!!
GOSHI (SCRUB) ゴシ
GOSHI ゴシ
BIKU (TWITCH) ビクッ
NEXT, AROUND YOUR BOTTOM... HUH? MAYBE I NEED SOME MORE BUBBLES.
AWA (BUBBLE) あわ
AWA あわ
NOW I'LL MAKE HIS BACK AND FRONT ALL NICE AND CLEAN—
MOKOKO (FLOOF) もこここ
…
MIRANDA …
MOKKO もっこ
きゅーん KYUUUN (WHIMPER)
きゅーん KYUUUN
MOKKO もっこ
MOKO もこ
SAW THAT COMING...

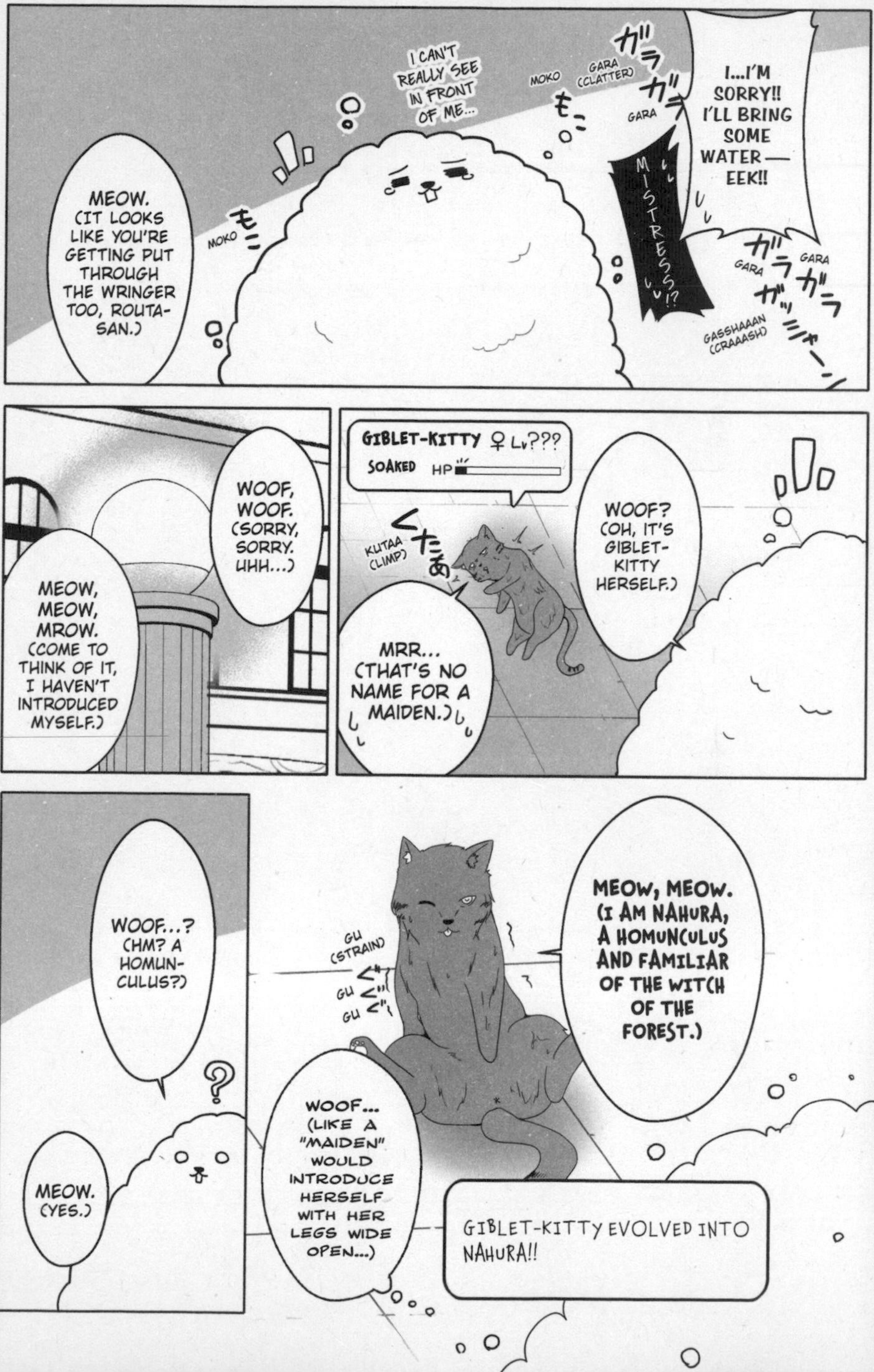
I...I'M SORRY!! I'LL BRING SOME WATER— EEK!!
MISTRESS!?
GARA (CLATTER)
GARA
GARA
GARA
GASSHAAAN (CRAAASH)
MOKO
I CAN'T REALLY SEE IN FRONT OF ME...
MOKO
MEOW. (IT LOOKS LIKE YOU'RE GETTING PUT THROUGH THE WRINGER TOO, ROUTA-SAN.)
GIBLET-KITTY ♀ Lv???
SOAKED HP
WOOF? (OH, IT'S GIBLET-KITTY HERSELF.)
KUTAA (LIMP)
MRR... (THAT'S NO NAME FOR A MAIDEN.)
WOOF, WOOF. (SORRY, SORRY. UHH...)
MEOW, MEOW, MROW. (COME TO THINK OF IT, I HAVEN'T INTRODUCED MYSELF.)
MEOW, MEOW. (I AM NAHURA, A HOMUNCULUS AND FAMILIAR OF THE WITCH OF THE FOREST.)
GU (STRAIN)
GU
GU
WOOF... (LIKE A "MAIDEN" WOULD INTRODUCE HERSELF WITH HER LEGS WIDE OPEN...)
GIBLET-KITTY EVOLVED INTO NAHURA!!
WOOF...? (HM? A HOMUNCULUS?)
MEOW. (YES.)

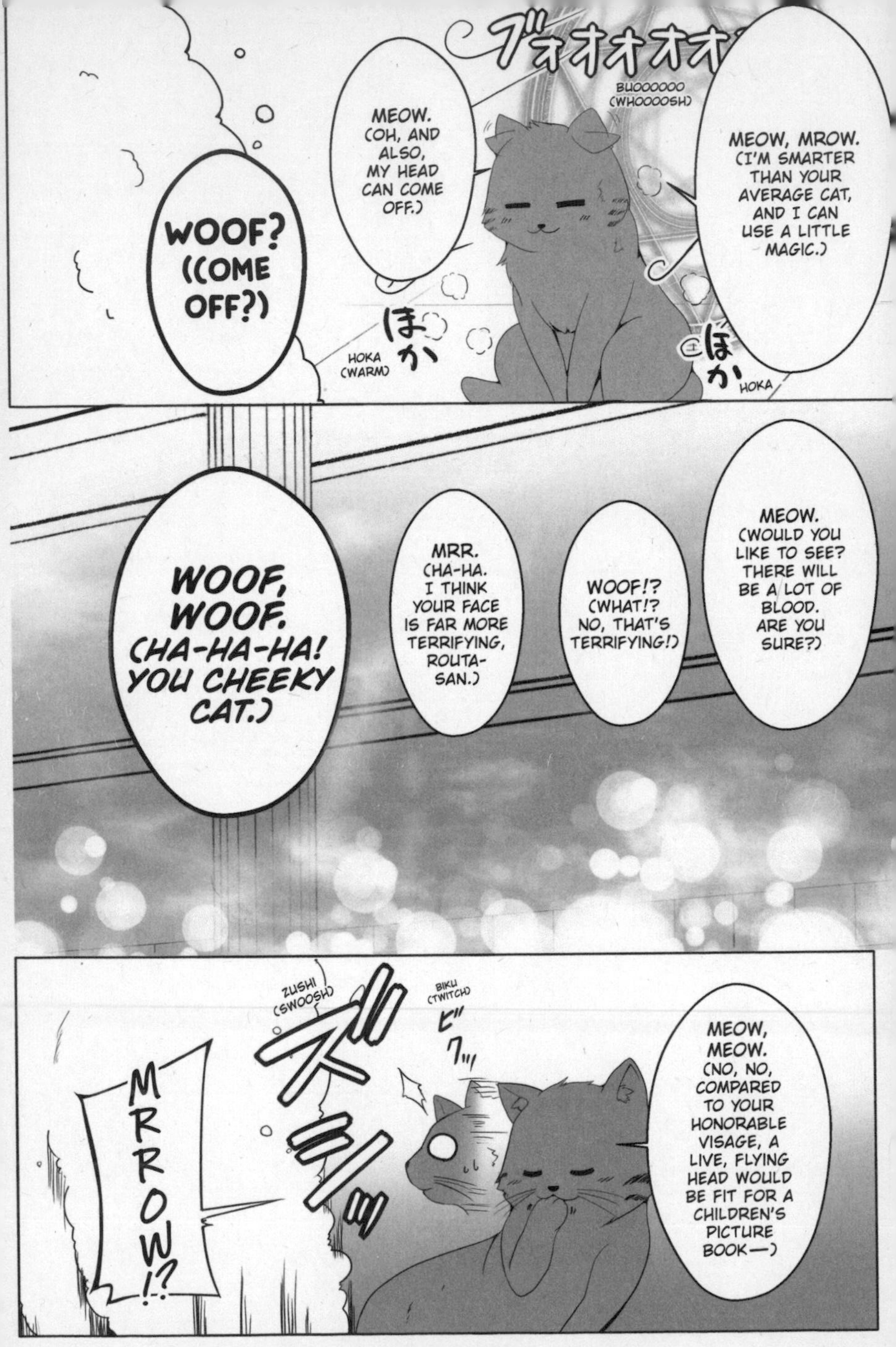
ブォオオオオ
BUOOOOOO (WHOOOOSH)
MEOW, MROW. (I'M SMARTER THAN YOUR AVERAGE CAT, AND I CAN USE A LITTLE MAGIC.)
ほか
HOKA
MEOW. (OH, AND ALSO, MY HEAD CAN COME OFF.)
ほか
HOKA (WARM)
WOOF? ((COME OFF?)
MEOW. (WOULD YOU LIKE TO SEE? THERE WILL BE A LOT OF BLOOD. ARE YOU SURE?)
WOOF!? (WHAT!? NO, THAT'S TERRIFYING!)
MRR. (HA-HA. I THINK YOUR FACE IS FAR MORE TERRIFYING, ROUTA-SAN.)
WOOF, WOOF. (HA-HA-HA! YOU CHEEKY CAT.)
MEOW, MEOW. (NO, NO, COMPARED TO YOUR HONORABLE VISAGE, A LIVE, FLYING HEAD WOULD BE FIT FOR A CHILDREN'S PICTURE BOOK—)
ビクッ
BIKU (TWITCH)
ズシ
ZUSHI (SWOOSH)
MRROW!?

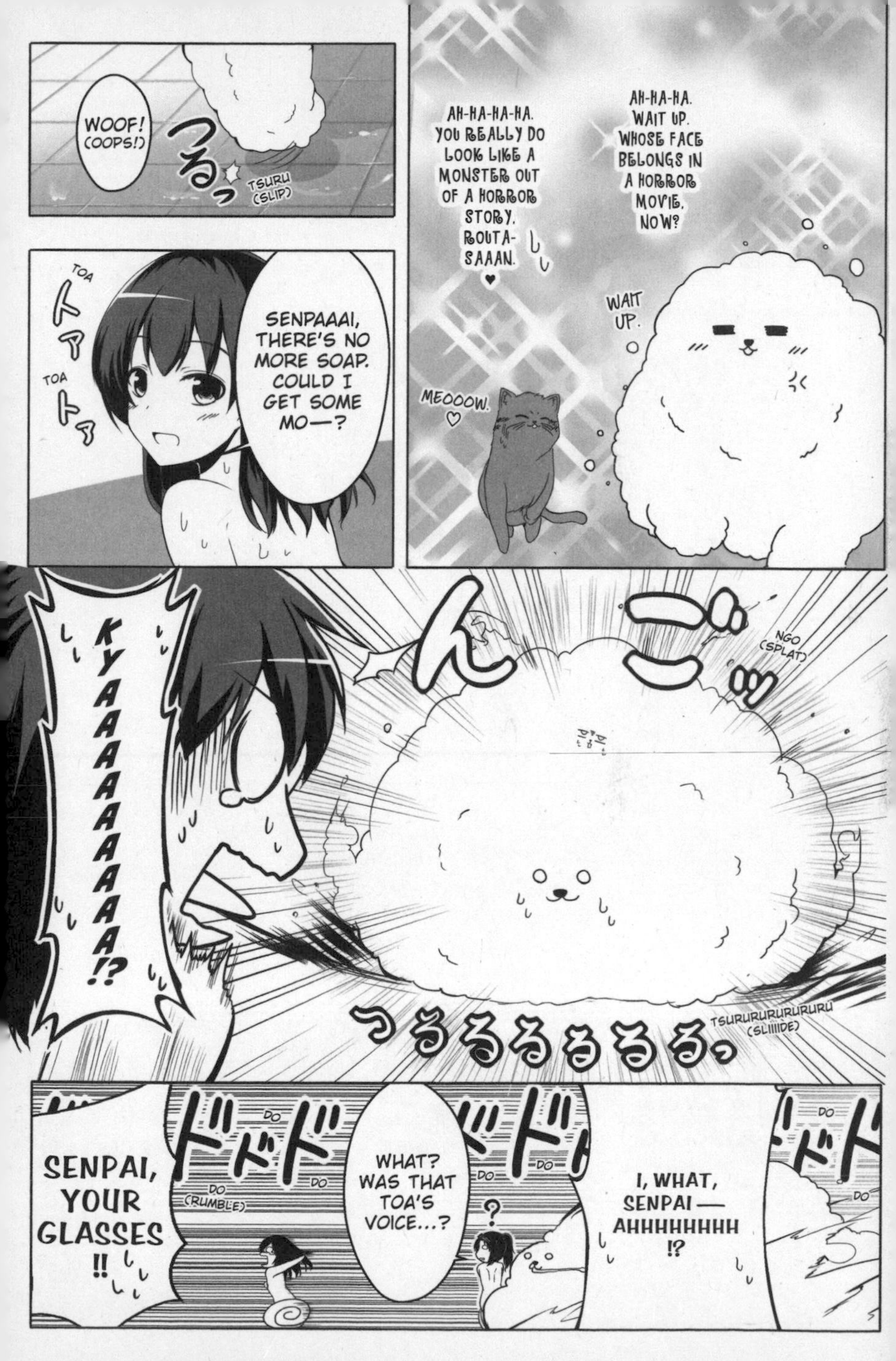
AH-HA-HA. WAIT UP. WHOSE FACE BELONGS IN A HORROR MOVIE, NOW?
AH-HA-HA-HA. YOU REALLY DO LOOK LIKE A MONSTER OUT OF A HORROR STORY, ROUTA-SAAAN. ♥
WAIT UP.
MEOOOW. ♡
WOOF! (OOPS!)
つるっ
TSURU (SLIP)
SENPAAAI, THERE'S NO MORE SOAP. COULD I GET SOME MO—?
トァ
TOA
トァ
TOA
んごッ
NGO (SPLAT)
KYAAAAAAAAAAAAA!?
つるるるるるるるっ
TSURURURURURURU (SLIIIIDE)
ドドド
DO
I, WHAT, SENPAI— AHHHHHHHH!?
ドドド
DO
DO
WHAT? WAS THAT TOA'S VOICE...?
ドドド
DO
DO
DO (RUMBLE)
SENPAI, YOUR GLASSES!!

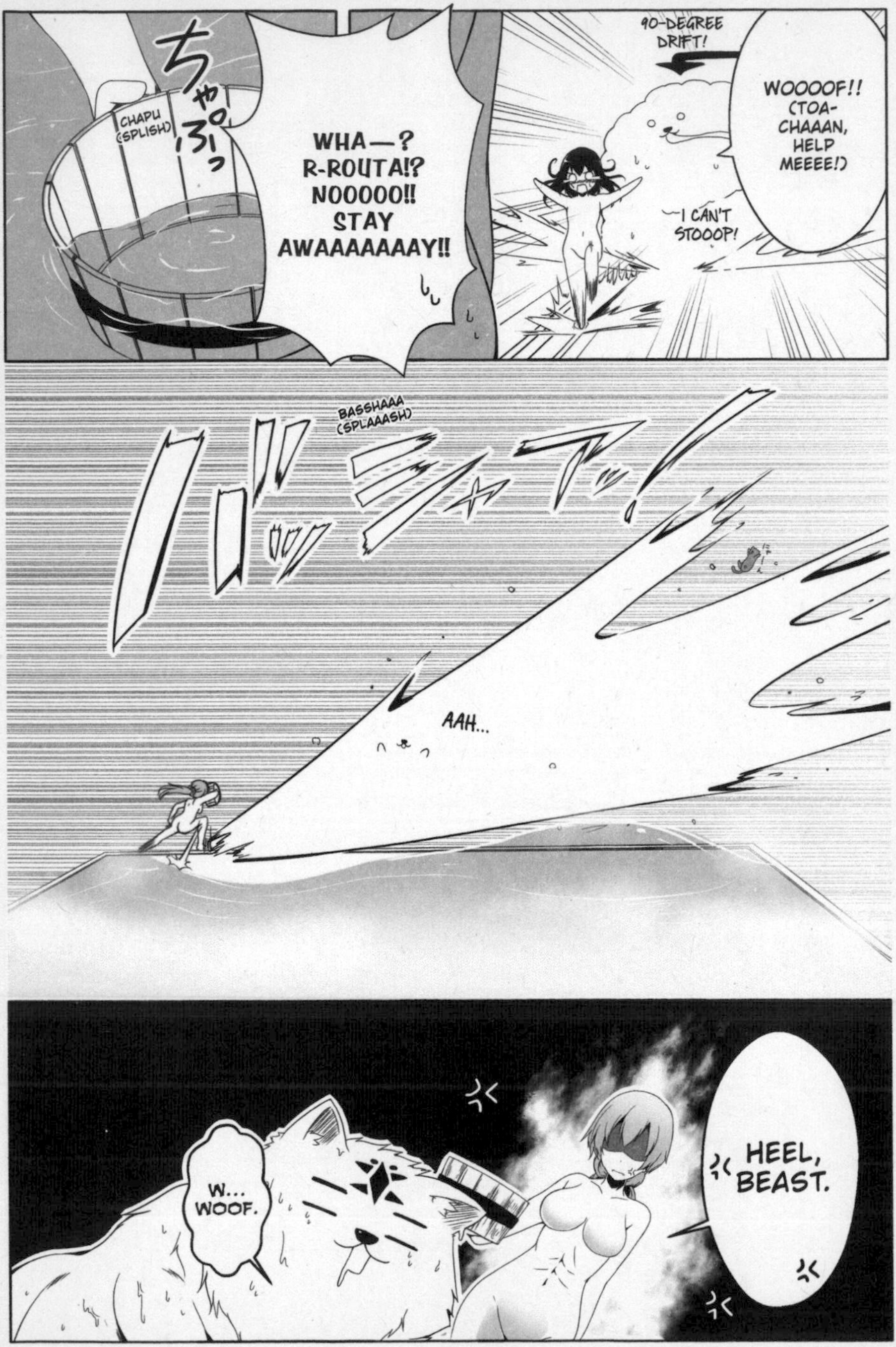
90-DEGREE DRIFT!
WOOOOF!! (TOA-CHAAAN, HELP MEEEE!)
I CAN'T STOOOP!
CHAPU (SPLISH)
WHA—? R-ROUTA!? NOOOOO!! STAY AWAAAAAAAY!!
BASSHAAA (SPLAAASH)
AAH...
HEEL, BEAST.
W... WOOF.

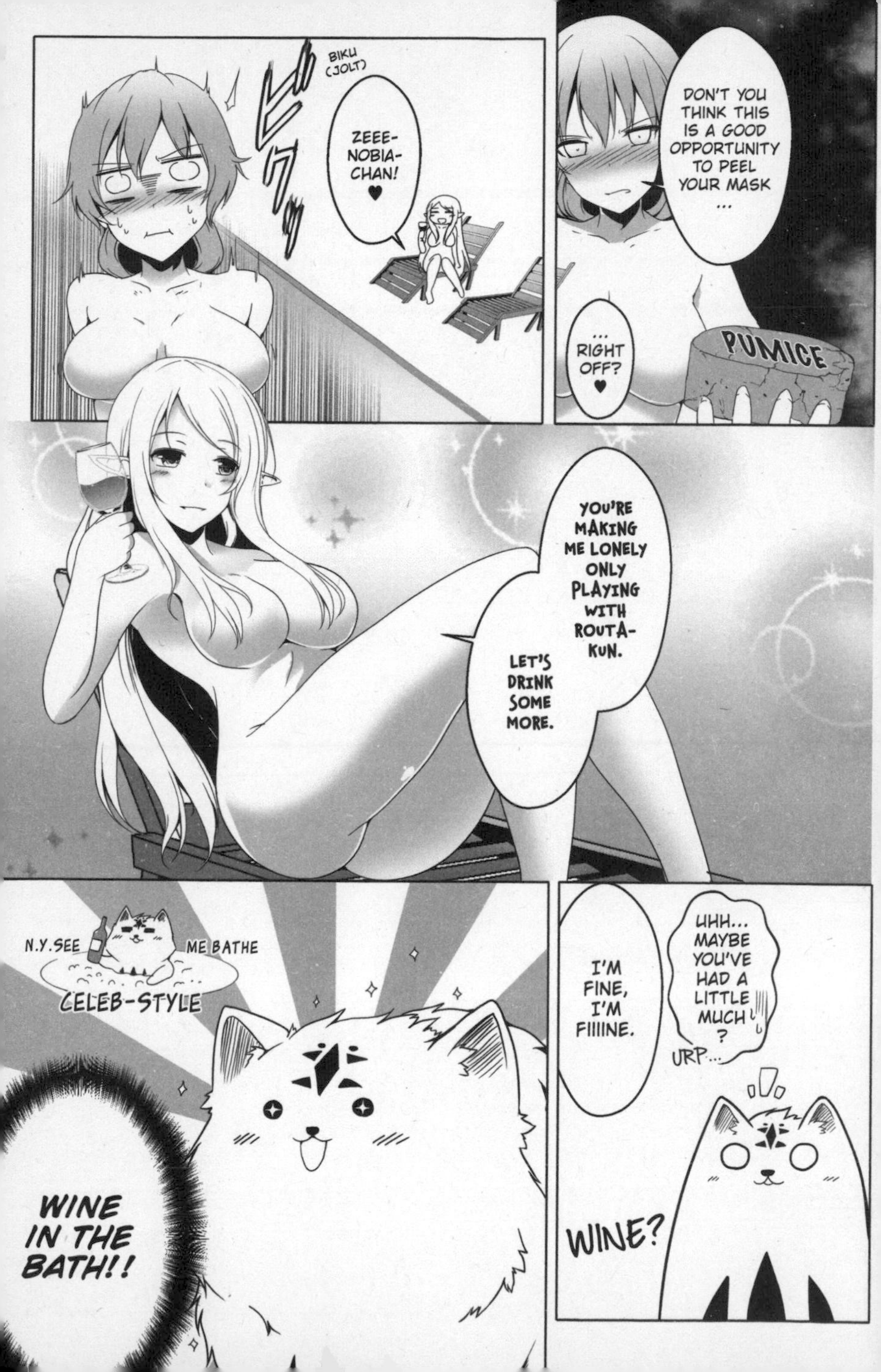
DON'T YOU THINK THIS IS A GOOD OPPORTUNITY TO PEEL YOUR MASK ...
... RIGHT OFF? ♥
PUMICE
BIKU (JOLT)
ZEEE-NOBIA-CHAN! ♥
YOU'RE MAKING ME LONELY ONLY PLAYING WITH ROUTA-KUN.
LET'S DRINK SOME MORE.
UHH... MAYBE YOU'VE HAD A LITTLE MUCH ?
I'M FINE, I'M FIIIINE.
URP...
WINE?
N.Y.SEE ME BATHE
CELEB-STYLE
WINE IN THE BATH!!

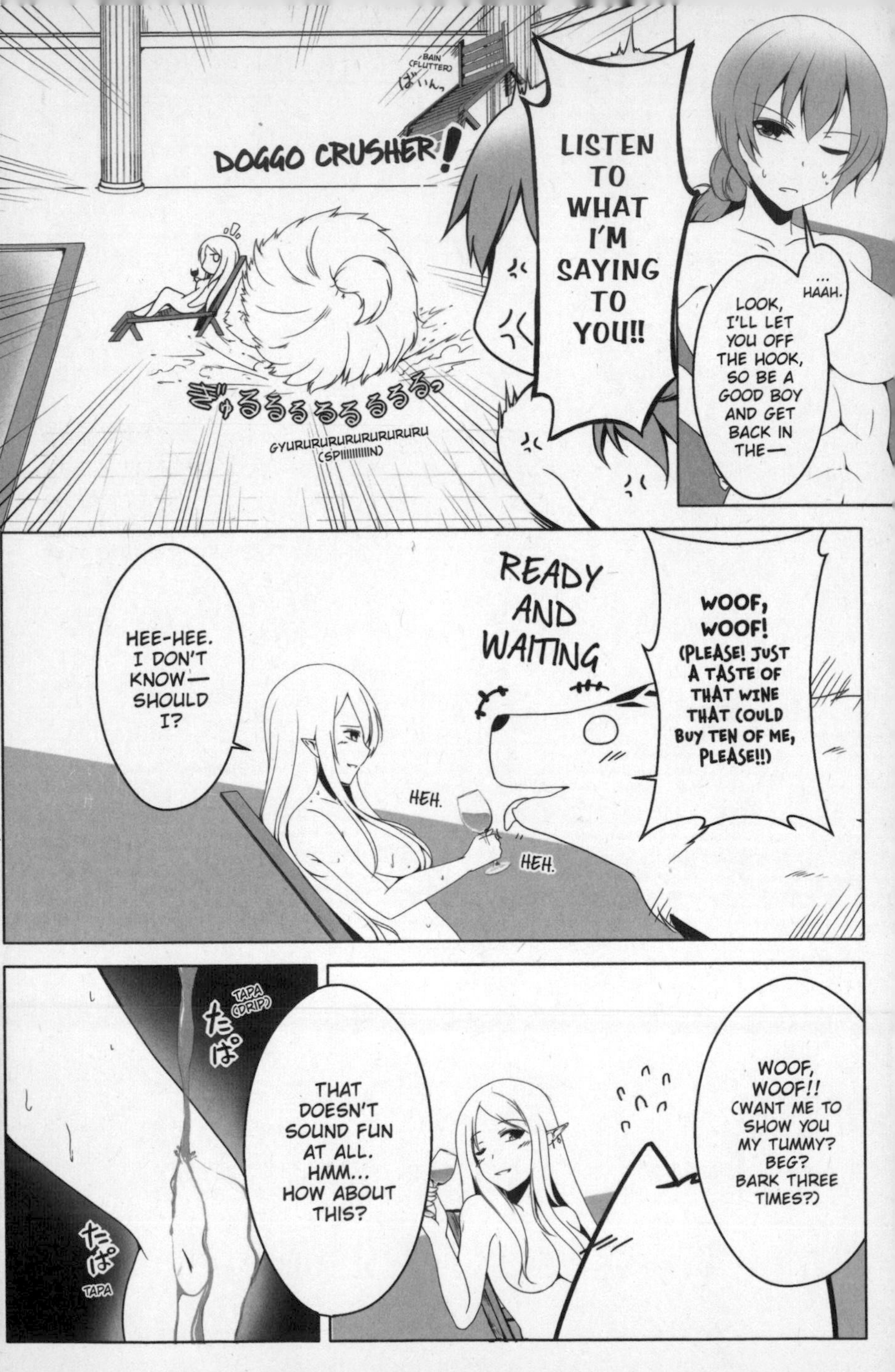
... HAAH.
LOOK, I'LL LET YOU OFF THE HOOK, SO BE A GOOD BOY AND GET BACK IN THE—
LISTEN TO WHAT I'M SAYING TO YOU!!
ばいん BAIN (FLUTTER)
DOGGO CRUSHER!
ぎゅるるるるるるるっ
GYURURURURURURURURU (SPIIIIIIIIIN)
READY AND WAITING
WOOF, WOOF! (PLEASE! JUST A TASTE OF THAT WINE THAT COULD BUY TEN OF ME, PLEASE!!)
HEH.
HEH.
HEE-HEE. I DON'T KNOW— SHOULD I?
WOOF, WOOF!! (WANT ME TO SHOW YOU MY TUMMY? BEG? BARK THREE TIMES?)
THAT DOESN'T SOUND FUN AT ALL. HMM... HOW ABOUT THIS?
たぱ TAPA (DRIP)
たぱ TAPA

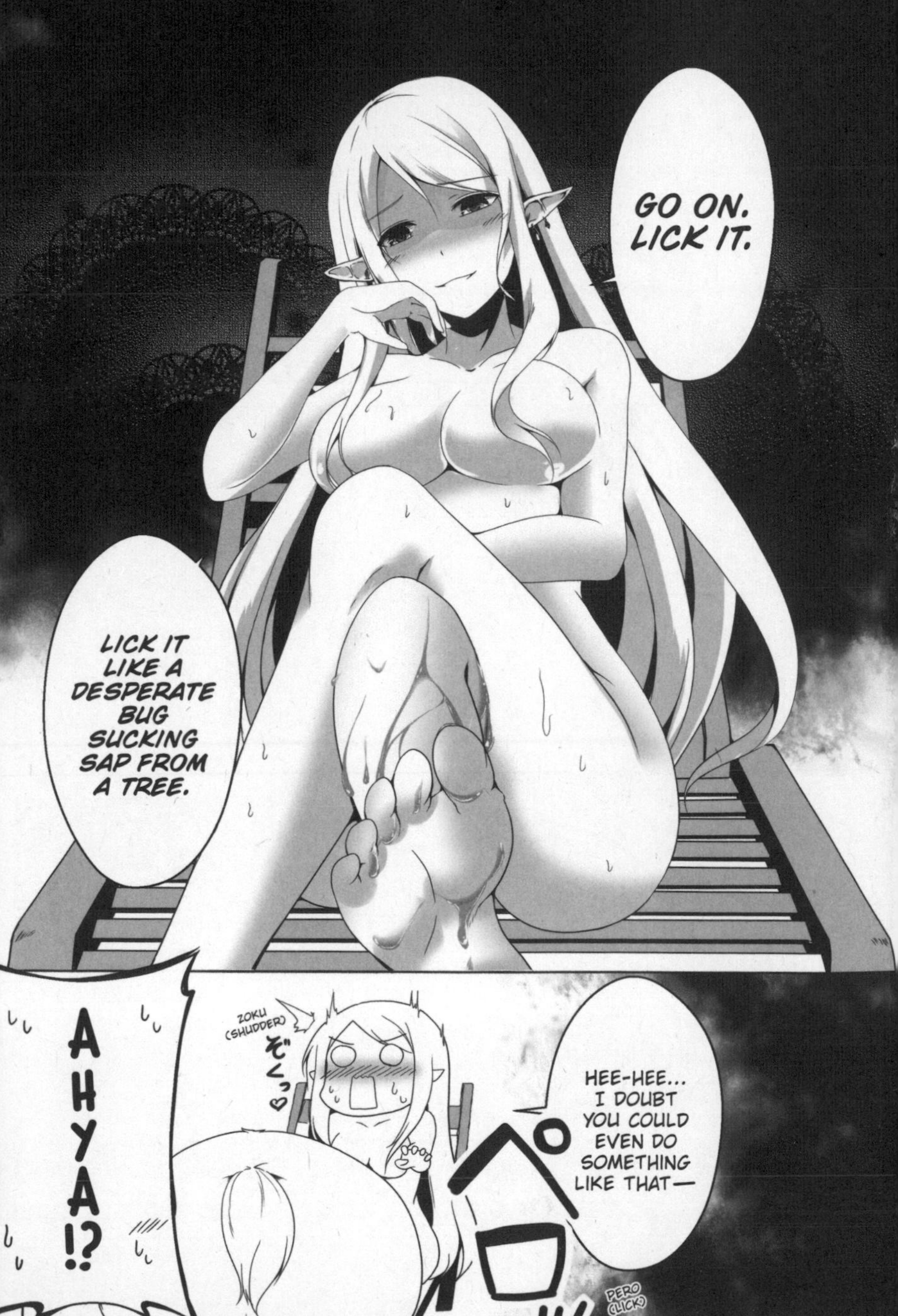
GO ON. LICK IT.
LICK IT LIKE A DESPERATE BUG SUCKING SAP FROM A TREE.
HEE-HEE... I DOUBT YOU COULD EVEN DO SOMETHING LIKE THAT—
ペロ
PERO (LICK)
ZOKU (SHUDDER)
ぞくっ
AHYA!?

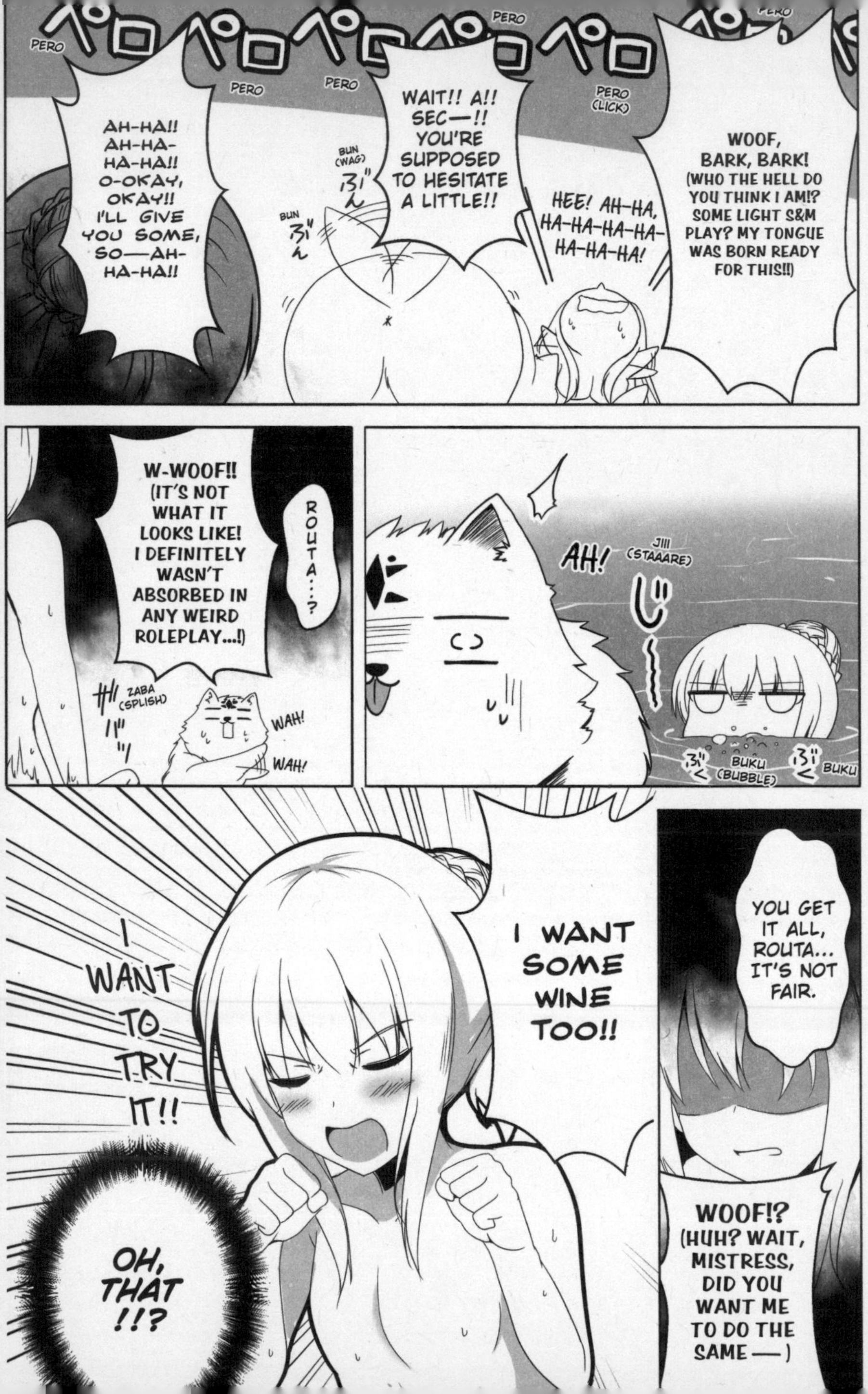
PERO
PERO (LICK)
WOOF, BARK, BARK! (WHO THE HELL DO YOU THINK I AM!? SOME LIGHT S&M PLAY? MY TONGUE WAS BORN READY FOR THIS!!)
HEE! AH-HA, HA-HA-HA-HA HA-HA-HA!
PERO
WAIT!! A!! SEC—!! YOU'RE SUPPOSED TO HESITATE A LITTLE!!
BUN (WAG)
BUN
PERO
PERO
PERO
AH-HA!! AH-HA-HA-HA!! O-OKAY, OKAY!! I'LL GIVE YOU SOME, SO—AH-HA-HA!!
AH!
JIII (STAAARE)
BUKU (BUBBLE)
BUKU
ROUTA...?
W-WOOF!! (IT'S NOT WHAT IT LOOKS LIKE! I DEFINITELY WASN'T ABSORBED IN ANY WEIRD ROLEPLAY...!)
ZABA (SPLISH)
WAH!
WAH!
YOU GET IT ALL, ROUTA... IT'S NOT FAIR.
WOOF!? (HUH? WAIT, MISTRESS, DID YOU WANT ME TO DO THE SAME—)
I WANT SOME WINE TOO!!
I WANT TO TRY IT!!
OH, THAT!!?

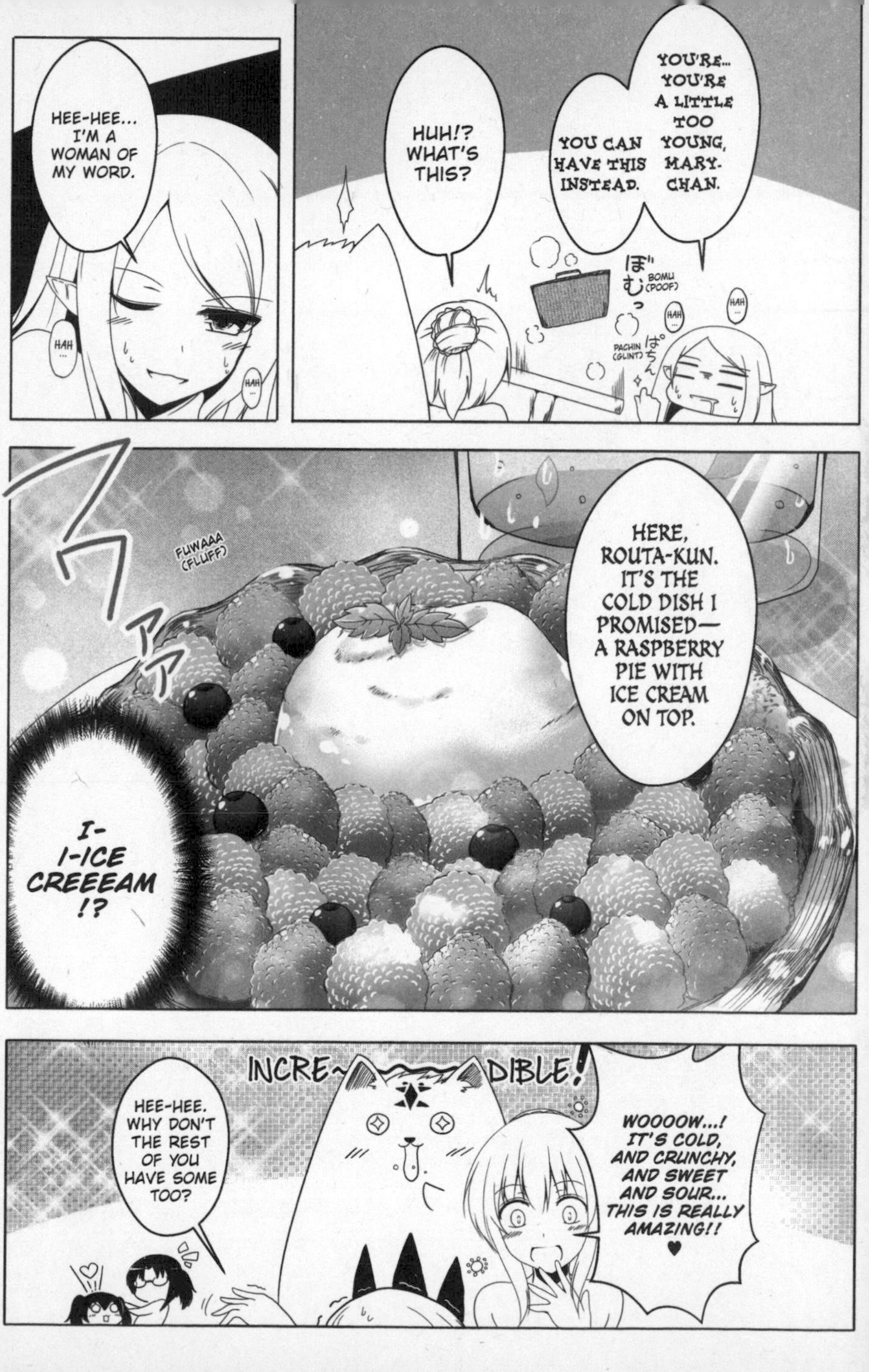
YOU'RE... YOU'RE A LITTLE TOO YOUNG, MARY-CHAN.
YOU CAN HAVE THIS INSTEAD.
HUH!? WHAT'S THIS?
ぼむっ BOMU (POOF)
HAH...
HAH...
ぱちん PACHIN (GLINT)
HEE-HEE... I'M A WOMAN OF MY WORD.
HAH...
HAH...
HERE, ROUTA-KUN. IT'S THE COLD DISH I PROMISED— A RASPBERRY PIE WITH ICE CREAM ON TOP.
FUWAAA (FLUFF)
I- I-ICE CREEEAM !?
INCRE~DIBLE!
WOOOOW...! IT'S COLD, AND CRUNCHY, AND SWEET AND SOUR... THIS IS REALLY AMAZING!! ♥
HEE-HEE. WHY DON'T THE REST OF YOU HAVE SOME TOO?

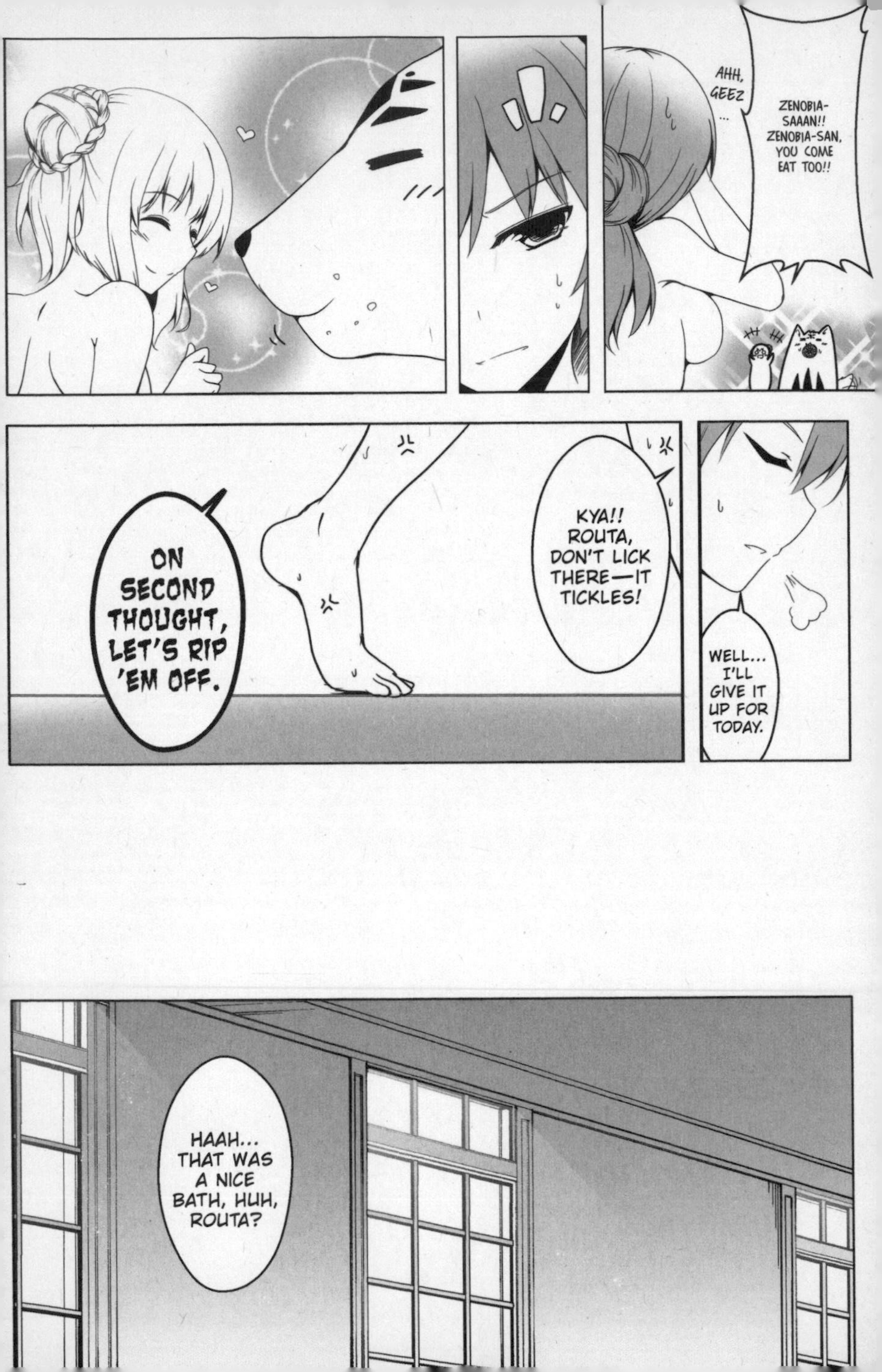
ZENOBIA-SAAAN!! ZENOBIA-SAN, YOU COME EAT TOO!!
AHH, GEEZ...
WELL... I'LL GIVE IT UP FOR TODAY.
KYA!! ROUTA, DON'T LICK THERE—IT TICKLES!
ON SECOND THOUGHT, LET'S RIP 'EM OFF.
HAAH... THAT WAS A NICE BATH, HUH, ROUTA?

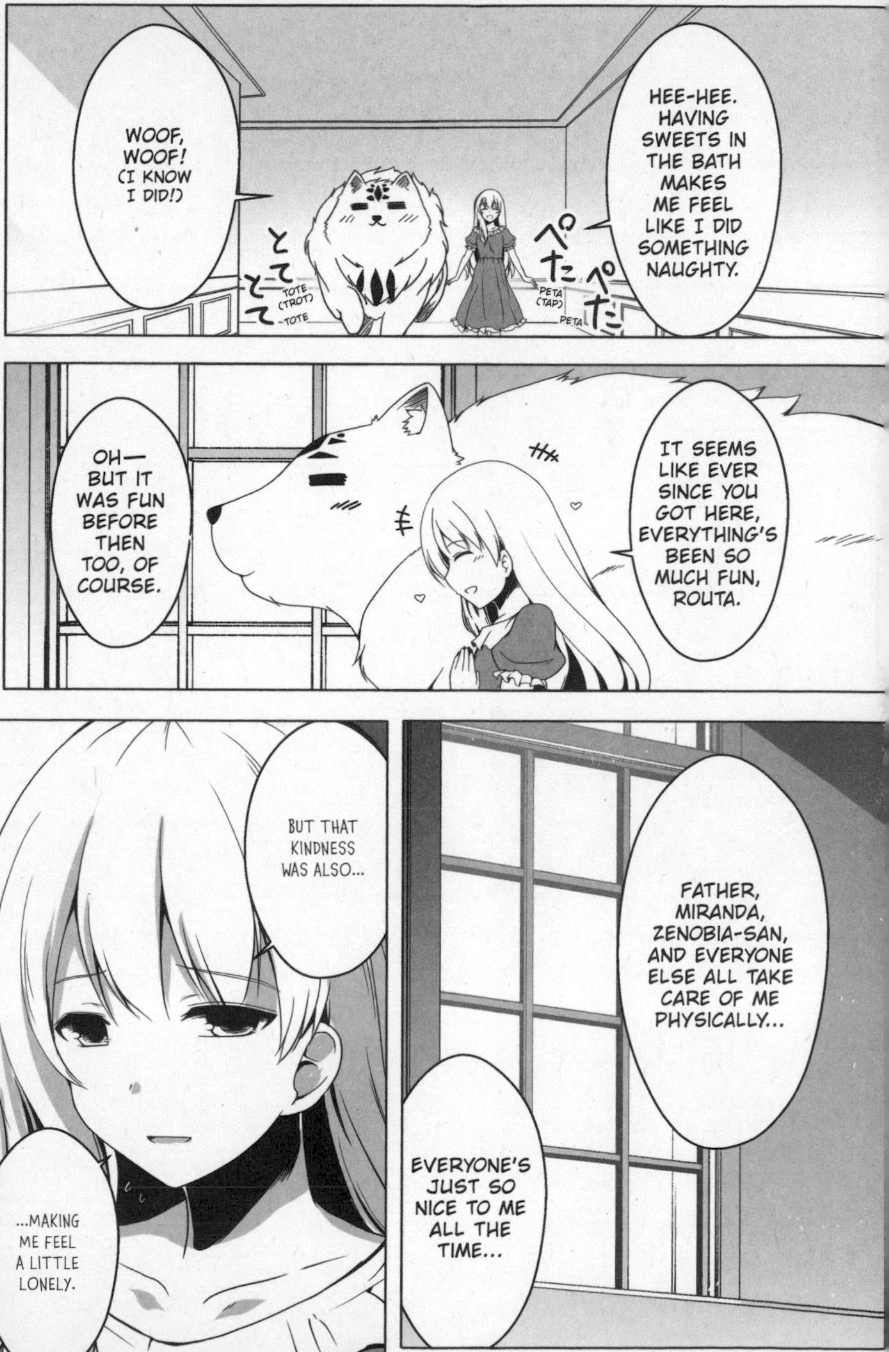
HEE-HEE. HAVING SWEETS IN THE BATH MAKES ME FEEL LIKE I DID SOMETHING NAUGHTY.
ぺたぺた
PETA (TAP) PETA
WOOF, WOOF! (I KNOW I DID!)
とてとて
TOTE (TROT) TOTE
IT SEEMS LIKE EVER SINCE YOU GOT HERE, EVERYTHING'S BEEN SO MUCH FUN, ROUTA.
OH— BUT IT WAS FUN BEFORE THEN TOO, OF COURSE.
FATHER, MIRANDA, ZENOBIA-SAN, AND EVERYONE ELSE ALL TAKE CARE OF ME PHYSICALLY...
EVERYONE'S JUST SO NICE TO ME ALL THE TIME...
BUT THAT KINDNESS WAS ALSO...
...MAKING ME FEEL A LITTLE LONELY.

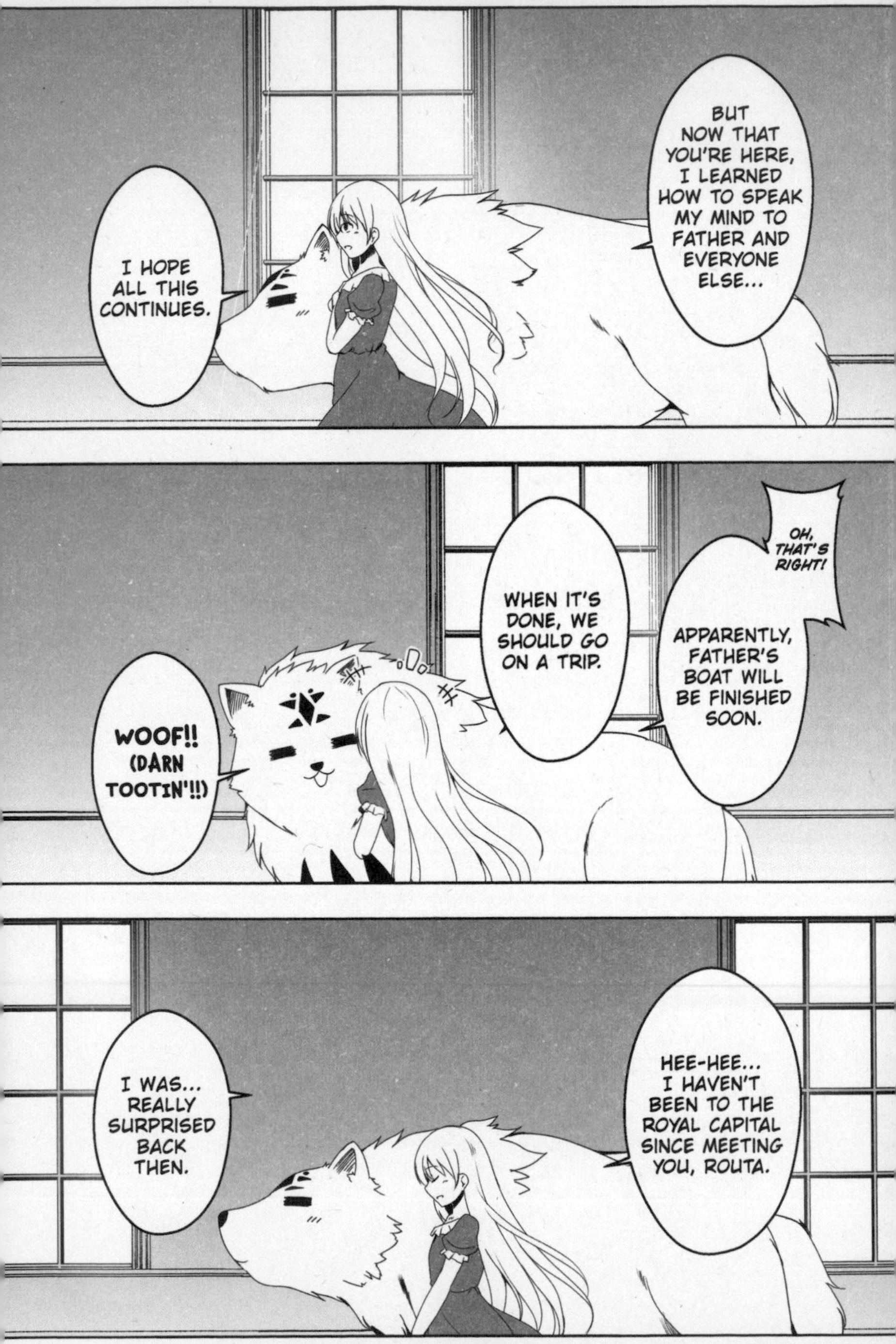
BUT NOW THAT YOU'RE HERE, I LEARNED HOW TO SPEAK MY MIND TO FATHER AND EVERYONE ELSE...
I HOPE ALL THIS CONTINUES.
OH, THAT'S RIGHT!
APPARENTLY, FATHER'S BOAT WILL BE FINISHED SOON.
WHEN IT'S DONE, WE SHOULD GO ON A TRIP.
WOOF!! (DARN TOOTIN'!!)
HEE-HEE... I HAVEN'T BEEN TO THE ROYAL CAPITAL SINCE MEETING YOU, ROUTA.
I WAS... REALLY SURPRISED BACK THEN.

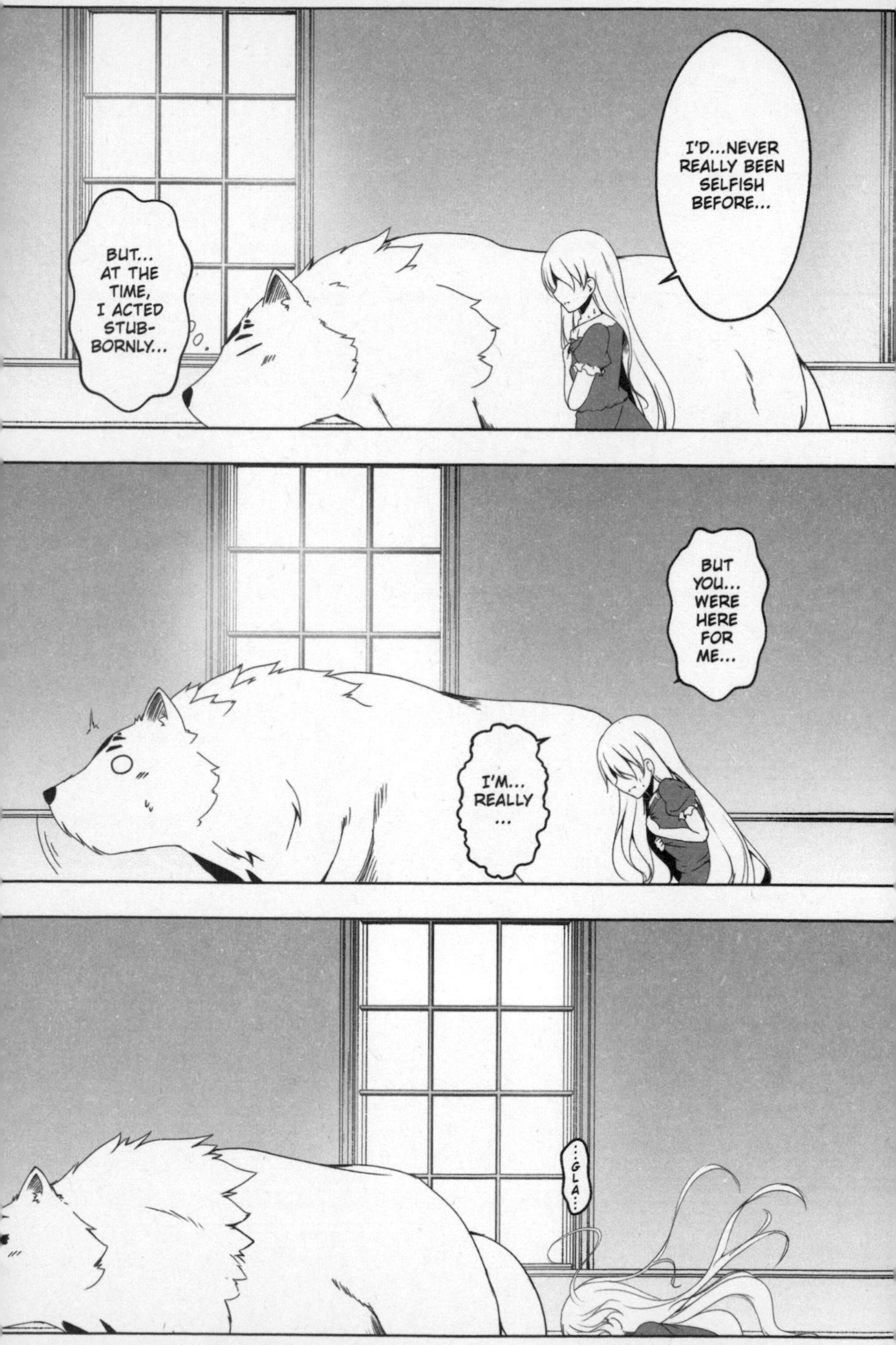
I'D...NEVER REALLY BEEN SELFISH BEFORE...
BUT... AT THE TIME, I ACTED STUB-BORNLY...
BUT YOU... WERE HERE FOR ME...
I'M... REALLY ...
...GLA...

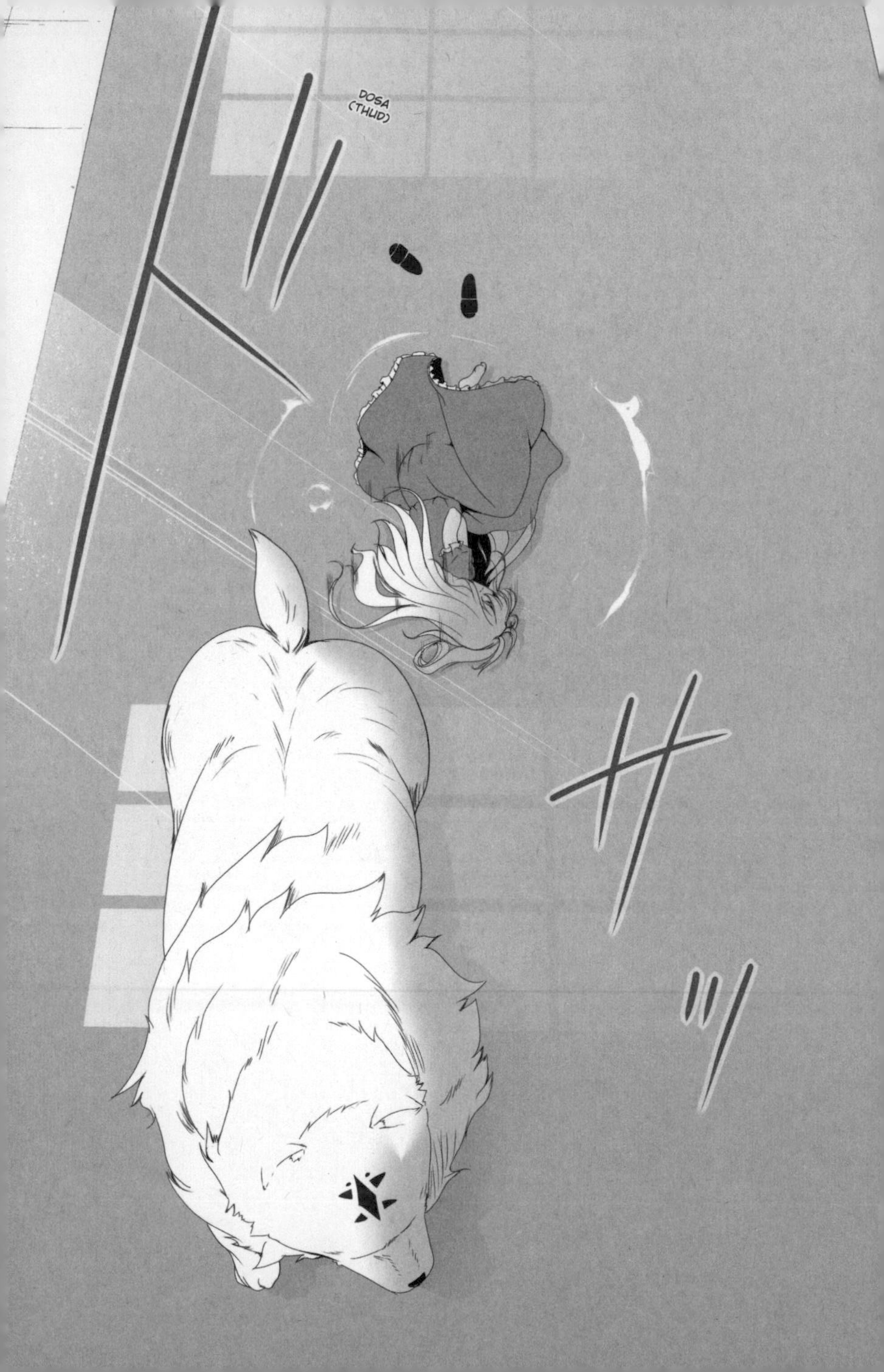
DOSA
(THUD)

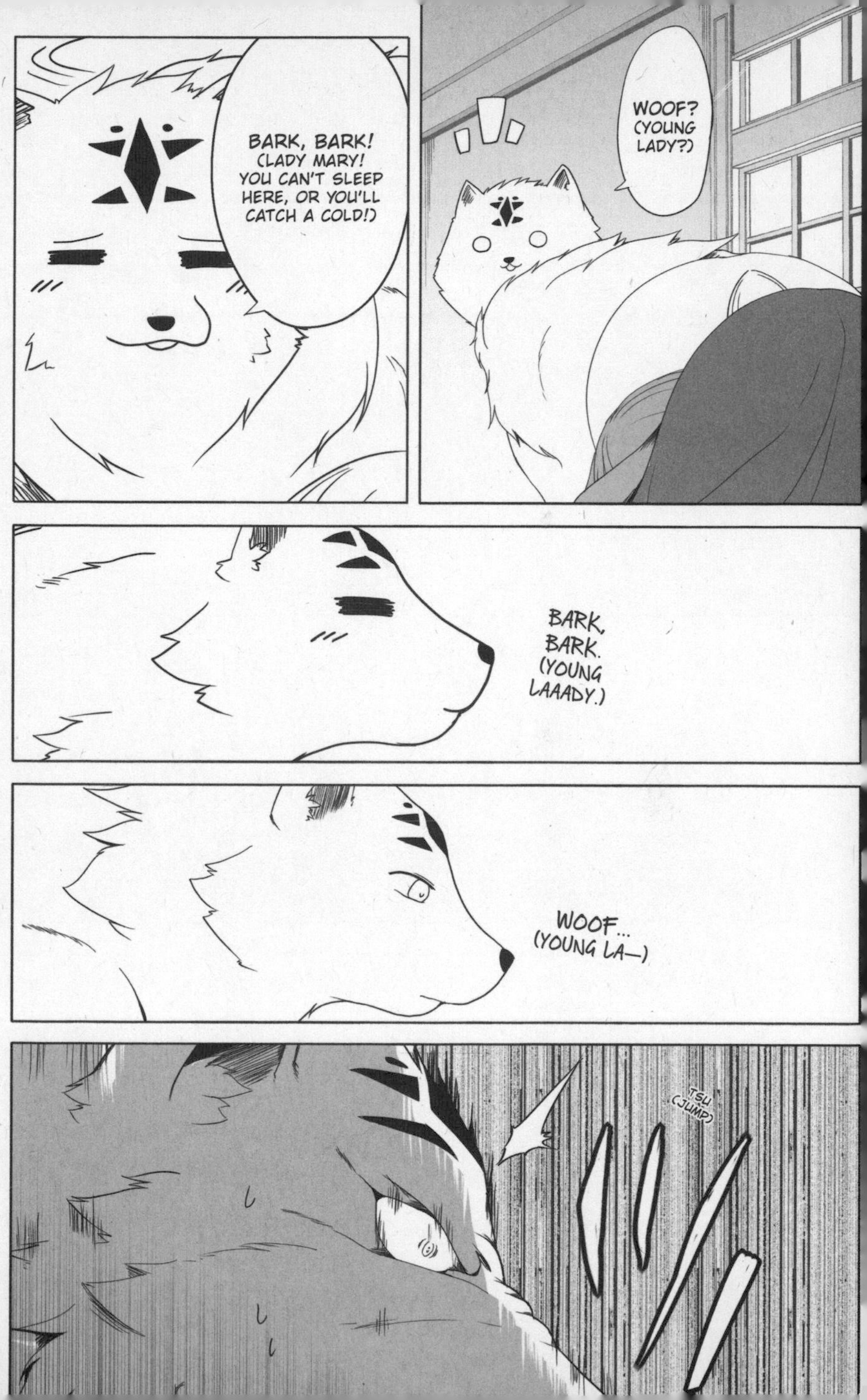
WOOF? (YOUNG LADY?)
BARK, BARK! (LADY MARY! YOU CAN'T SLEEP HERE, OR YOU'LL CATCH A COLD!)
BARK, BARK. (YOUNG LAAADY.)
WOOF... (YOUNG LA—)
TSU (JUMP)

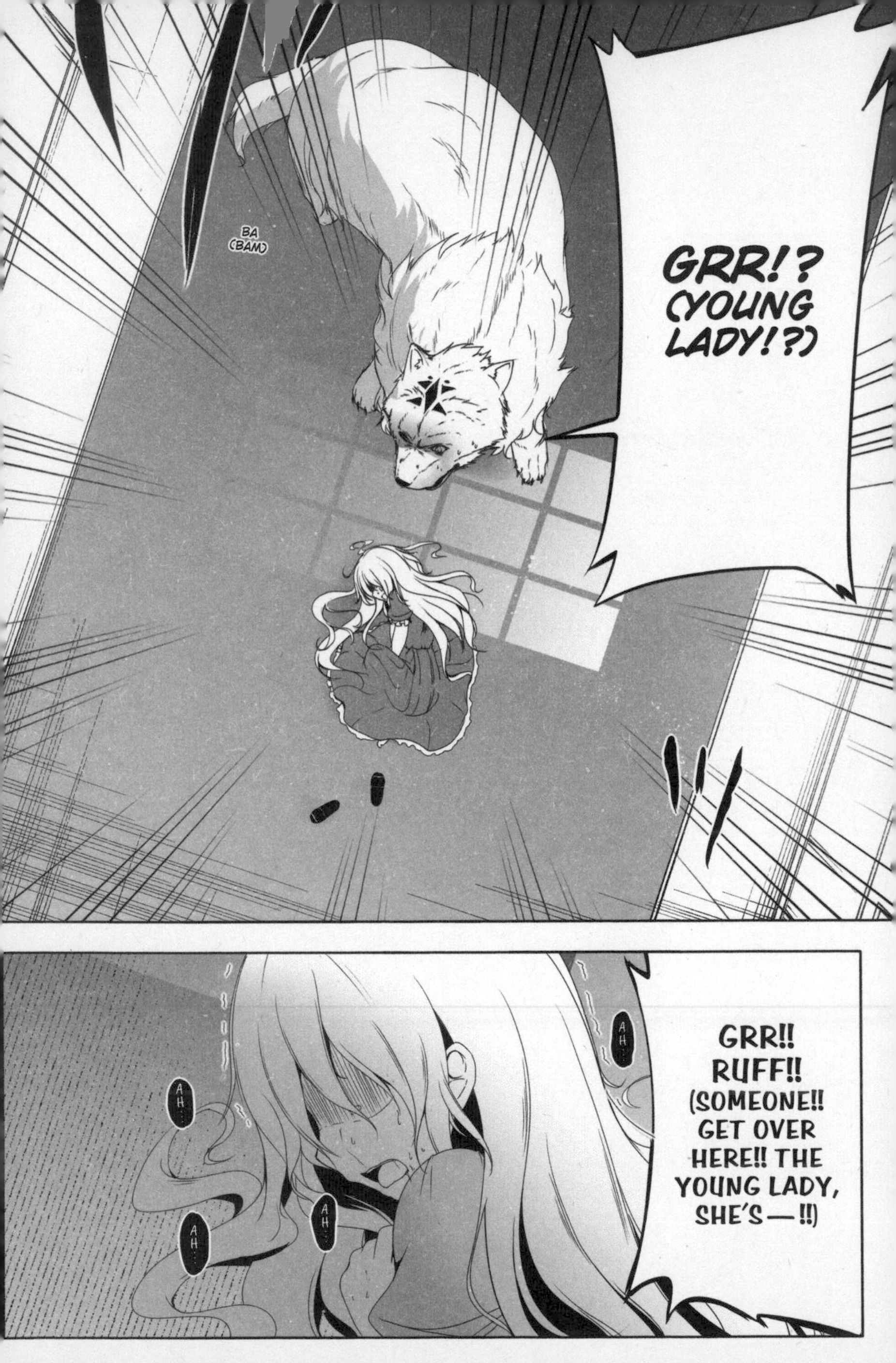

GRR!? (YOUNG LADY!?)
BA (BAM)
GRR!! RUFF!! (SOMEONE!! GET OVER HERE!! THE YOUNG LADY, SHE'S—!!)
AH…
AH…
AH…
AH…

Woof
Woof
Story

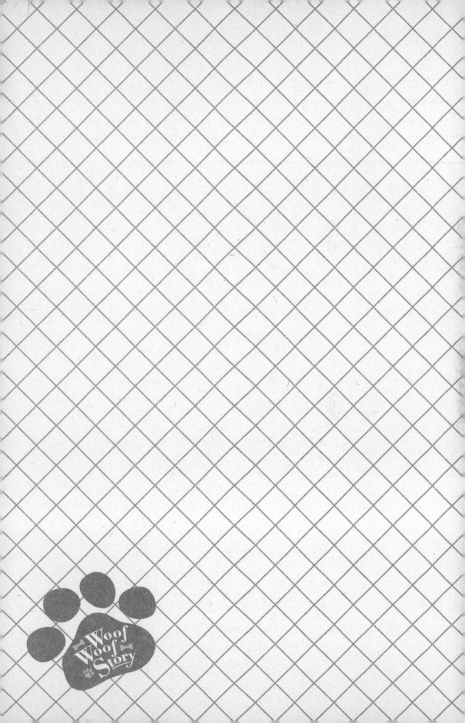

Woof Woof Story

I TOLD YOU TO TURN ME INTO A *Pampered Pooch,* NOT FENRIR!

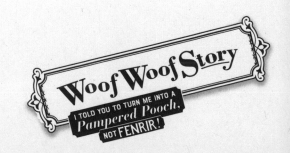

Chapter 9

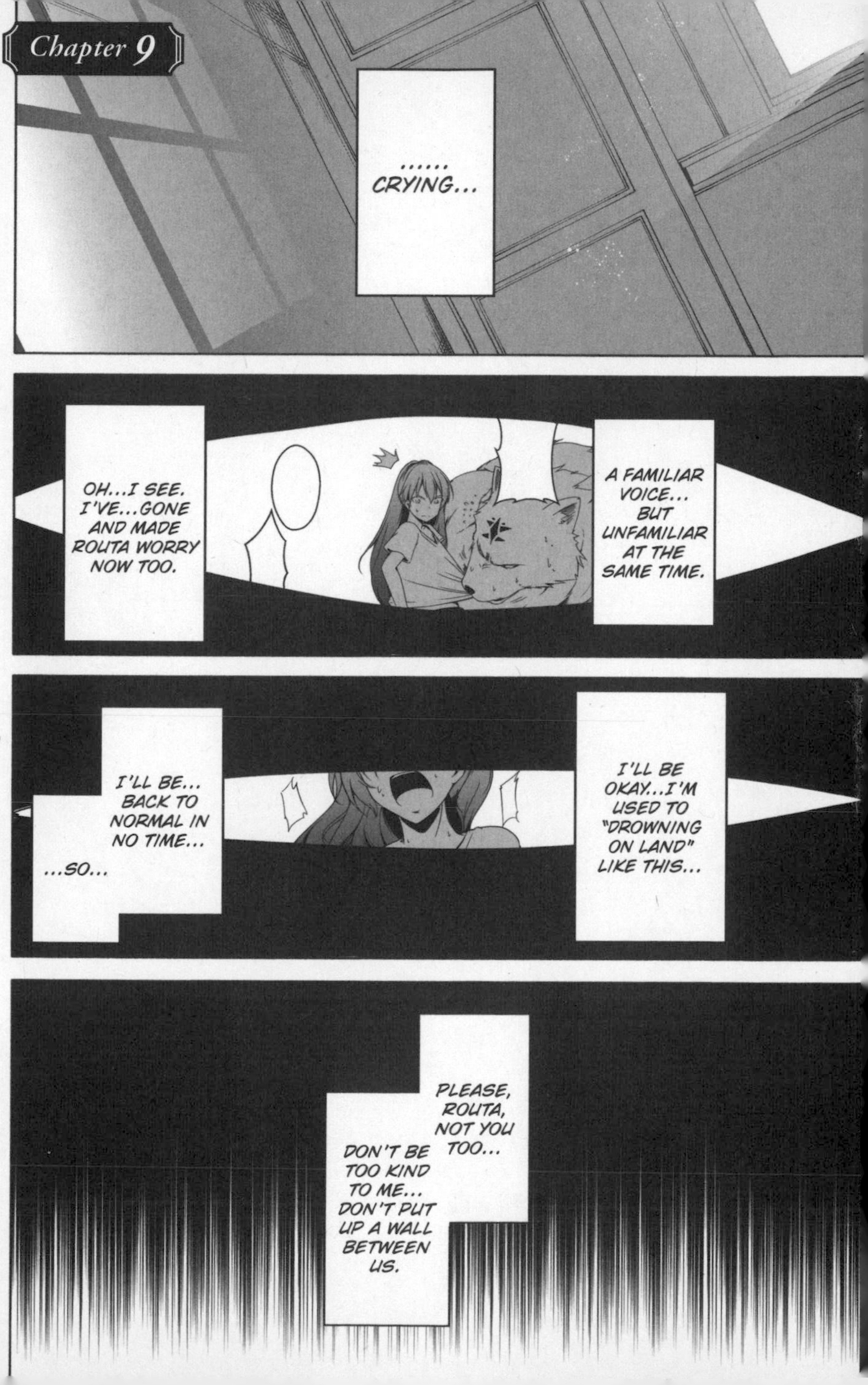
......
CRYING...
A FAMILIAR VOICE... BUT UNFAMILIAR AT THE SAME TIME.
OH...I SEE. I'VE...GONE AND MADE ROUTA WORRY NOW TOO.
I'LL BE OKAY...I'M USED TO "DROWNING ON LAND" LIKE THIS...
I'LL BE... BACK TO NORMAL IN NO TIME...
...SO...
PLEASE, ROUTA, NOT YOU TOO...
DON'T BE TOO KIND TO ME... DON'T PUT UP A WALL BETWEEN US.

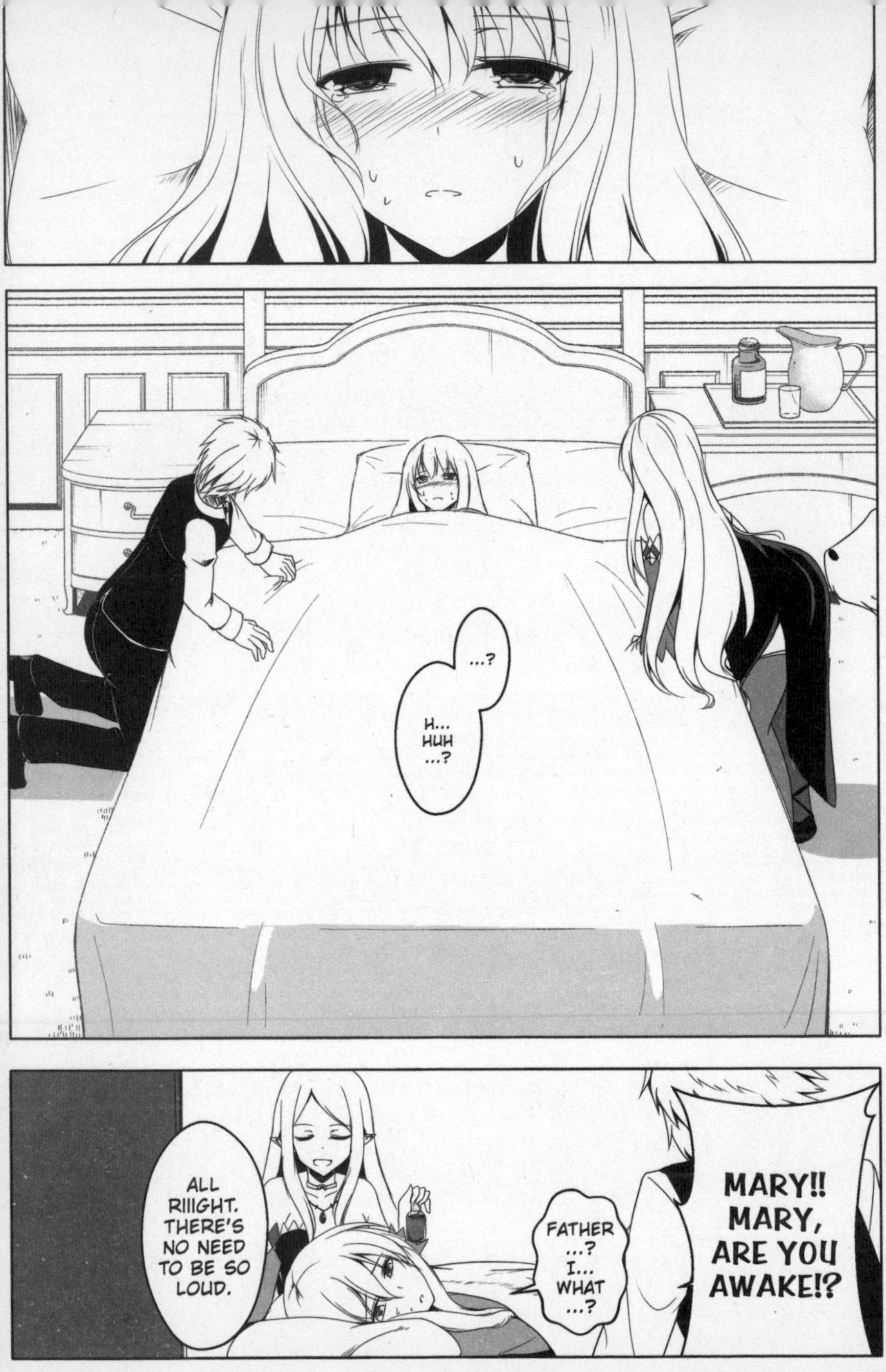
...?
H... HUH ...?
MARY!! MARY, ARE YOU AWAKE!?
FATHER ...? I... WHAT ...?
ALL RIIIGHT. THERE'S NO NEED TO BE SO LOUD.

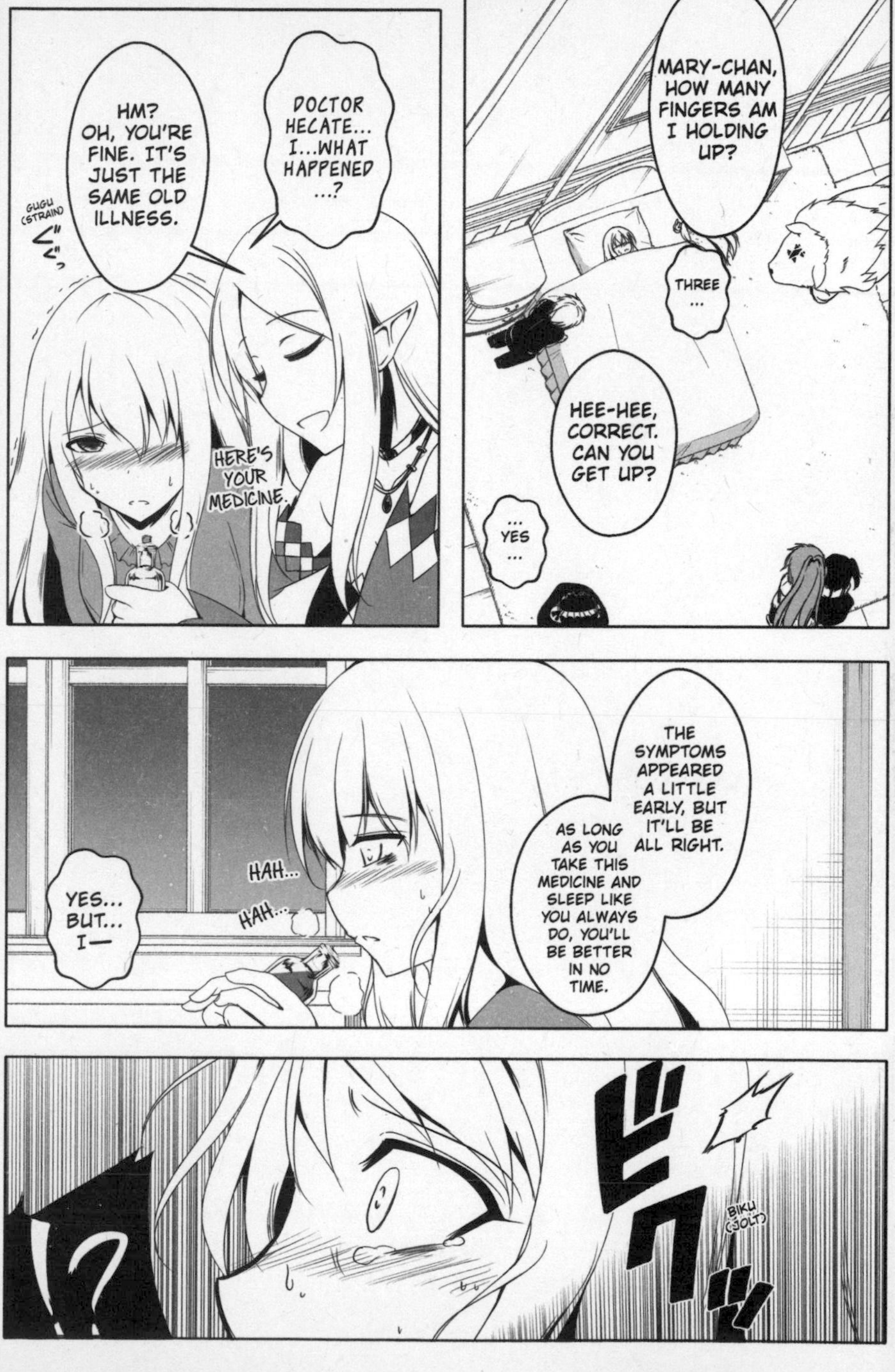
MARY-CHAN, HOW MANY FINGERS AM I HOLDING UP?
THREE...
HEE-HEE, CORRECT. CAN YOU GET UP?
...YES...
DOCTOR HECATE... I...WHAT HAPPENED...?
HM? OH, YOU'RE FINE. IT'S JUST THE SAME OLD ILLNESS.
GUGU (STRAIN)
HERE'S YOUR MEDICINE.
THE SYMPTOMS APPEARED A LITTLE EARLY, BUT IT'LL BE ALL RIGHT.
AS LONG AS YOU TAKE THIS MEDICINE AND SLEEP LIKE YOU ALWAYS DO, YOU'LL BE BETTER IN NO TIME.
HAH...
HAH...
YES... BUT... I—
BIKU (JOLT)
!?

KOFF!!

NGH...

HAH...

HAH...

AH...

GATA (CLATTER)

MARY!?

KOFF!! KOFF!! KOFF!!

I'VE...

JIWA (TEAR)

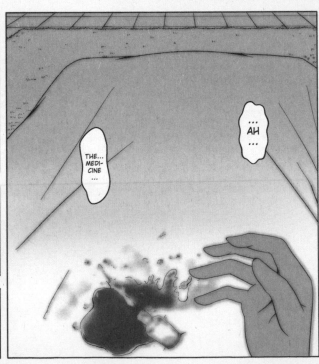

THE... MEDI- CINE...

...AH...

GU (GRIT)

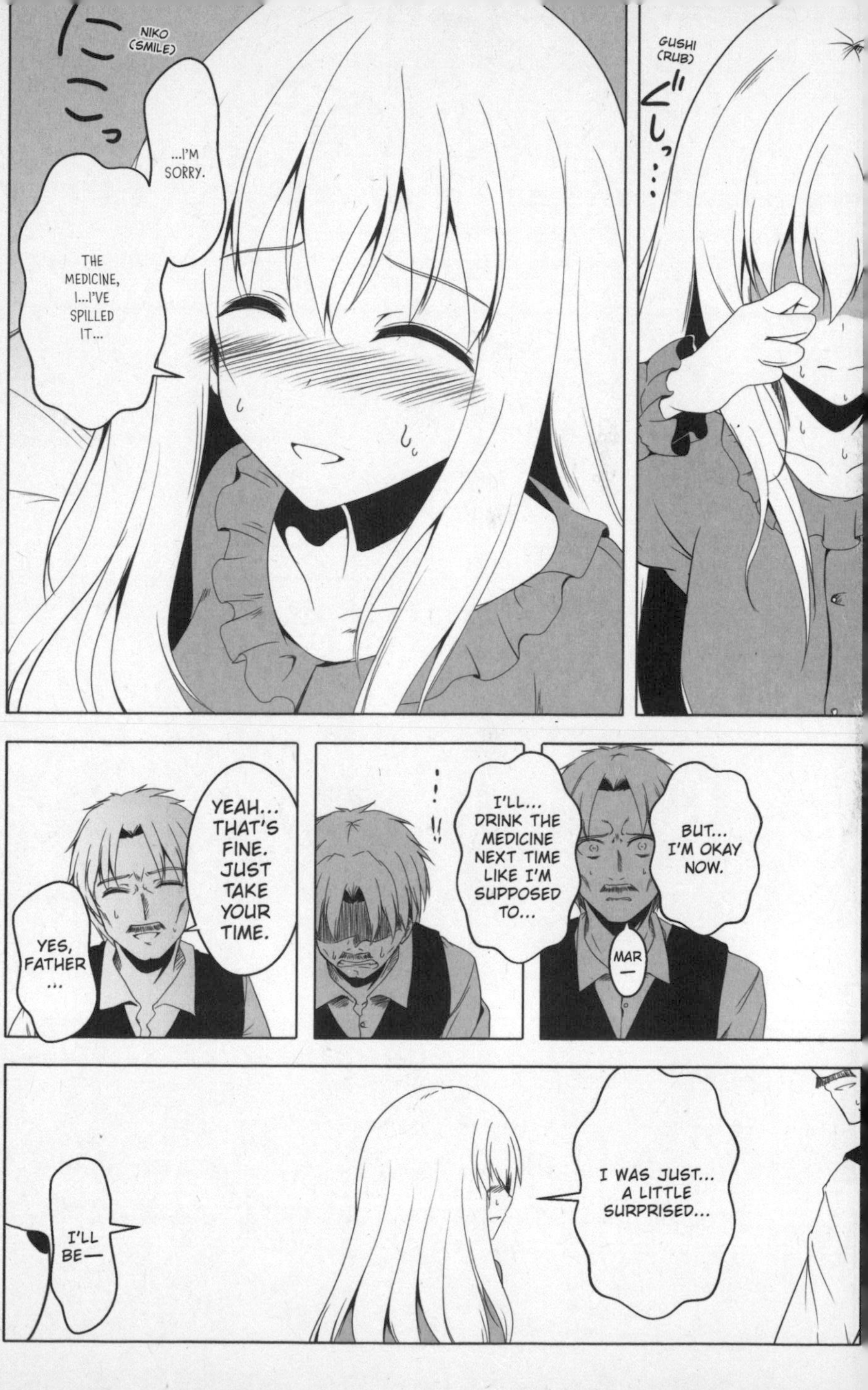
ぐしっ…
GUSHI (RUB)
にこっ
NIKO (SMILE)
...I'M SORRY.
THE MEDICINE, I...I'VE SPILLED IT...
BUT... I'M OKAY NOW.
I'LL... DRINK THE MEDICINE NEXT TIME LIKE I'M SUPPOSED TO...
MAR—
...!!
YEAH... THAT'S FINE. JUST TAKE YOUR TIME.
YES, FATHER...
I WAS JUST... A LITTLE SURPRISED...
I'LL BE—

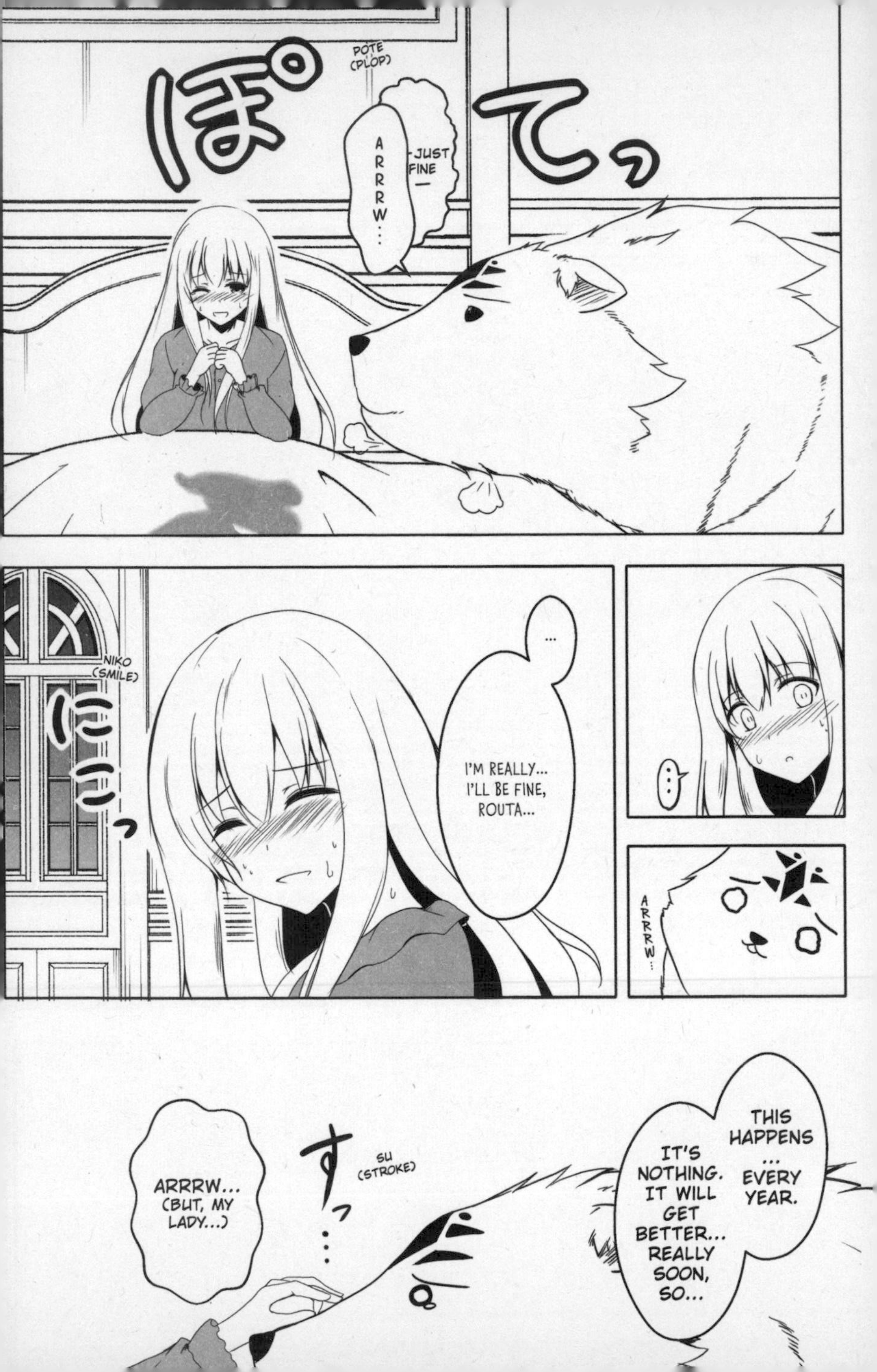
POTE (PLOP)
ARRRW...
—JUST FINE—
...
ARRRW...
...
I'M REALLY... I'LL BE FINE, ROUTA...
NIKO (SMILE)
THIS HAPPENS... EVERY YEAR.
IT'S NOTHING. IT WILL GET BETTER... REALLY SOON, SO...
SU (STROKE)
ARRRW... (BUT, MY LADY...)

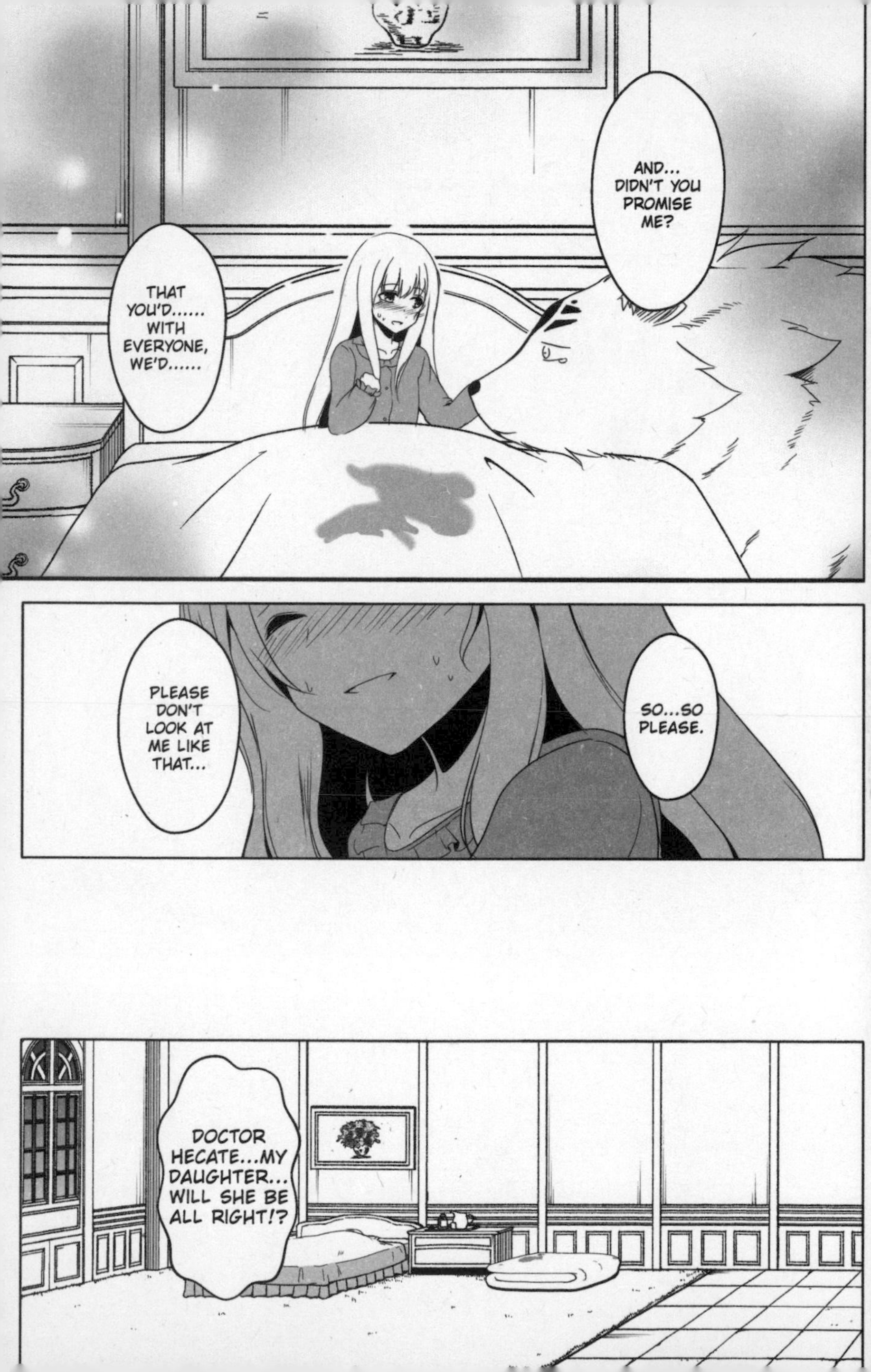
AND... DIDN'T YOU PROMISE ME?
THAT YOU'D...... WITH EVERYONE, WE'D......
SO...SO PLEASE.
PLEASE DON'T LOOK AT ME LIKE THAT...
DOCTOR HECATE...MY DAUGHTER... WILL SHE BE ALL RIGHT!?

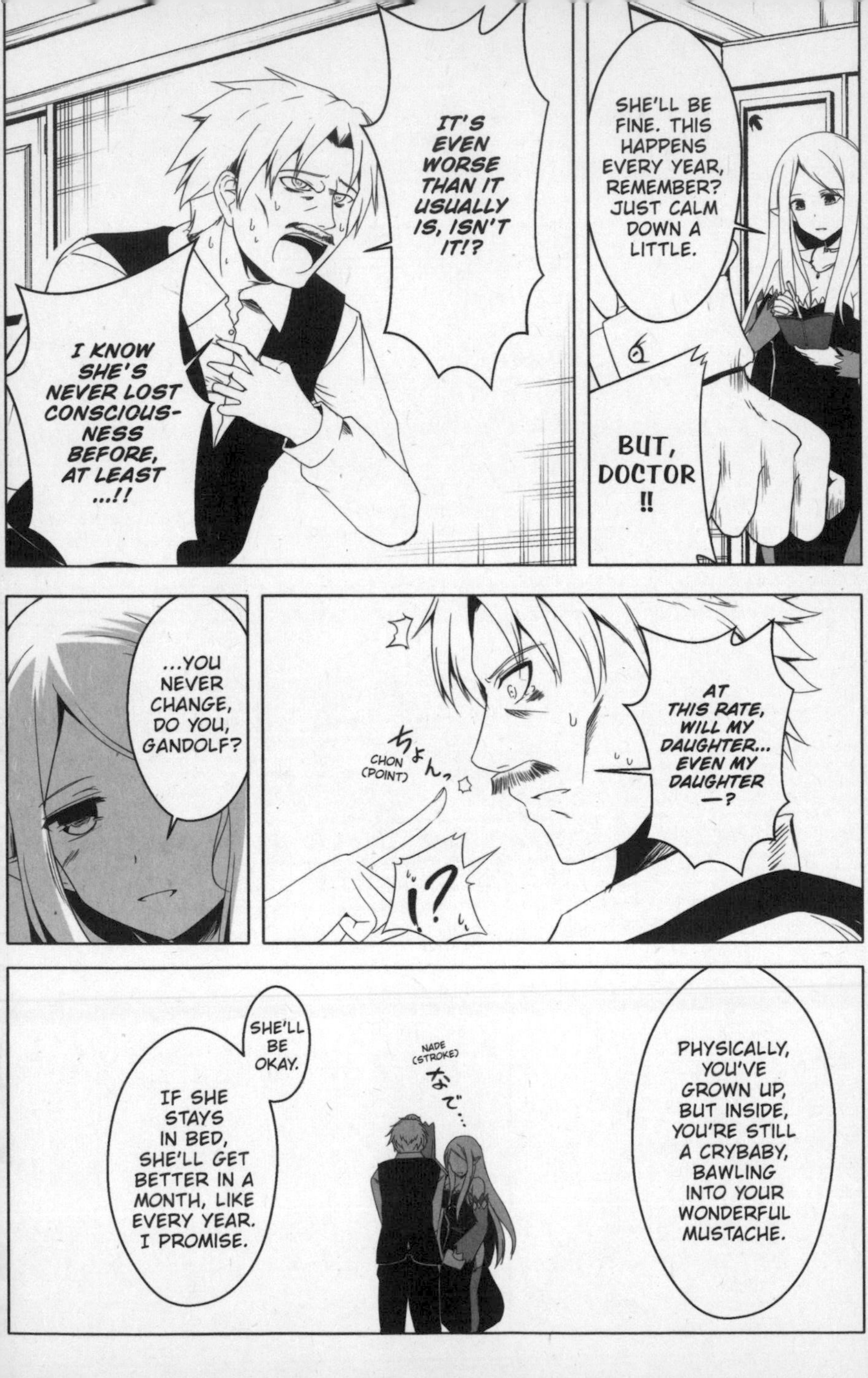
SHE'LL BE FINE. THIS HAPPENS EVERY YEAR, REMEMBER? JUST CALM DOWN A LITTLE.
BUT, DOCTOR!!
IT'S EVEN WORSE THAN IT USUALLY IS, ISN'T IT!?
I KNOW SHE'S NEVER LOST CONSCIOUS-NESS BEFORE, AT LEAST...!!
AT THIS RATE, WILL MY DAUGHTER... EVEN MY DAUGHTER—?
ちょん
CHON (POINT)
!?
...YOU NEVER CHANGE, DO YOU, GANDOLF?
PHYSICALLY, YOU'VE GROWN UP, BUT INSIDE, YOU'RE STILL A CRYBABY, BAWLING INTO YOUR WONDERFUL MUSTACHE.
NADE (STROKE)
なで…
SHE'LL BE OKAY.
IF SHE STAYS IN BED, SHE'LL GET BETTER IN A MONTH, LIKE EVERY YEAR. I PROMISE.

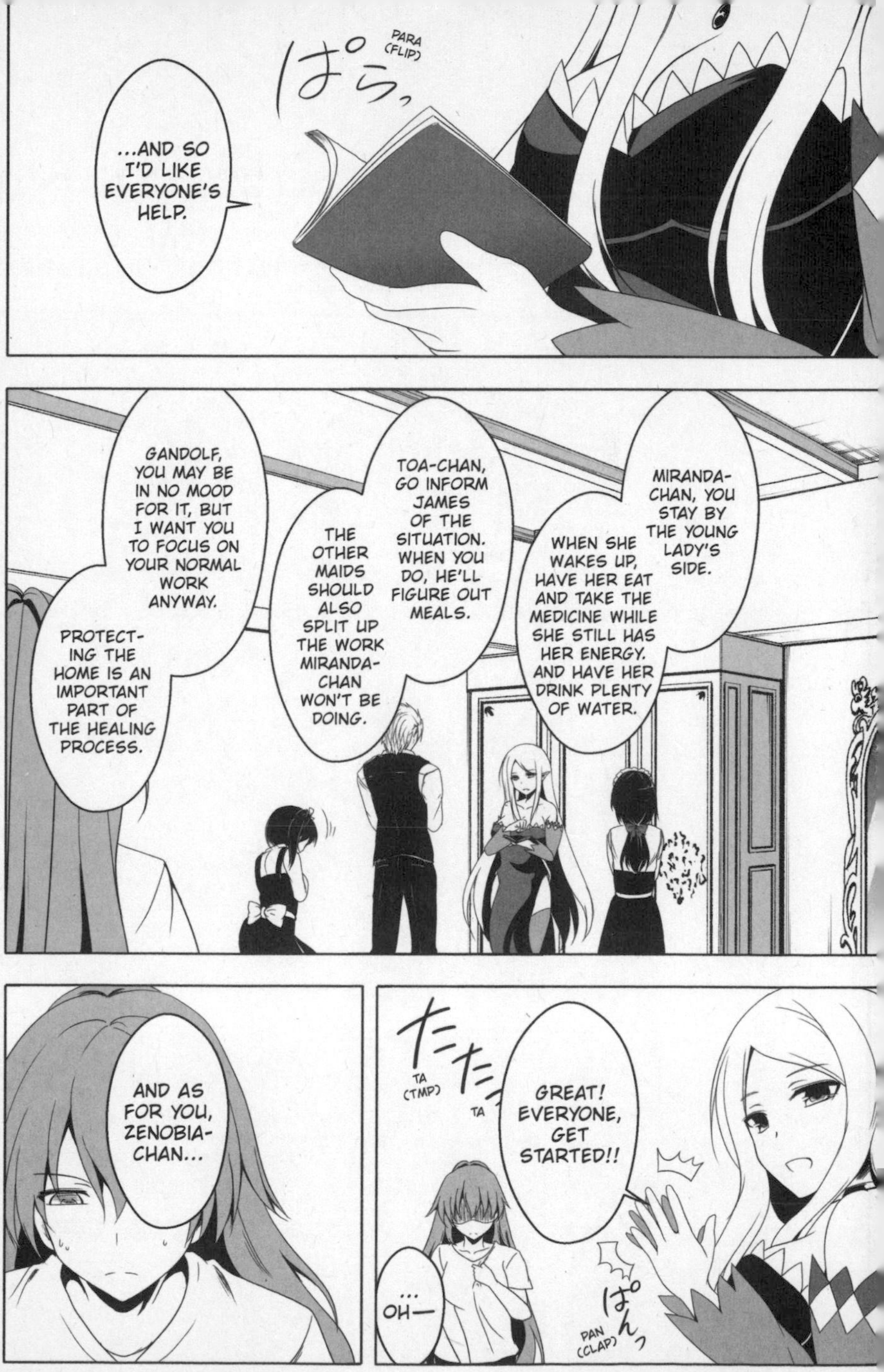
ぱらっ
PARA (FLIP)
...AND SO I'D LIKE EVERYONE'S HELP.
MIRANDA-CHAN, YOU STAY BY THE YOUNG LADY'S SIDE.
WHEN SHE WAKES UP, HAVE HER EAT AND TAKE THE MEDICINE WHILE SHE STILL HAS HER ENERGY. AND HAVE HER DRINK PLENTY OF WATER.
TOA-CHAN, GO INFORM JAMES OF THE SITUATION. WHEN YOU DO, HE'LL FIGURE OUT MEALS.
THE OTHER MAIDS SHOULD ALSO SPLIT UP THE WORK MIRANDA-CHAN WON'T BE DOING.
GANDOLF, YOU MAY BE IN NO MOOD FOR IT, BUT I WANT YOU TO FOCUS ON YOUR NORMAL WORK ANYWAY.
PROTECT-ING THE HOME IS AN IMPORTANT PART OF THE HEALING PROCESS.
たたっ
TA (TMP)
TA
GREAT! EVERYONE, GET STARTED!!
ぱんっ
PAN (CLAP)
...OH—
AND AS FOR YOU, ZENOBIA-CHAN...

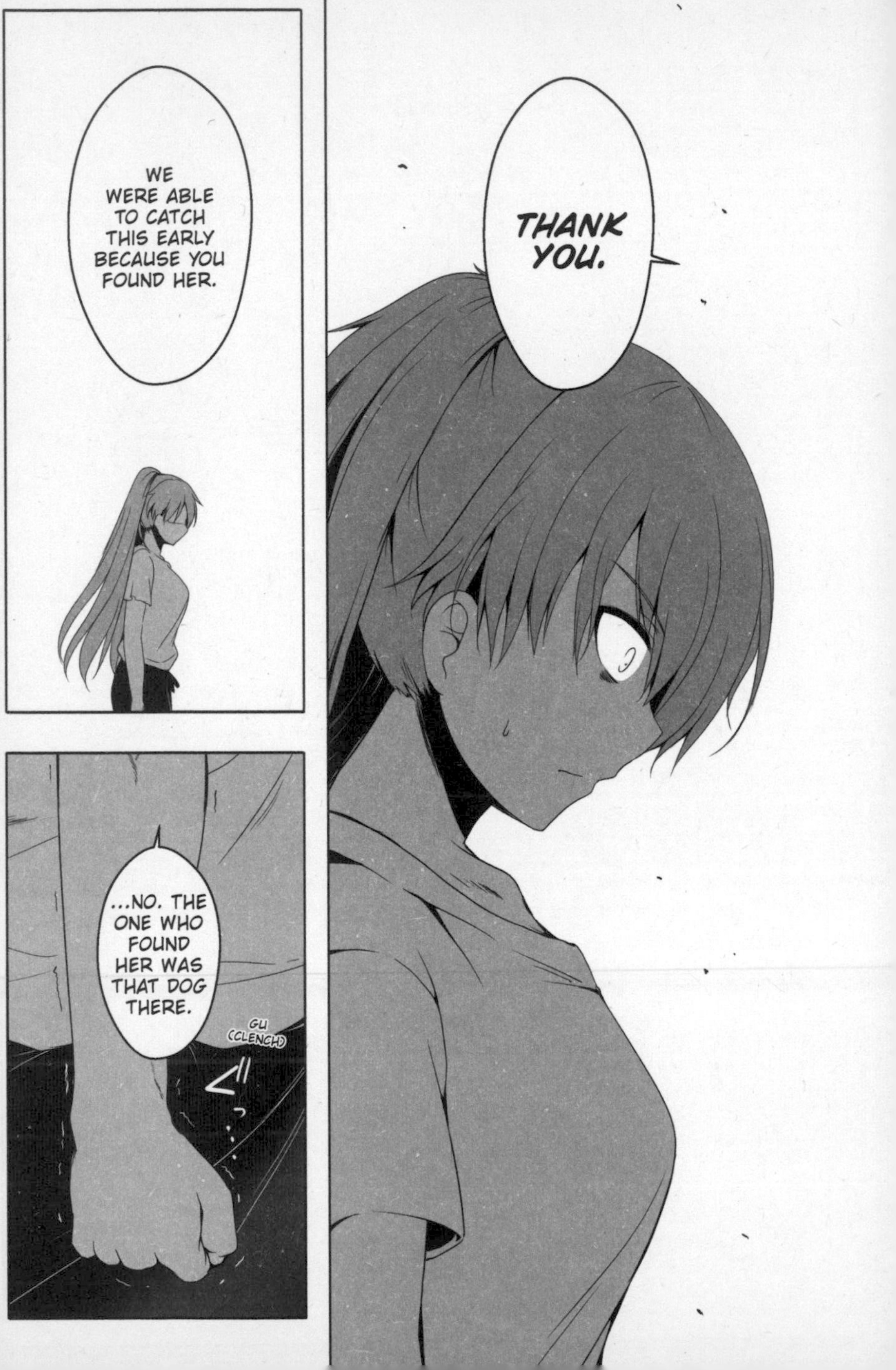
THANK YOU.
WE WERE ABLE TO CATCH THIS EARLY BECAUSE YOU FOUND HER.
...NO. THE ONE WHO FOUND HER WAS THAT DOG THERE.
GU (CLENCH)

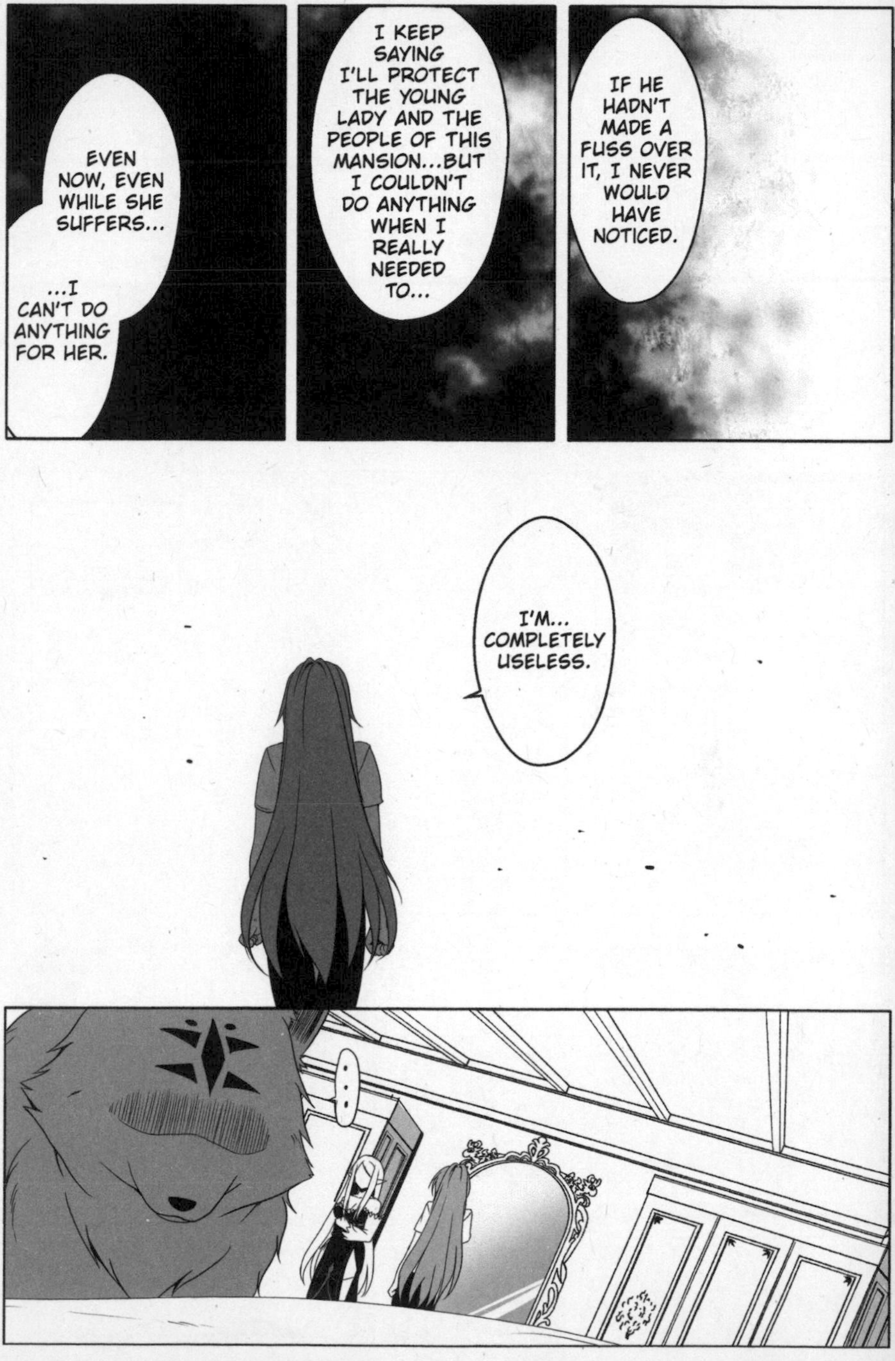
IF HE HADN'T MADE A FUSS OVER IT, I NEVER WOULD HAVE NOTICED.
I KEEP SAYING I'LL PROTECT THE YOUNG LADY AND THE PEOPLE OF THIS MANSION...BUT I COULDN'T DO ANYTHING WHEN I REALLY NEEDED TO...
EVEN NOW, EVEN WHILE SHE SUFFERS...
...I CAN'T DO ANYTHING FOR HER.
I'M... COMPLETELY USELESS.
...

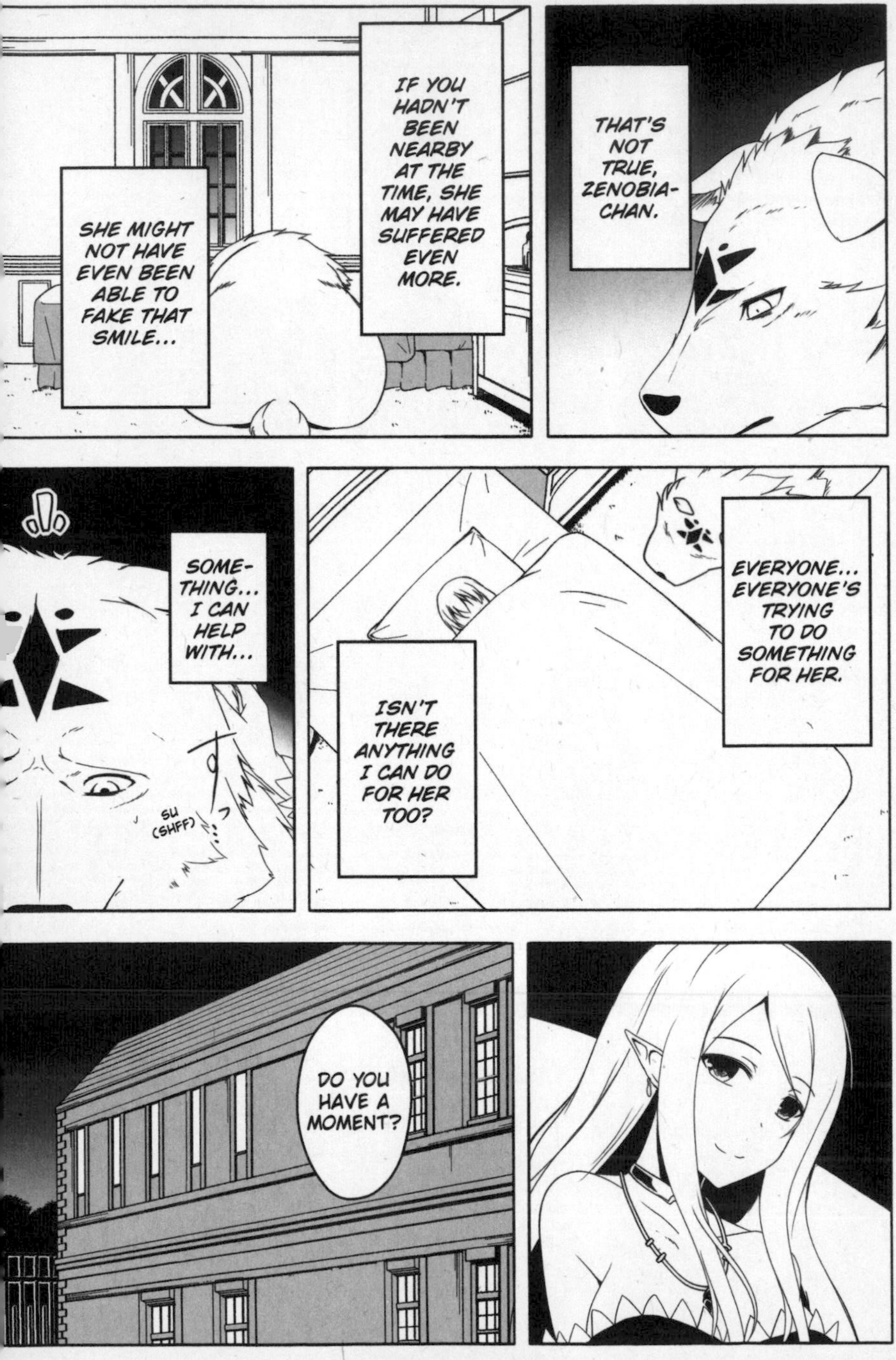
THAT'S NOT TRUE, ZENOBIA-CHAN.
IF YOU HADN'T BEEN NEARBY AT THE TIME, SHE MAY HAVE SUFFERED EVEN MORE.
SHE MIGHT NOT HAVE EVEN BEEN ABLE TO FAKE THAT SMILE...
EVERYONE... EVERYONE'S TRYING TO DO SOMETHING FOR HER.
ISN'T THERE ANYTHING I CAN DO FOR HER TOO?
SOME-THING... I CAN HELP WITH...
SU (SHFF)
DO YOU HAVE A MOMENT?

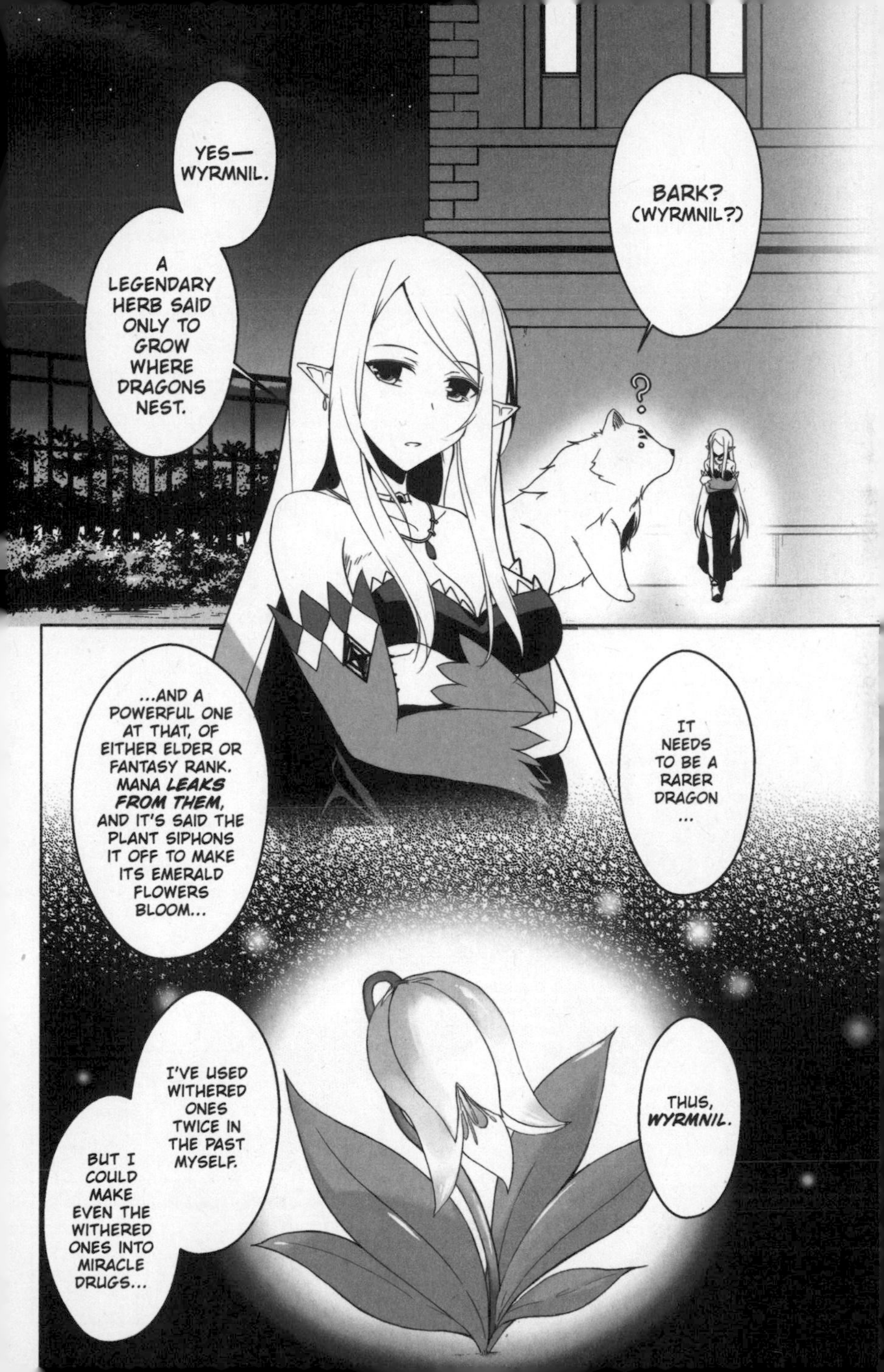
BARK? (WYRMNIL?)
YES— WYRMNIL.
A LEGENDARY HERB SAID ONLY TO GROW WHERE DRAGONS NEST.
IT NEEDS TO BE A RARER DRAGON...
...AND A POWERFUL ONE AT THAT, OF EITHER ELDER OR FANTASY RANK. MANA *LEAKS FROM THEM,* AND IT'S SAID THE PLANT SIPHONS IT OFF TO MAKE ITS EMERALD FLOWERS BLOOM...
THUS, *WYRMNIL.*
I'VE USED WITHERED ONES TWICE IN THE PAST MYSELF.
BUT I COULD MAKE EVEN THE WITHERED ONES INTO MIRACLE DRUGS...

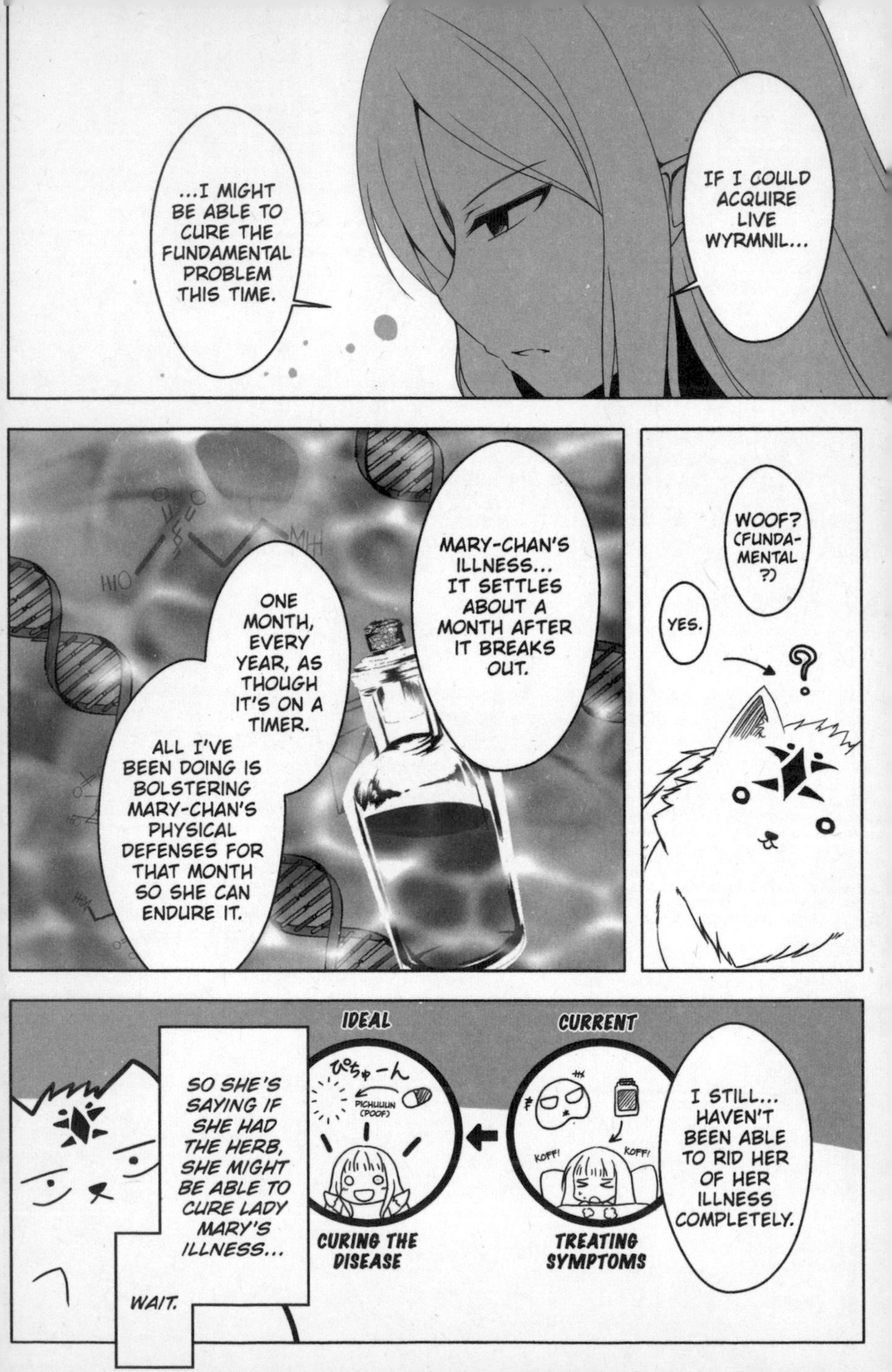
IF I COULD ACQUIRE LIVE WYRMNIL...
...I MIGHT BE ABLE TO CURE THE FUNDAMENTAL PROBLEM THIS TIME.
WOOF? (FUNDAMENTAL?)
YES.
MARY-CHAN'S ILLNESS... IT SETTLES ABOUT A MONTH AFTER IT BREAKS OUT.
ONE MONTH, EVERY YEAR, AS THOUGH IT'S ON A TIMER.
ALL I'VE BEEN DOING IS BOLSTERING MARY-CHAN'S PHYSICAL DEFENSES FOR THAT MONTH SO SHE CAN ENDURE IT.
I STILL... HAVEN'T BEEN ABLE TO RID HER OF HER ILLNESS COMPLETELY.
CURRENT
KOFF!
KOFF!
TREATING SYMPTOMS
IDEAL
ぴちゅーん
PICHUUUN (POOF)
CURING THE DISEASE
SO SHE'S SAYING IF SHE HAD THE HERB, SHE MIGHT BE ABLE TO CURE LADY MARY'S ILLNESS...
WAIT.

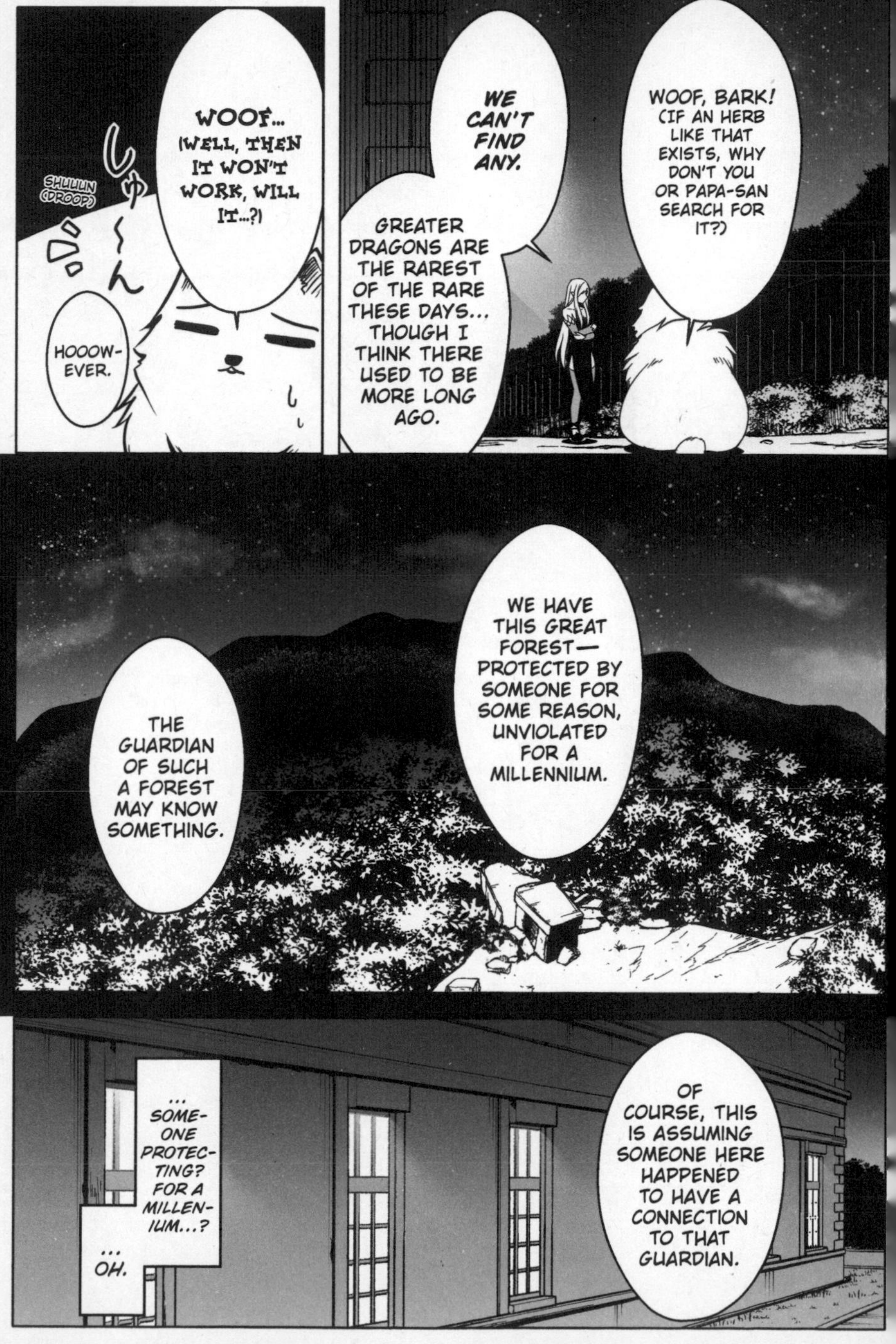
WOOF, BARK! (IF AN HERB LIKE THAT EXISTS, WHY DON'T YOU OR PAPA-SAN SEARCH FOR IT?)
WE CAN'T FIND ANY.
GREATER DRAGONS ARE THE RAREST OF THE RARE THESE DAYS... THOUGH I THINK THERE USED TO BE MORE LONG AGO.
WOOF... (WELL, THEN IT WON'T WORK, WILL IT...?)
SHUUUN (DROOP)
HOOOW-EVER.
WE HAVE THIS GREAT FOREST—PROTECTED BY SOMEONE FOR SOME REASON, UNVIOLATED FOR A MILLENNIUM.
THE GUARDIAN OF SUCH A FOREST MAY KNOW SOMETHING.
OF COURSE, THIS IS ASSUMING SOMEONE HERE HAPPENED TO HAVE A CONNECTION TO THAT GUARDIAN.
...SOME-ONE PROTEC-TING? FOR A MILLEN-IUM...?
...OH.

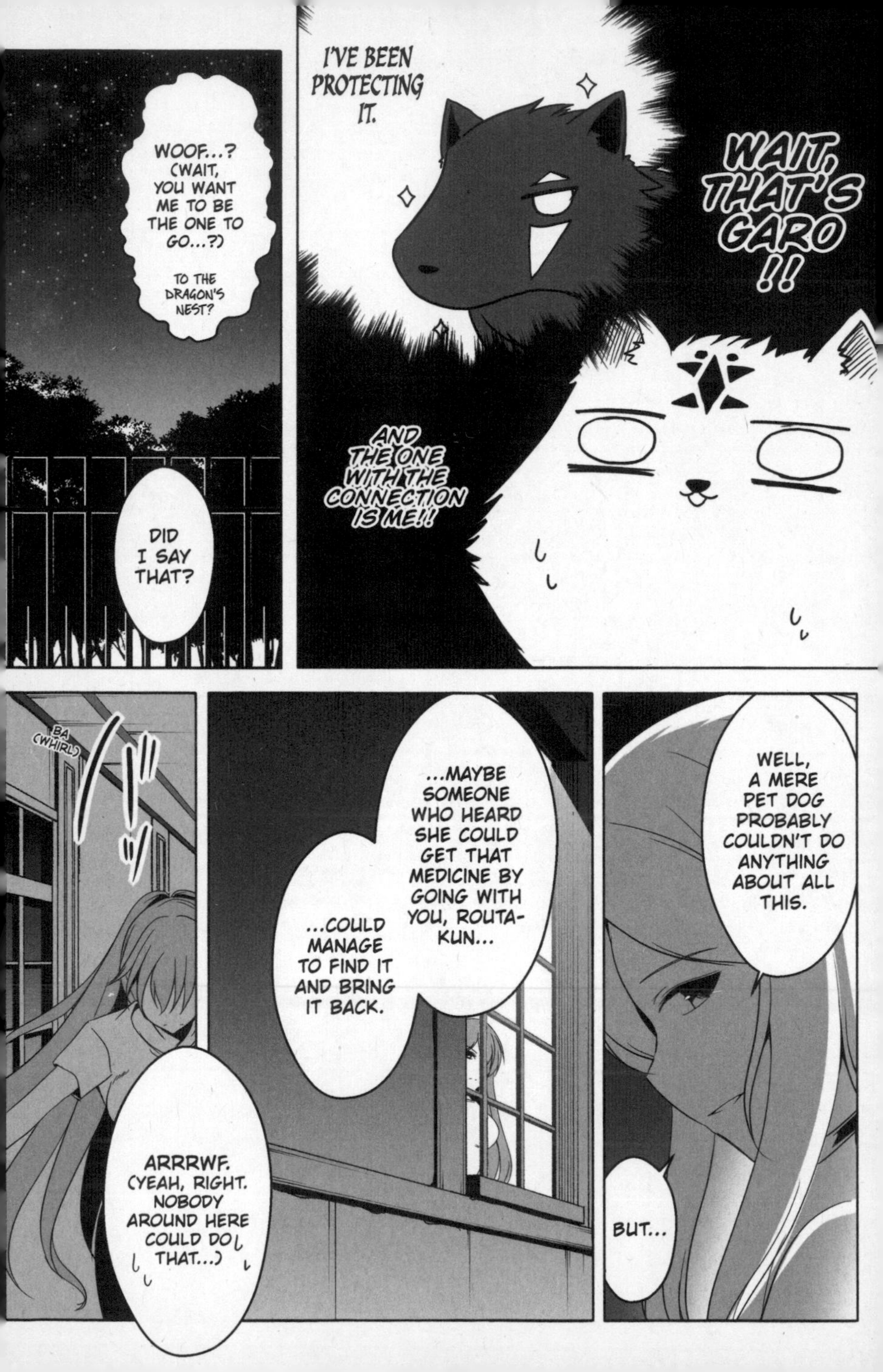
WAIT, THAT'S GARO!!
I'VE BEEN PROTECTING IT.
AND THE ONE WITH THE CONNECTION IS ME!!
WOOF...? (WAIT, YOU WANT ME TO BE THE ONE TO GO...?)
TO THE DRAGON'S NEST?
DID I SAY THAT?
WELL, A MERE PET DOG PROBABLY COULDN'T DO ANYTHING ABOUT ALL THIS.
BUT...
...MAYBE SOMEONE WHO HEARD SHE COULD GET THAT MEDICINE BY GOING WITH YOU, ROUTA-KUN...
...COULD MANAGE TO FIND IT AND BRING IT BACK.
BA (WHIRL)
ARRRWF. (YEAH, RIGHT. NOBODY AROUND HERE COULD DO THAT...)

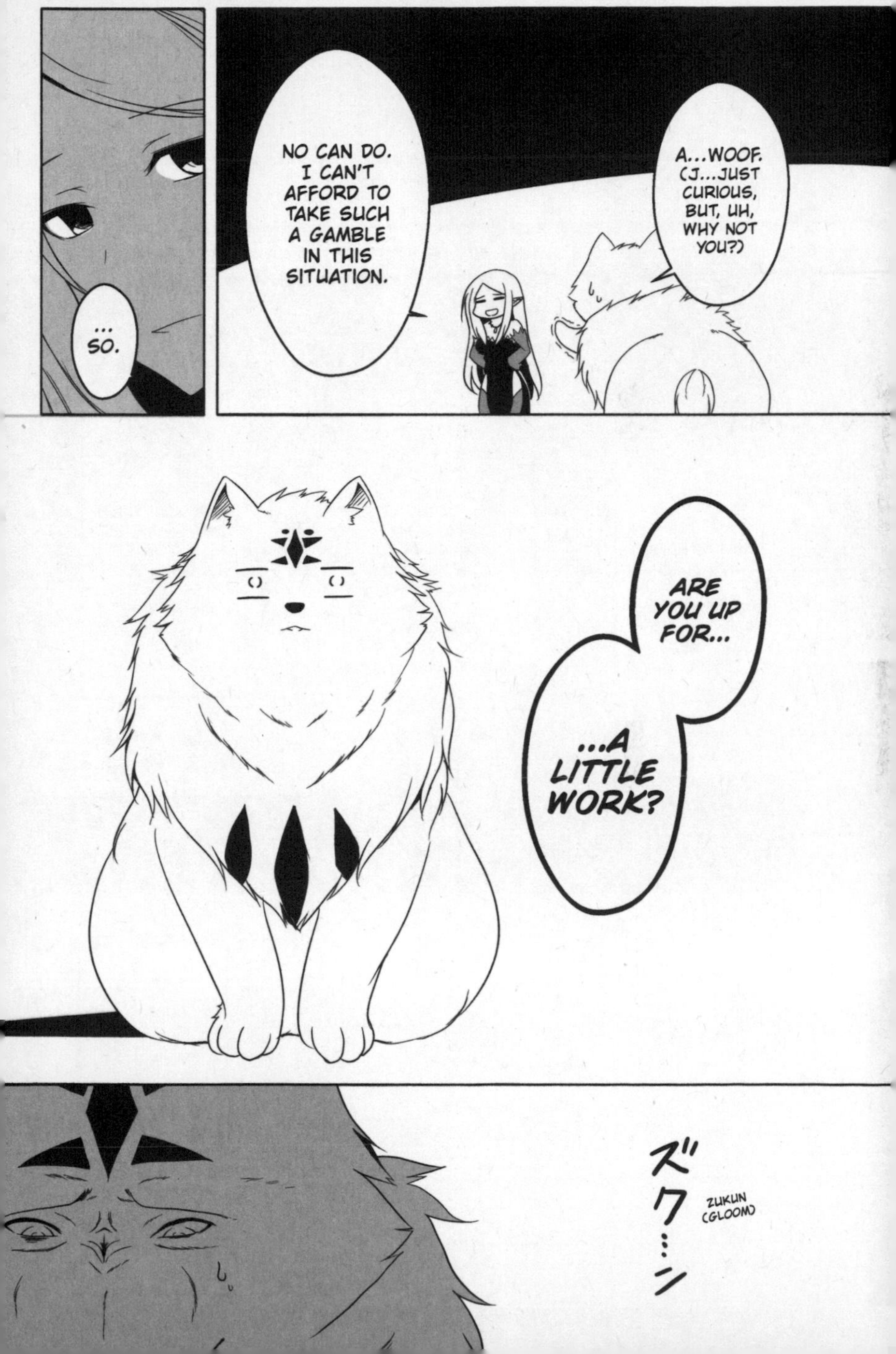
A...WOOF. (J...JUST CURIOUS, BUT, UH, WHY NOT YOU?)
NO CAN DO. I CAN'T AFFORD TO TAKE SUCH A GAMBLE IN THIS SITUATION.
... SO.
ARE YOU UP FOR...
...A LITTLE WORK?
ズクーン
ZUKUN (GLOOM)

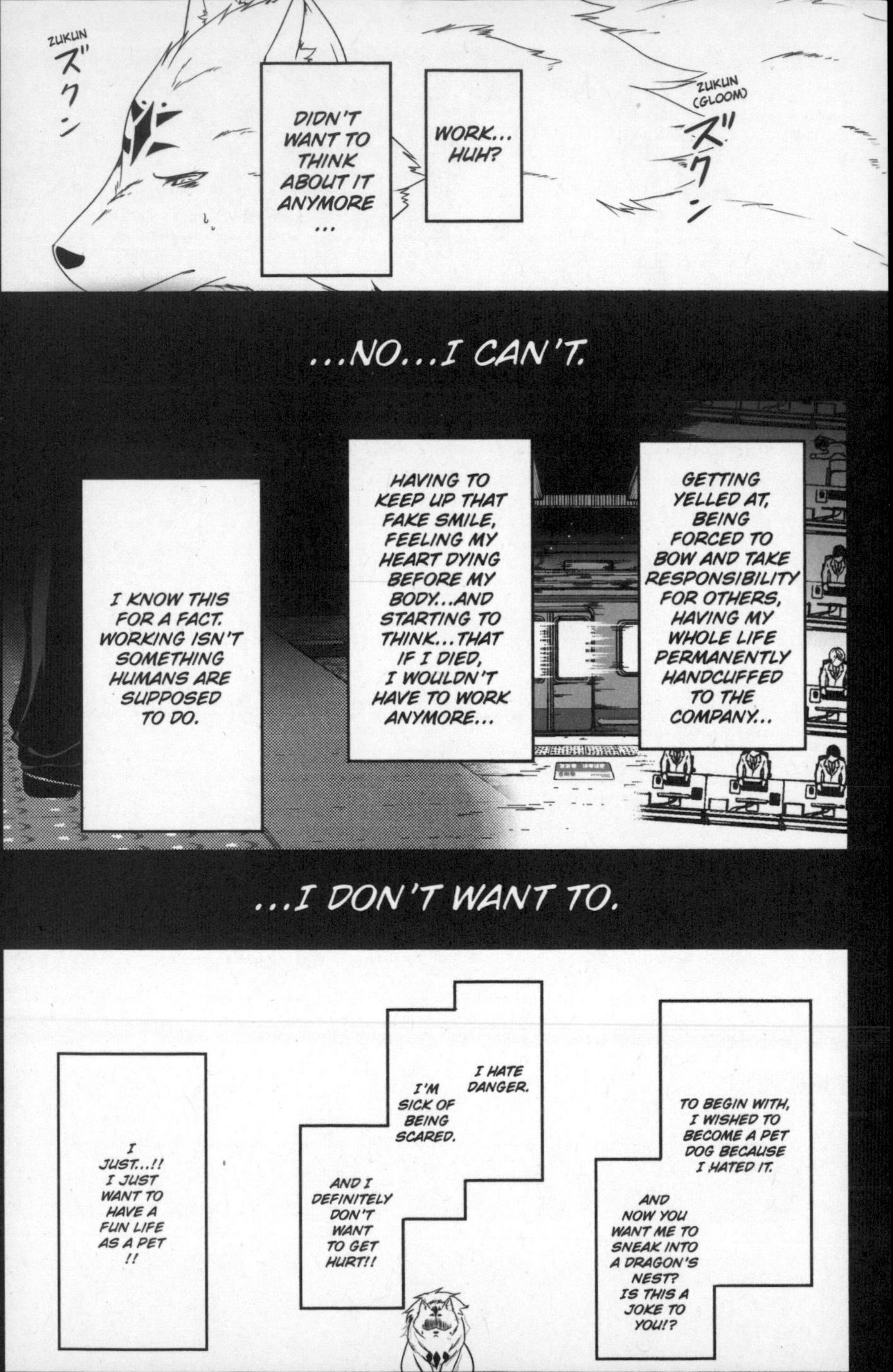
ZUKUN (GLOOM)
ズクン
WORK... HUH?
DIDN'T WANT TO THINK ABOUT IT ANYMORE ...
ZUKUN
ズクン
...NO...I CAN'T.
GETTING YELLED AT, BEING FORCED TO BOW AND TAKE RESPONSIBILITY FOR OTHERS, HAVING MY WHOLE LIFE PERMANENTLY HANDCUFFED TO THE COMPANY...
HAVING TO KEEP UP THAT FAKE SMILE, FEELING MY HEART DYING BEFORE MY BODY...AND STARTING TO THINK...THAT IF I DIED, I WOULDN'T HAVE TO WORK ANYMORE...
I KNOW THIS FOR A FACT. WORKING ISN'T SOMETHING HUMANS ARE SUPPOSED TO DO.
...I DON'T WANT TO.
TO BEGIN WITH, I WISHED TO BECOME A PET DOG BECAUSE I HATED IT.
AND NOW YOU WANT ME TO SNEAK INTO A DRAGON'S NEST? IS THIS A JOKE TO YOU!?
I HATE DANGER.
I'M SICK OF BEING SCARED.
AND I DEFINITELY DON'T WANT TO GET HURT!!
I JUST...!! I JUST WANT TO HAVE A FUN LIFE AS A PET !!

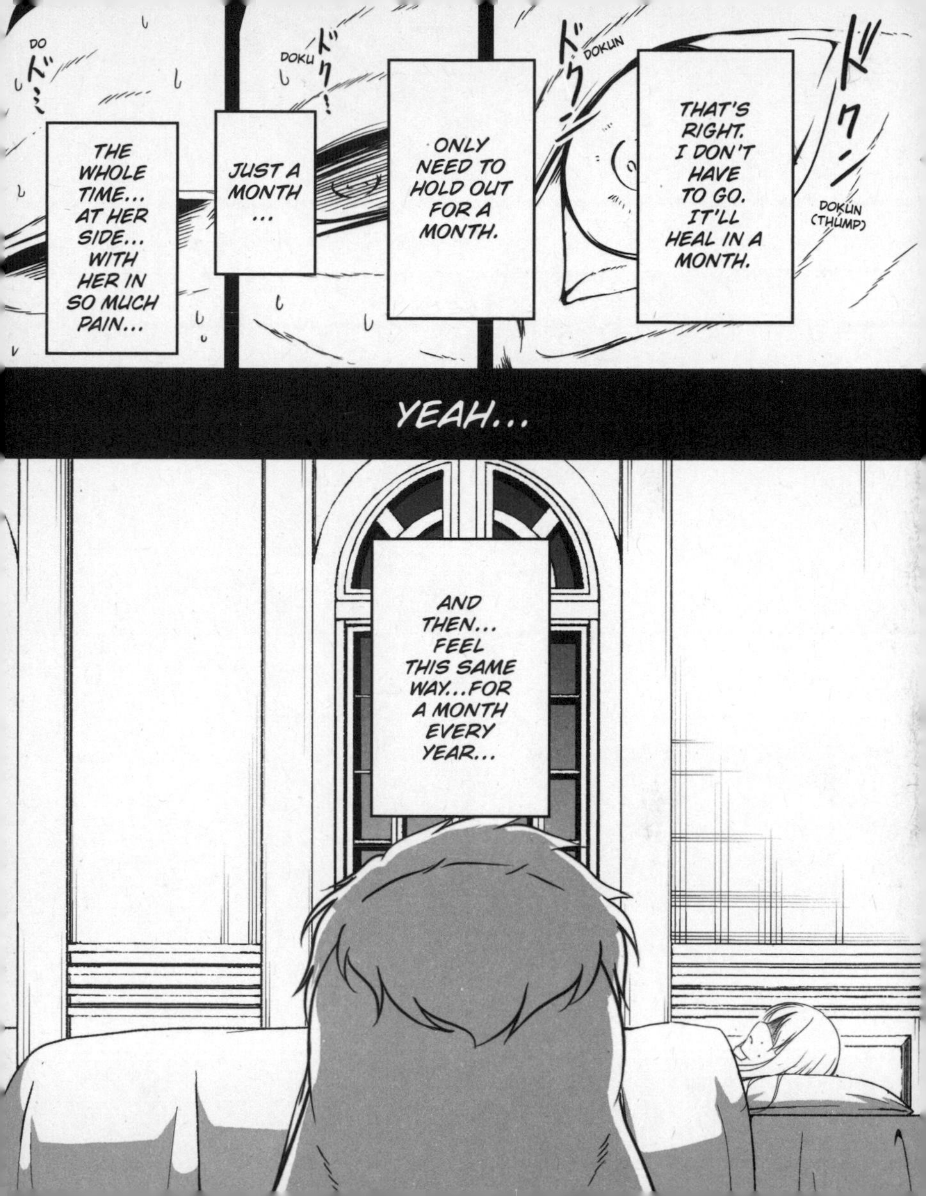
DOKUN (THUMP)
THAT'S RIGHT. I DON'T HAVE TO GO. IT'LL HEAL IN A MONTH.
DOKUN
ONLY NEED TO HOLD OUT FOR A MONTH.
DOKU
JUST A MONTH...
DO
THE WHOLE TIME... AT HER SIDE... WITH HER IN SO MUCH PAIN...
YEAH...
AND THEN... FEEL THIS SAME WAY...FOR A MONTH EVERY YEAR...

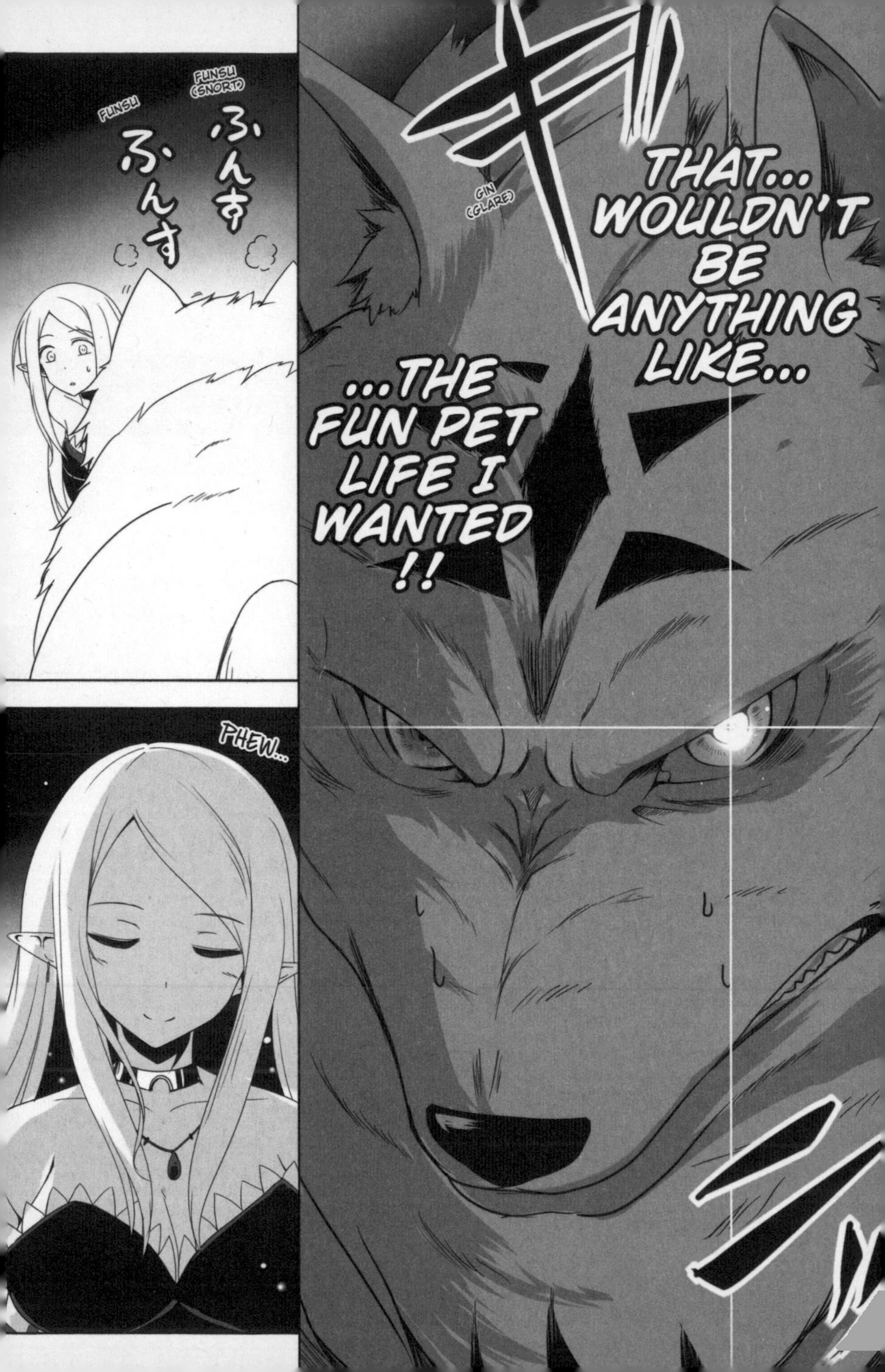
GIN (GLARE)
THAT... WOULDN'T BE ANYTHING LIKE...
...THE FUN PET LIFE I WANTED!!
FUNSU (SNORT)
ふんす
FUNSU
ふんす
PHEW...

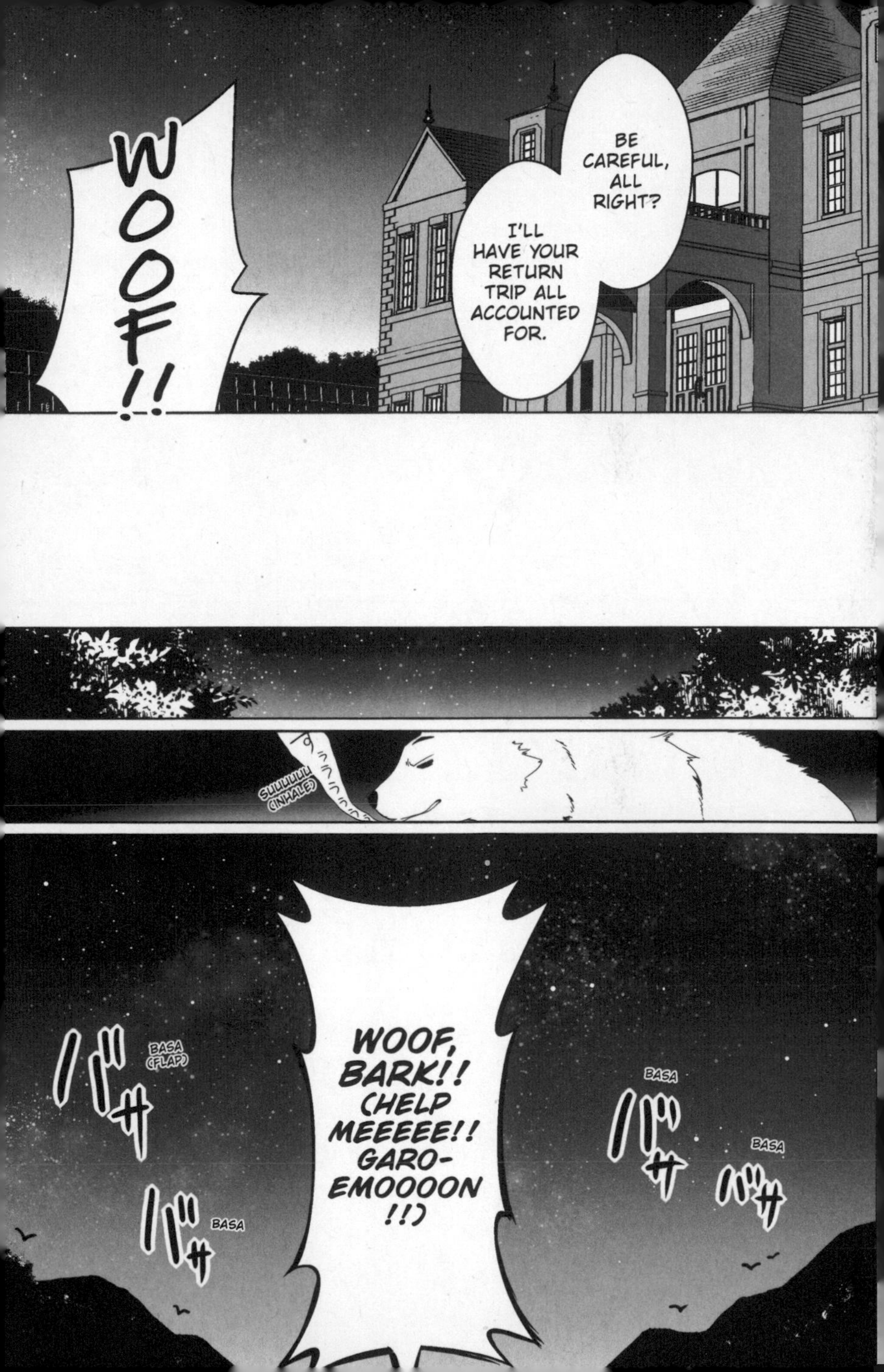
BE CAREFUL, ALL RIGHT?
I'LL HAVE YOUR RETURN TRIP ALL ACCOUNTED FOR.
WOOF!!
SUUUUUU (INHALE)
BASA
BASA
WOOF, BARK!! (HELP MEEEEE!! GARO-EMOOOON!!)
BASA (FLAP)
BASA

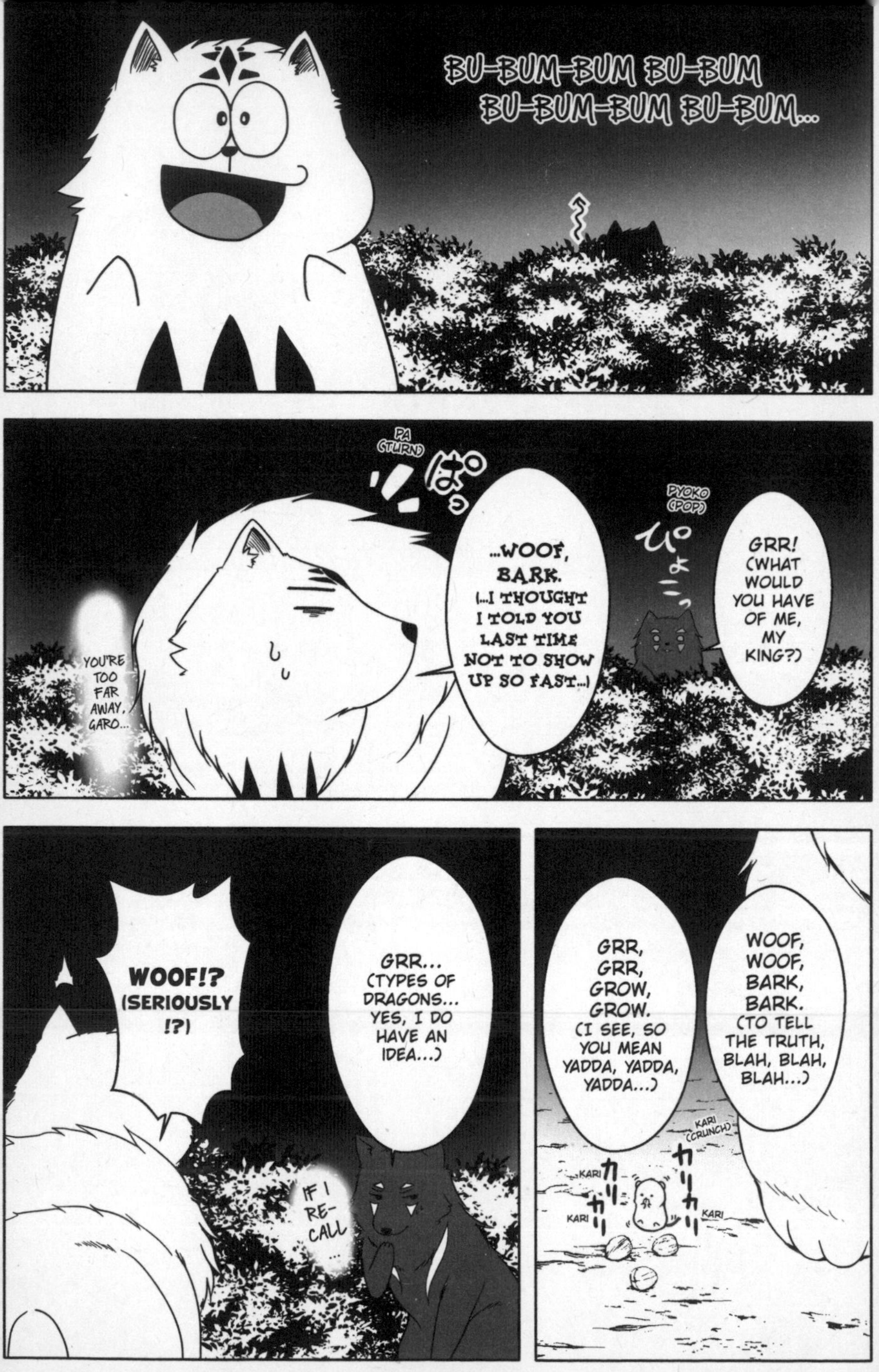
BU-BUM-BUM BU-BUM
BU-BUM-BUM BU-BUM...
PYOKO (POP)
ぴょこっ
GRR! (WHAT WOULD YOU HAVE OF ME, MY KING?)
PA (TURN)
ぱっ
...WOOF, BARK. (...I THOUGHT I TOLD YOU LAST TIME NOT TO SHOW UP SO FAST...)
YOU'RE TOO FAR AWAY, GARO...
WOOF, WOOF, BARK, BARK. (TO TELL THE TRUTH, BLAH, BLAH, BLAH...)
GRR, GRR, GROW, GROW. (I SEE, SO YOU MEAN YADDA, YADDA, YADDA...)
KARI (CRUNCH)
カリカリ
KARI
カリカリ
KARI
KARI
GRR... (TYPES OF DRAGONS... YES, I DO HAVE AN IDEA...)
IF I RE-CALL...
WOOF!? (SERIOUSLY!?)

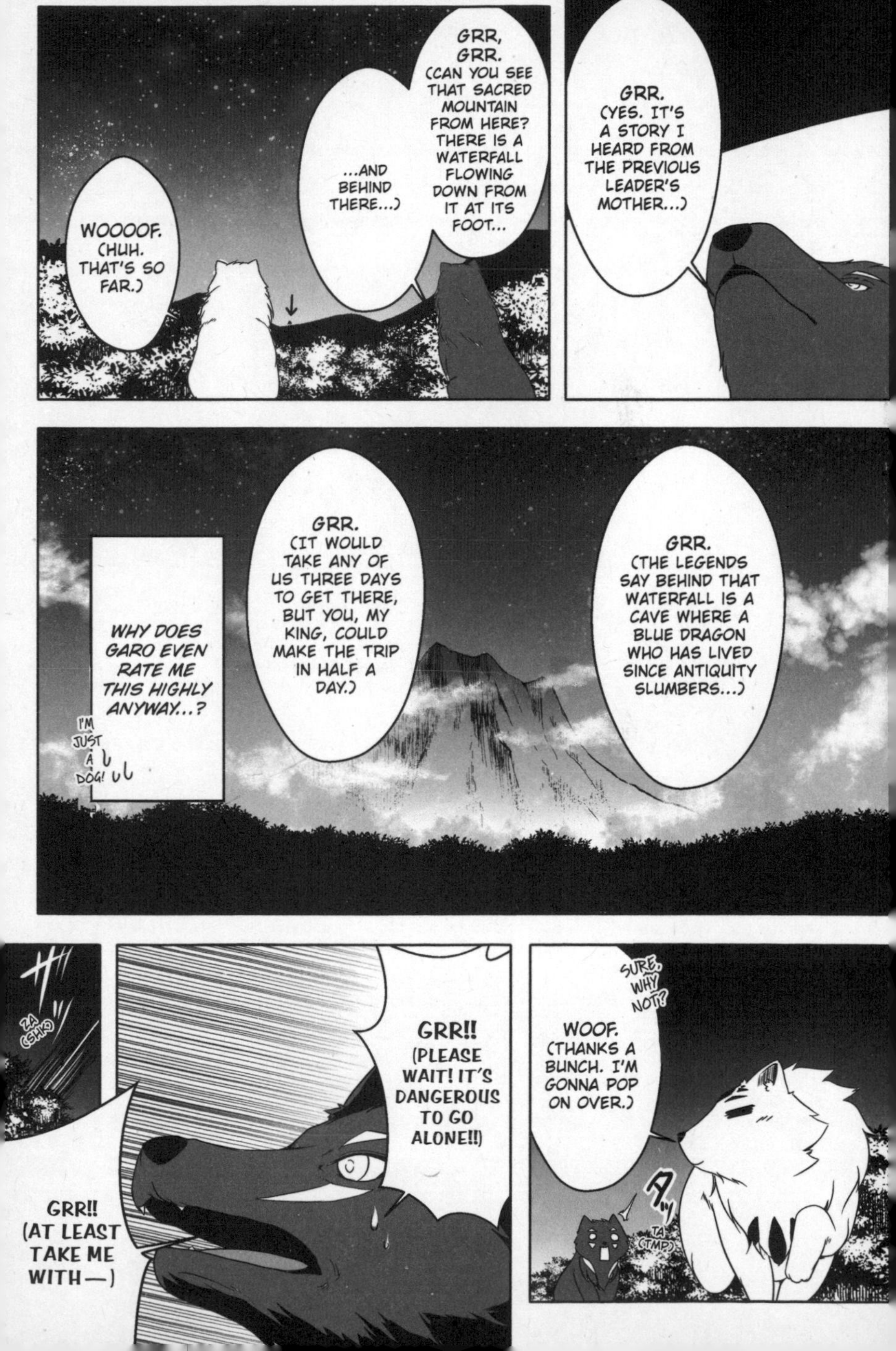
GRR. (YES. IT'S A STORY I HEARD FROM THE PREVIOUS LEADER'S MOTHER...)
GRR, GRR. (CAN YOU SEE THAT SACRED MOUNTAIN FROM HERE? THERE IS A WATERFALL FLOWING DOWN FROM IT AT ITS FOOT...
...AND BEHIND THERE...)
WOOOOF. (HUH. THAT'S SO FAR.)
GRR. (THE LEGENDS SAY BEHIND THAT WATERFALL IS A CAVE WHERE A BLUE DRAGON WHO HAS LIVED SINCE ANTIQUITY SLUMBERS...)
GRR. (IT WOULD TAKE ANY OF US THREE DAYS TO GET THERE, BUT YOU, MY KING, COULD MAKE THE TRIP IN HALF A DAY.)
WHY DOES GARO EVEN RATE ME THIS HIGHLY ANYWAY...?
I'M JUST A DOG!
SURE, WHY NOT?
WOOF. (THANKS A BUNCH. I'M GONNA POP ON OVER.)
A
TA (TMP)
GRR!! (PLEASE WAIT! IT'S DANGEROUS TO GO ALONE!!)
GRR!! (AT LEAST TAKE ME WITH—)
ZA (SHK)

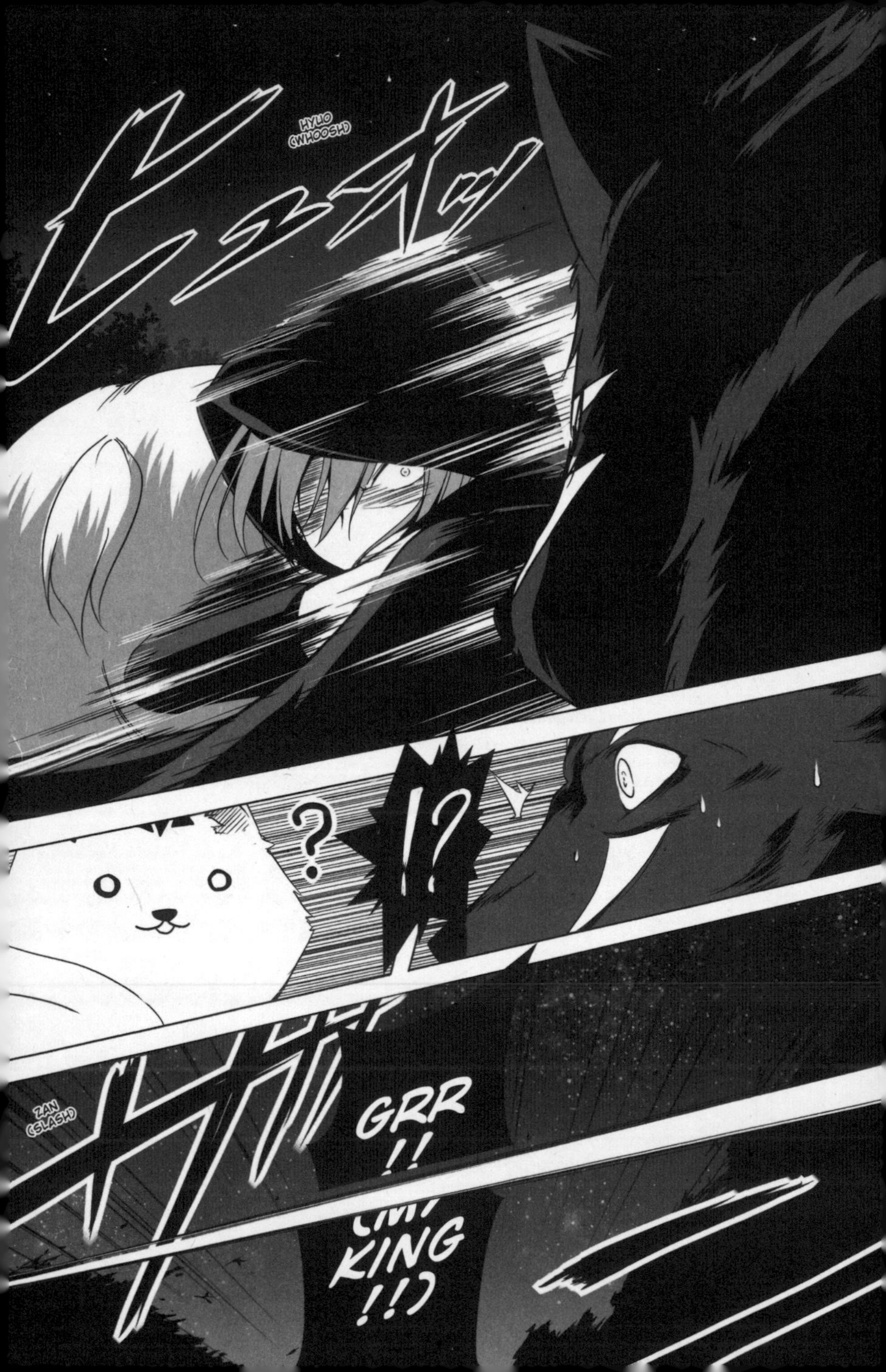
HYUO (WHOOSH)
!?
?
GRR!! (MY KING!!)
ZAN (SLASH)

Chapter 10

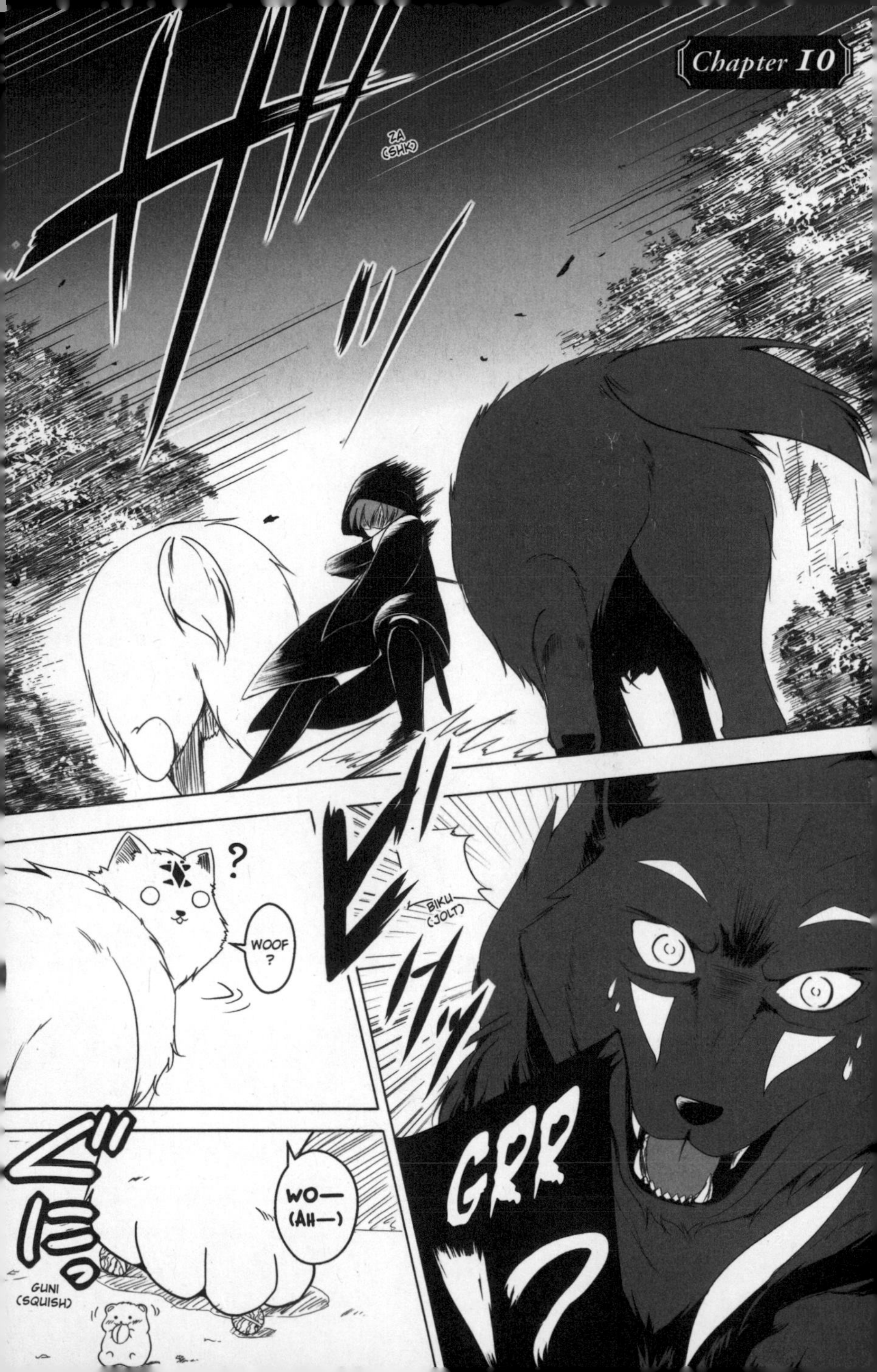
ZA
(SHK)
BIKU
(JOLT)
GRR
?
WOOF
?
WO—
(AH—)
GUNI
(SQUISH)

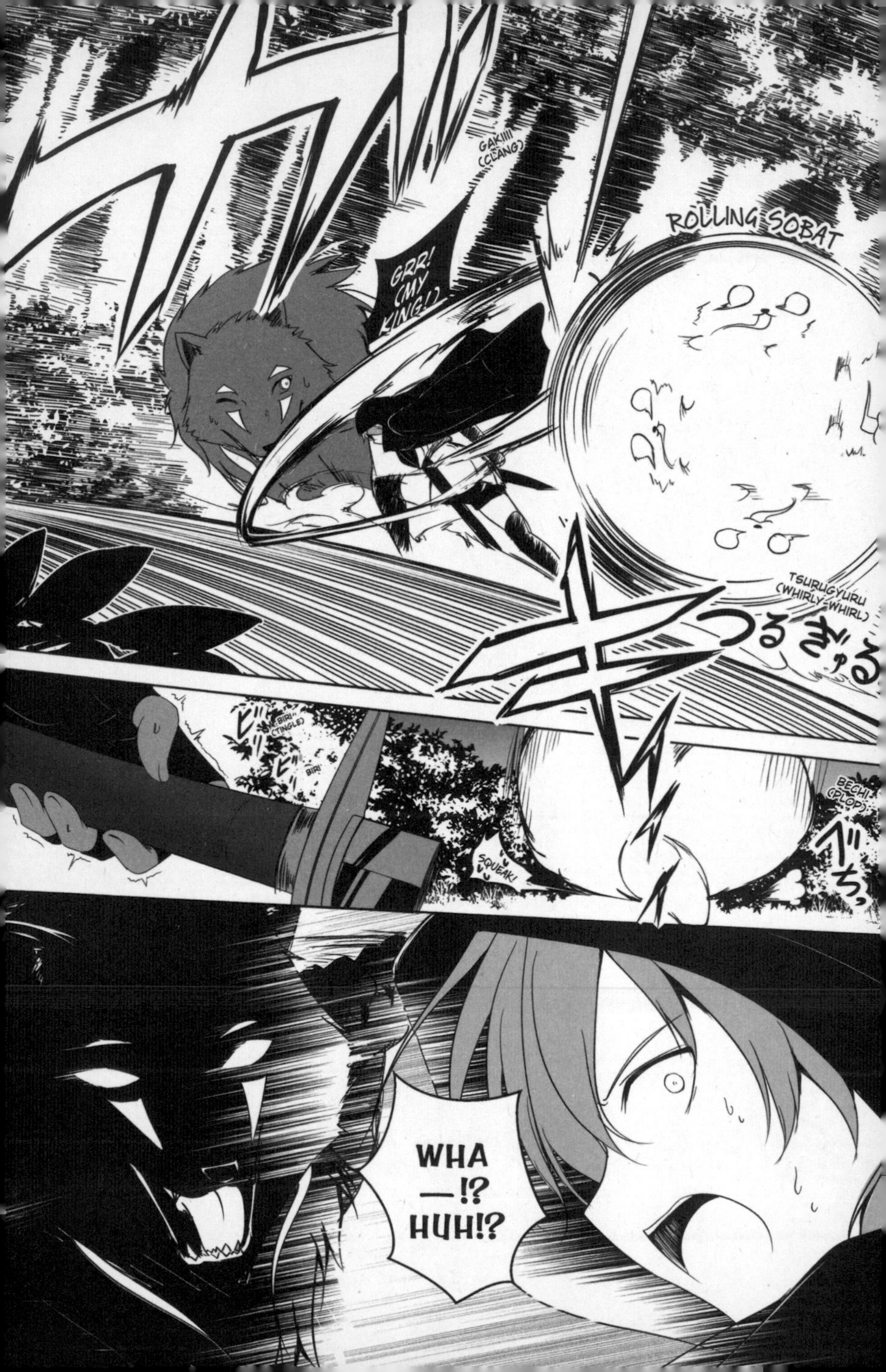
ROLLING SOBAT
GAKIIII (CLANG)
GRR! (MY KING!)
TSURUGYURU (WHIRLY WHIRL)
つるぎゅる
BECHI (PLOP)
べち
SQUEAK!
BIRI (TINGLE)
ビリ
BIRI
ビリ
WHA—!? HUH!?

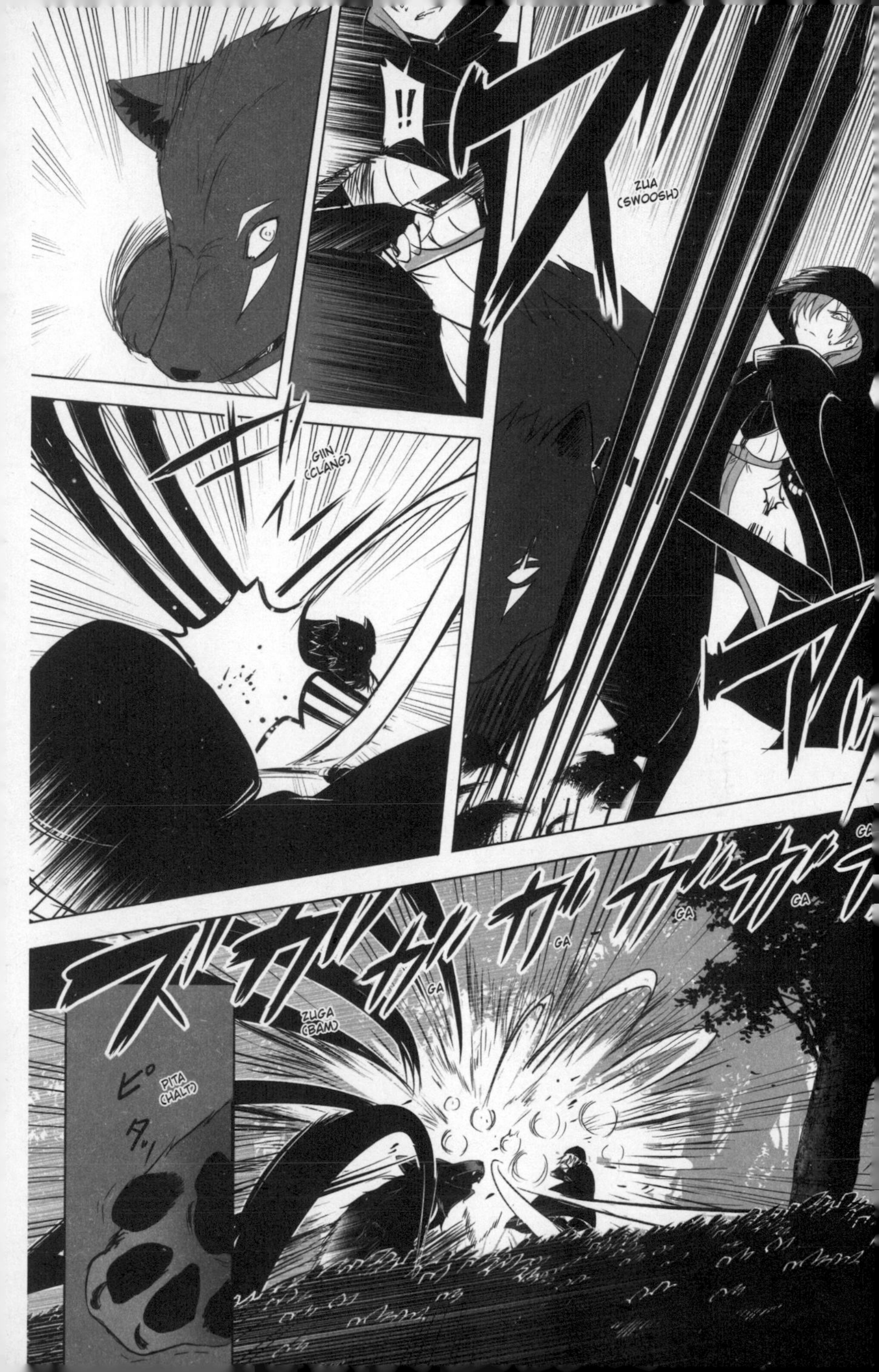

ZUA
(SWOOSH)
!!
GIIN
(CLANG)
GA
GA
GA
GA
GA
ZUGA
(BAM)
ピタッ
PITA
(HALT)

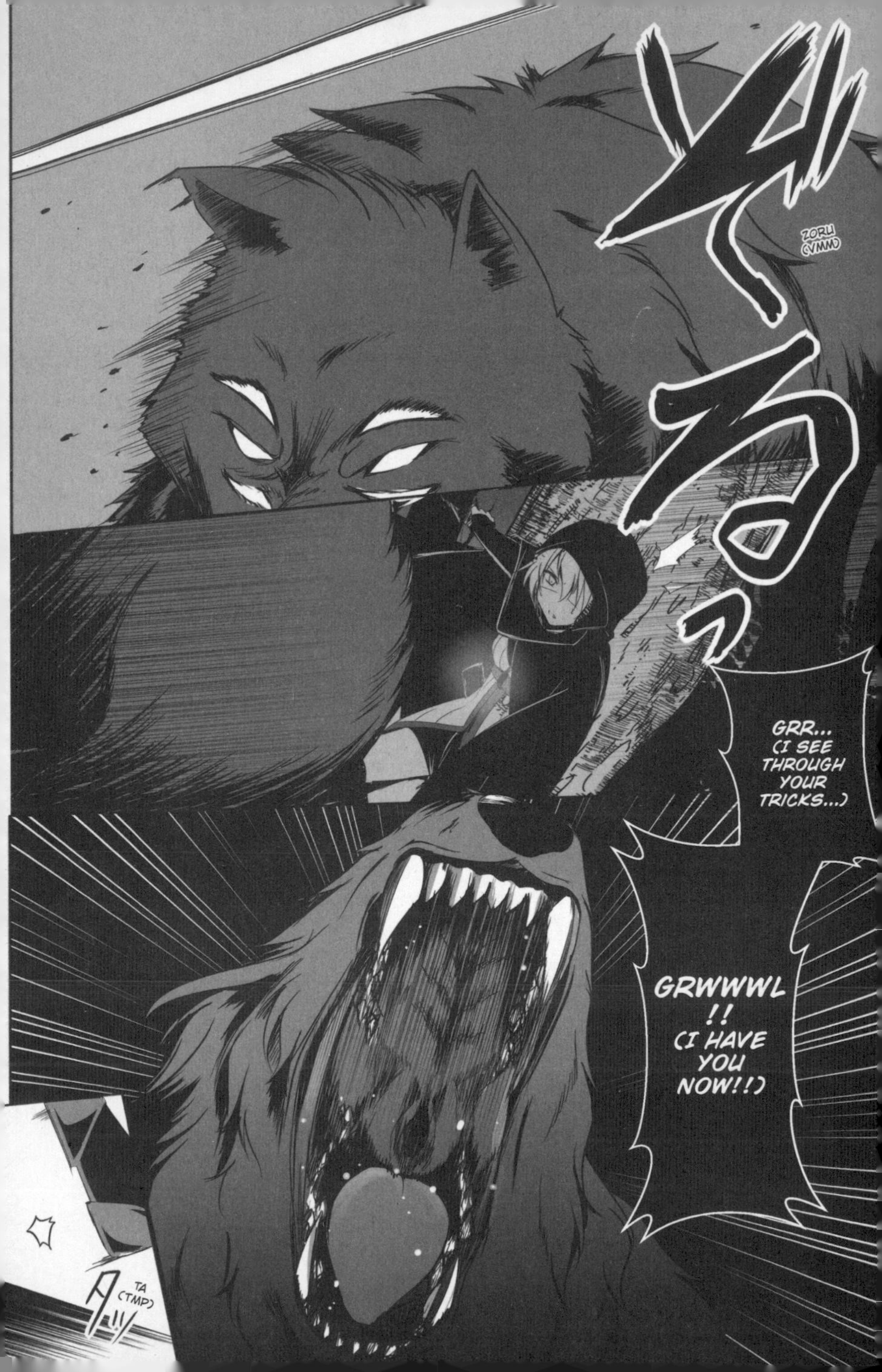
ZORU
(VMM)
GRR...
(I SEE THROUGH YOUR TRICKS...)
GRWWWL!!
(I HAVE YOU NOW!!)
TA
(TMP)

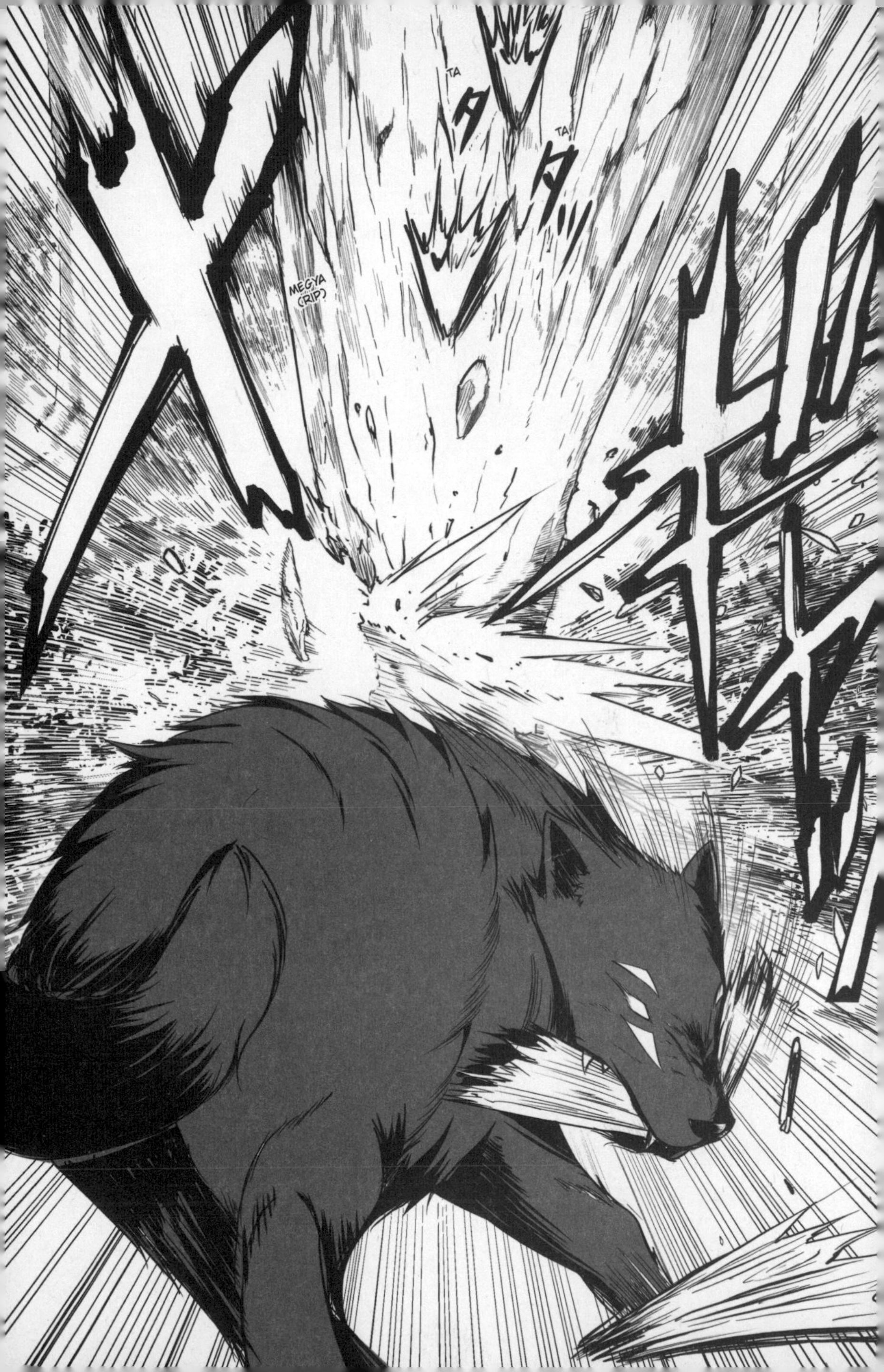
TA
TA
MEGYA
(RIP)

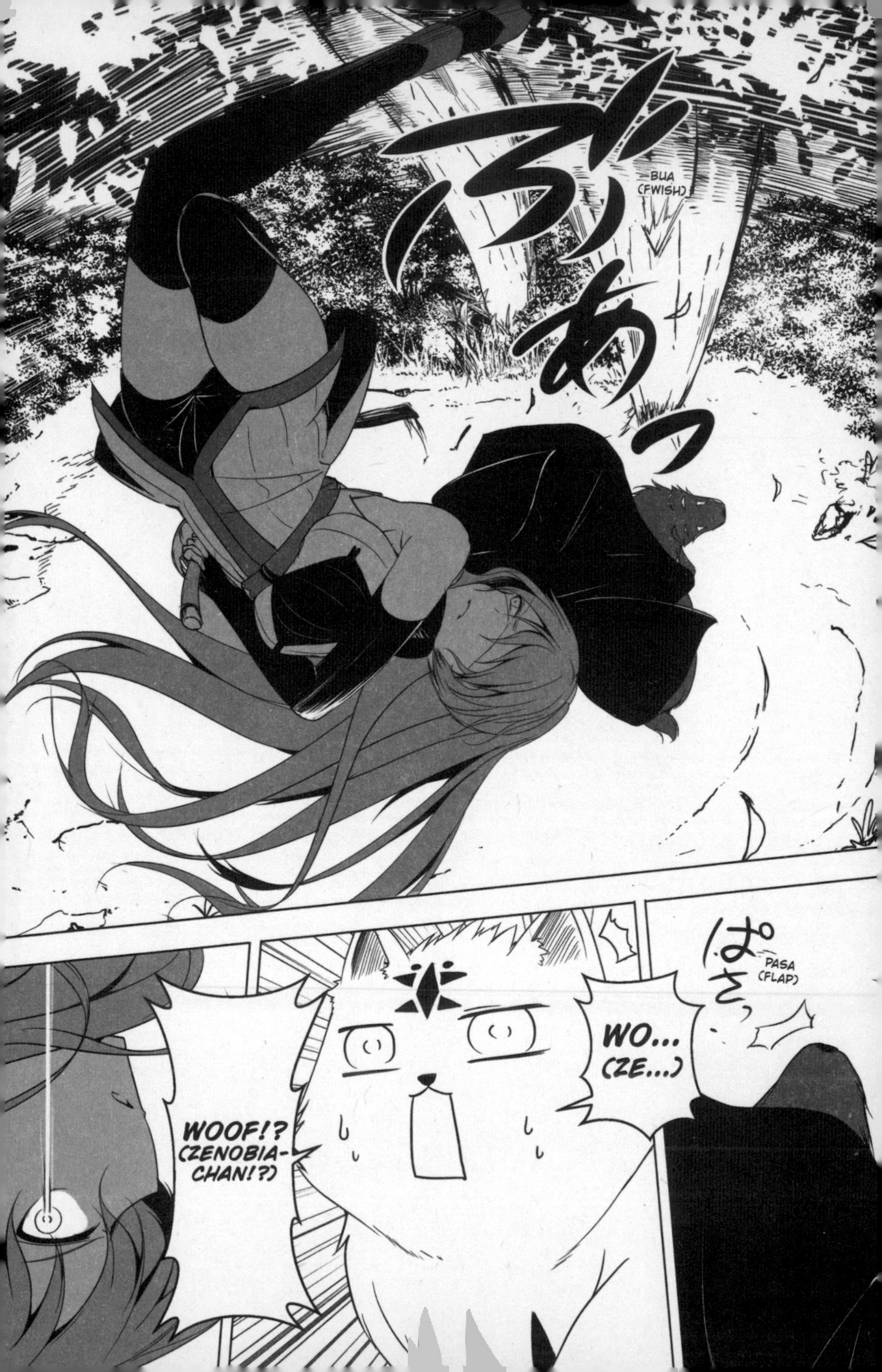
ぶあっ
BUA (FWISH)
ぱさっ
PASA (FLAP)
WO... (ZE...)
WOOF!? (ZENOBIA-CHAN!?)

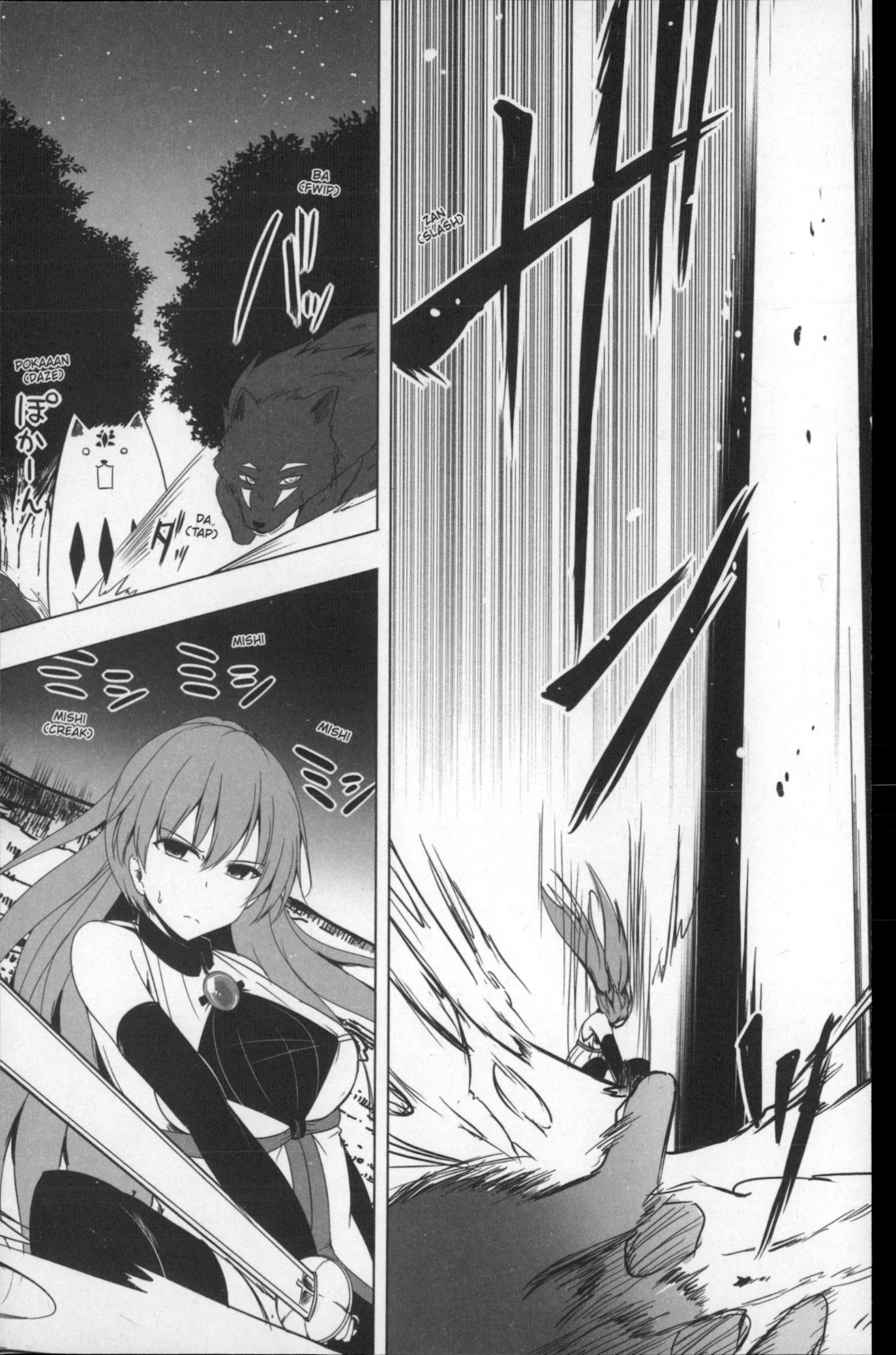
ZAN (SLASH)
BA (FWIP)
POKAAAN (DAZE)
ぽかーん
DA (TAP)
MISHI
MISHI
MISHI (CREAK)

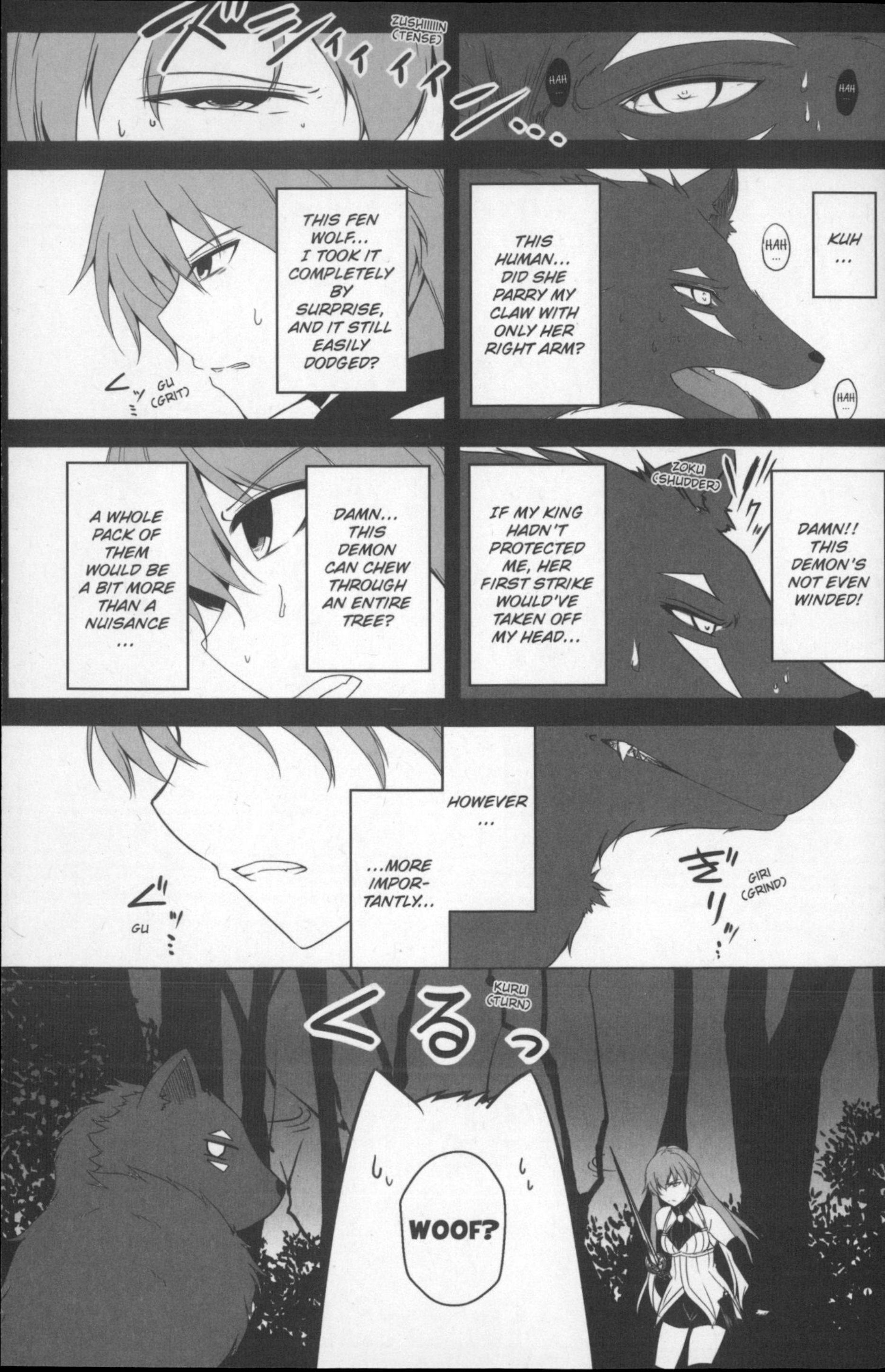
HAH...
HAH...
ZUSHIIIIIN (TENSE)
KUH...
HAH...
THIS HUMAN... DID SHE PARRY MY CLAW WITH ONLY HER RIGHT ARM?
HAH...
THIS FEN WOLF... I TOOK IT COMPLETELY BY SURPRISE, AND IT STILL EASILY DODGED?
GU (GRIT)
DAMN!! THIS DEMON'S NOT EVEN WINDED!
ZOKU (SHUDDER)
IF MY KING HADN'T PROTECTED ME, HER FIRST STRIKE WOULD'VE TAKEN OFF MY HEAD...
DAMN... THIS DEMON CAN CHEW THROUGH AN ENTIRE TREE?
A WHOLE PACK OF THEM WOULD BE A BIT MORE THAN A NUISANCE...
GIRI (GRIND)
HOWEVER...
...MORE IMPORTANTLY...
GU
KURU (TURN)
WOOF?

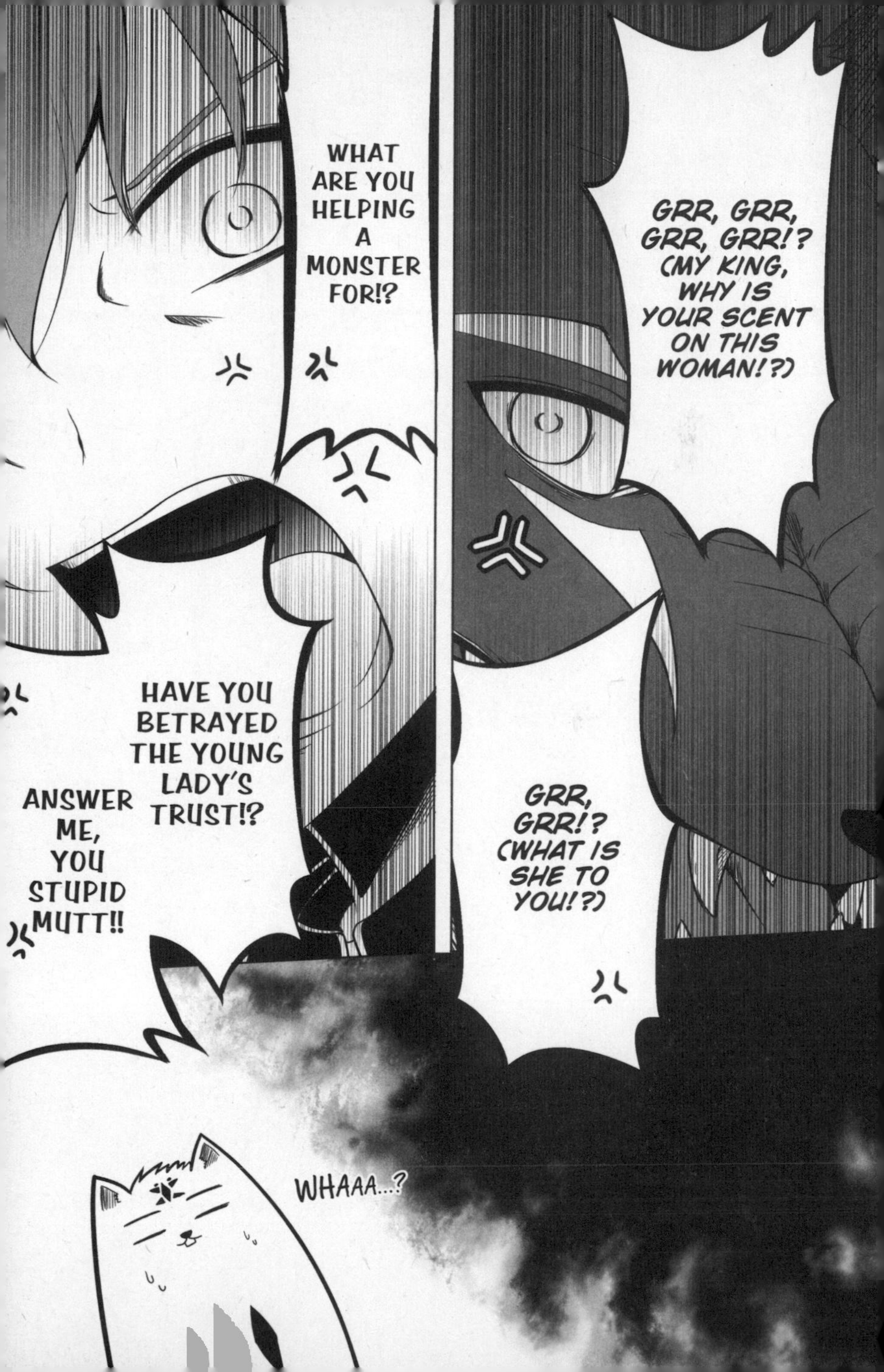
GRR, GRR, GRR, GRR!? (MY KING, WHY IS YOUR SCENT ON THIS WOMAN!?)
GRR, GRR!? (WHAT IS SHE TO YOU!?)
WHAT ARE YOU HELPING A MONSTER FOR!?
HAVE YOU BETRAYED THE YOUNG LADY'S TRUST!?
ANSWER ME, YOU STUPID MUTT!!
WHAAA...?

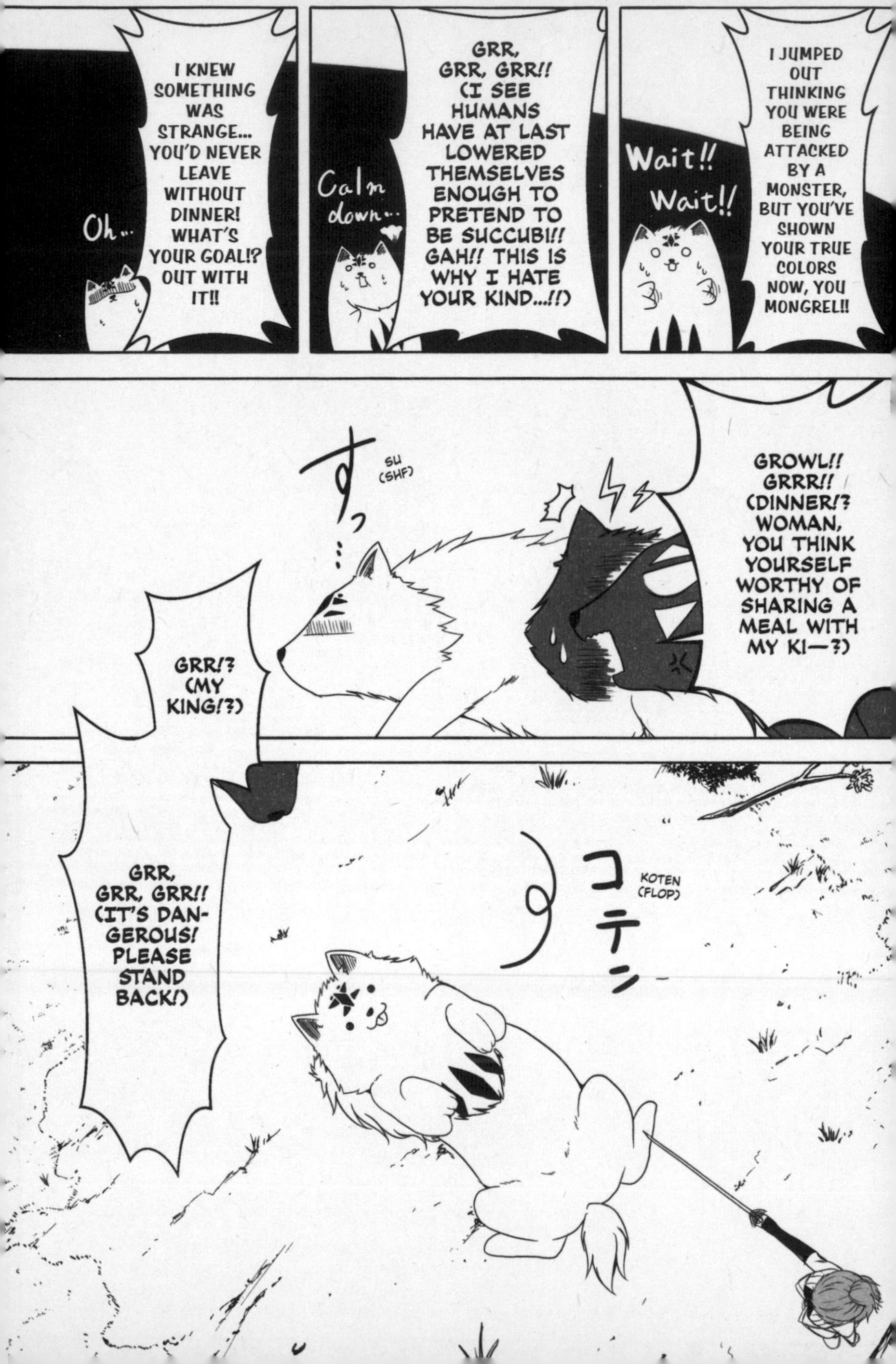
I JUMPED OUT THINKING YOU WERE BEING ATTACKED BY A MONSTER, BUT YOU'VE SHOWN YOUR TRUE COLORS NOW, YOU MONGREL!!
Wait!! Wait!!
GRR, GRR, GRR!! (I SEE HUMANS HAVE AT LAST LOWERED THEMSELVES ENOUGH TO PRETEND TO BE SUCCUBI!! GAH!! THIS IS WHY I HATE YOUR KIND...!!)
Calm down...
I KNEW SOMETHING WAS STRANGE... YOU'D NEVER LEAVE WITHOUT DINNER! WHAT'S YOUR GOAL!? OUT WITH IT!!
Oh...
GROWL!! GRRR!! (DINNER!? WOMAN, YOU THINK YOURSELF WORTHY OF SHARING A MEAL WITH MY KI—?)
すっ
SU (SHF)
GRR!? (MY KING!?)
コテン
KOTEN (FLOP)
GRR, GRR, GRR!! (IT'S DAN-GEROUS! PLEASE STAND BACK!)

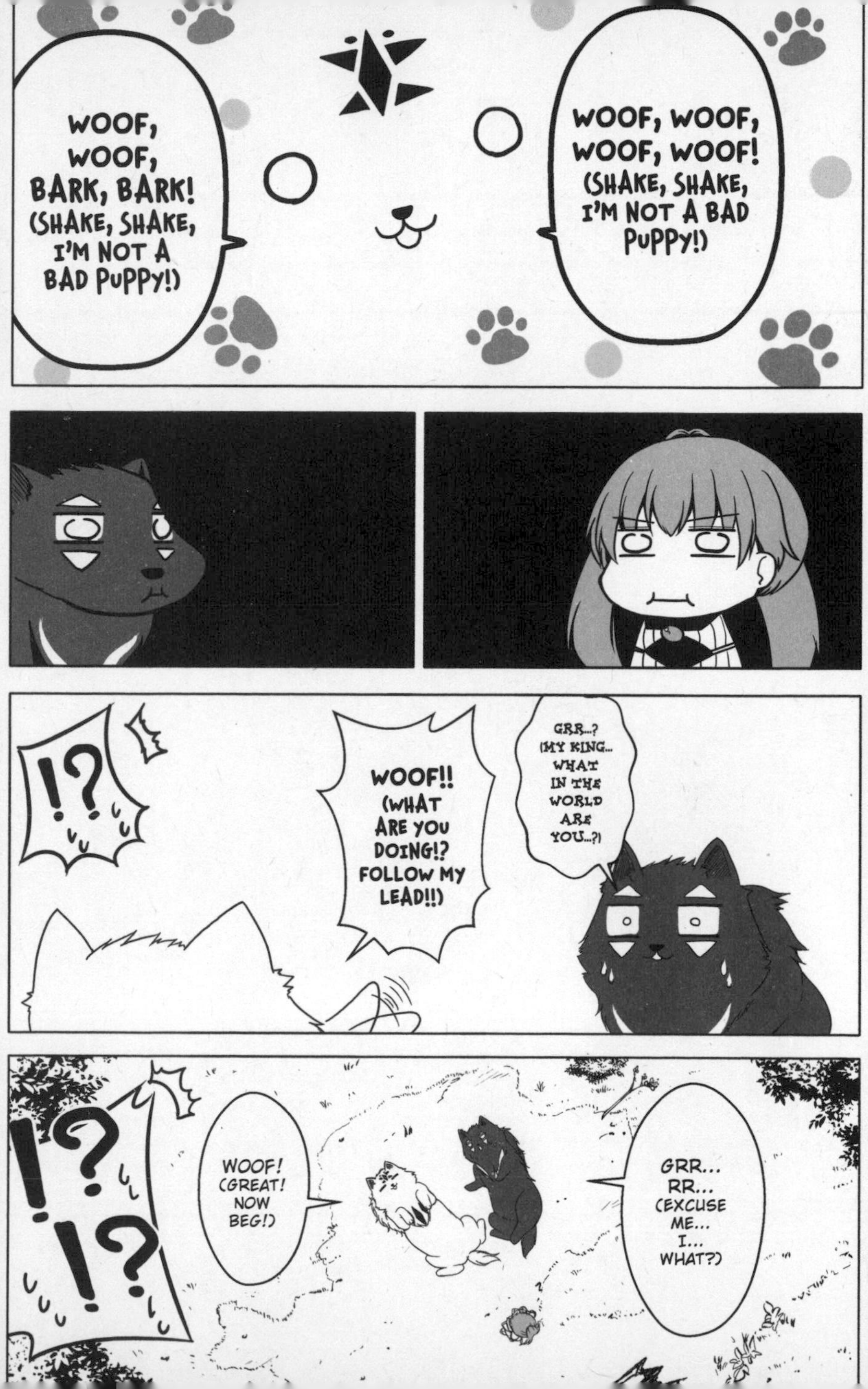
WOOF, WOOF, WOOF, WOOF! (SHAKE, SHAKE, I'M NOT A BAD PUPPY!)
WOOF, WOOF, BARK, BARK! (SHAKE, SHAKE, I'M NOT A BAD PUPPY!)
GRR...? (MY KING... WHAT IN THE WORLD ARE YOU...?)
WOOF!! (WHAT ARE YOU DOING!? FOLLOW MY LEAD!!)
!?
GRR... RR... (EXCUSE ME... I... WHAT?)
WOOF! (GREAT! NOW BEG!)
!?!?

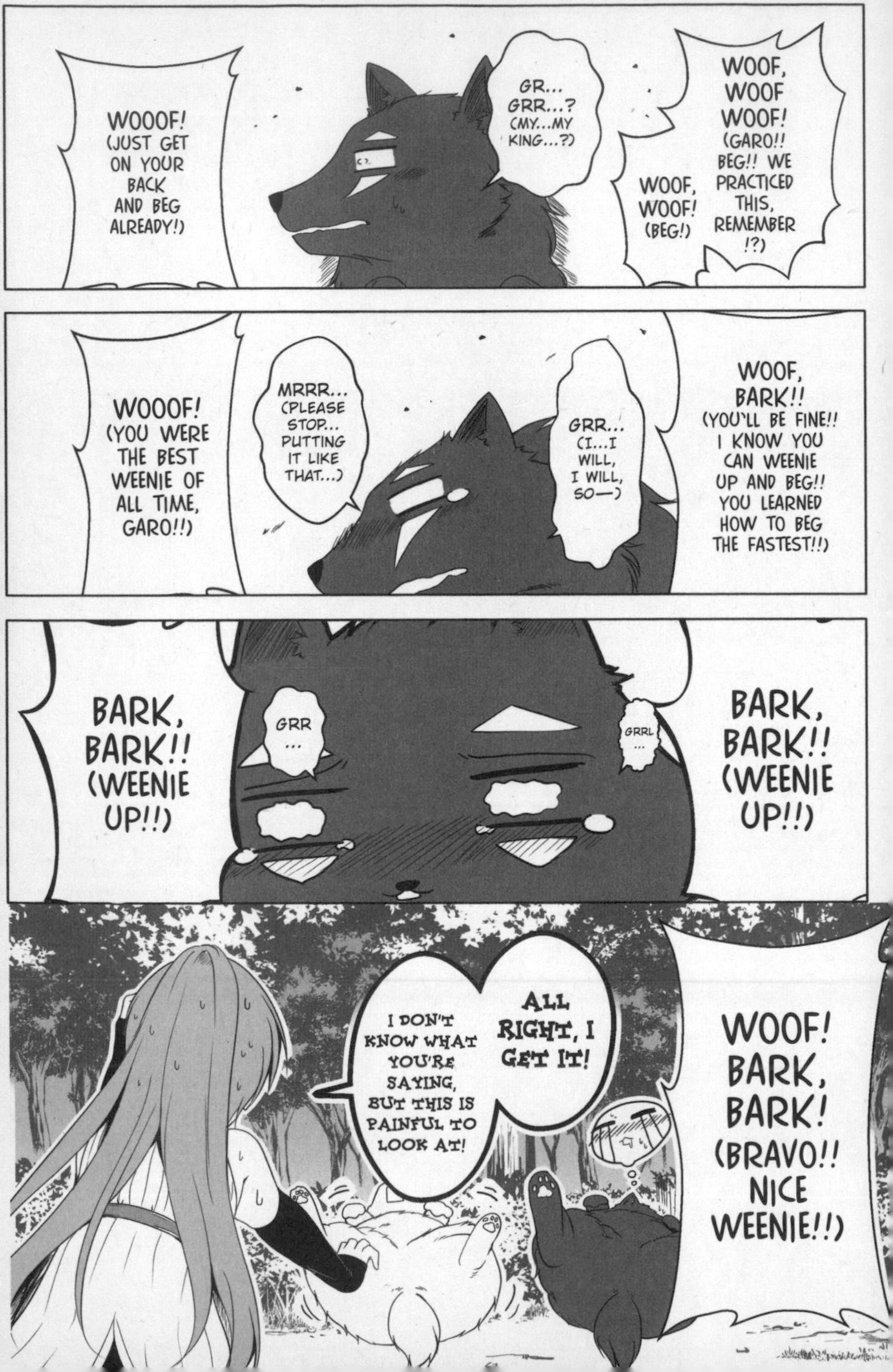
WOOF, WOOF WOOF! (GARO!! BEG!! WE PRACTICED THIS, REMEMBER!?)
WOOF, WOOF! (BEG!)
GR... GRR...? (MY...MY KING...?)
WOOOF! (JUST GET ON YOUR BACK AND BEG ALREADY!)
WOOF, BARK!! (YOU'LL BE FINE!! I KNOW YOU CAN WEENIE UP AND BEG!! YOU LEARNED HOW TO BEG THE FASTEST!!)
GRR... (I...I WILL, I WILL, SO—)
MRRR... (PLEASE STOP... PUTTING IT LIKE THAT...)
WOOOF! (YOU WERE THE BEST WEENIE OF ALL TIME, GARO!!)
BARK, BARK!! (WEENIE UP!!)
GRRL ...
GRR ...
BARK, BARK!! (WEENIE UP!!)
WOOF! BARK, BARK! (BRAVO!! NICE WEENIE!!)
ALL RIGHT, I GET IT!
I DON'T KNOW WHAT YOU'RE SAYING, BUT THIS IS PAINFUL TO LOOK AT!

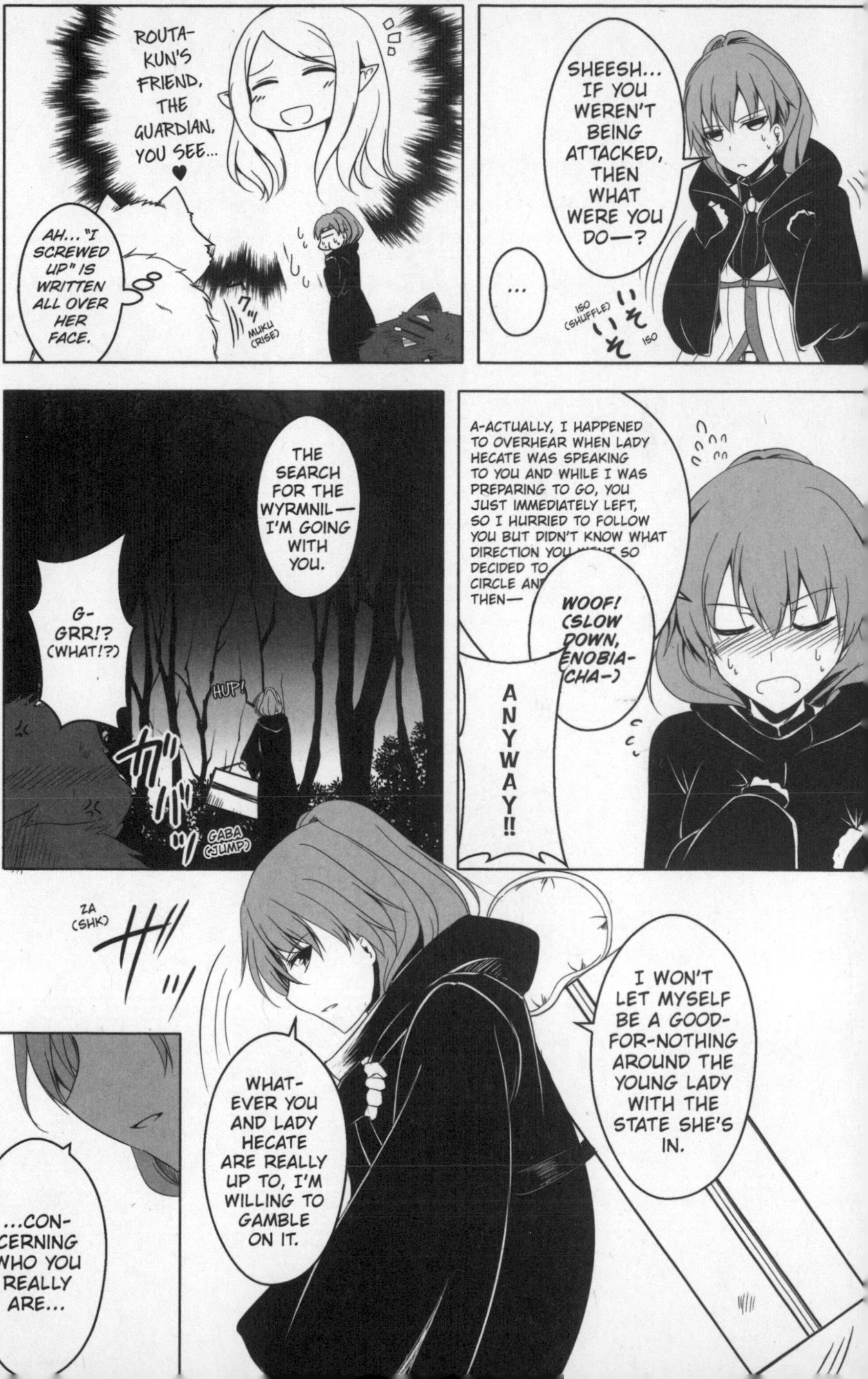
SHEESH... IF YOU WEREN'T BEING ATTACKED, THEN WHAT WERE YOU DO—?
ISO ISO (SHUFFLE)
...
ROUTA-KUN'S FRIEND, THE GUARDIAN, YOU SEE... ♥
MUKU (RISE)
AH... "I SCREWED UP" IS WRITTEN ALL OVER HER FACE.
A-ACTUALLY, I HAPPENED TO OVERHEAR WHEN LADY HECATE WAS SPEAKING TO YOU AND WHILE I WAS PREPARING TO GO, YOU JUST IMMEDIATELY LEFT, SO I HURRIED TO FOLLOW YOU BUT DIDN'T KNOW WHAT DIRECTION YOU SO DECIDED TO CIRCLE AN THEN—
WOOF! (SLOW DOWN, ENOBIA-CHA-)
ANYWAY!!
THE SEARCH FOR THE WYRMNIL— I'M GOING WITH YOU.
G-GRR!? (WHAT!?)
HUP!
GABA (JUMP)
ZA (SHK)
I WON'T LET MYSELF BE A GOOD-FOR-NOTHING AROUND THE YOUNG LADY WITH THE STATE SHE'S IN.
WHAT-EVER YOU AND LADY HECATE ARE REALLY UP TO, I'M WILLING TO GAMBLE ON IT.
...CON-CERNING WHO YOU REALLY ARE...

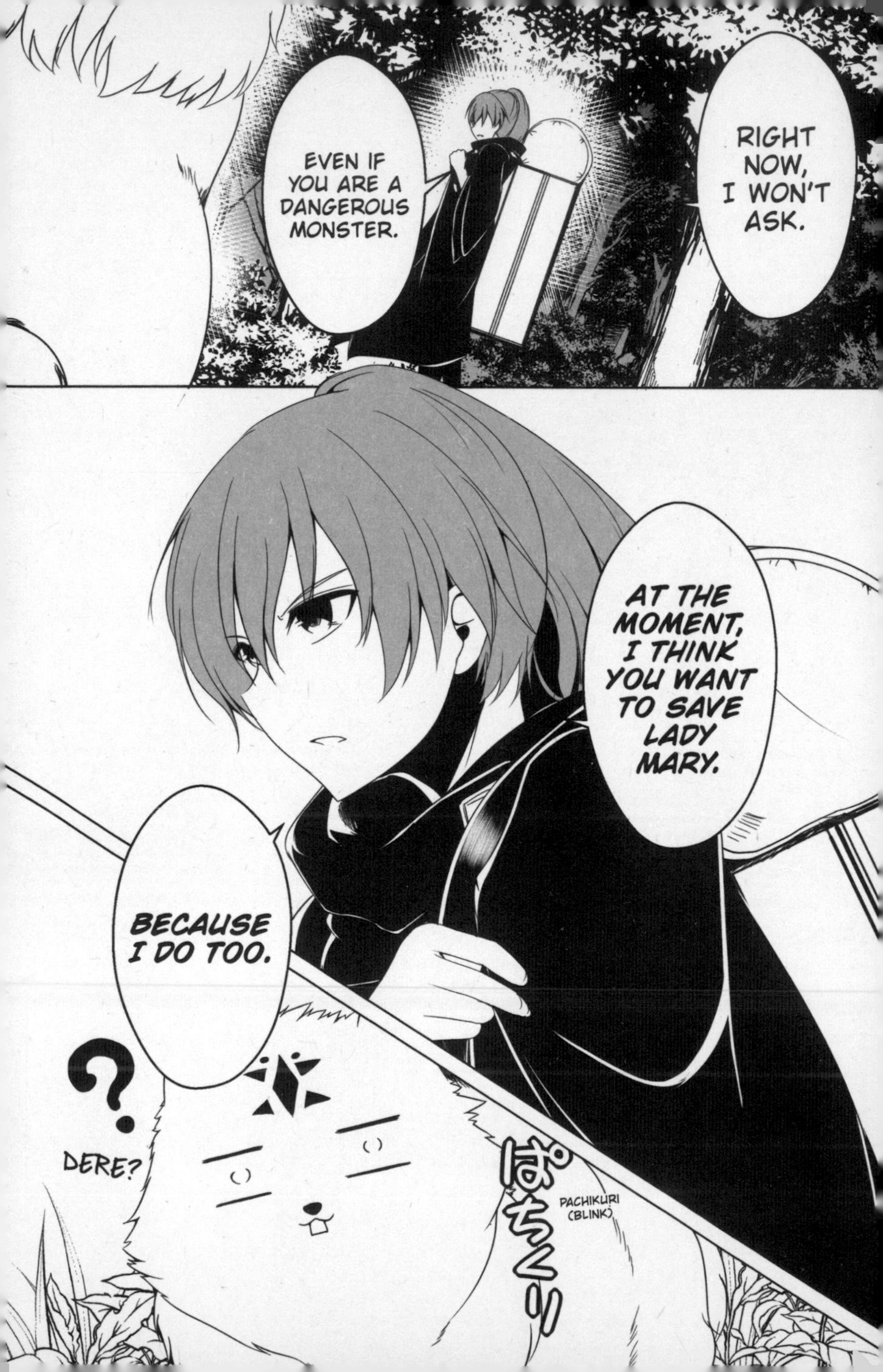
RIGHT NOW, I WON'T ASK.
EVEN IF YOU ARE A DANGEROUS MONSTER.
AT THE MOMENT, I THINK YOU WANT TO SAVE LADY MARY.
BECAUSE I DO TOO.
ぱちくり
PACHIKURI (BLINK)
DERE?

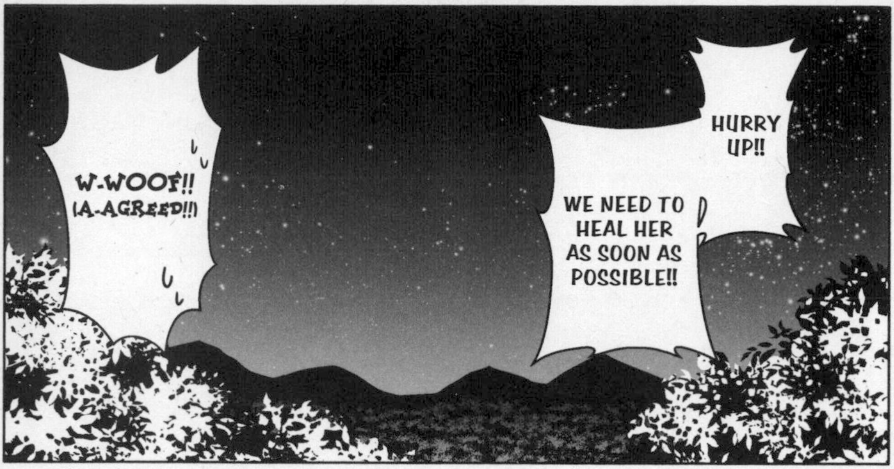
HURRY UP!!
WE NEED TO HEAL HER AS SOON AS POSSIBLE!!
W-WOOF!! (A-AGREED!!)

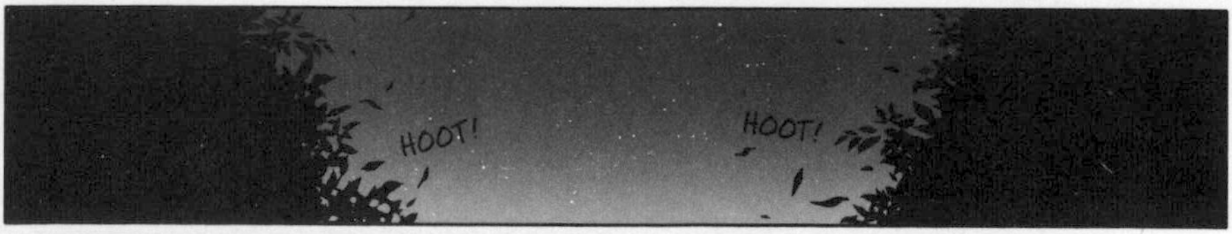
HOOT!
HOOT!

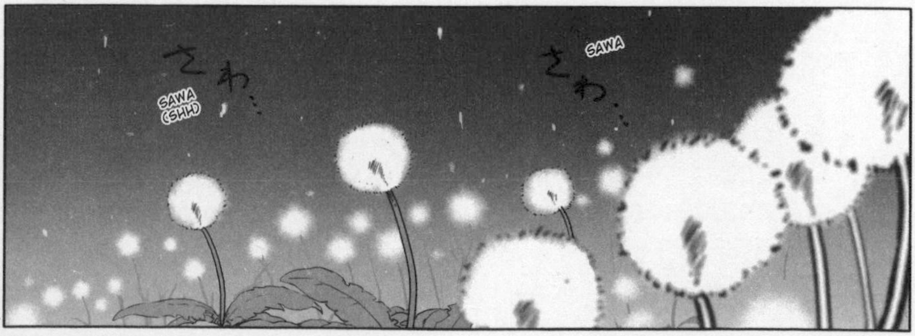
さわ…
SAWA
さわ…
SAWA (SHH)

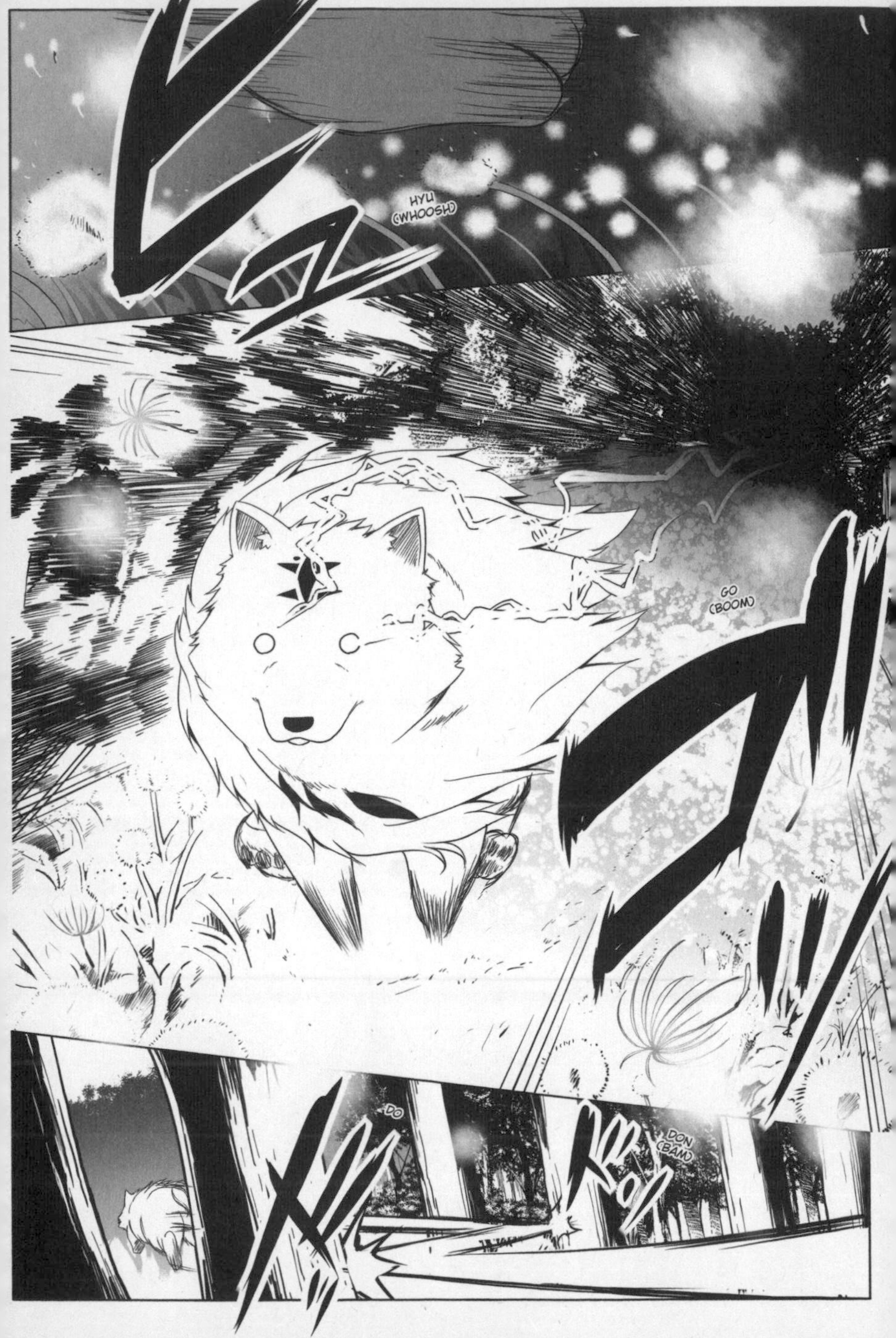
HYU
(WHOOSH)
GO
(BOOM)
DON
(BAM)
DO

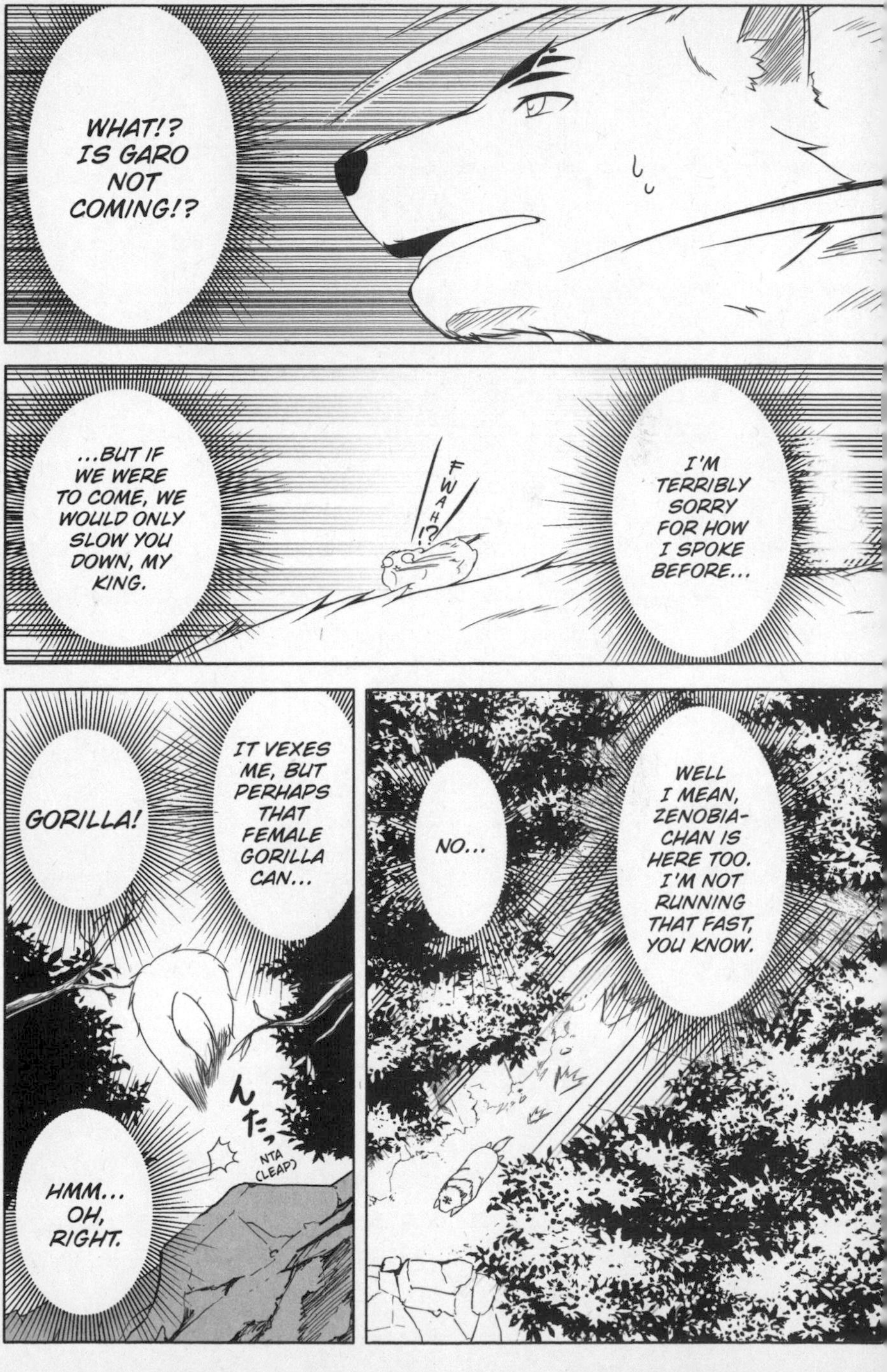
WHAT!? IS GARO NOT COMING!?
I'M TERRIBLY SORRY FOR HOW I SPOKE BEFORE...
FWAH!?
...BUT IF WE WERE TO COME, WE WOULD ONLY SLOW YOU DOWN, MY KING.
WELL I MEAN, ZENOBIA-CHAN IS HERE TOO. I'M NOT RUNNING THAT FAST, YOU KNOW.
NO...
IT VEXES ME, BUT PERHAPS THAT FEMALE GORILLA CAN...
GORILLA!
んたっ
NTA (LEAP)
HMM... OH, RIGHT.

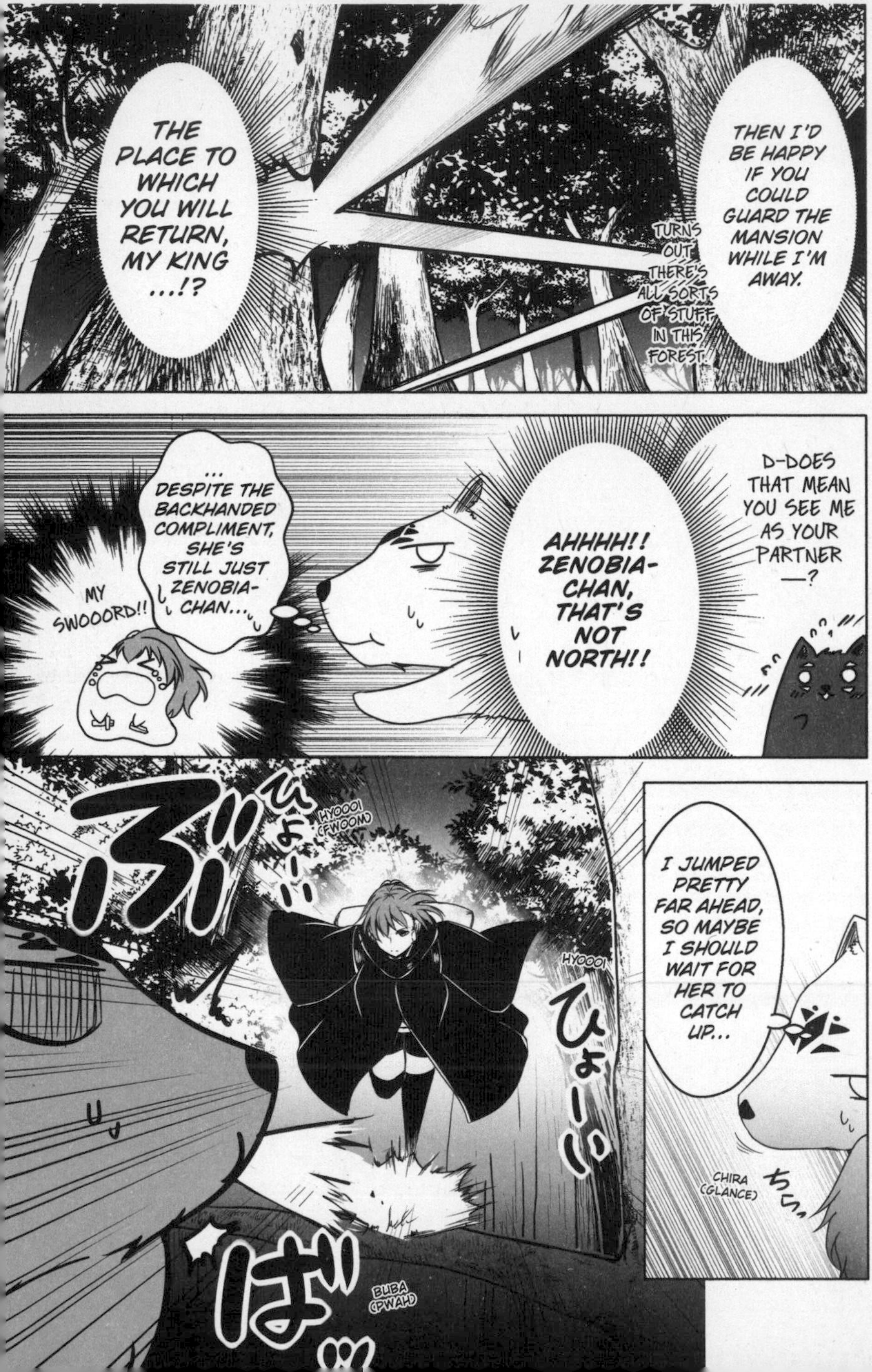
THEN I'D BE HAPPY IF YOU COULD GUARD THE MANSION WHILE I'M AWAY.
TURNS OUT THERE'S ALL SORTS OF STUFF IN THIS FOREST.
THE PLACE TO WHICH YOU WILL RETURN, MY KING ...!?
D-DOES THAT MEAN YOU SEE ME AS YOUR PARTNER —?
AHHHH!! ZENOBIA-CHAN, THAT'S NOT NORTH!!
... DESPITE THE BACKHANDED COMPLIMENT, SHE'S STILL JUST ZENOBIA-CHAN...
MY SWOOORD!!
I JUMPED PRETTY FAR AHEAD, SO MAYBE I SHOULD WAIT FOR HER TO CATCH UP...
CHIRA (GLANCE)
HYOOOI (FWOOM)
HYOOOI
BUBA (PWAH)

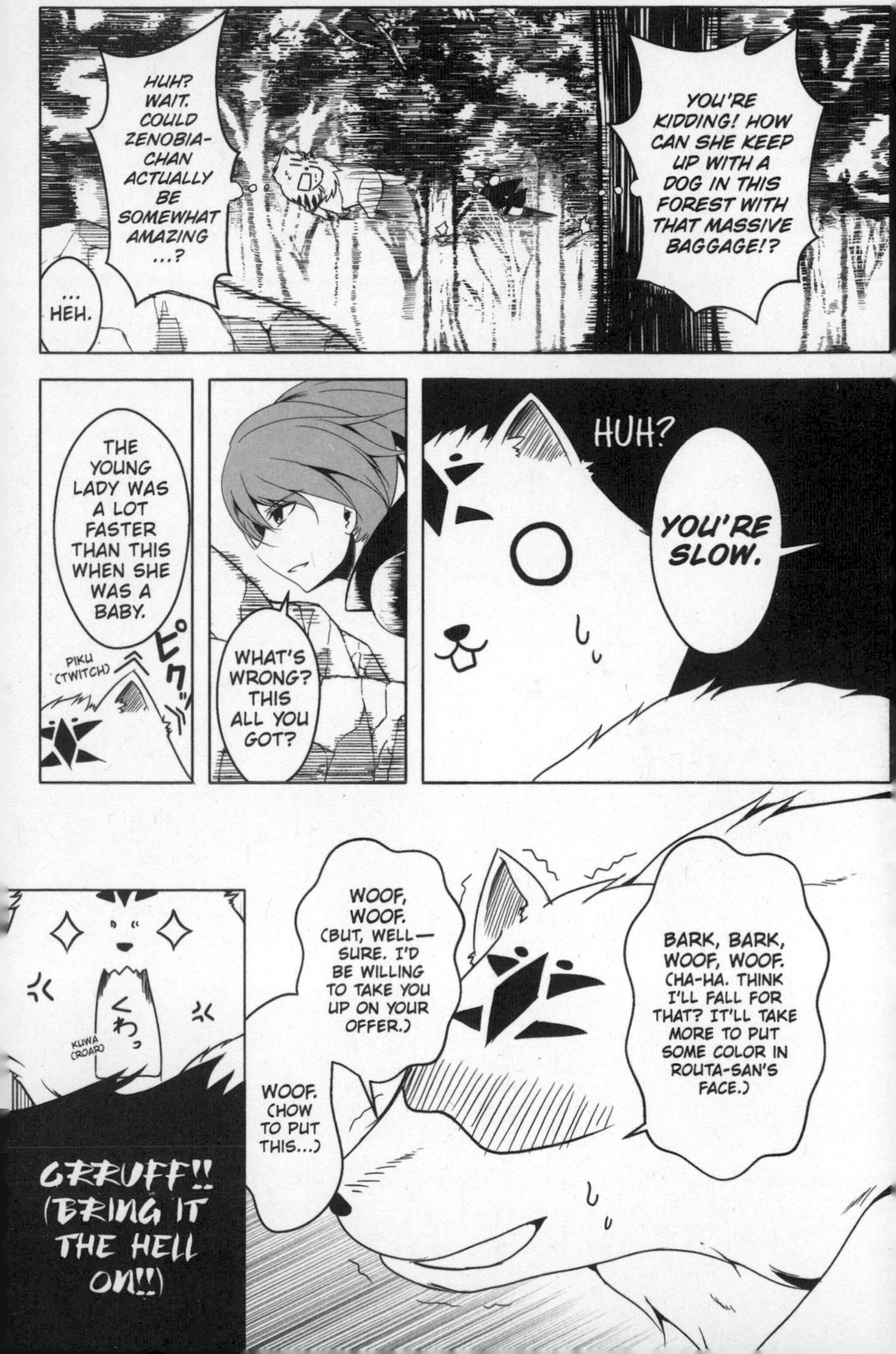
YOU'RE KIDDING! HOW CAN SHE KEEP UP WITH A DOG IN THIS FOREST WITH THAT MASSIVE BAGGAGE!?
HUH? WAIT. COULD ZENOBIA-CHAN ACTUALLY BE SOMEWHAT AMAZING ...?
... HEH.
HUH?
YOU'RE SLOW.
WHAT'S WRONG? THIS ALL YOU GOT?
THE YOUNG LADY WAS A LOT FASTER THAN THIS WHEN SHE WAS A BABY.
PIKU (TWITCH)
BARK, BARK, WOOF, WOOF. (HA-HA. THINK I'LL FALL FOR THAT? IT'LL TAKE MORE TO PUT SOME COLOR IN ROUTA-SAN'S FACE.)
WOOF, WOOF. (BUT, WELL— SURE. I'D BE WILLING TO TAKE YOU UP ON YOUR OFFER.)
WOOF. (HOW TO PUT THIS...)
KUWA (ROAR)
GRRUFF!! (BRING IT THE HELL ON!!)

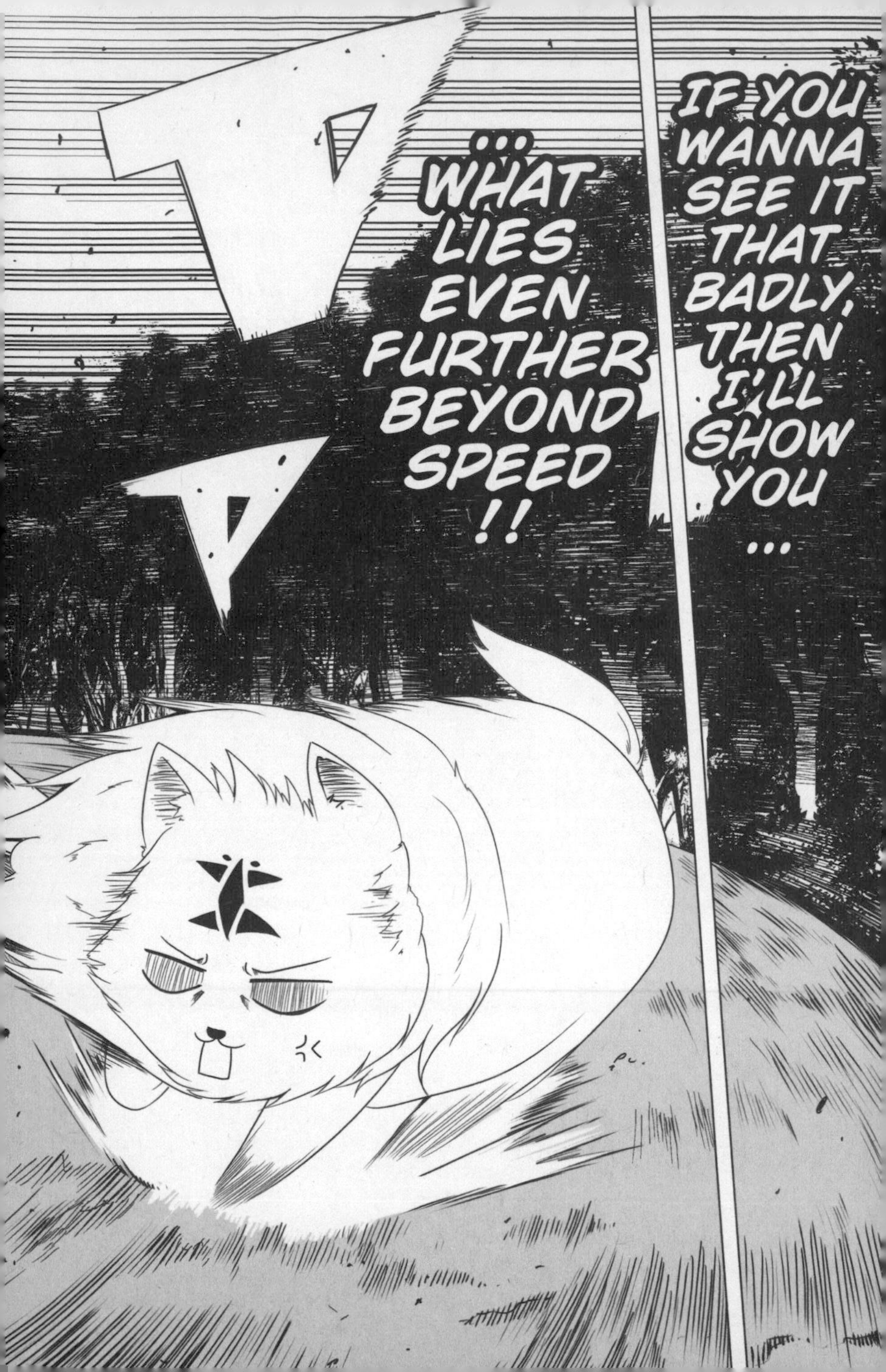
IF YOU WANNA SEE IT THAT BADLY, THEN I'LL SHOW YOU ...
...WHAT LIES EVEN FURTHER BEYOND SPEED !!

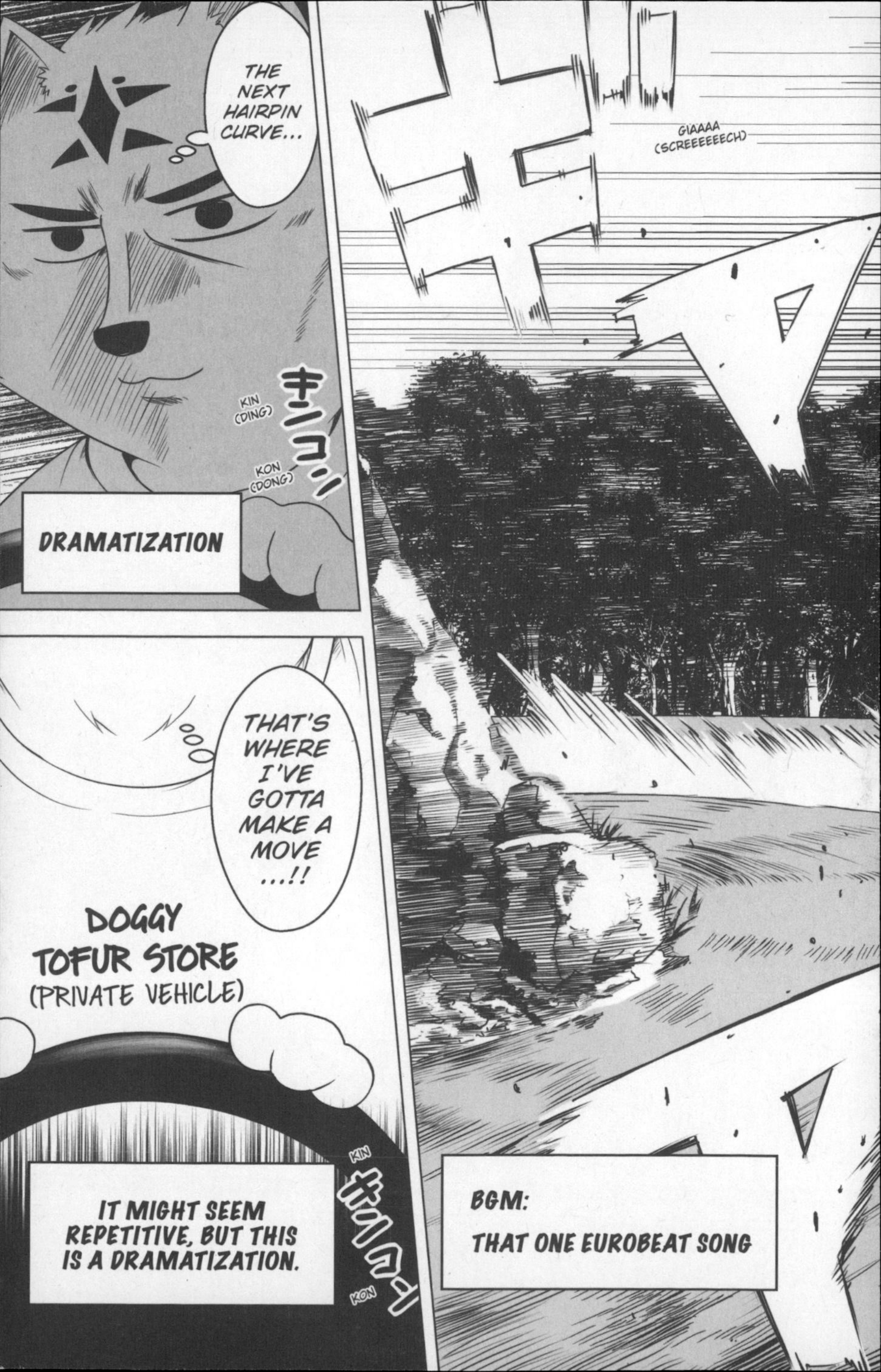
GIAAAA
(SCREEEEEECH)
BGM:
THAT ONE EUROBEAT SONG
THE NEXT HAIRPIN CURVE...
KIN (DING)
KON (DONG)
DRAMATIZATION
THAT'S WHERE I'VE GOTTA MAKE A MOVE ...!!
DOGGY TOFUR STORE
(PRIVATE VEHICLE)
KIN
KON
IT MIGHT SEEM REPETITIVE, BUT THIS IS A DRAMATIZATION.

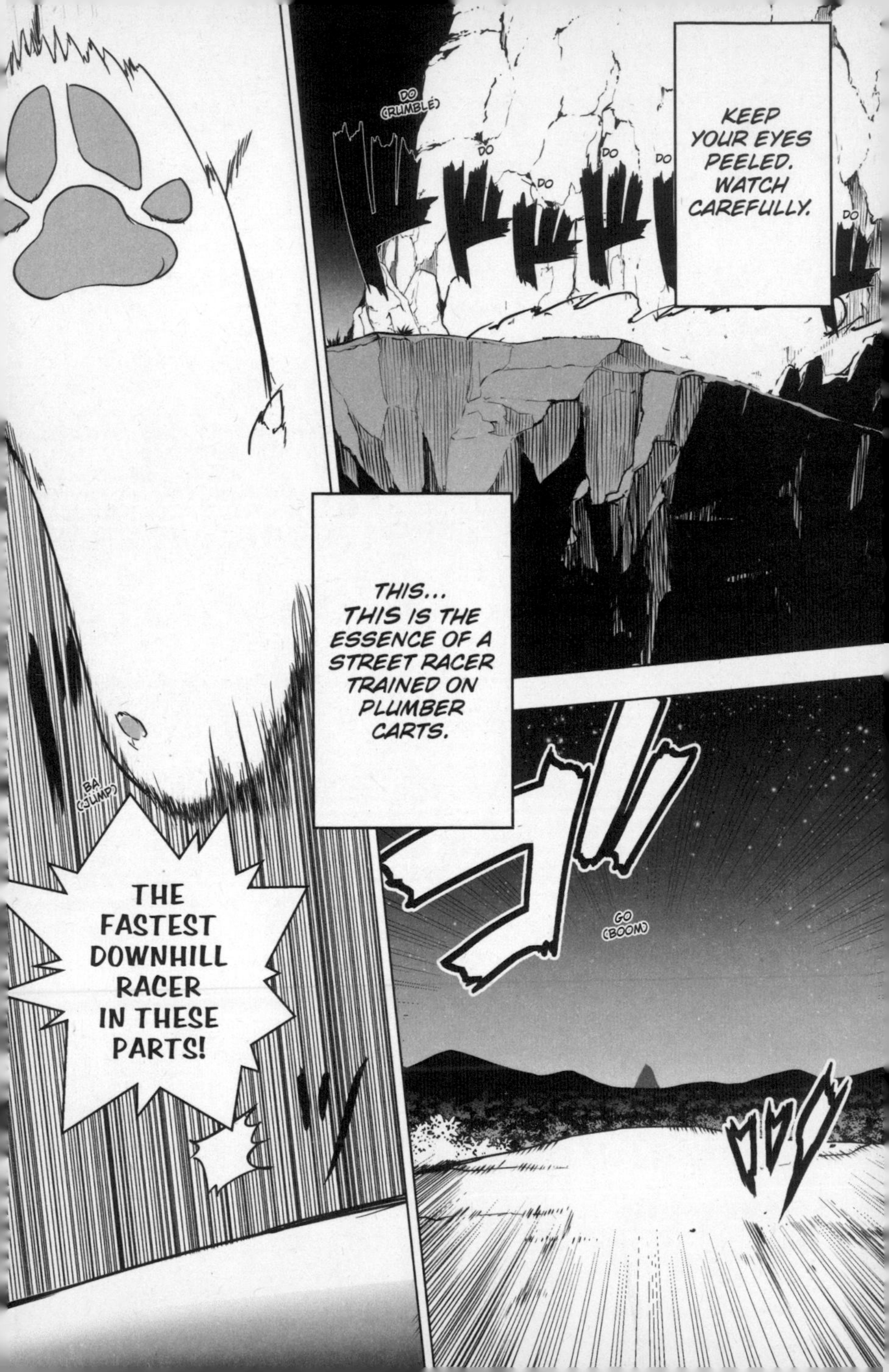

KEEP YOUR EYES PEELED. WATCH CAREFULLY.
DO
DO
DO
DO
DO
DO (RUMBLE)
THIS... THIS IS THE ESSENCE OF A STREET RACER TRAINED ON PLUMBER CARTS.
GO (BOOM)
BA (JUMP)
THE FASTEST DOWNHILL RACER IN THESE PARTS!

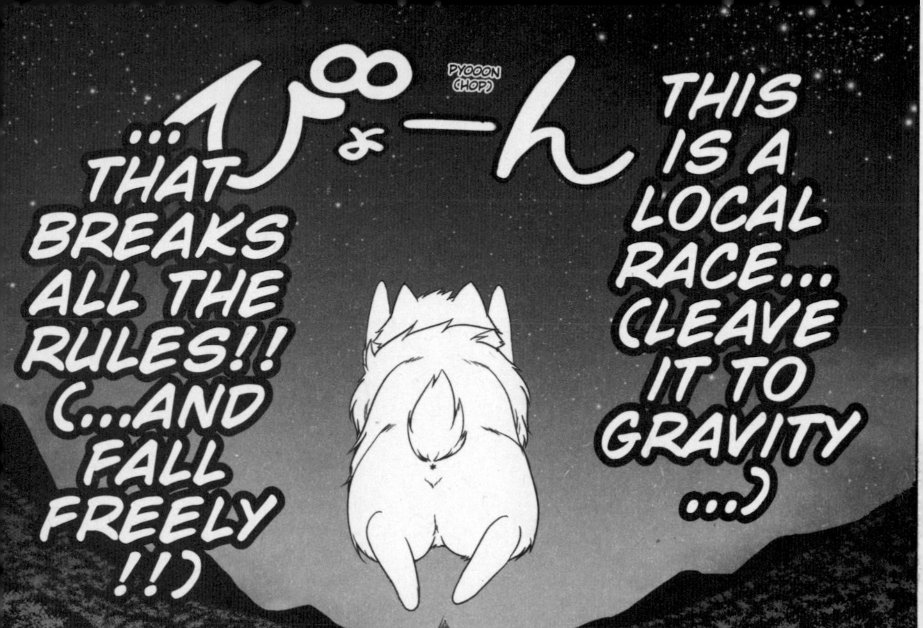
THIS IS A LOCAL RACE... (LEAVE IT TO GRAVITY...)
ぴょーん
PYOOON (HOP)
...THAT BREAKS ALL THE RULES!! (...AND FALL FREELY!!)

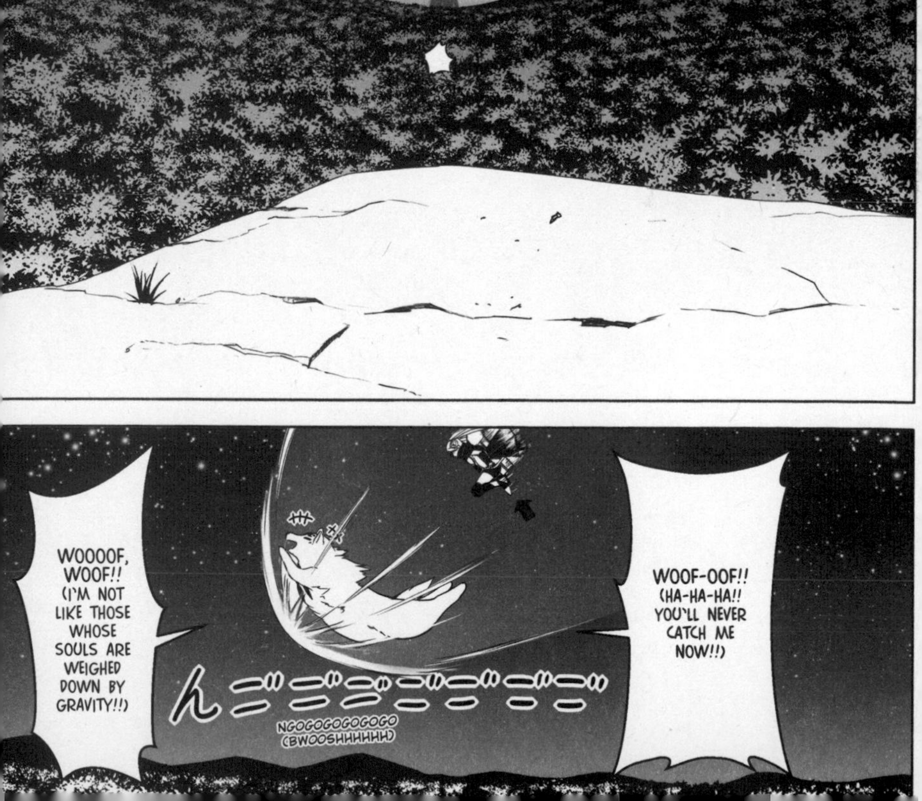
WOOF-OOF!! (HA-HA-HA!! YOU'LL NEVER CATCH ME NOW!!)
WOOOOF, WOOF!! (I'M NOT LIKE THOSE WHOSE SOULS ARE WEIGHED DOWN BY GRAVITY!!)
NGOGOGOGOGOGOGO (BWOOSHHHHHHH)

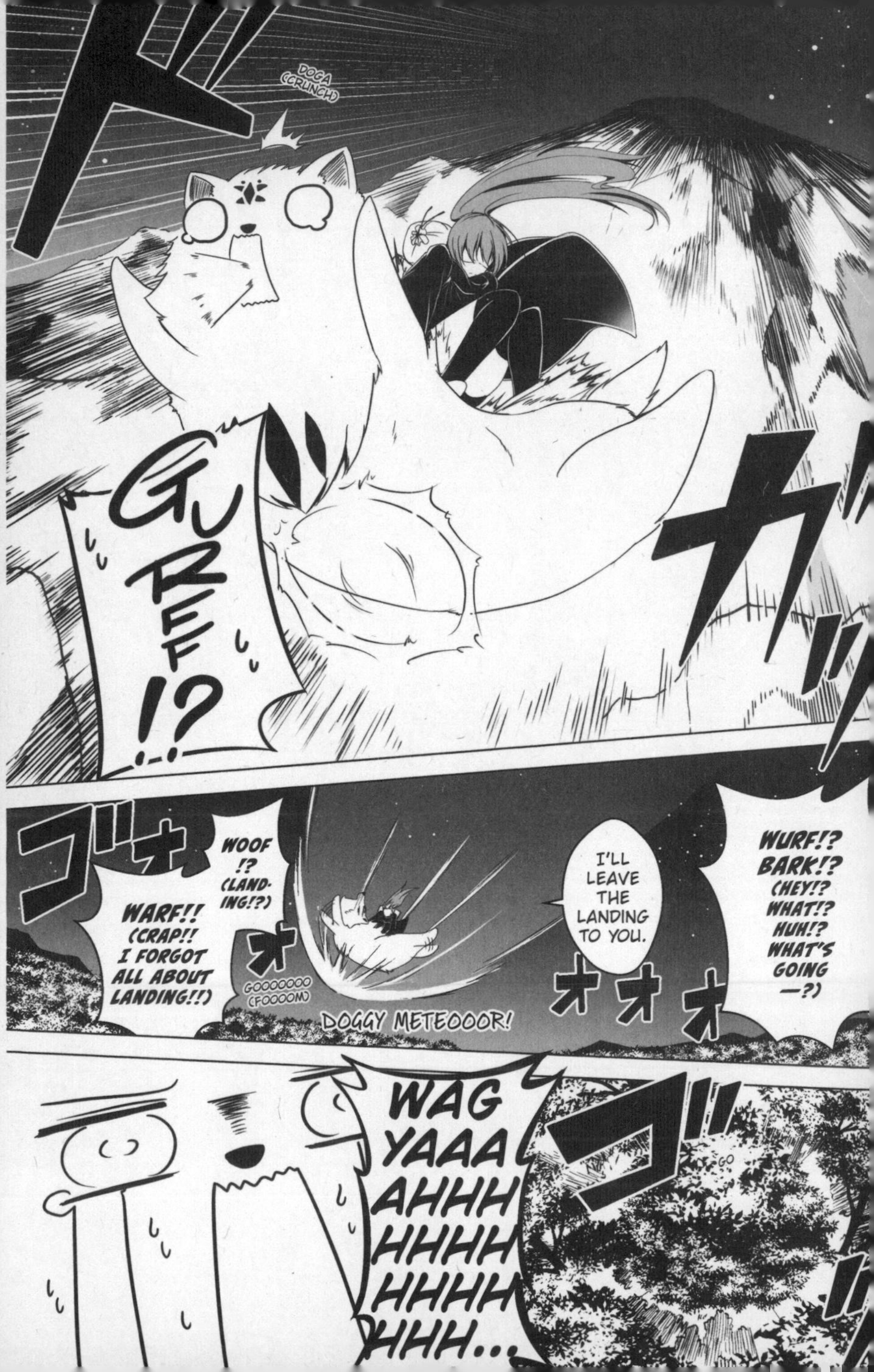
ド
DOGA (CRUNCH)
ガッ
GURFF!?
WURF!? BARK!? (HEY!? WHAT!? HUH!? WHAT'S GOING—?)
I'LL LEAVE THE LANDING TO YOU.
オオオ
DOGGY METEOOOR!
GOOOOOOO (FOOOOM)
オ
WOOF!? (LANDING!?)
WARF!! (CRAP!! I FORGOT ALL ABOUT LANDING!!)
ゴォ
ゴ
GO
WAG YAAAAHHHHHHHHHHHHHH...

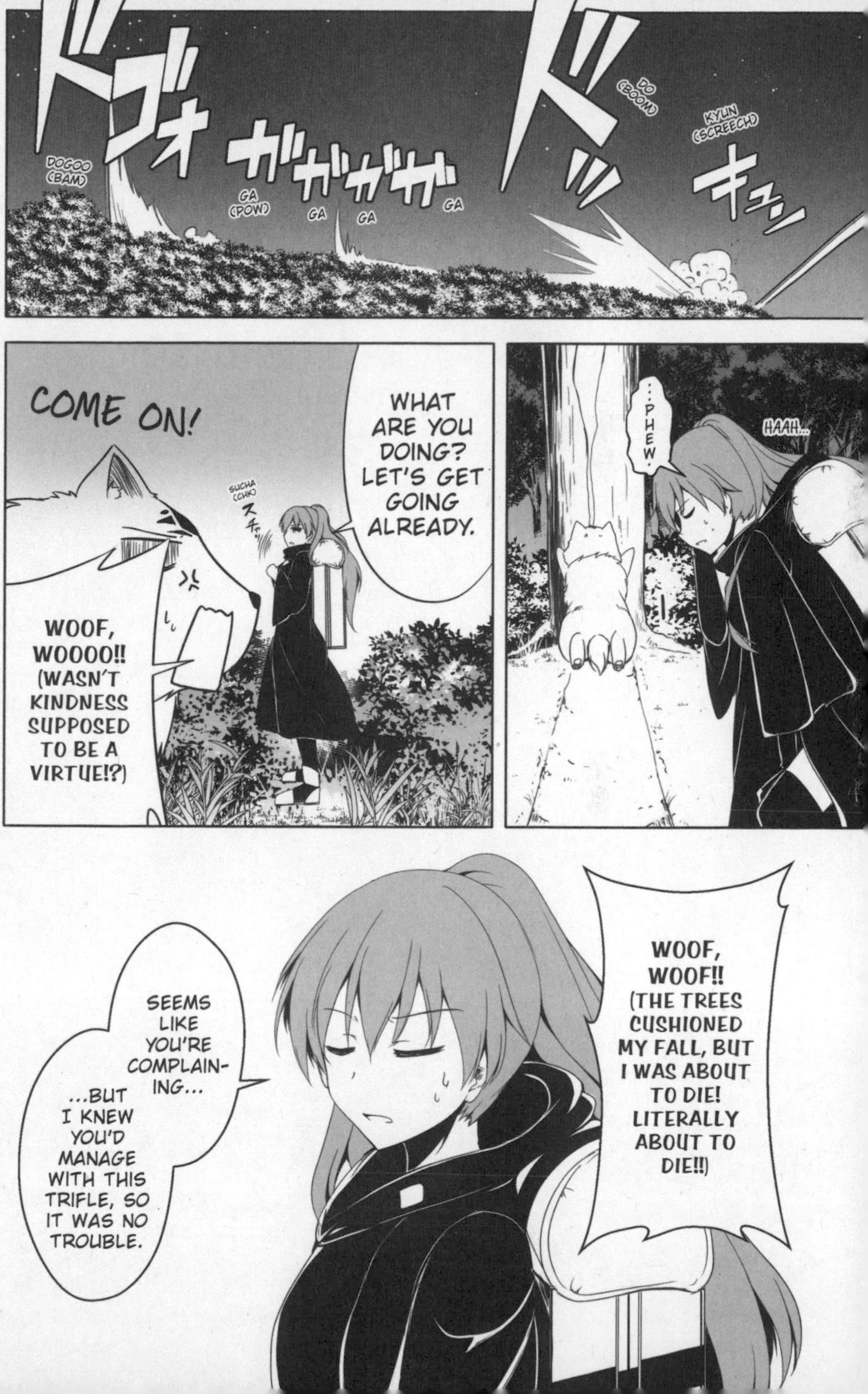
キュン
KYUN (SCREECH)
ドッ
DO (BOOM)
ガガガガ
GA (POW) GA GA GA
ドゴオ
DOGOO (BAM)
...PHEW.
HAAH...
WHAT ARE YOU DOING? LET'S GET GOING ALREADY.
SUCHA (CHK)
COME ON!
WOOF, WOOOO!! (WASN'T KINDNESS SUPPOSED TO BE A VIRTUE!?)
WOOF, WOOF!! (THE TREES CUSHIONED MY FALL, BUT I WAS ABOUT TO DIE! LITERALLY ABOUT TO DIE!!)
SEEMS LIKE YOU'RE COMPLAINING...
...BUT I KNEW YOU'D MANAGE WITH THIS TRIFLE, SO IT WAS NO TROUBLE.

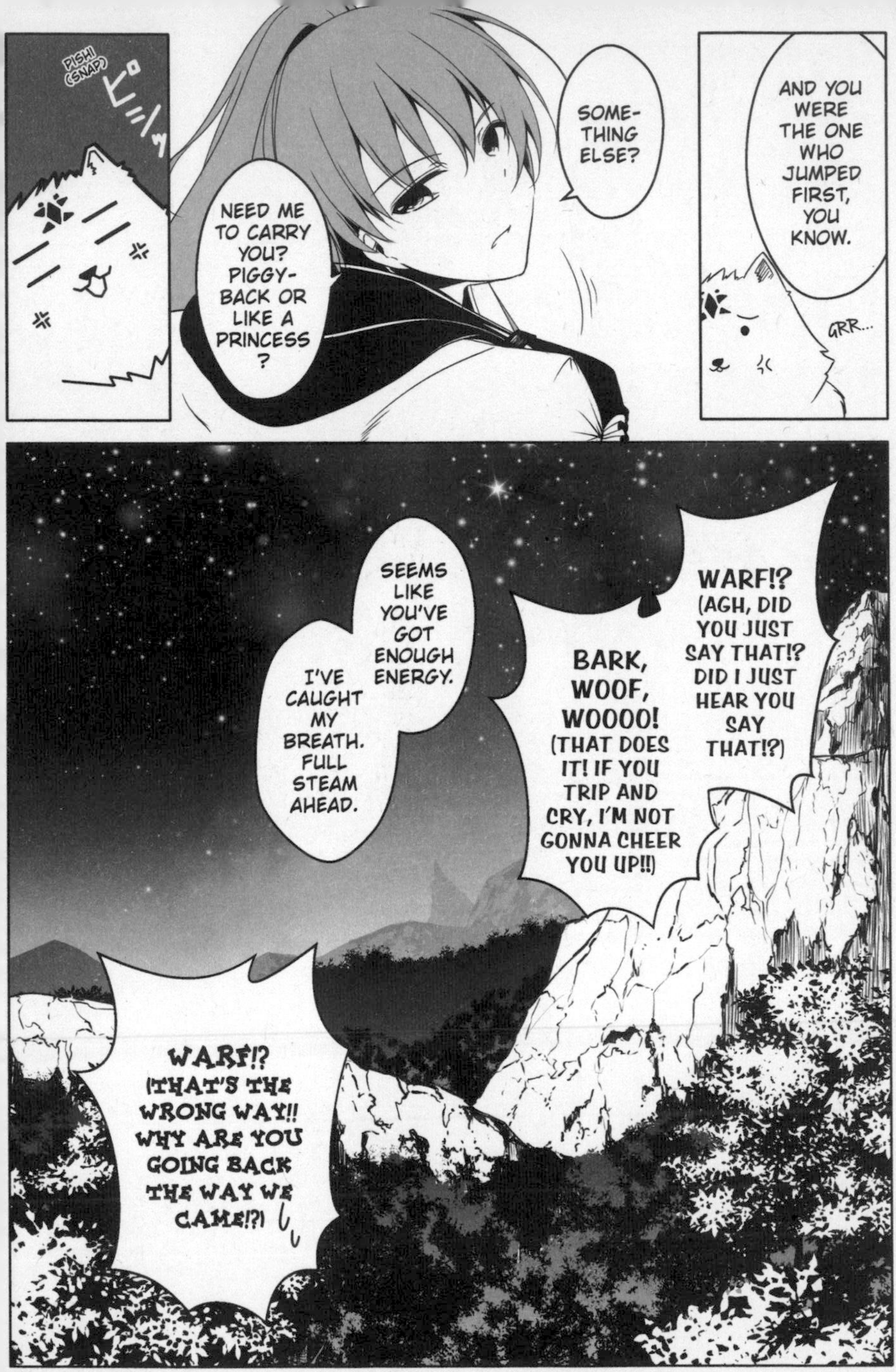
AND YOU WERE THE ONE WHO JUMPED FIRST, YOU KNOW.
GRR...
SOME-THING ELSE?
NEED ME TO CARRY YOU? PIGGY-BACK OR LIKE A PRINCESS?
PISHI (SNAP)
WARF!? (AGH, DID YOU JUST SAY THAT!? DID I JUST HEAR YOU SAY THAT!?)
BARK, WOOF, WOOOO! (THAT DOES IT! IF YOU TRIP AND CRY, I'M NOT GONNA CHEER YOU UP!!)
SEEMS LIKE YOU'VE GOT ENOUGH ENERGY.
I'VE CAUGHT MY BREATH. FULL STEAM AHEAD.
WARF!? (THAT'S THE WRONG WAY!! WHY ARE YOU GOING BACK THE WAY WE CAME!?)

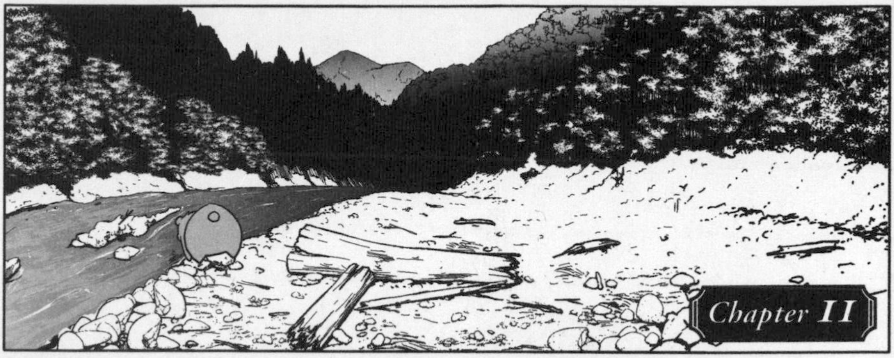
Chapter II

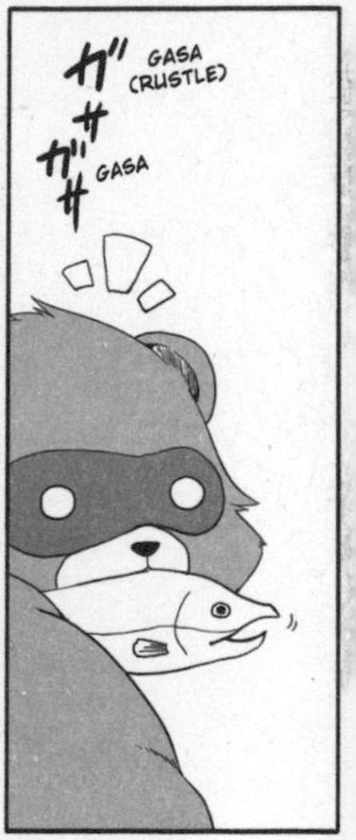
ガサ
GASA (RUSTLE)
ガサ
GASA

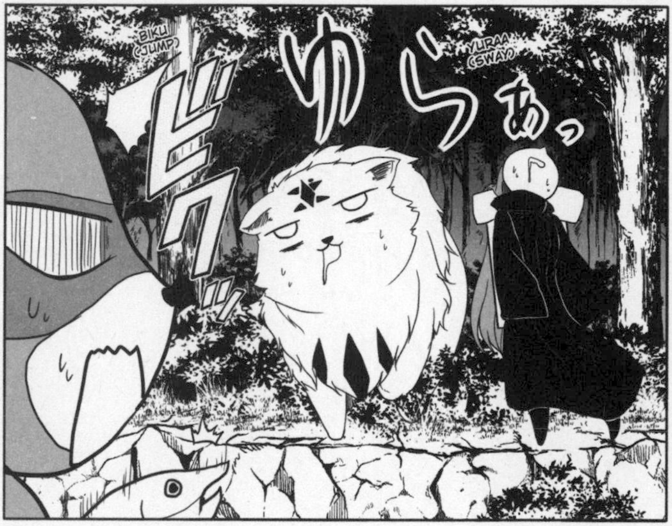
ゆらぁっ
YURAA (SWAY)
ビクッ
BIKU (JUMP)

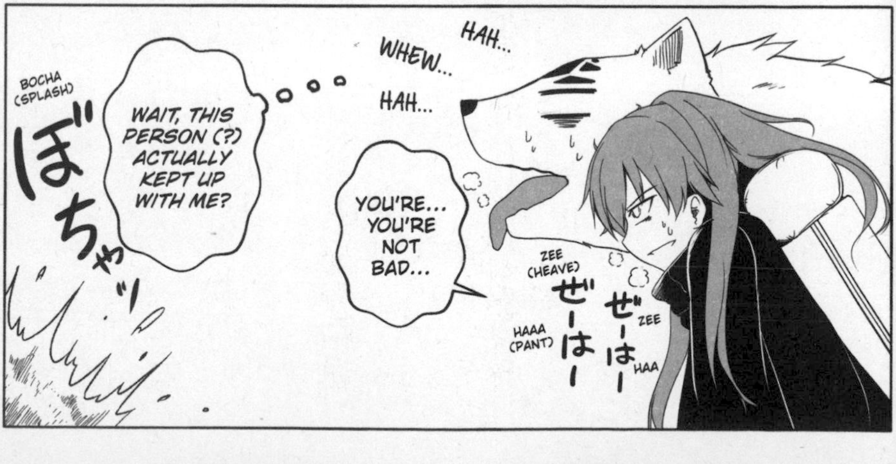
HAH...
WHEW...
HAH...
ぜーはー
ZEE
HAA
ぜーはー
ZEE (HEAVE)
HAAA (PANT)
YOU'RE... YOU'RE NOT BAD...
WAIT, THIS PERSON (?) ACTUALLY KEPT UP WITH ME?
BOCHA (SPLASH)
ぼちゃッ

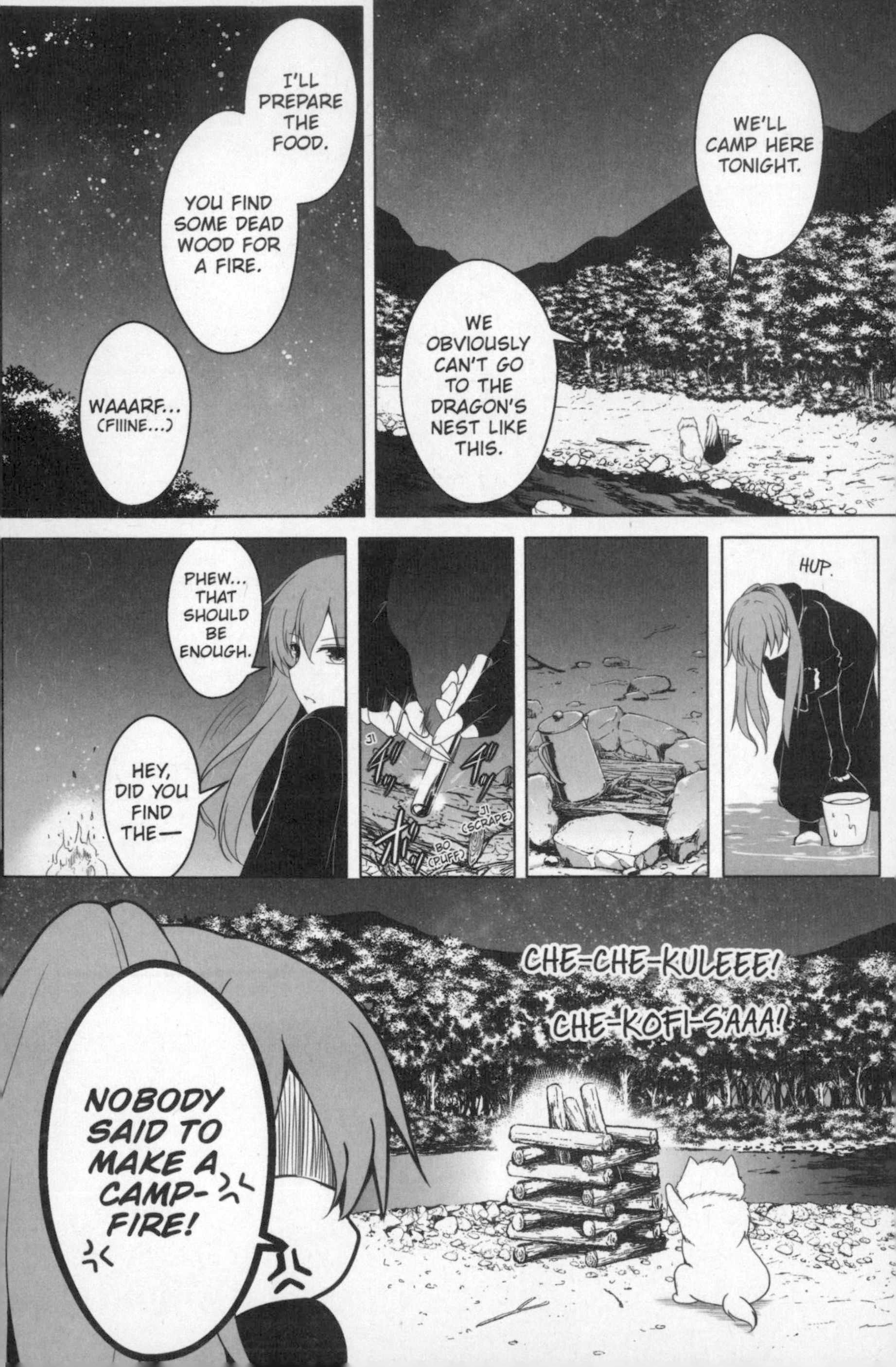
WE'LL CAMP HERE TONIGHT.
WE OBVIOUSLY CAN'T GO TO THE DRAGON'S NEST LIKE THIS.
I'LL PREPARE THE FOOD.
YOU FIND SOME DEAD WOOD FOR A FIRE.
WAAARF... (FIIINE...)
HUP.
JI
JI (SCRAPE)
BO (PUFF)
PHEW... THAT SHOULD BE ENOUGH.
HEY, DID YOU FIND THE—
CHE-CHE-KULEEE!
CHE-KOFI-SAAA!
NOBODY SAID TO MAKE A CAMP-FIRE!

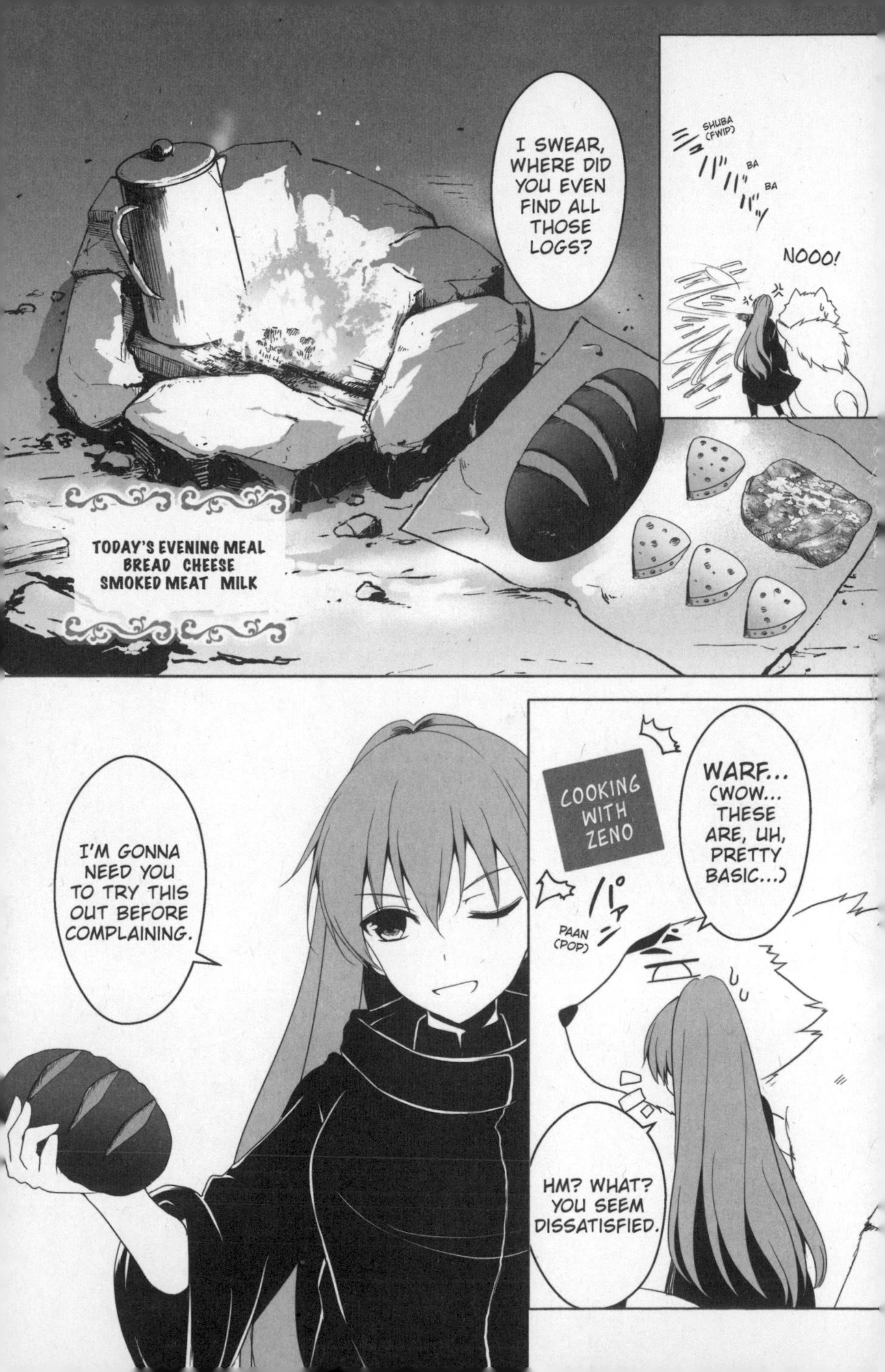
SHUBA (FWIP)
BA
BA
NOOO!
I SWEAR, WHERE DID YOU EVEN FIND ALL THOSE LOGS?
TODAY'S EVENING MEAL
BREAD CHEESE
SMOKED MEAT MILK
WARF... (WOW... THESE ARE, UH, PRETTY BASIC...)
COOKING WITH ZENO
PAAN (POP)
HM? WHAT? YOU SEEM DISSATISFIED.
I'M GONNA NEED YOU TO TRY THIS OUT BEFORE COMPLAINING.

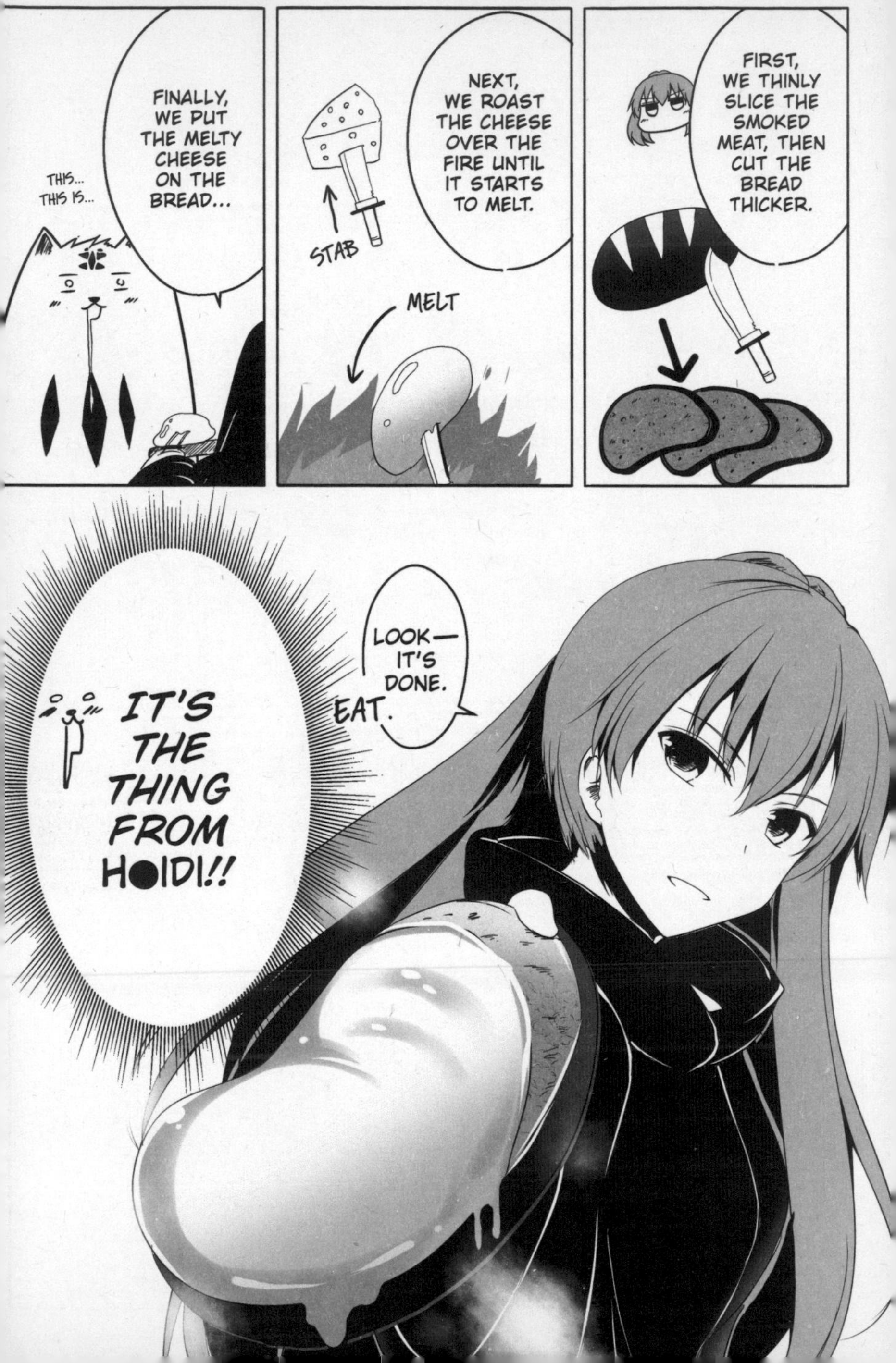
FIRST, WE THINLY SLICE THE SMOKED MEAT, THEN CUT THE BREAD THICKER.
NEXT, WE ROAST THE CHEESE OVER THE FIRE UNTIL IT STARTS TO MELT.
STAB
MELT
FINALLY, WE PUT THE MELTY CHEESE ON THE BREAD...
THIS... THIS IS...
LOOK— IT'S DONE.
EAT.
IT'S THE THING FROM H●IDI!!

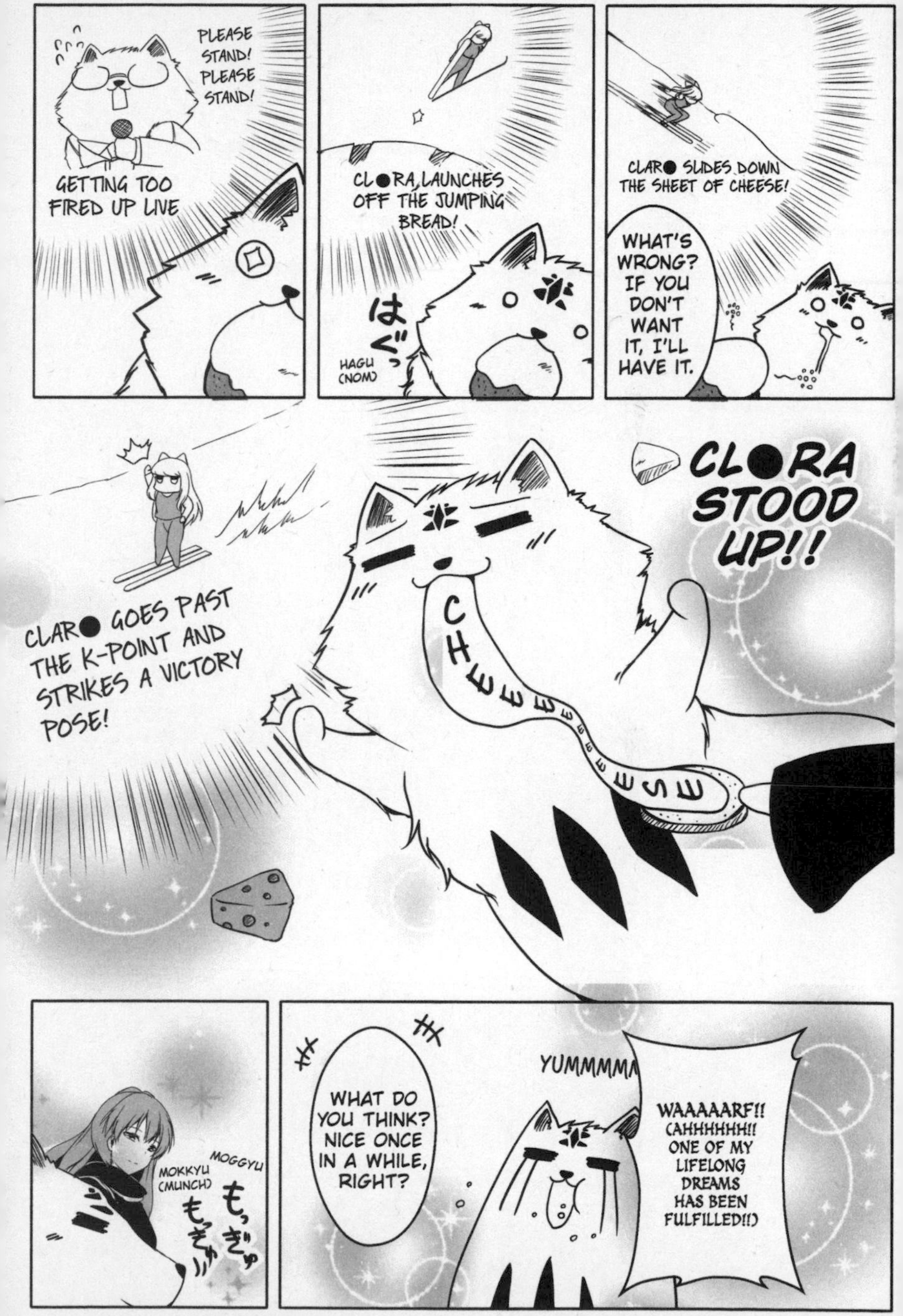
CLAR● SLIDES DOWN THE SHEET OF CHEESE!
WHAT'S WRONG? IF YOU DON'T WANT IT, I'LL HAVE IT.
CL●RA LAUNCHES OFF THE JUMPING BREAD!
はぐっ
HAGU (NOM)
PLEASE STAND! PLEASE STAND!
GETTING TOO FIRED UP LIVE
CL●RA STOOD UP!!
CHEEEEEEESE
CLAR● GOES PAST THE K-POINT AND STRIKES A VICTORY POSE!
YUMMMMA
WAAAAARF!! (AHHHHHH!! ONE OF MY LIFELONG DREAMS HAS BEEN FULFILLED!!)
WHAT DO YOU THINK? NICE ONCE IN A WHILE, RIGHT?
もっぎゅ
もっぎゅ
MOGGYU
MOKKYU (MUNCH)

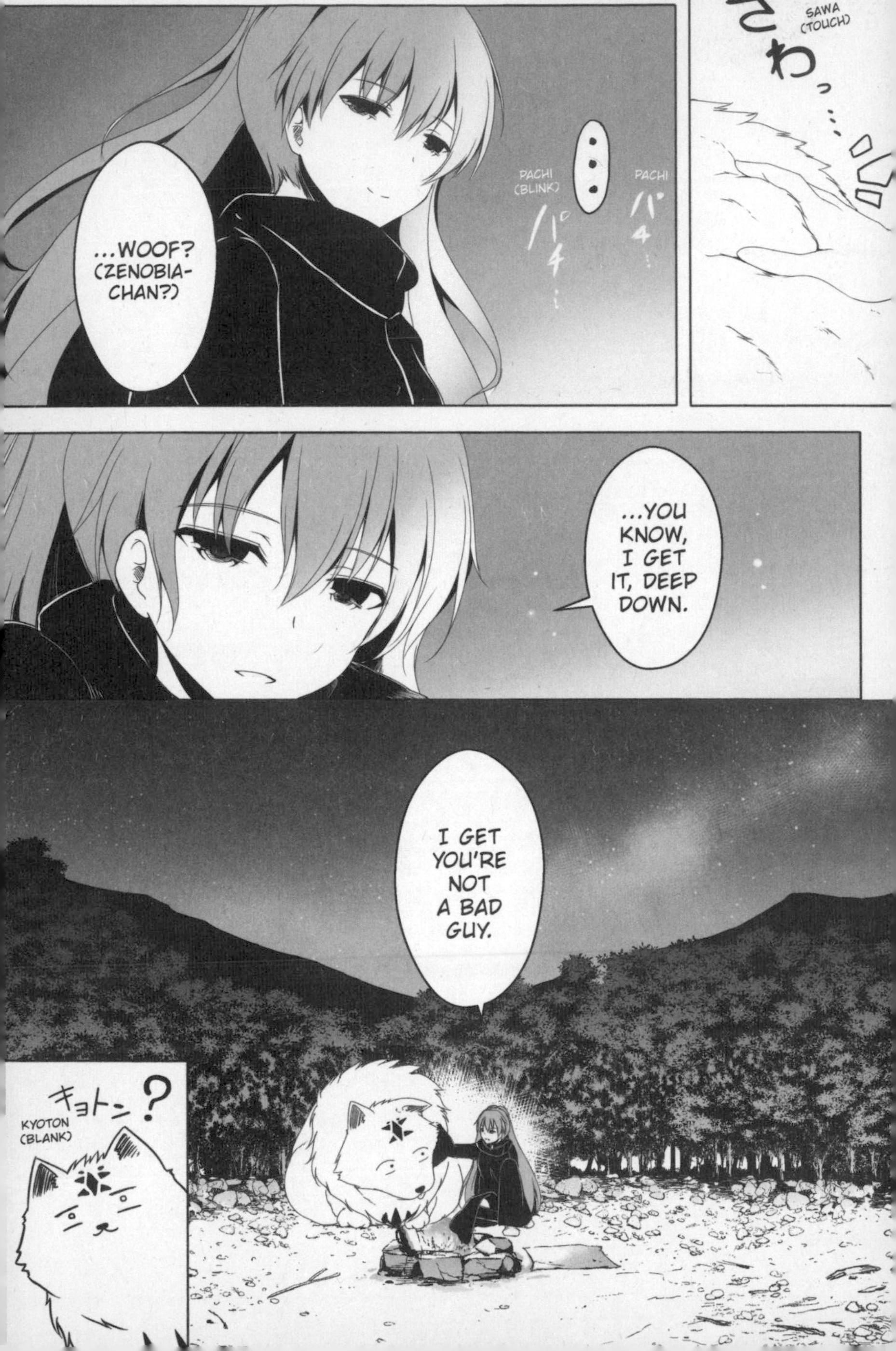
さわっ…
SAWA (TOUCH)
パチ…
PACHI
パチ…
PACHI (BLINK)
…
…WOOF? (ZENOBIA-CHAN?)
…YOU KNOW, I GET IT, DEEP DOWN.
I GET YOU'RE NOT A BAD GUY.
キョトン?
KYOTON (BLANK)

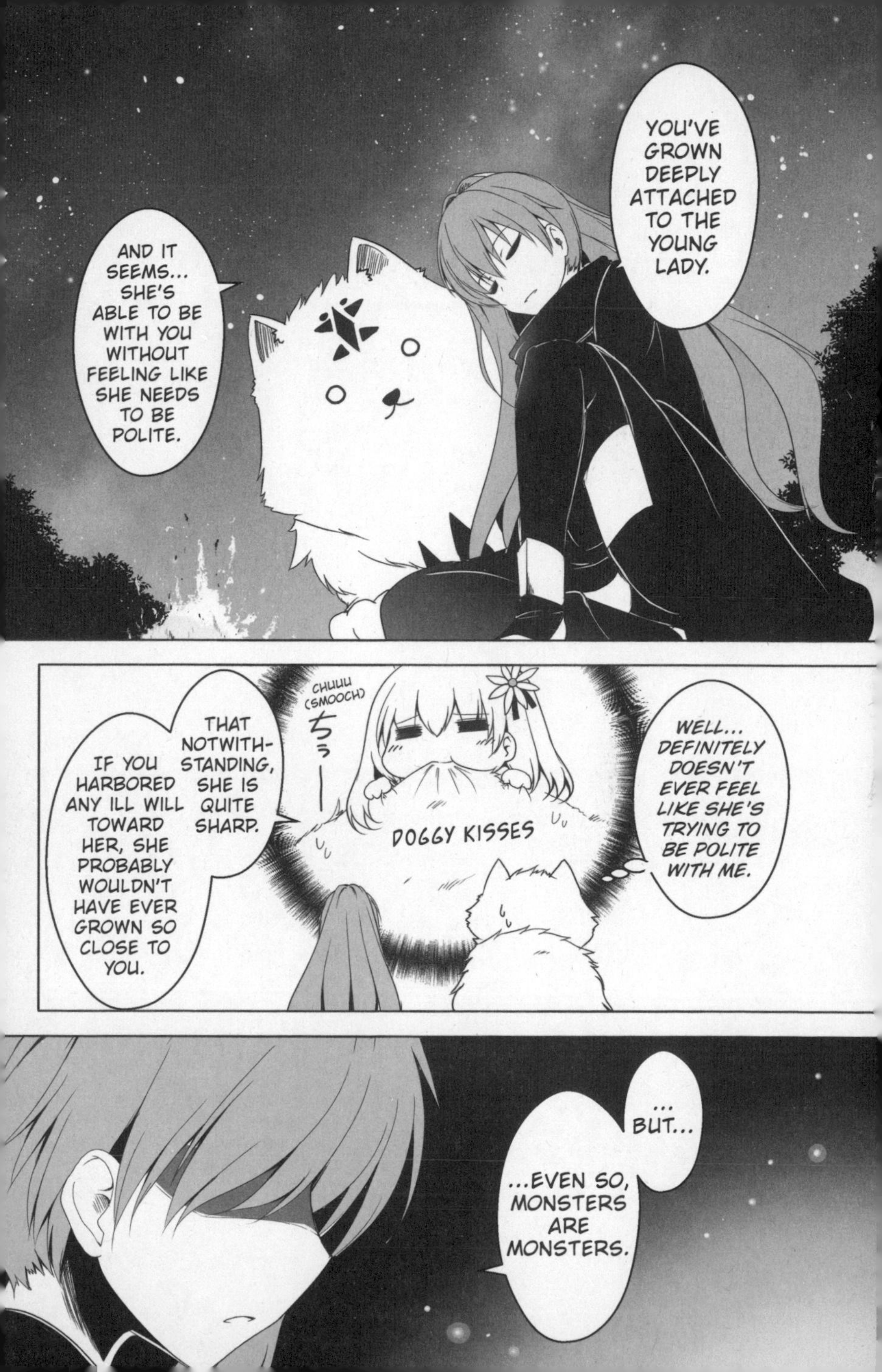

YOU'VE GROWN DEEPLY ATTACHED TO THE YOUNG LADY.
AND IT SEEMS... SHE'S ABLE TO BE WITH YOU WITHOUT FEELING LIKE SHE NEEDS TO BE POLITE.
WELL... DEFINITELY DOESN'T EVER FEEL LIKE SHE'S TRYING TO BE POLITE WITH ME.
CHUUU (SMOOCH)
ちぅー
DOGGY KISSES
THAT NOTWITH-STANDING, SHE IS QUITE SHARP.
IF YOU HARBORED ANY ILL WILL TOWARD HER, SHE PROBABLY WOULDN'T HAVE EVER GROWN SO CLOSE TO YOU.
... BUT...
...EVEN SO, MONSTERS ARE MONSTERS.

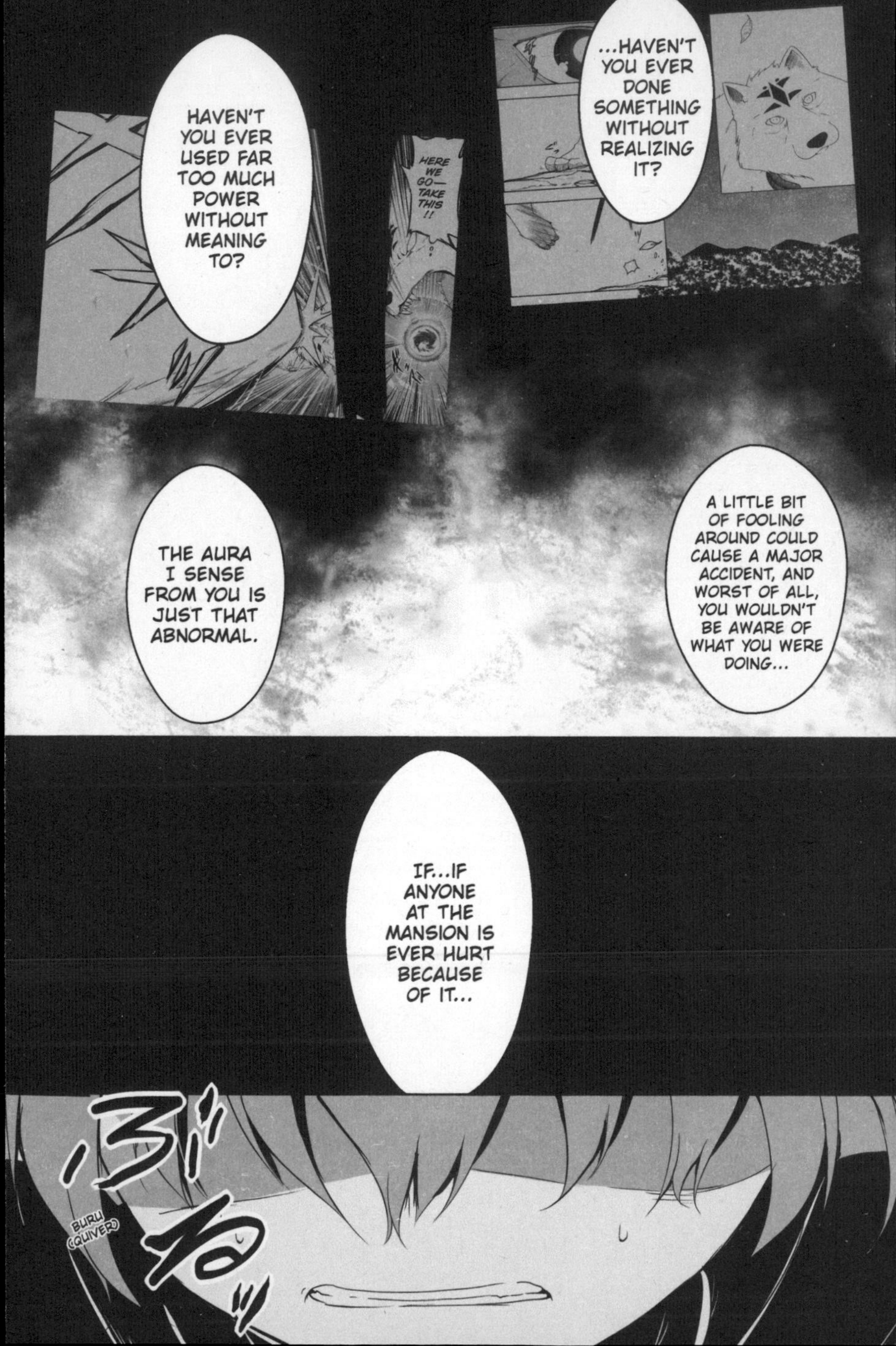
...HAVEN'T YOU EVER DONE SOMETHING WITHOUT REALIZING IT?
HERE WE GO—TAKE THIS!!
HAVEN'T YOU EVER USED FAR TOO MUCH POWER WITHOUT MEANING TO?
A LITTLE BIT OF FOOLING AROUND COULD CAUSE A MAJOR ACCIDENT, AND WORST OF ALL, YOU WOULDN'T BE AWARE OF WHAT YOU WERE DOING...
THE AURA I SENSE FROM YOU IS JUST THAT ABNORMAL.
IF...IF ANYONE AT THE MANSION IS EVER HURT BECAUSE OF IT...
BURU (QUIVER)

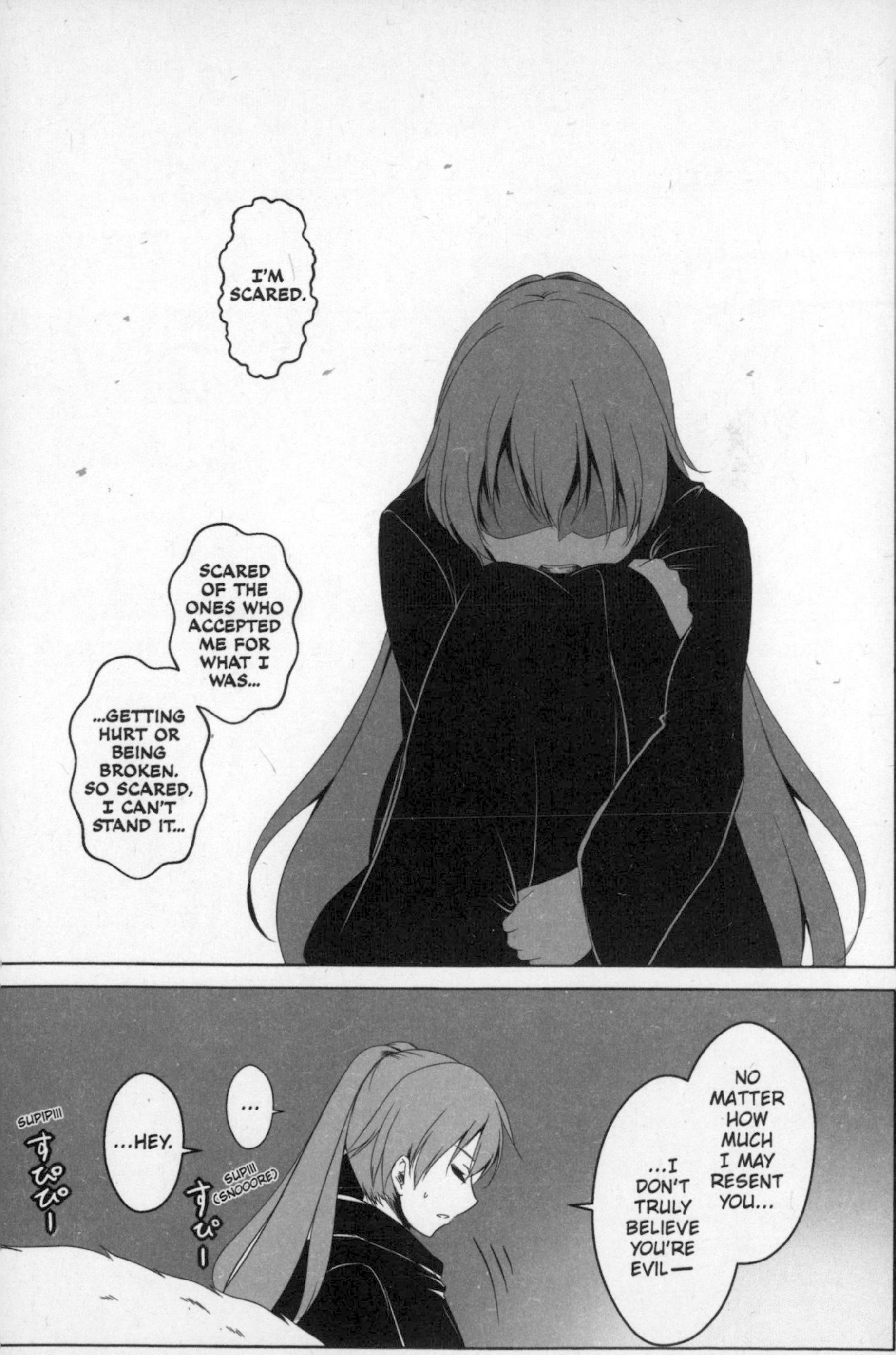
I'M SCARED.
SCARED OF THE ONES WHO ACCEPTED ME FOR WHAT I WAS...
...GETTING HURT OR BEING BROKEN. SO SCARED, I CAN'T STAND IT...
NO MATTER HOW MUCH I MAY RESENT YOU...
...I DON'T TRULY BELIEVE YOU'RE EVIL—
...
SUPIII (SNOOORE)
すぴー
...HEY.
SUPIPIII
すぴぴー

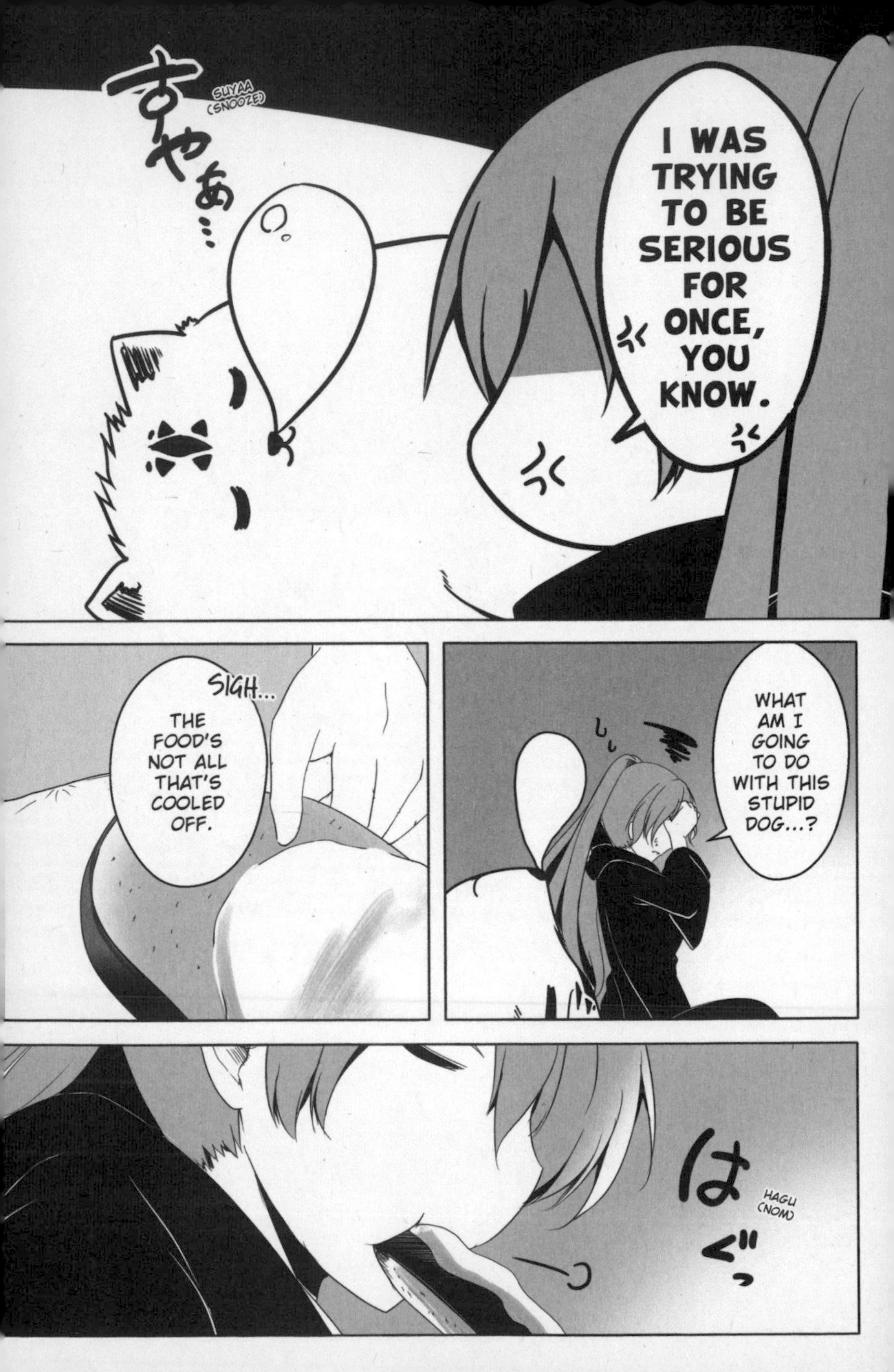
I WAS TRYING TO BE SERIOUS FOR ONCE, YOU KNOW.
すやぁ…
SUYAA (SNOOZE)
WHAT AM I GOING TO DO WITH THIS STUPID DOG...?
SIGH...
THE FOOD'S NOT ALL THAT'S COOLED OFF.
はぐっ
HAGU (NOM)

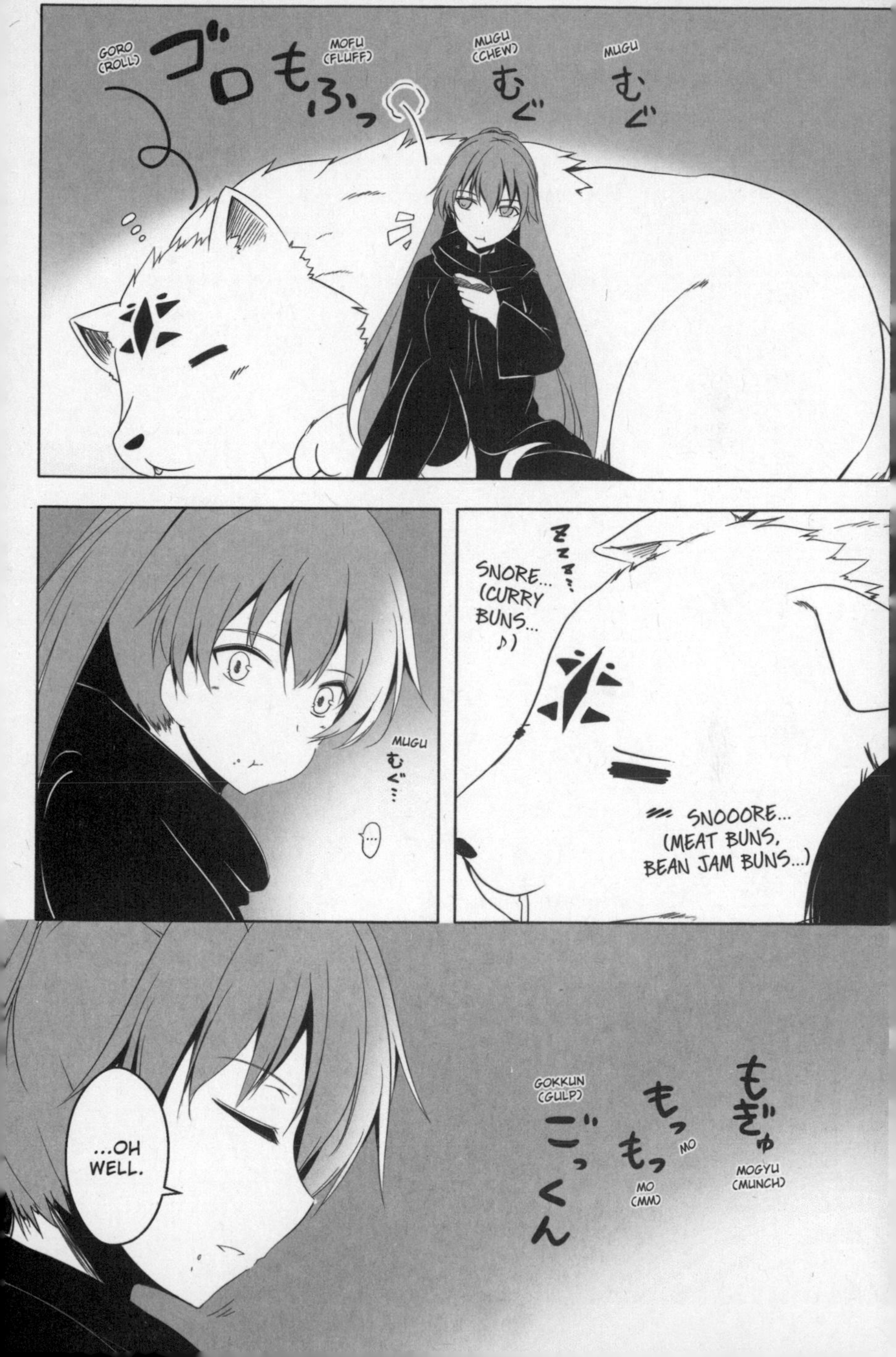
MUGU
むぐ
MUGU (CHEW)
むぐ
MOFU (FLUFF)
もふっ
GORO (ROLL)
ゴロ
SNORE... (CURRY BUNS... ♪)
SNOOORE... (MEAT BUNS, BEAN JAM BUNS...)
MUGU
むぐ...
...
もぎゅ
MOGYU (MUNCH)
もっ
MO
もっ
MO (MM)
ごっくん
GOKKUN (GULP)
...OH WELL.

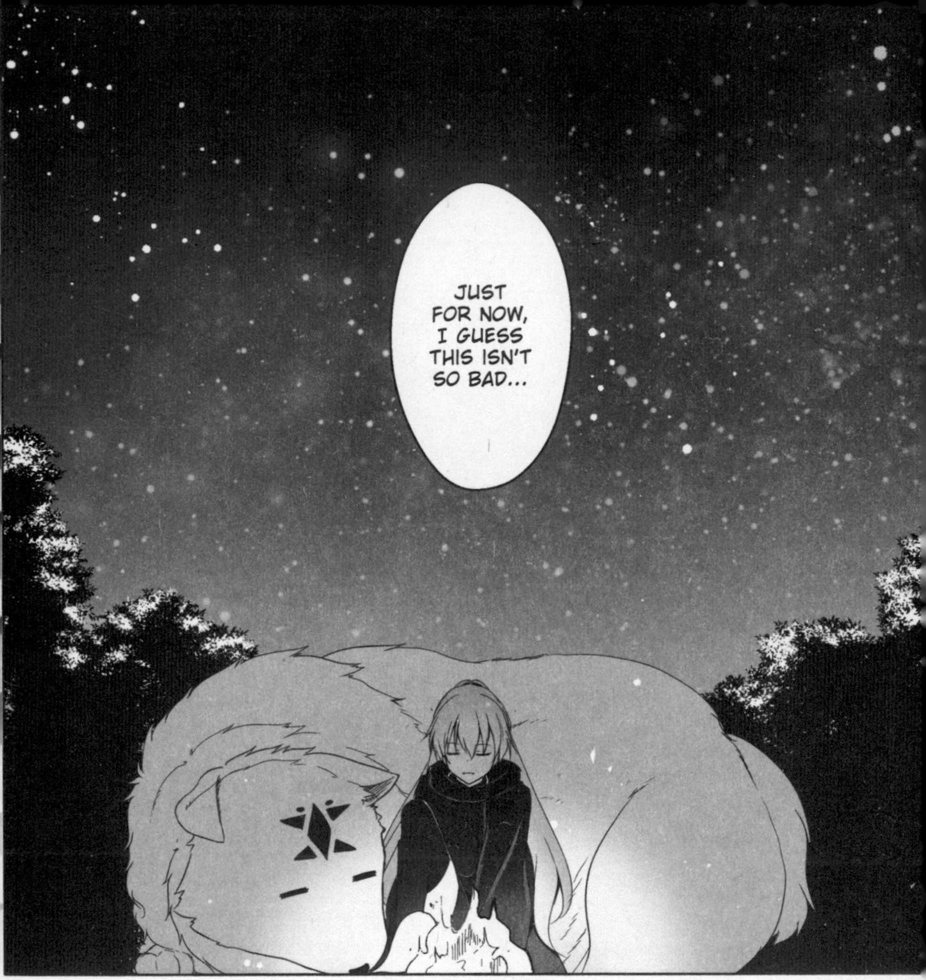
JUST FOR NOW, I GUESS THIS ISN'T SO BAD...

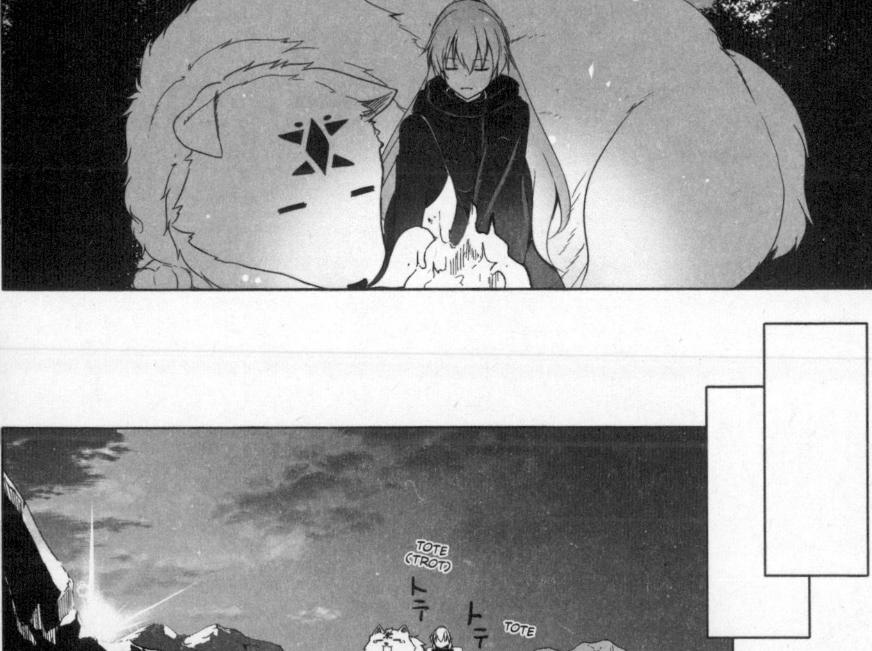
トテ
TOTE
トテ
TOTE (TROT)

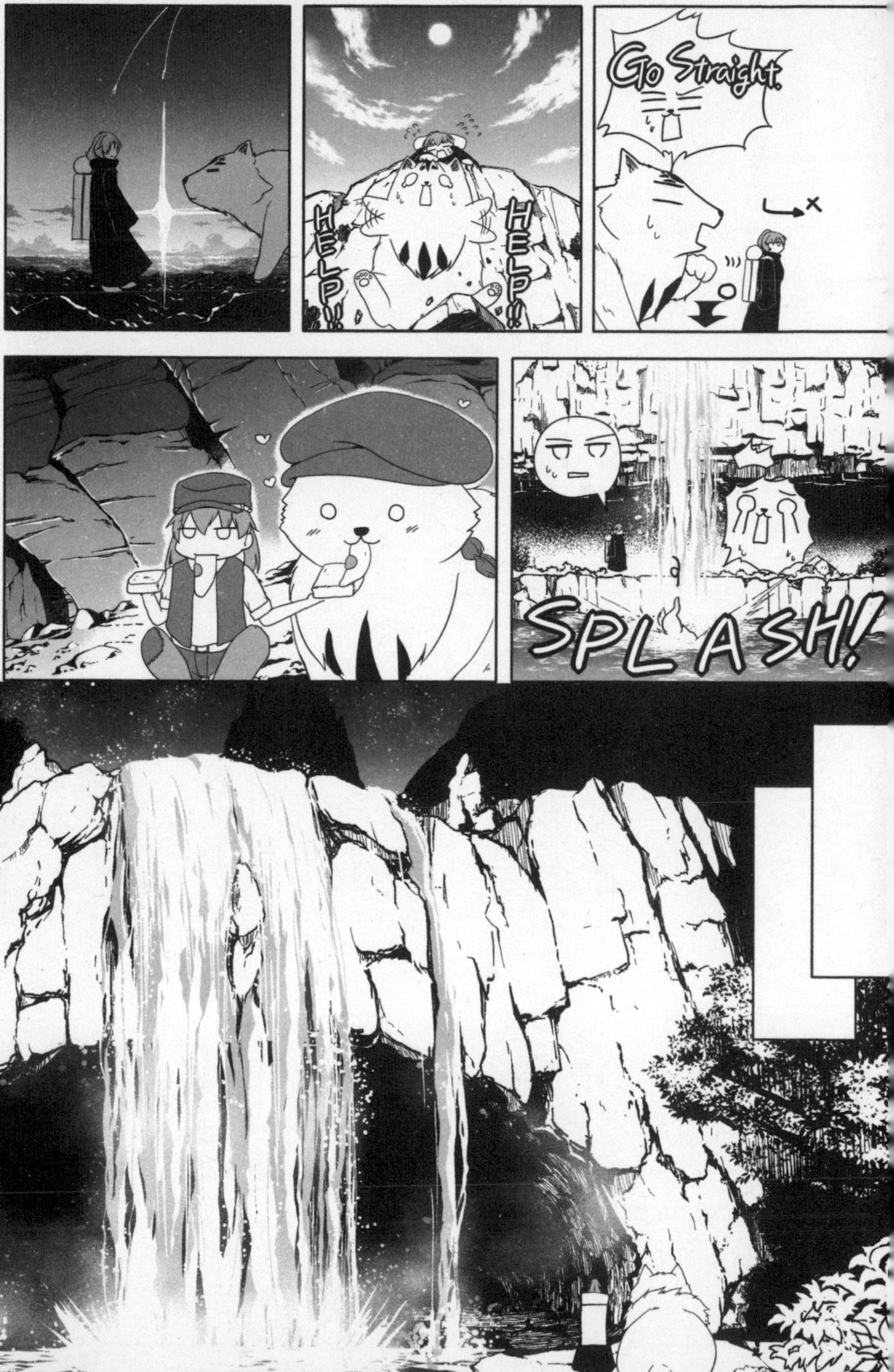
Go Straight.
HELP!!
HELP!!
SPLASH!

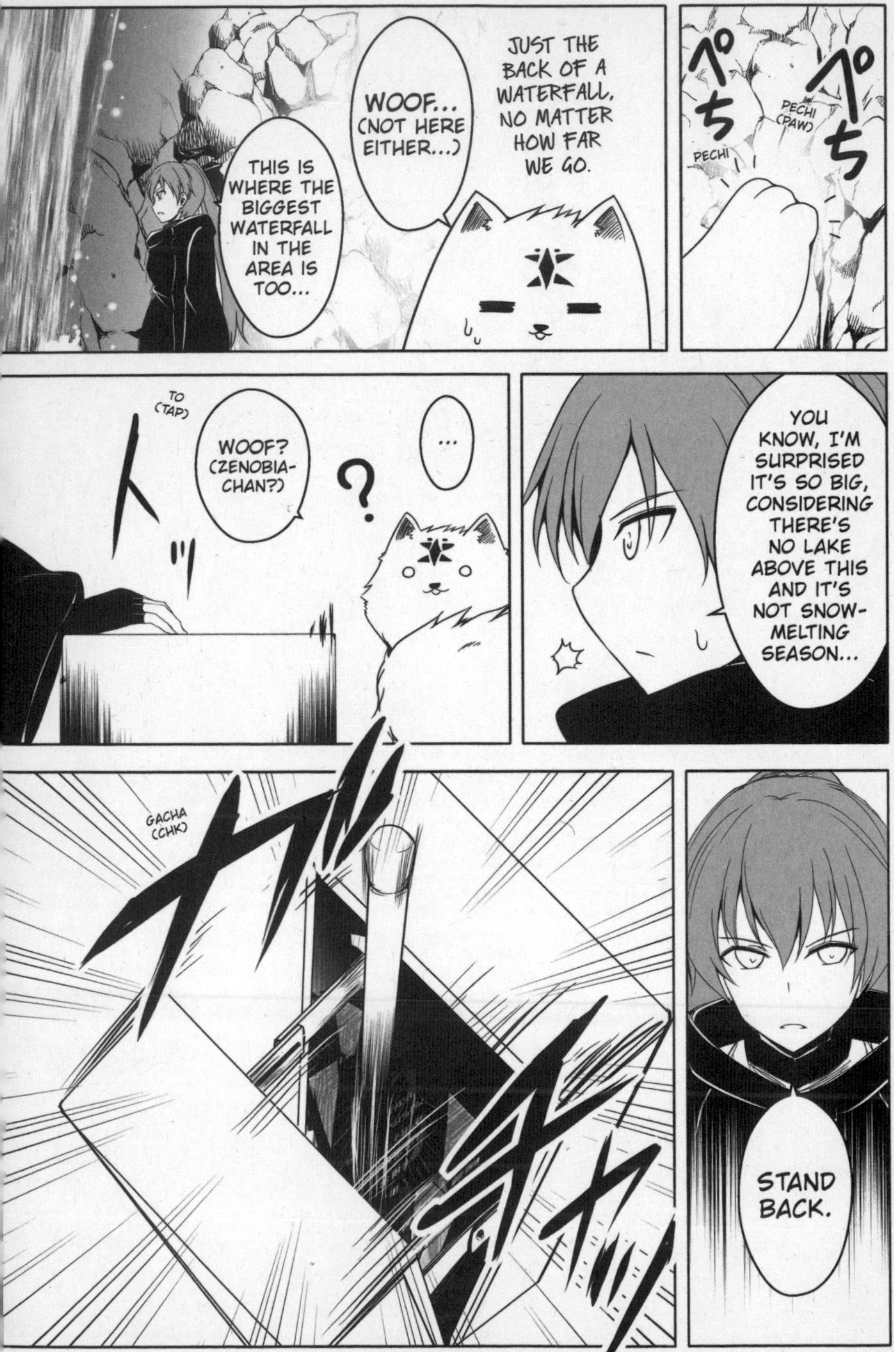
ぺち
PECHI (PAW)
ぺち
PECHI
JUST THE BACK OF A WATERFALL, NO MATTER HOW FAR WE GO.
WOOF... (NOT HERE EITHER...)
THIS IS WHERE THE BIGGEST WATERFALL IN THE AREA IS TOO...
YOU KNOW, I'M SURPRISED IT'S SO BIG, CONSIDERING THERE'S NO LAKE ABOVE THIS AND IT'S NOT SNOW-MELTING SEASON...
...
WOOF? (ZENOBIA-CHAN?)
トッ
TO (TAP)
STAND BACK.
GACHA (CHK)

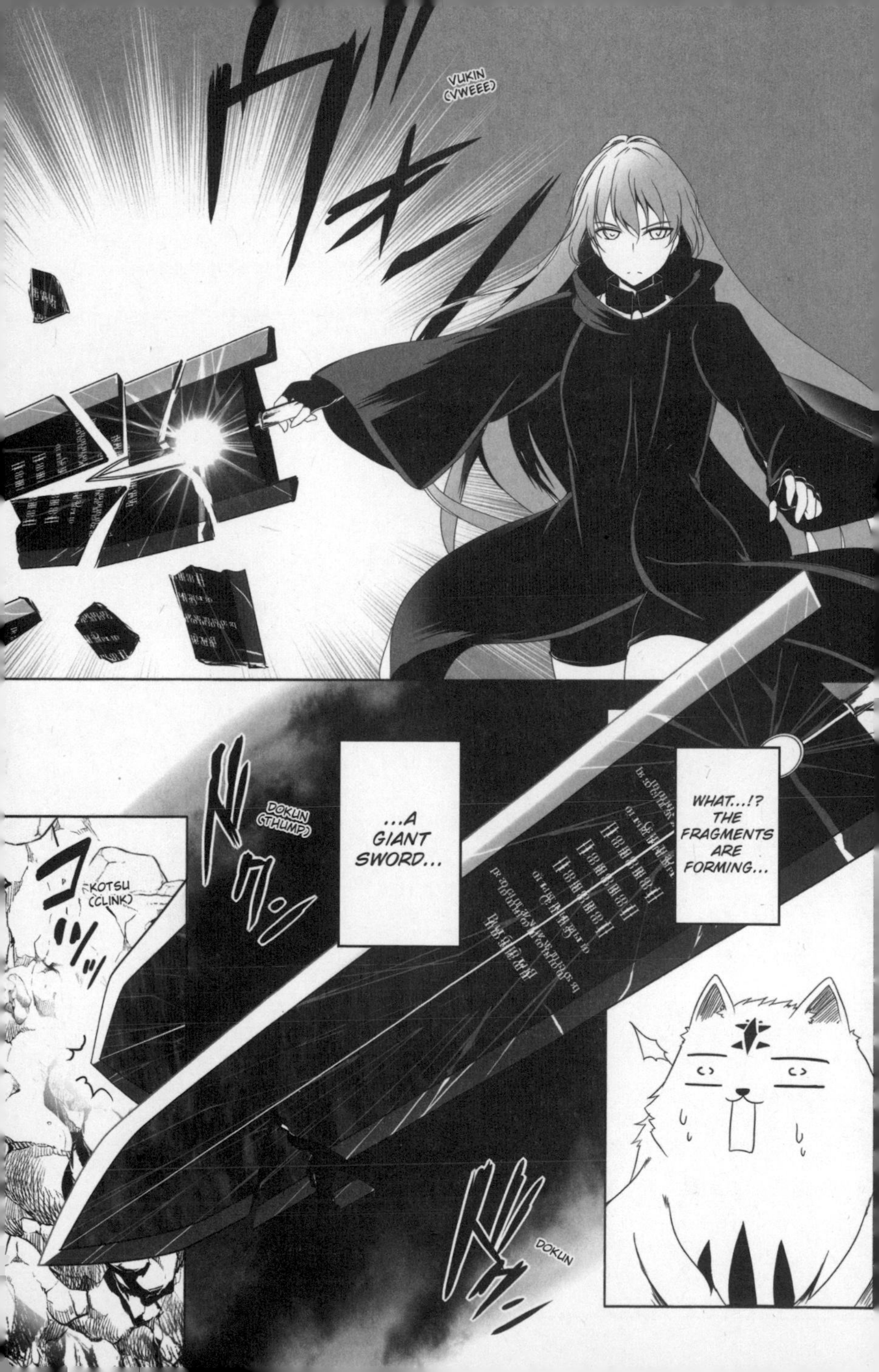
VUKIN (VWEEE)
WHAT...!? THE FRAGMENTS ARE FORMING...
...A GIANT SWORD...
DOKUN (THUMP)
KOTSU (CLINK)
DOKUN

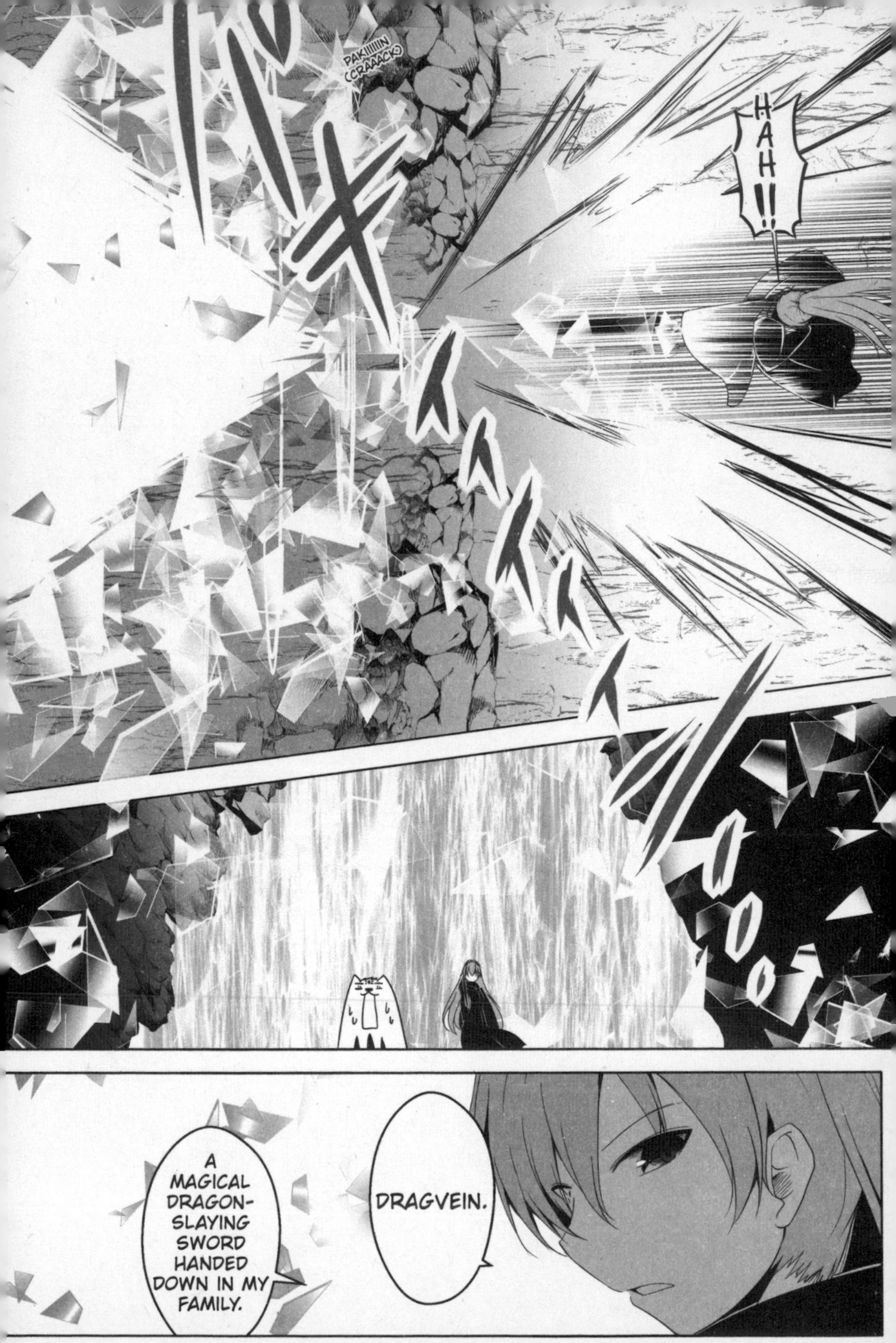
HAH!!
PAKIIIIIIIN (CRAAACK)
DRAGVEIN.
A MAGICAL DRAGON-SLAYING SWORD HANDED DOWN IN MY FAMILY.

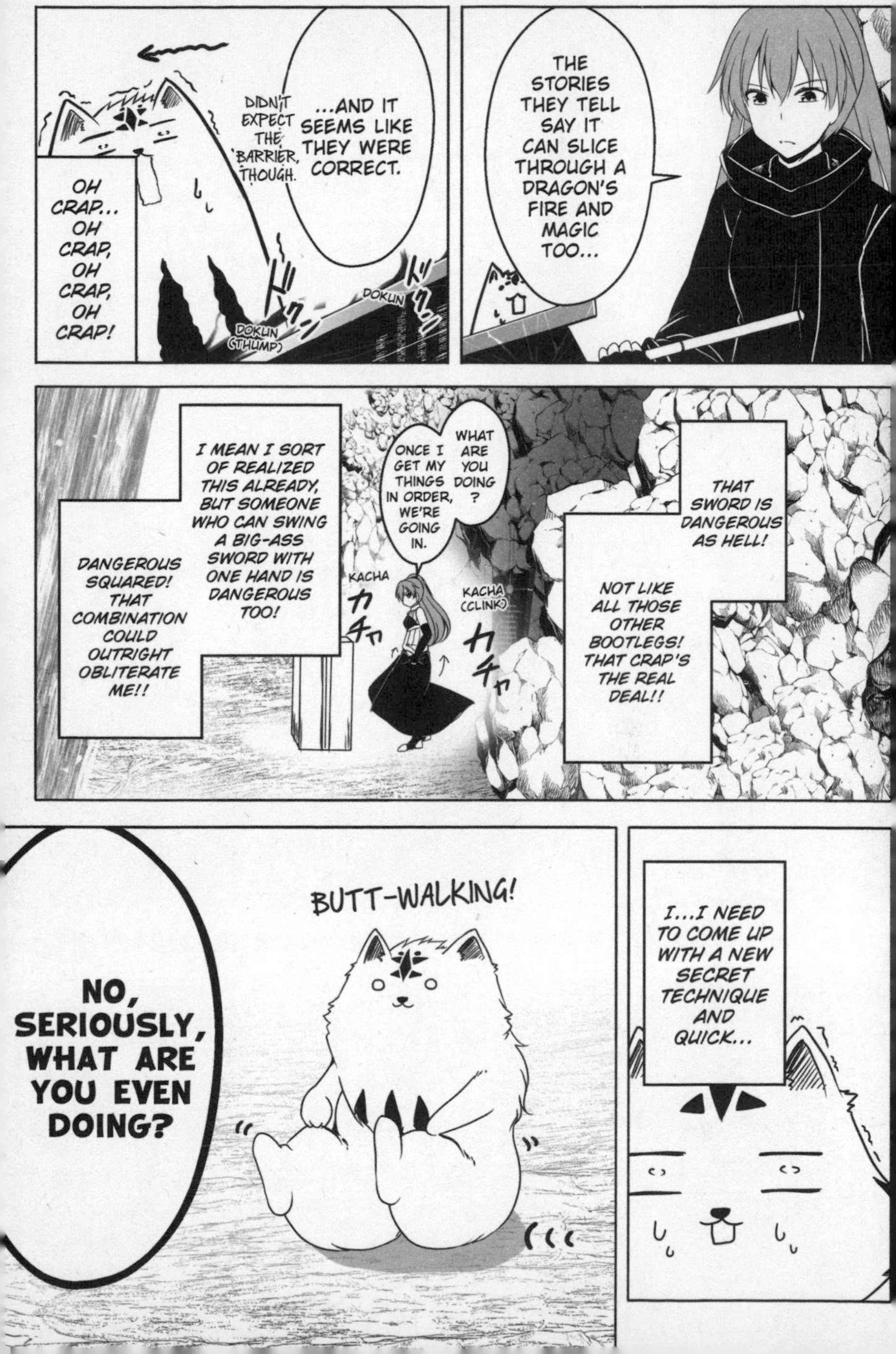
THE STORIES THEY TELL SAY IT CAN SLICE THROUGH A DRAGON'S FIRE AND MAGIC TOO...
...AND IT SEEMS LIKE THEY WERE CORRECT.
DIDN'T EXPECT THE BARRIER, THOUGH.
DOKUN
DOKUN (THUMP)
OH CRAP... OH CRAP, OH CRAP, OH CRAP!
THAT SWORD IS DANGEROUS AS HELL!
NOT LIKE ALL THOSE OTHER BOOTLEGS! THAT CRAP'S THE REAL DEAL!!
WHAT ARE YOU DOING?
ONCE I GET MY THINGS IN ORDER, WE'RE GOING IN.
KACHA (CLINK)
KACHA
I MEAN I SORT OF REALIZED THIS ALREADY, BUT SOMEONE WHO CAN SWING A BIG-ASS SWORD WITH ONE HAND IS DANGEROUS TOO!
DANGEROUS SQUARED! THAT COMBINATION COULD OUTRIGHT OBLITERATE ME!!
I...I NEED TO COME UP WITH A NEW SECRET TECHNIQUE AND QUICK...
BUTT-WALKING!
NO, SERIOUSLY, WHAT ARE YOU EVEN DOING?

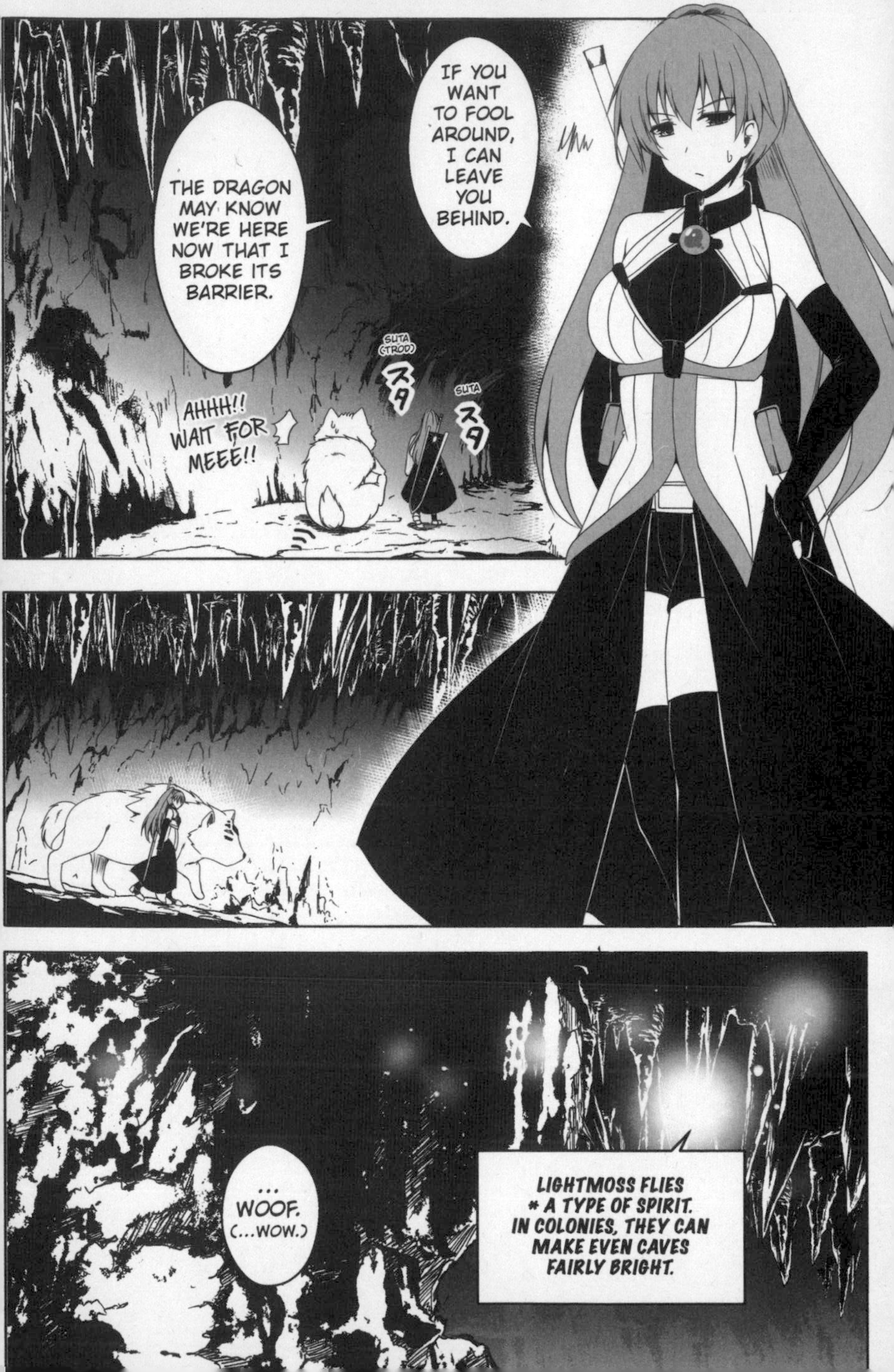
IF YOU WANT TO FOOL AROUND, I CAN LEAVE YOU BEHIND.
THE DRAGON MAY KNOW WE'RE HERE NOW THAT I BROKE ITS BARRIER.
SUTA
スタ
SUTA (TROD)
スタ
AHHH!! WAIT FOR MEEE!!
LIGHTMOSS FLIES
* A TYPE OF SPIRIT. IN COLONIES, THEY CAN MAKE EVEN CAVES FAIRLY BRIGHT.
... WOOF. (...WOW.)

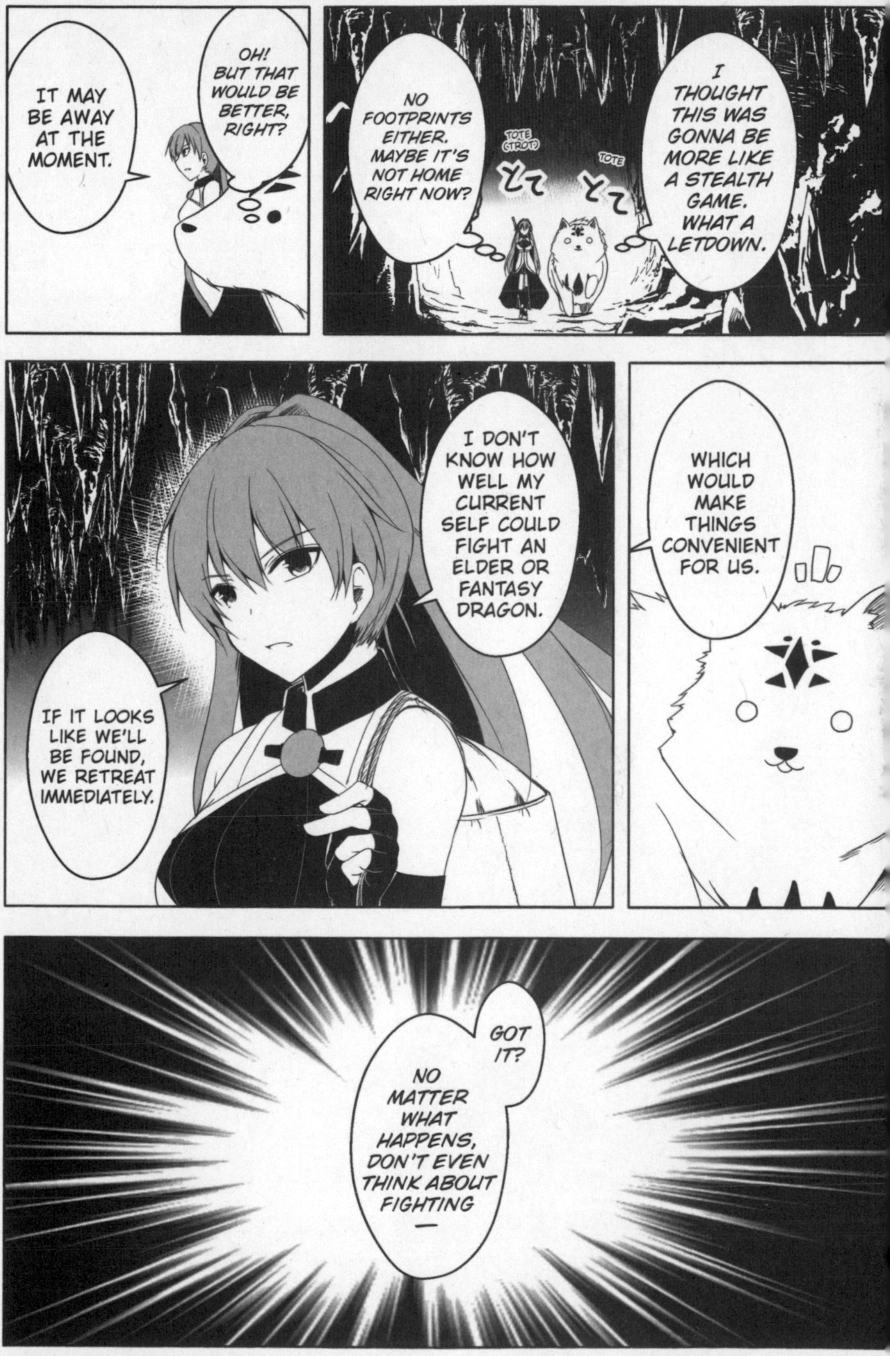
I THOUGHT THIS WAS GONNA BE MORE LIKE A STEALTH GAME. WHAT A LETDOWN.
TOTE
とて
TOTE (TROT)
とて
NO FOOTPRINTS EITHER. MAYBE IT'S NOT HOME RIGHT NOW?
OH! BUT THAT WOULD BE BETTER, RIGHT?
IT MAY BE AWAY AT THE MOMENT.
WHICH WOULD MAKE THINGS CONVENIENT FOR US.
I DON'T KNOW HOW WELL MY CURRENT SELF COULD FIGHT AN ELDER OR FANTASY DRAGON.
IF IT LOOKS LIKE WE'LL BE FOUND, WE RETREAT IMMEDIATELY.
GOT IT?
NO MATTER WHAT HAPPENS, DON'T EVEN THINK ABOUT FIGHTING —

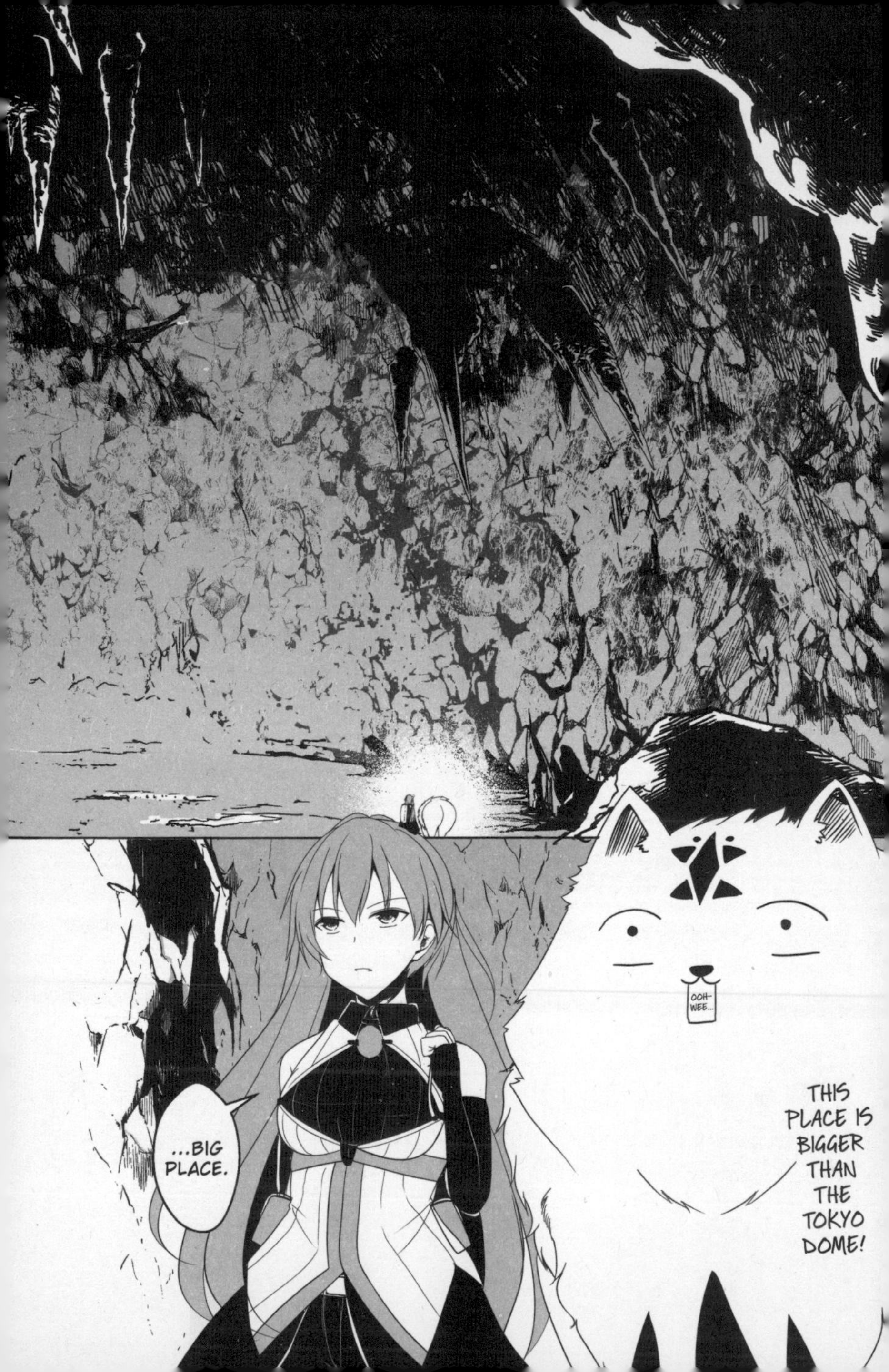
OOH-WEE...
THIS PLACE IS BIGGER THAN THE TOKYO DOME!
...BIG PLACE.

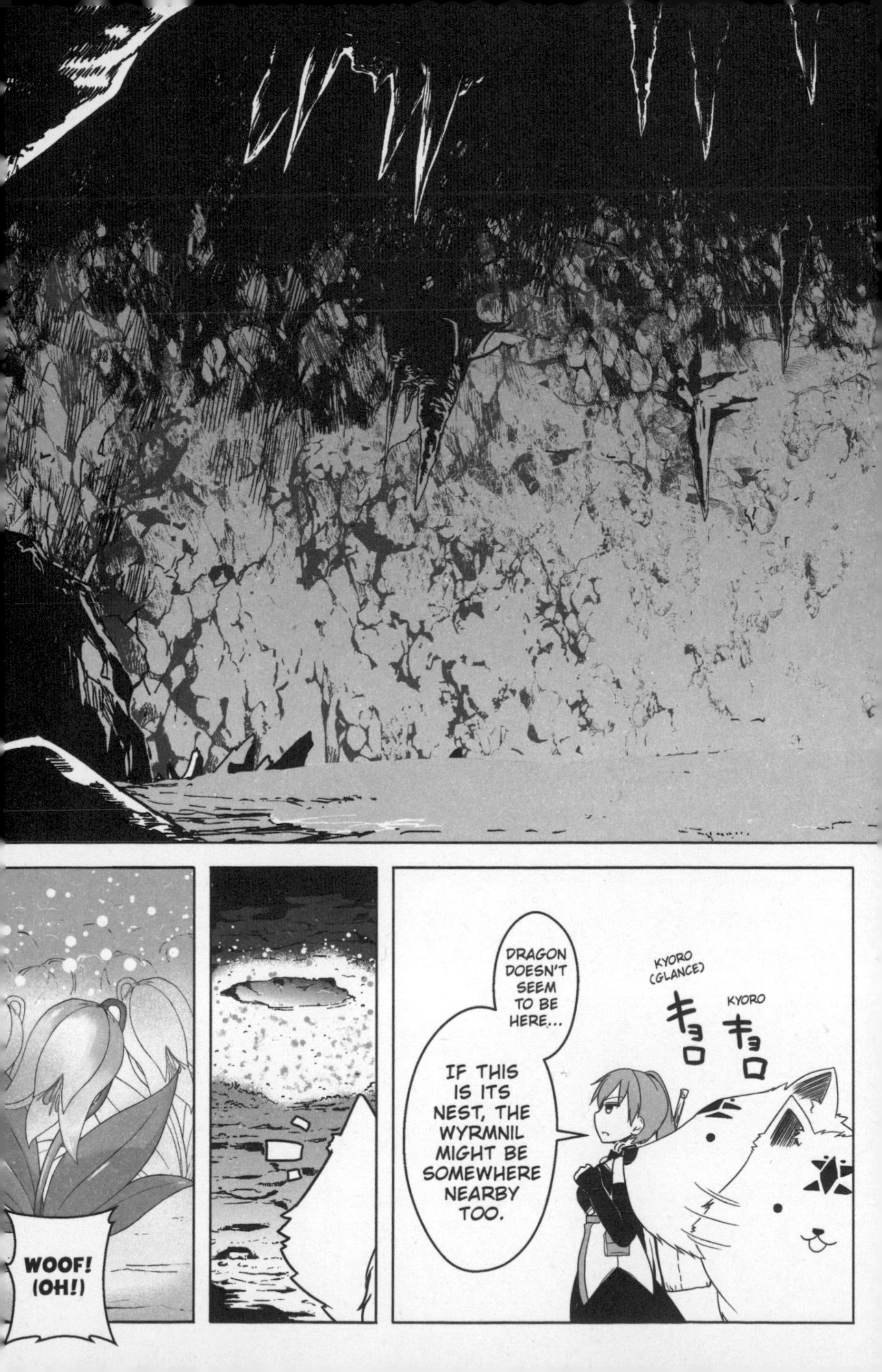
KYORO (GLANCE)
KYORO
DRAGON DOESN'T SEEM TO BE HERE...
IF THIS IS ITS NEST, THE WYRMNIL MIGHT BE SOMEWHERE NEARBY TOO.
WOOF! (OH!)

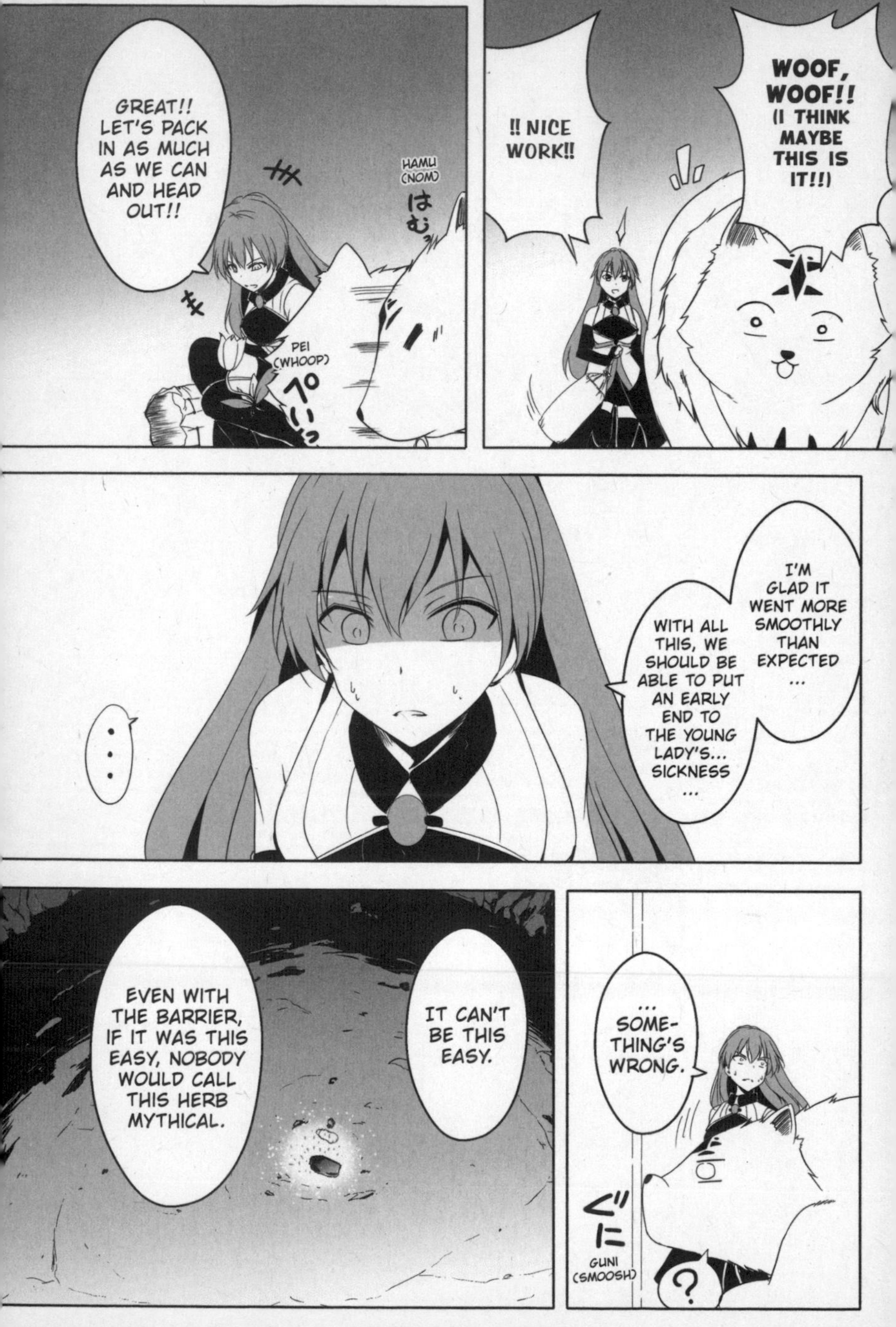
WOOF, WOOF!! (I THINK MAYBE THIS IS IT!!)
!! NICE WORK!!
!
HAMU (NOM)
はむっ
GREAT!! LET'S PACK IN AS MUCH AS WE CAN AND HEAD OUT!!
PEI (WHOOP)
ぺいっ
I'M GLAD IT WENT MORE SMOOTHLY THAN EXPECTED...
WITH ALL THIS, WE SHOULD BE ABLE TO PUT AN EARLY END TO THE YOUNG LADY'S... SICKNESS...
...
... SOME-THING'S WRONG.
ぐに
GUNI (SMOOSH)
?
IT CAN'T BE THIS EASY.
EVEN WITH THE BARRIER, IF IT WAS THIS EASY, NOBODY WOULD CALL THIS HERB MYTHICAL.

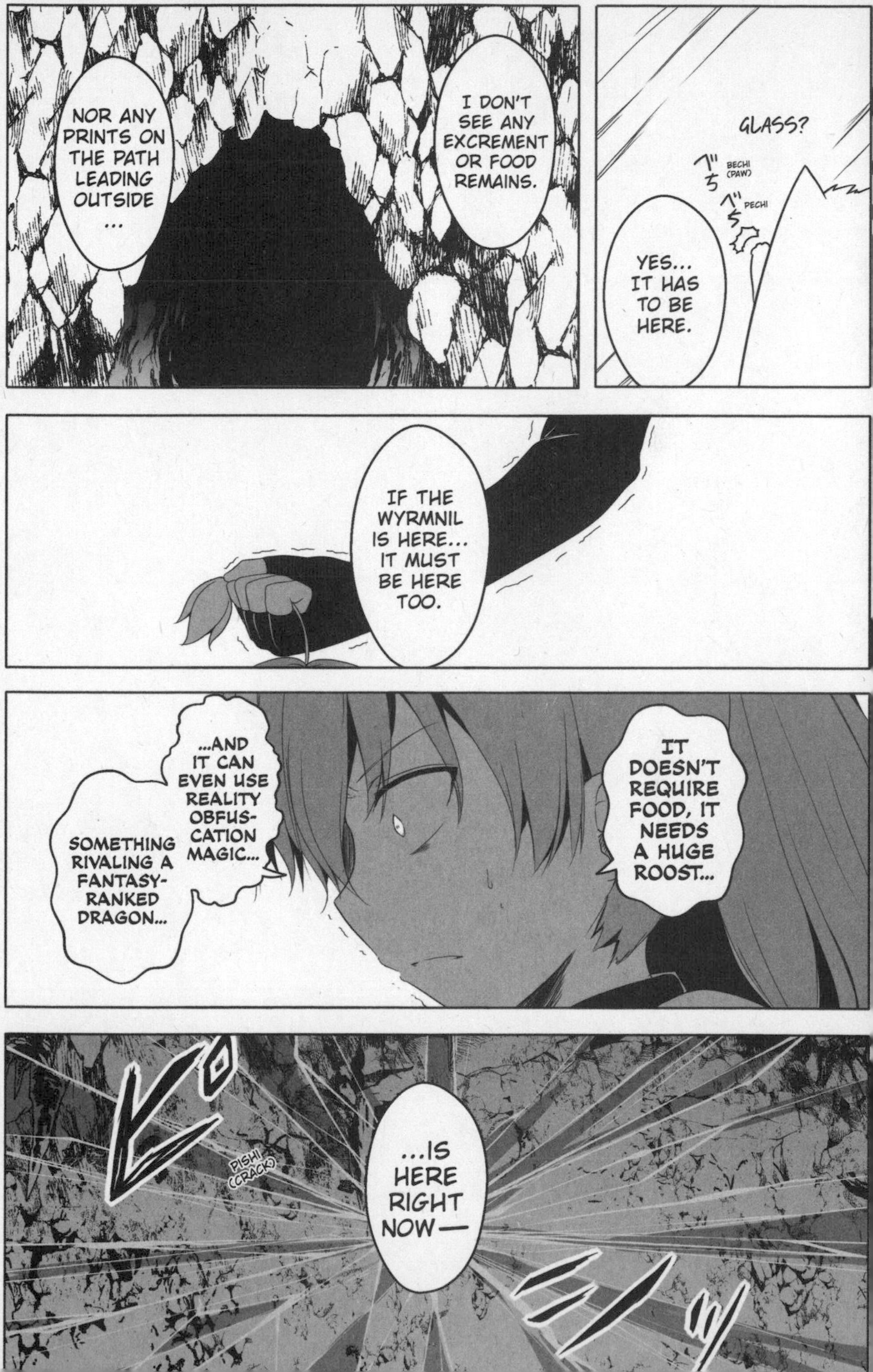
GLASS?
BECHI (PAW)
PECHI
YES... IT HAS TO BE HERE.
I DON'T SEE ANY EXCREMENT OR FOOD REMAINS.
NOR ANY PRINTS ON THE PATH LEADING OUTSIDE ...
IF THE WYRMNIL IS HERE... IT MUST BE HERE TOO.
IT DOESN'T REQUIRE FOOD, IT NEEDS A HUGE ROOST...
...AND IT CAN EVEN USE REALITY OBFUS-CATION MAGIC...
SOMETHING RIVALING A FANTASY-RANKED DRAGON...
...IS HERE RIGHT NOW—
PISHI (CRACK)

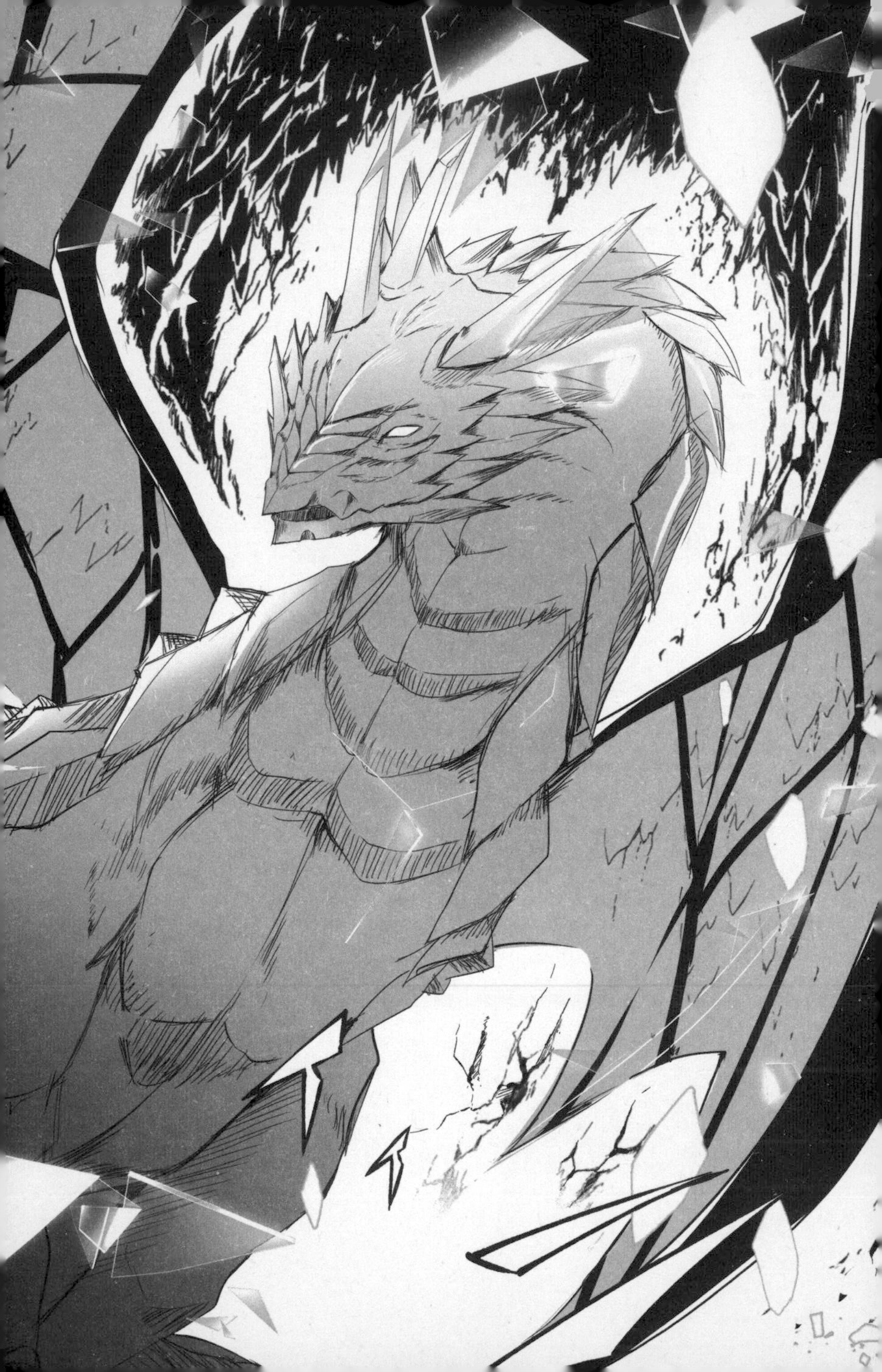

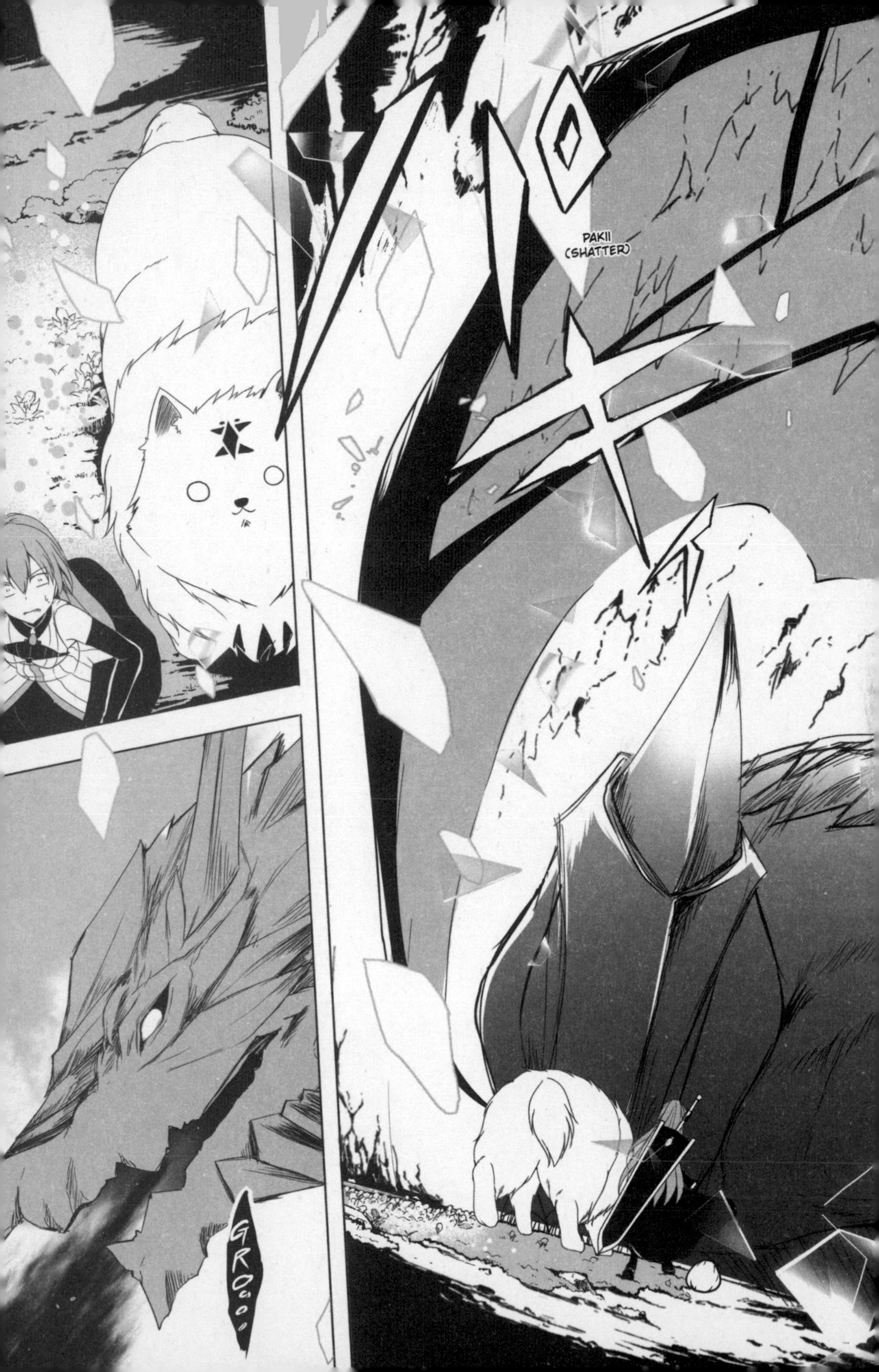
PAKII
(SHATTER)
GROooo

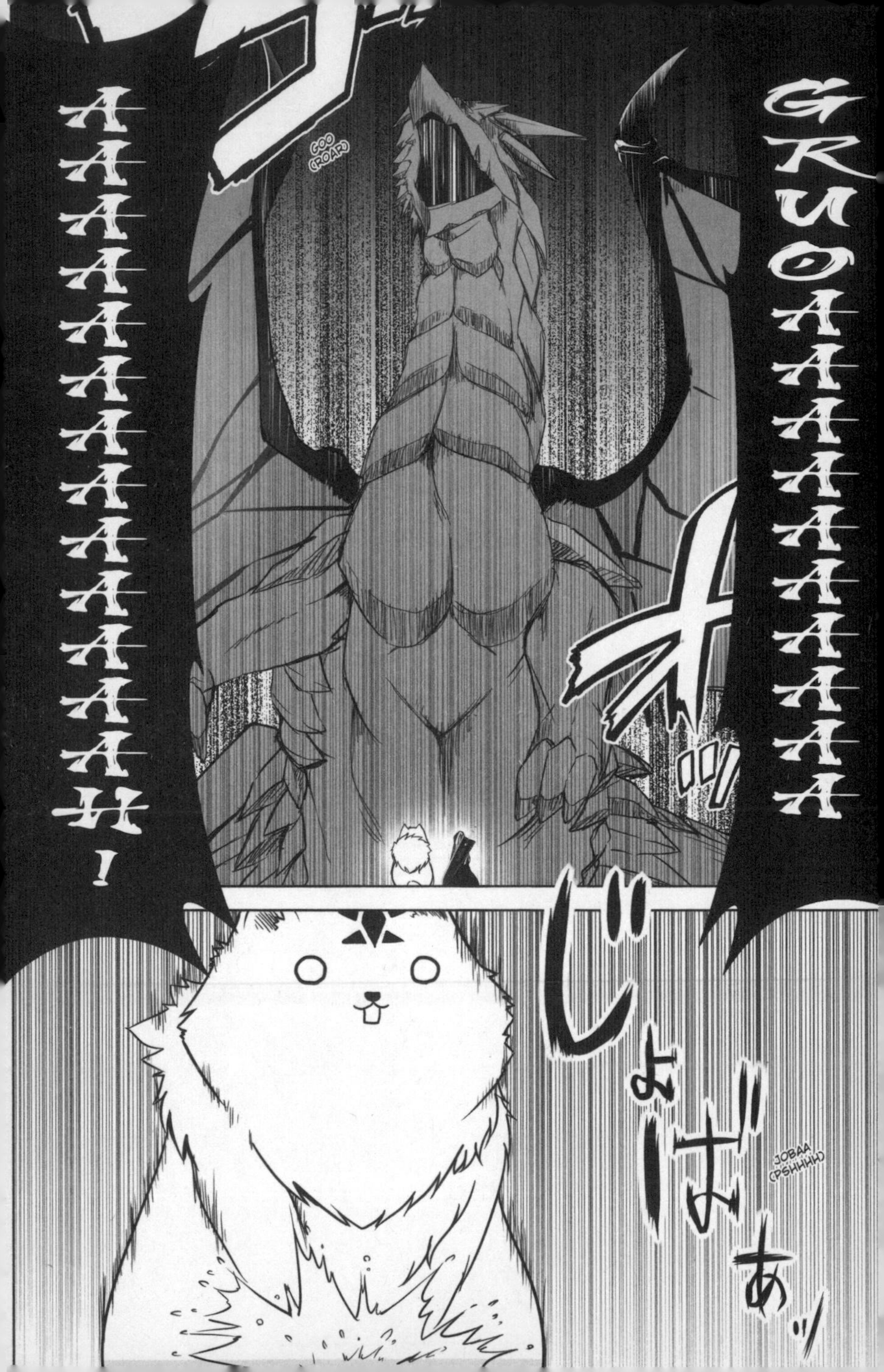
GRUOAAAAAAAAAA
AAAAAAAAAAAAAH!
オッ
GOO (ROAR)
じょばあッ
JOBAA (PSHHHH)

Woof Woof Story

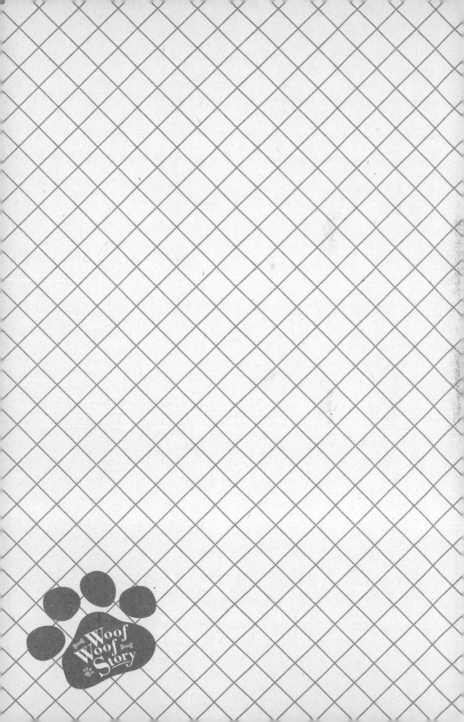

Woof Woof Story

I TOLD YOU TO TURN ME INTO A Pampered Pooch, NOT FENRIR!

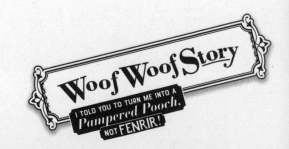

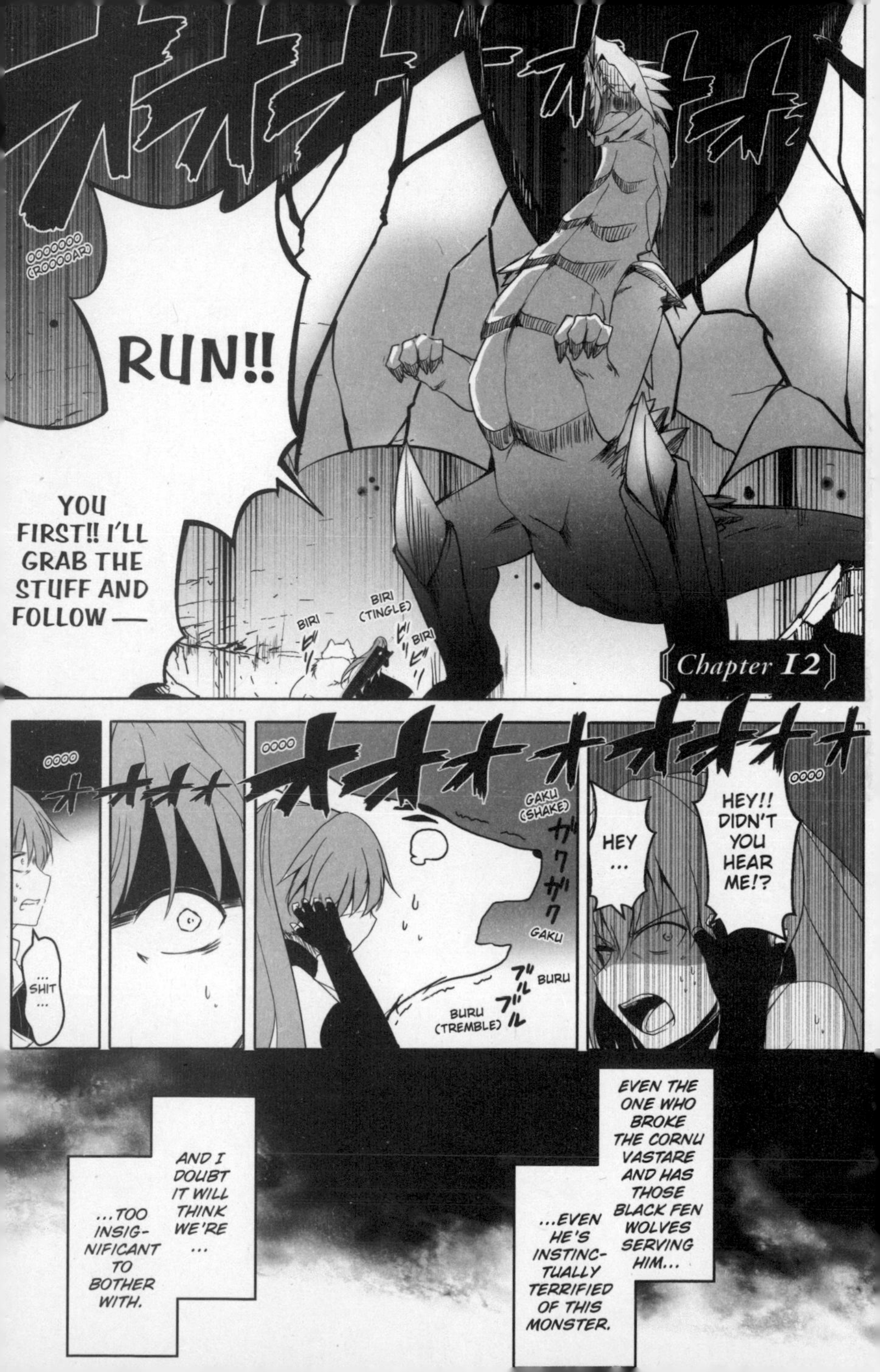
OOOOOOO (ROOOOAR)
Chapter 12
RUN!!
YOU FIRST!! I'LL GRAB THE STUFF AND FOLLOW—
BIRI (TINGLE)
BIRI
BIRI
OOOO
HEY!! DIDN'T YOU HEAR ME!?
HEY ...
OOOO
GAKU (SHAKE)
GAKU
BURU
BURU (TREMBLE)
OOOO
... SHIT ...
EVEN THE ONE WHO BROKE THE CORNU VASTARE AND HAS THOSE BLACK FEN WOLVES SERVING HIM...
...EVEN HE'S INSTINCTUALLY TERRIFIED OF THIS MONSTER.
AND I DOUBT IT WILL THINK WE'RE ...
...TOO INSIGNIFICANT TO BOTHER WITH.

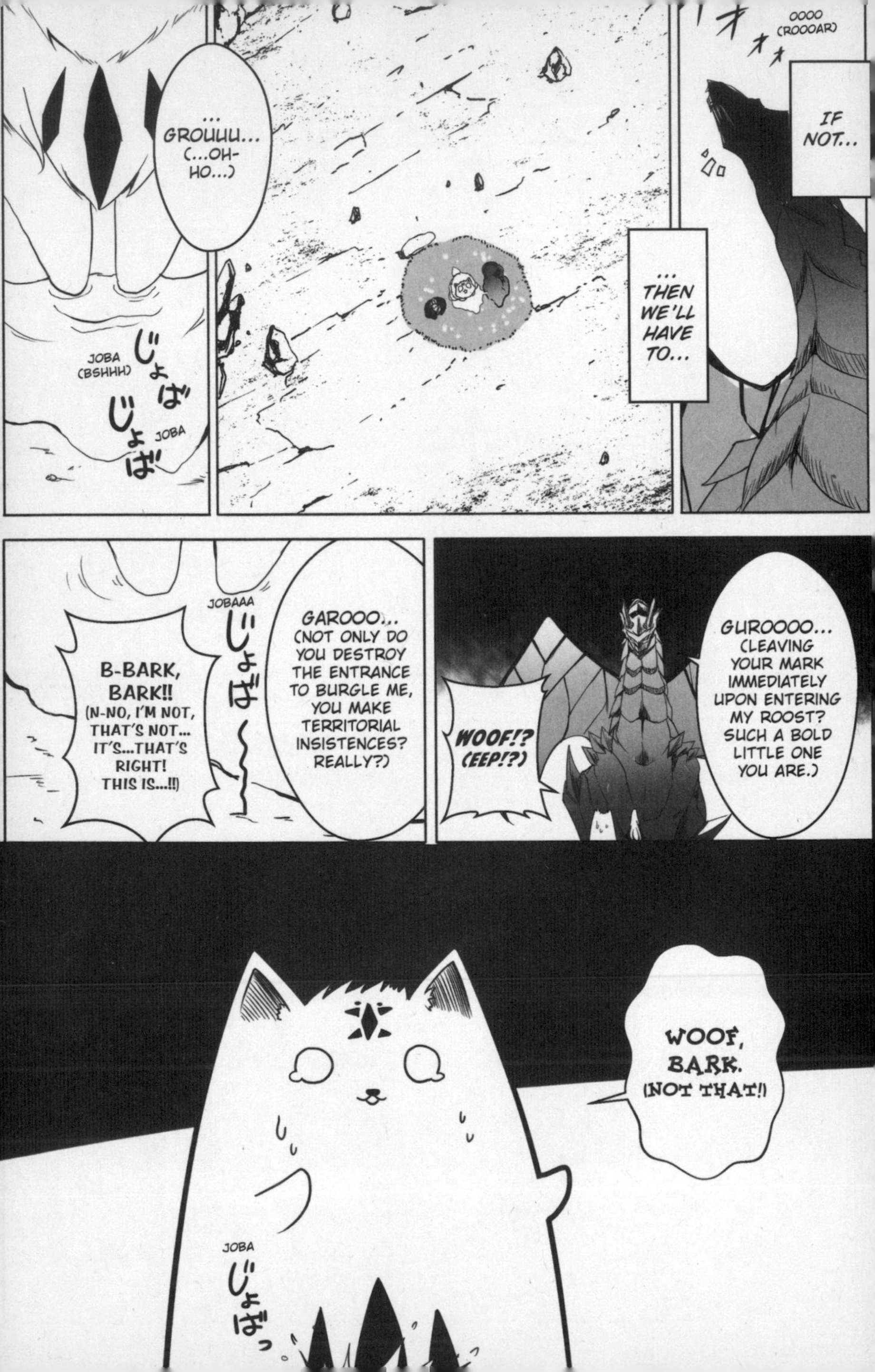
オオオ
OOOO (ROOOAR)
IF NOT...
...THEN WE'LL HAVE TO...
...GROUUU... (...OH-HO...)
JOBA (BSHHH)
じょば
じょば
JOBA
GUROOOO... (LEAVING YOUR MARK IMMEDIATELY UPON ENTERING MY ROOST? SUCH A BOLD LITTLE ONE YOU ARE.)
WOOF!? (EEP!?)
GAROOO... (NOT ONLY DO YOU DESTROY THE ENTRANCE TO BURGLE ME, YOU MAKE TERRITORIAL INSISTENCES? REALLY?)
JOBAAA
じょばー
B-BARK, BARK!! (N-NO, I'M NOT, THAT'S NOT... IT'S...THAT'S RIGHT! THIS IS...!!)
WOOF, BARK. (NOT THAT!)
JOBA
じょばっ

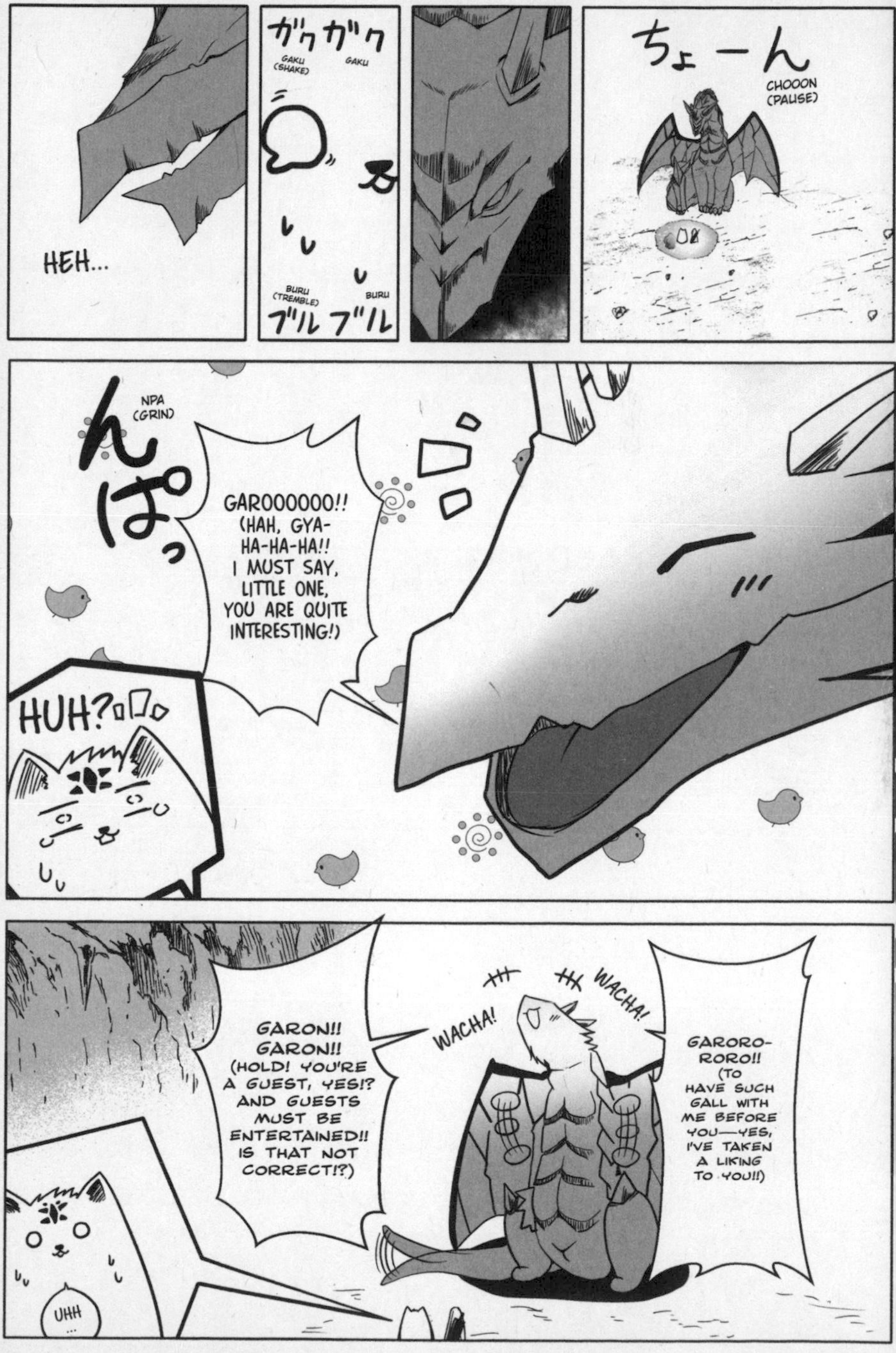
ちょーん
CHOOON (PAUSE)
ガクガク
GAKU (SHAKE) GAKU
ブルブル
BURU (TREMBLE) BURU
HEH...
んぱっ
NPA (GRIN)
GAROOOOOOO!! (HAH, GYA-HA-HA-HA!! I MUST SAY, LITTLE ONE, YOU ARE QUITE INTERESTING!)
HUH?
GARORO-RORO!! (TO HAVE SUCH GALL WITH ME BEFORE YOU—YES, I'VE TAKEN A LIKING TO YOU!!)
WACHA!
WACHA!
GARON!! GARON!! (HOLD! YOU'RE A GUEST, YES!? AND GUESTS MUST BE ENTERTAINED!! IS THAT NOT CORRECT!?)
UHH ...

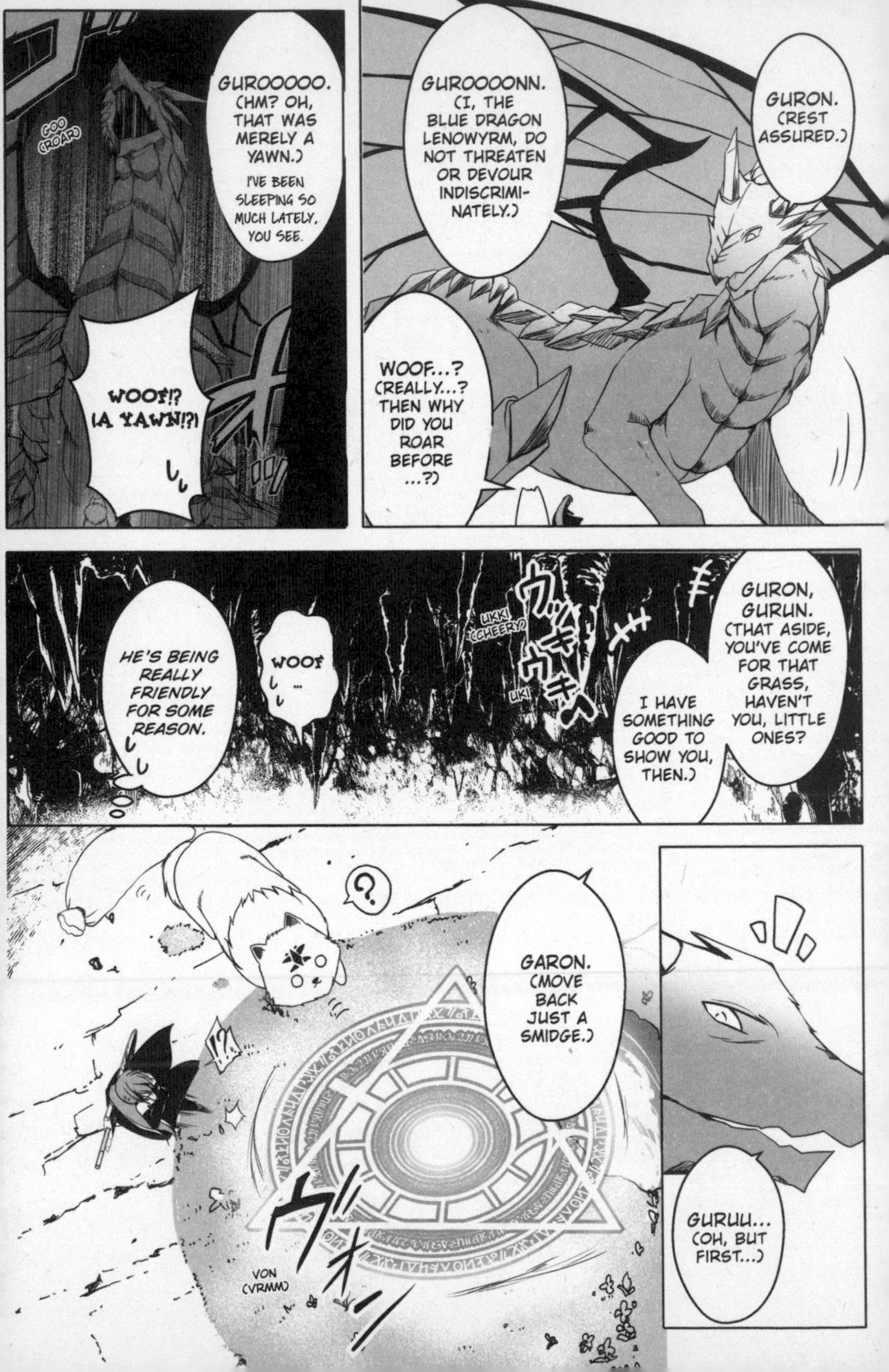
GURON. (REST ASSURED.)
GUROOOONN. (I, THE BLUE DRAGON LENOWYRM, DO NOT THREATEN OR DEVOUR INDISCRIMINATELY.)
WOOF...? (REALLY...? THEN WHY DID YOU ROAR BEFORE ...?)
GUROOOOO. (HM? OH, THAT WAS MERELY A YAWN.)
I'VE BEEN SLEEPING SO MUCH LATELY, YOU SEE.
GOO (ROAR)
WOOF!? (A YAWN!?)
GURON, GURUN. (THAT ASIDE, YOU'VE COME FOR THAT GRASS, HAVEN'T YOU, LITTLE ONES?
I HAVE SOMETHING GOOD TO SHOW YOU, THEN.)
UKKI (CHEERY)
UKI
WOOF ...
HE'S BEING REALLY FRIENDLY FOR SOME REASON.
GURUU... (OH, BUT FIRST...)
GARON. (MOVE BACK JUST A SMIDGE.)
?
!?
VON (VRMM)

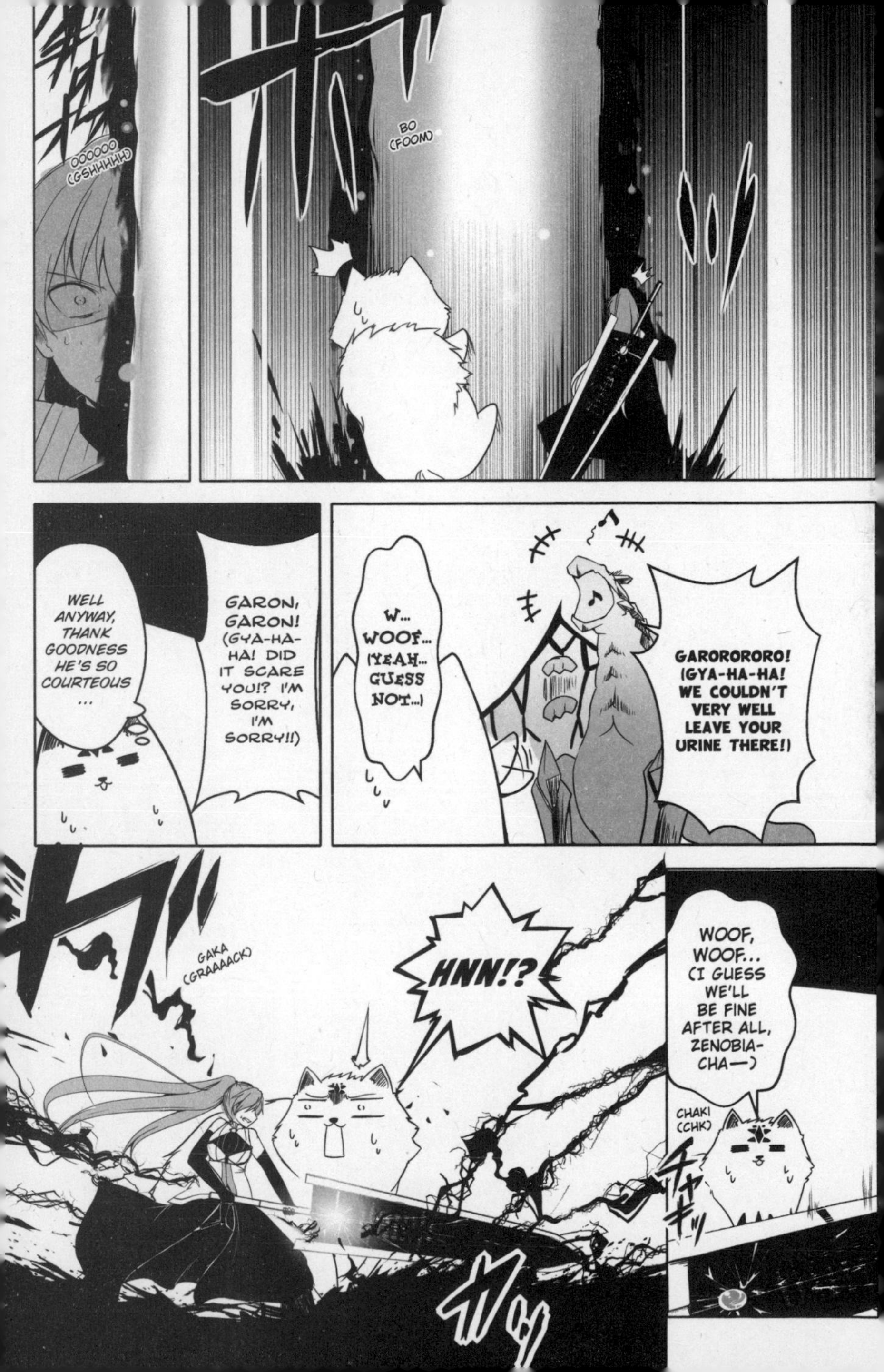
BO (FOOM)
OOOOOO (GSHHHHHH)
GAROROROROI (GYA-HA-HA! WE COULDN'T VERY WELL LEAVE YOUR URINE THERE!)
W... WOOF... (YEAH... GUESS NOT...)
GARON, GARON! (GYA-HA-HA! DID IT SCARE YOU!? I'M SORRY, I'M SORRY!!)
WELL ANYWAY, THANK GOODNESS HE'S SO COURTEOUS ...
WOOF, WOOF... (I GUESS WE'LL BE FINE AFTER ALL, ZENOBIA-CHA—)
CHAKI (CHK)
HNN!?
GAKA (GRAAAACK)

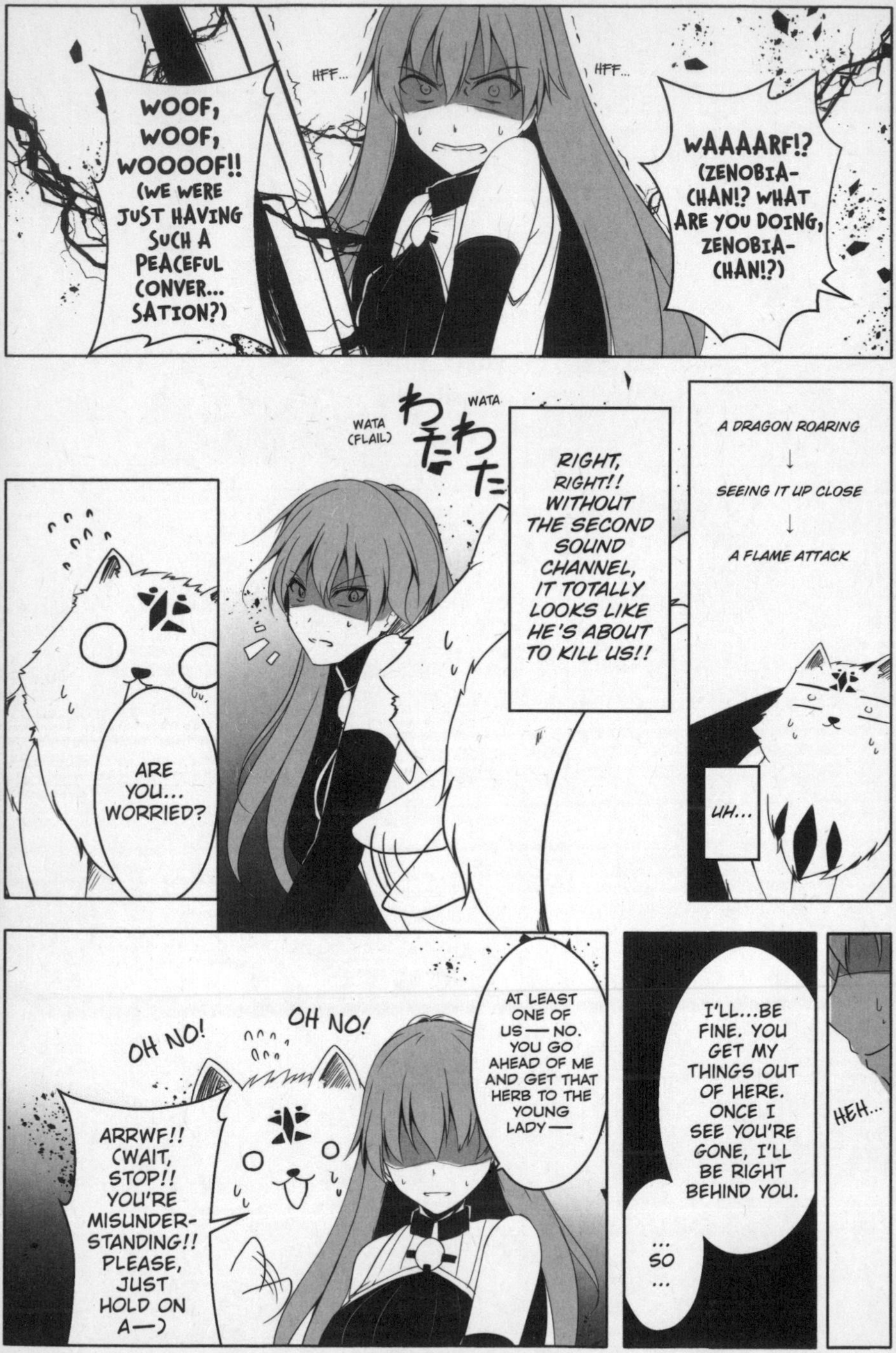
HFF...
WAAAARF!? (ZENOBIA-CHAN!? WHAT ARE YOU DOING, ZENOBIA-CHAN!?)
HFF...
WOOF, WOOF, WOOOOF!! (WE WERE JUST HAVING SUCH A PEACEFUL (CONVER... SATION?)
A DRAGON ROARING
↓
SEEING IT UP CLOSE
↓
A FLAME ATTACK
UH...
RIGHT, RIGHT!! WITHOUT THE SECOND SOUND CHANNEL, IT TOTALLY LOOKS LIKE HE'S ABOUT TO KILL US!!
わたわた
WATA
WATA (FLAIL)
ARE YOU... WORRIED?
HEH...
I'LL...BE FINE. YOU GET MY THINGS OUT OF HERE. ONCE I SEE YOU'RE GONE, I'LL BE RIGHT BEHIND YOU.
...SO...
AT LEAST ONE OF US— NO. YOU GO AHEAD OF ME AND GET THAT HERB TO THE YOUNG LADY—
OH NO!
OH NO!
ARRWF!! (WAIT, STOP!! YOU'RE MISUNDER-STANDING!! PLEASE, JUST HOLD ON A—)

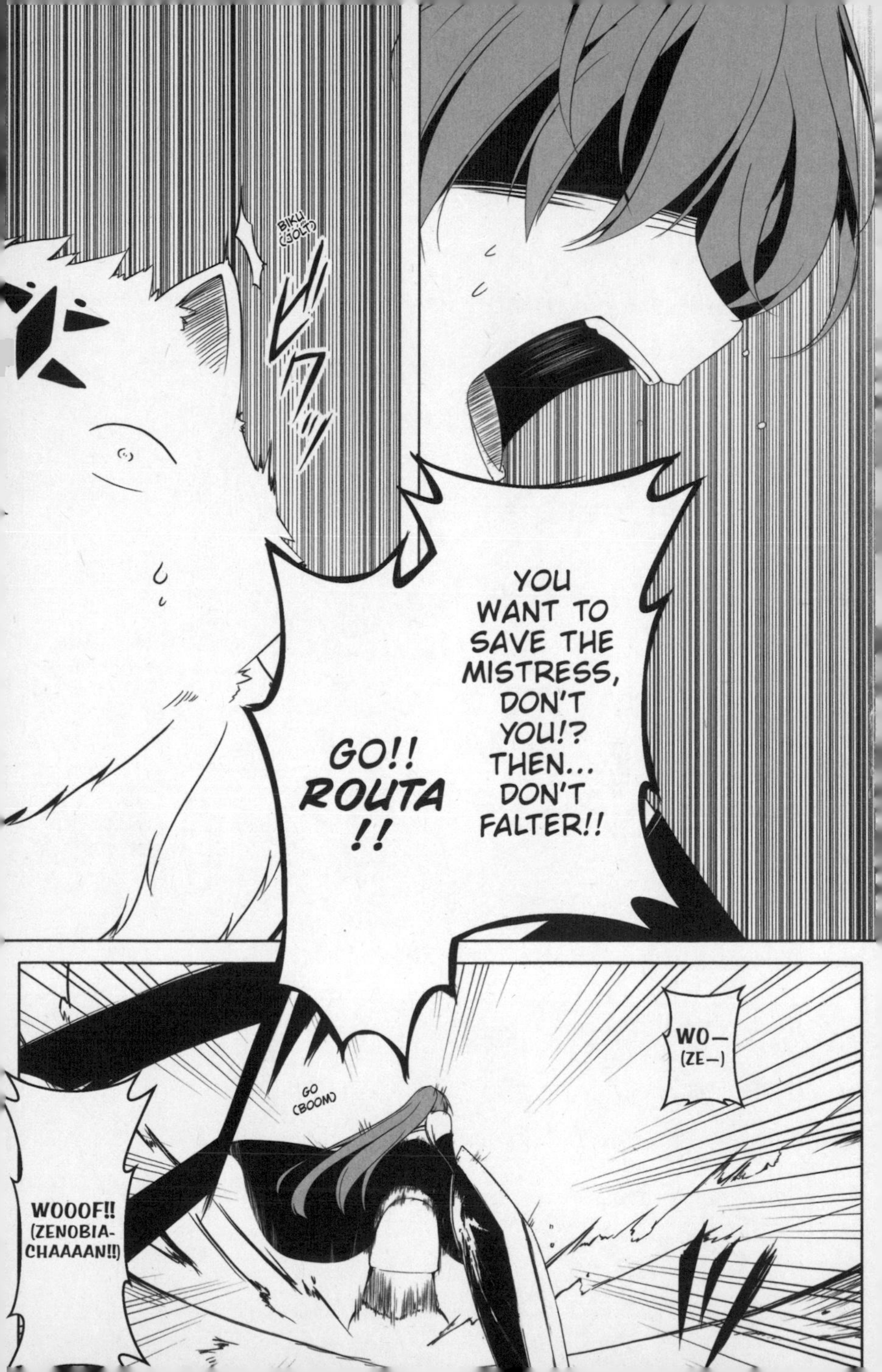
YOU WANT TO SAVE THE MISTRESS, DON'T YOU!? THEN... DON'T FALTER!!
GO!! ROUTA !!
BIKU (JOLT)
WO— (ZE—)
GO (BOOM)
WOOOF!! (ZENOBIA-CHAAAAN!!)

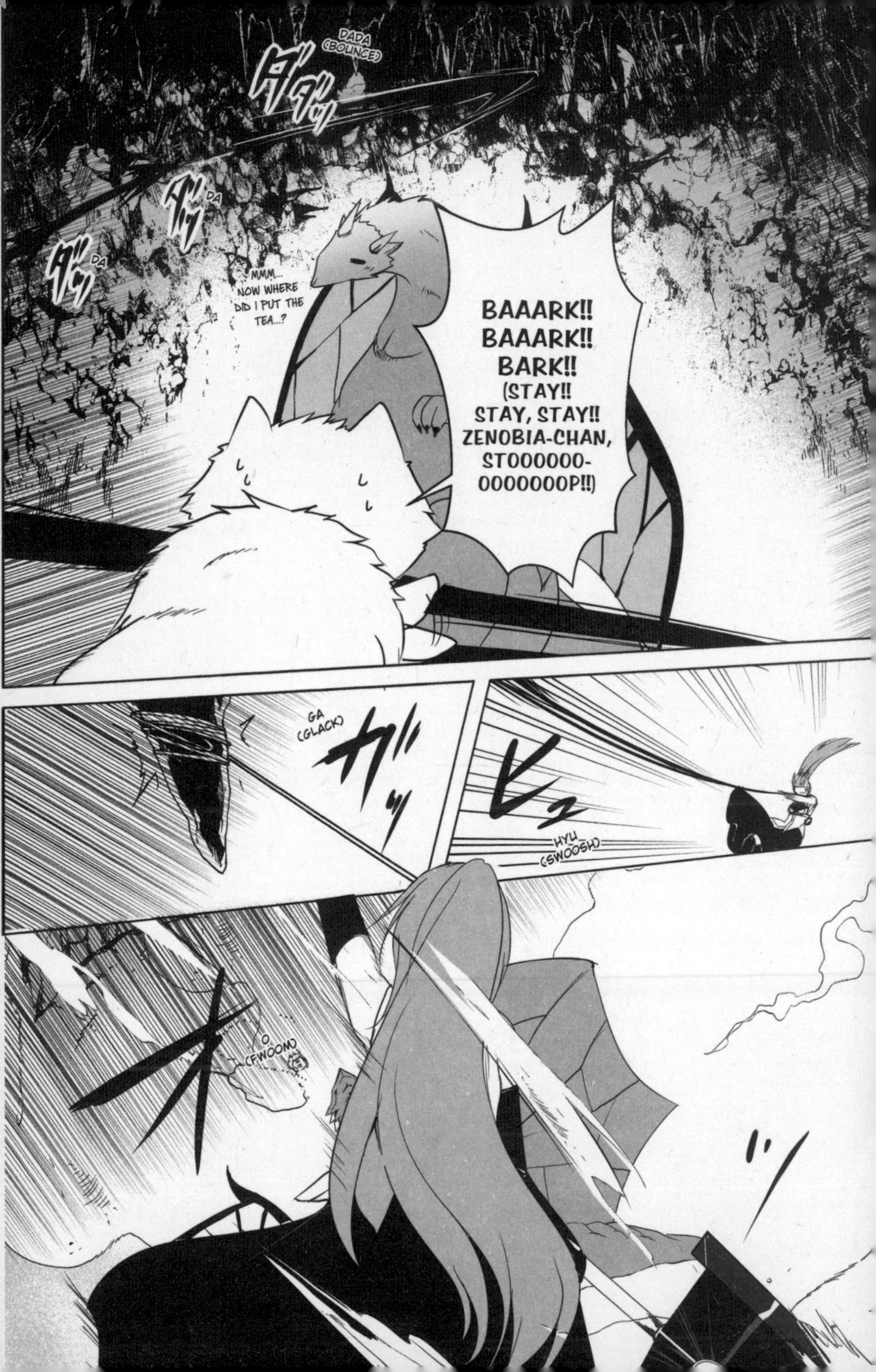
BAAARK!! BAAARK!! BARK!!
(STAY!! STAY, STAY!! ZENOBIA-CHAN, STOOOOOO-OOOOOOOP!!)
DADA (BOUNCE)
DA
MMM... NOW WHERE DID I PUT THE TEA...?
DA
HYU (SWOOSH)
GA (GLACK)
O (FWOOM)

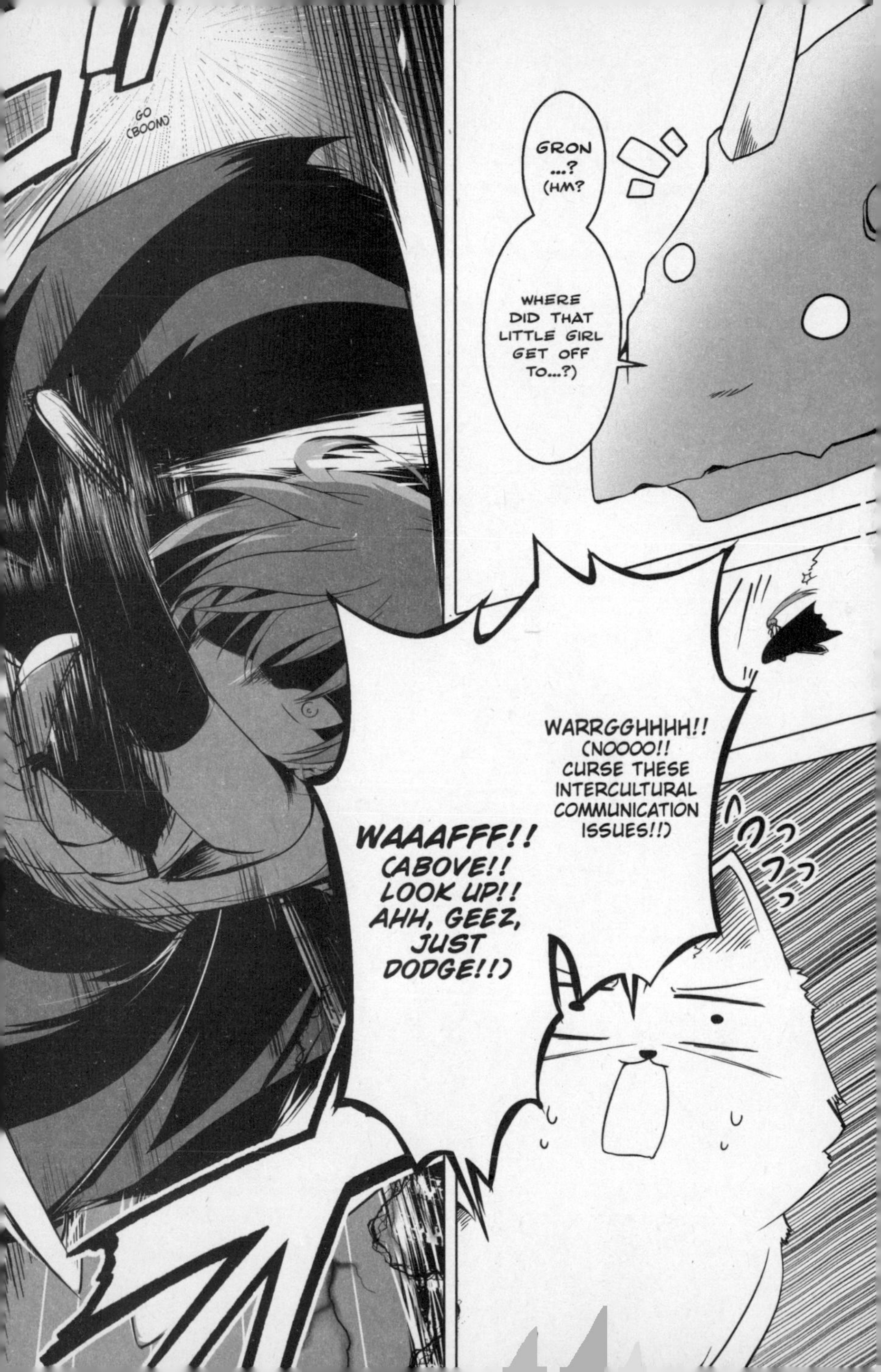
GRON ...? (HM? WHERE DID THAT LITTLE GIRL GET OFF TO...?)
WARRGHHHH!! (NOOOO!! CURSE THESE INTERCULTURAL COMMUNICATION ISSUES!!)
WAAAFFF!! (ABOVE!! LOOK UP!! AHH, GEEZ, JUST DODGE!!)
GO (BOOM)

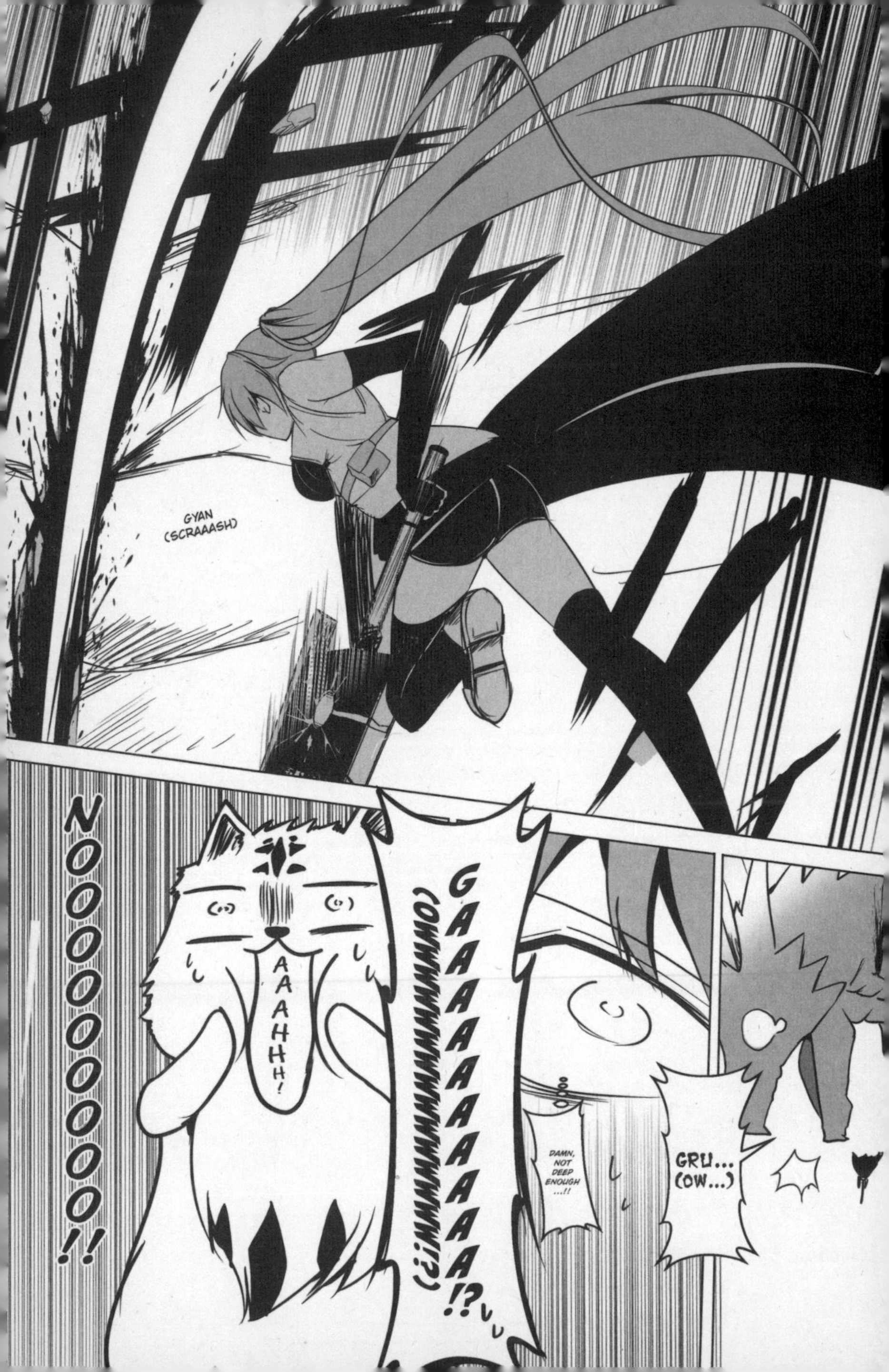
GYAN
(SCRAAASH)
GRU...
(OW...)
DAMN, NOT DEEP ENOUGH...!!
GAAAAAAAAAAAAAA!?
(OWMMMMMMMMMMMMMMMMMMMM!!?)
AAAHHH!
NOOOOOOOOOOOOO!!

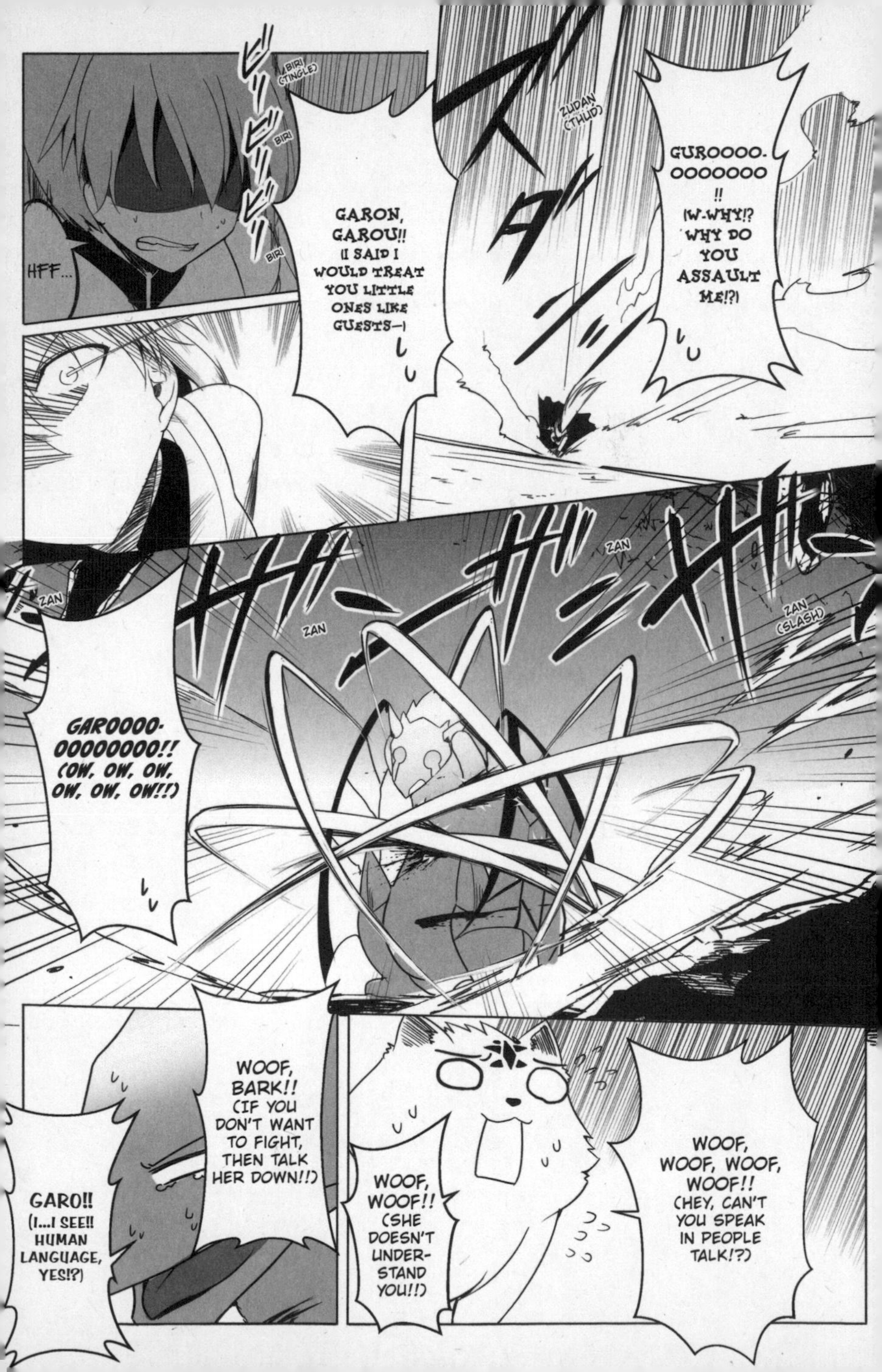
ZUDAN (THUD)
GUROOOO-OOOOOOO!! (W-WHY!? WHY DO YOU ASSAULT ME!?)
BIRI (TINGLE) BIRI BIRI
HFF...
GARON, GAROU!! (I SAID I WOULD TREAT YOU LITTLE ONES LIKE GUESTS—)
ZAN (SLASH) ZAN ZAN ZAN
GAROOOO-OOOOOOOO!! (OW, OW, OW, OW, OW, OW!!)
WOOF, WOOF, WOOF, WOOF!! (HEY, CAN'T YOU SPEAK IN PEOPLE TALK!?)
WOOF, WOOF!! (SHE DOESN'T UNDER-STAND YOU!!)
WOOF, BARK!! (IF YOU DON'T WANT TO FIGHT, THEN TALK HER DOWN!!)
GARO!! (I...I SEE!! HUMAN LANGUAGE, YES!?)

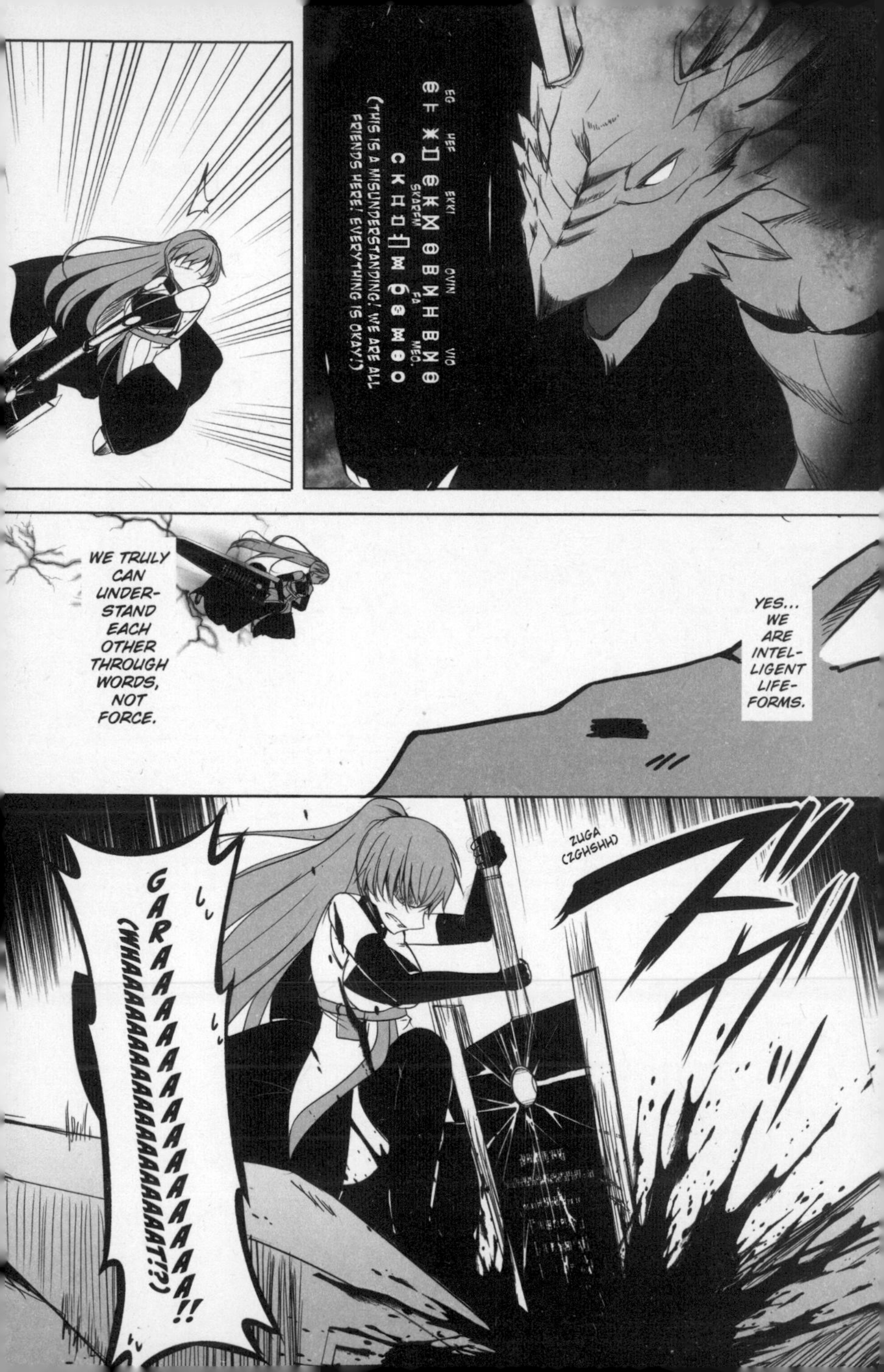
EG HEF EKKI OVIN VIO
SKAPEM FA MEC.
(THIS IS A MISUNDERSTANDING! WE ARE ALL FRIENDS HERE! EVERYTHING IS OKAY!)
YES... WE ARE INTELLIGENT LIFE-FORMS.
WE TRULY CAN UNDERSTAND EACH OTHER THROUGH WORDS, NOT FORCE.
ZUGA (ZGHSHH)
GARAAAAAAAAAAAAAAAAAAAA!! (WHAAAAAAAAAAAAAAAAAAAT!?)

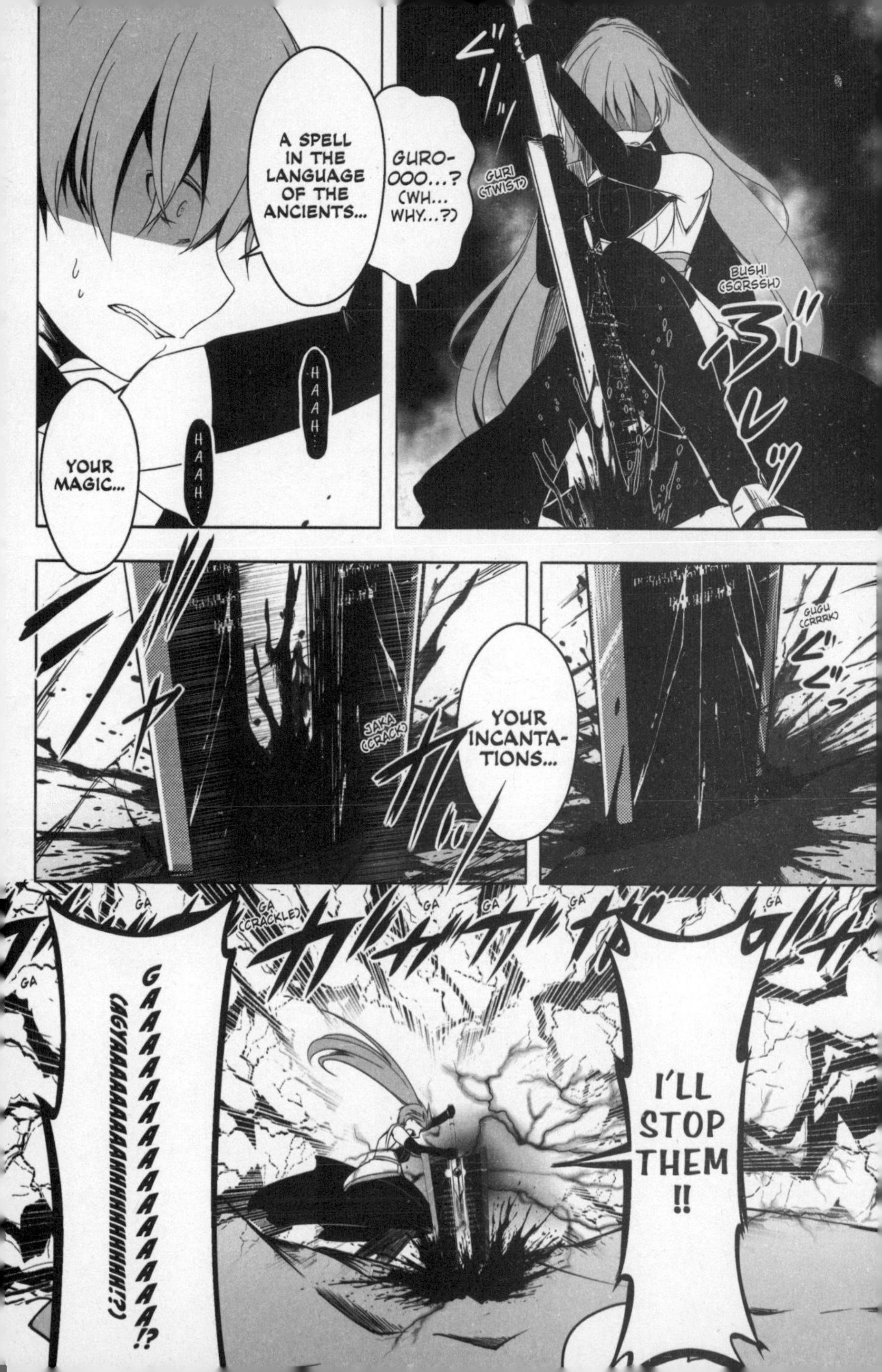
GURI (TWIST)
BUSHI (SQRSSH)
GURO-OOO…? (WH… WHY…?)
A SPELL IN THE LANGUAGE OF THE ANCIENTS…
HAAAH…
HAAAH…
YOUR MAGIC…
GUGU (CRRRK)
JAKA (CRACK)
YOUR INCANTATIONS…
GA
GA (CRACKLE)
GA
GA
GA
GA
GA
I'LL STOP THEM!!
GAAAAAAAAAAAAAAAA!?
(GYAAAAAAAAAAHHHHHHHH!?)

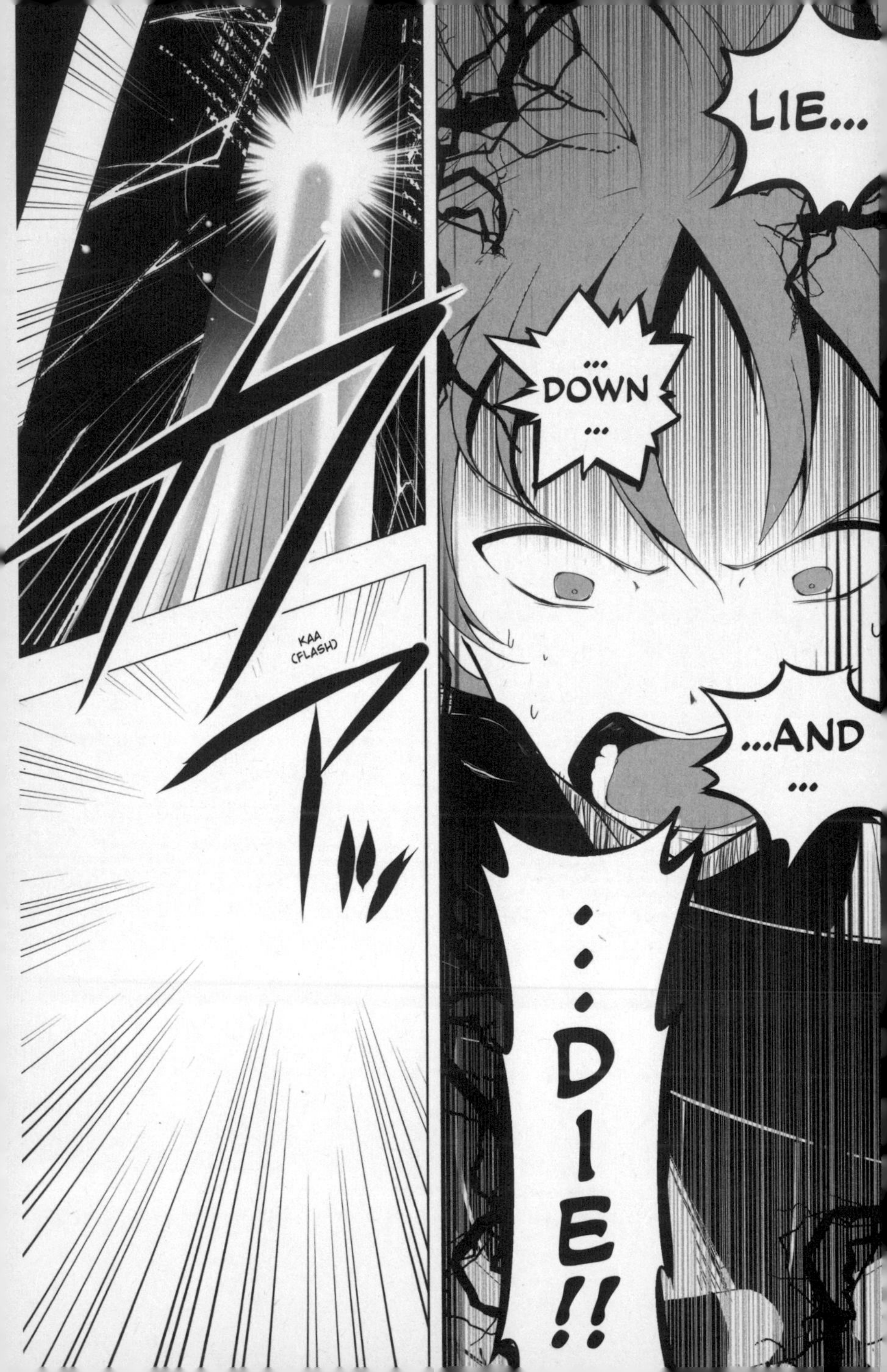
LIE...
...DOWN...
...AND...
...DIE!!
KAA (FLASH)

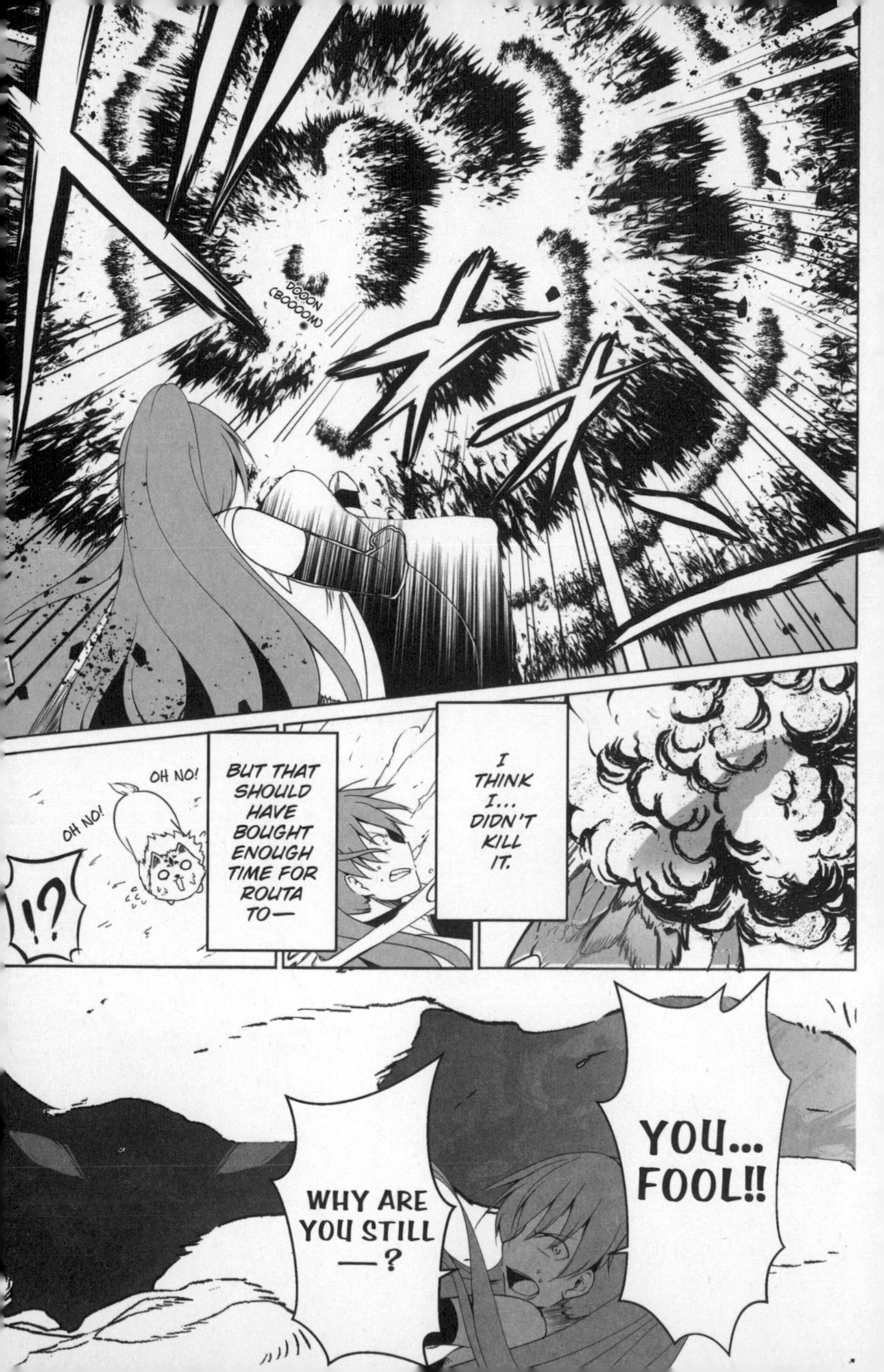
DOOON (BOOOOM)
I THINK I... DIDN'T KILL IT.
BUT THAT SHOULD HAVE BOUGHT ENOUGH TIME FOR ROUTA TO—
OH NO!
OH NO!
!?
YOU... FOOL!!
WHY ARE YOU STILL —?

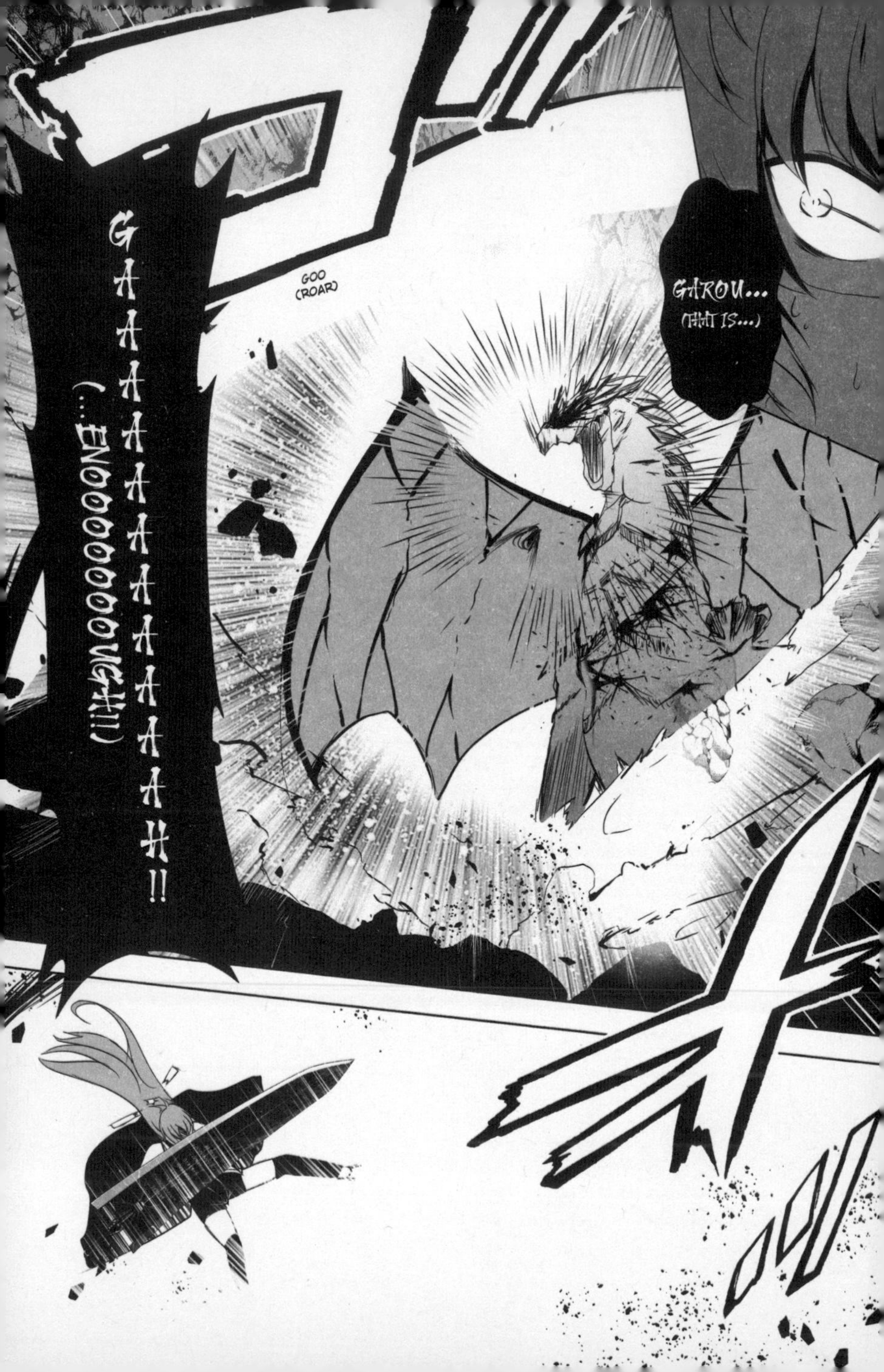
GAROU...
(THAT IS...)
GOO
(ROAR)
GAAAAAAAAAAAH!!
(...ENOOOOOOOUGH!!)

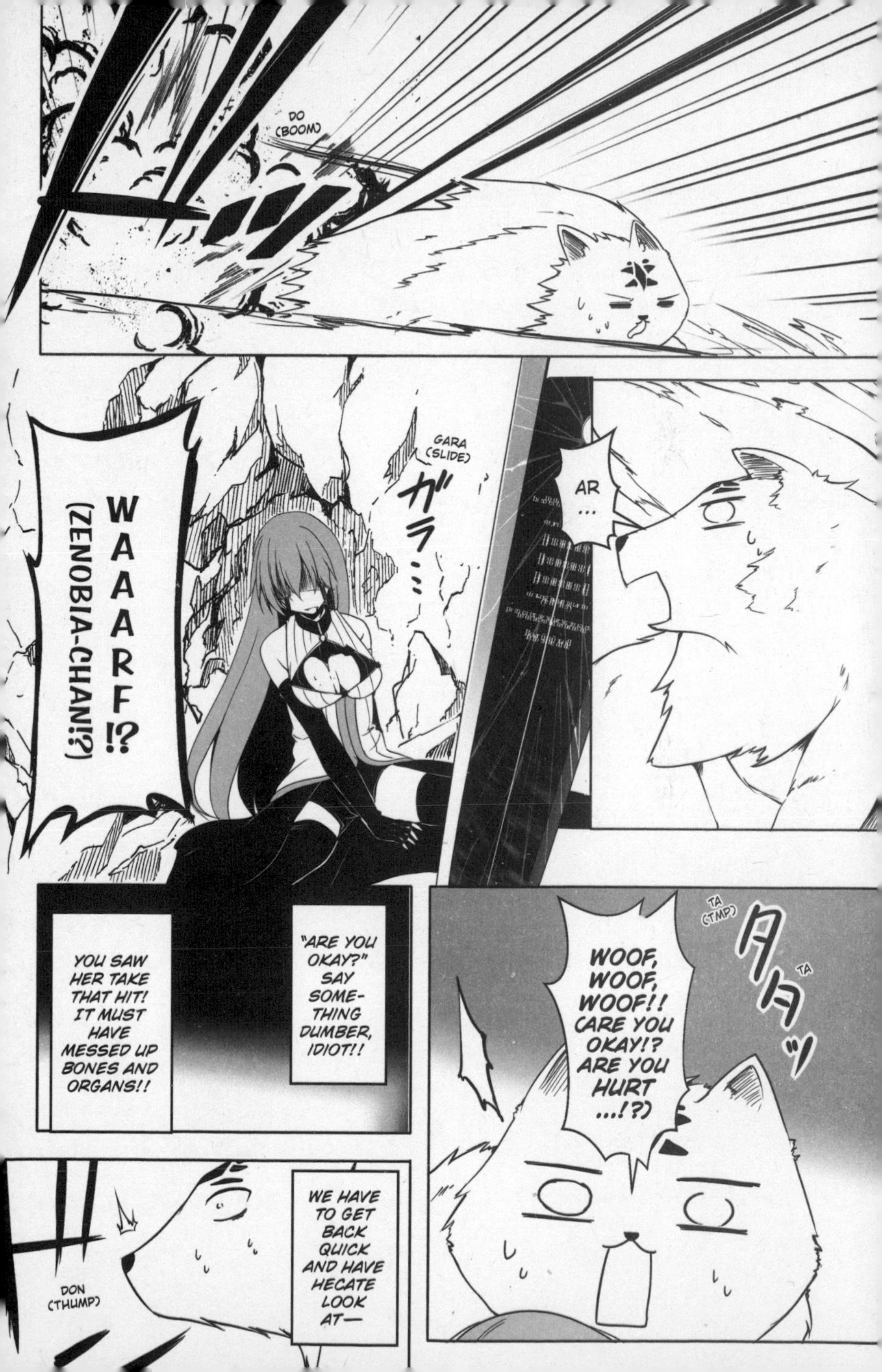
DO
(BOOM)
AR
...
GARA
(SLIDE)
WAAAARF!?
(ZENOBIA-CHAN!?)
TA
(TMP)
TA
WOOF, WOOF, WOOF!! (ARE YOU OKAY!? ARE YOU HURT ...!?)
"ARE YOU OKAY?" SAY SOME-THING DUMBER, IDIOT!!
YOU SAW HER TAKE THAT HIT! IT MUST HAVE MESSED UP BONES AND ORGANS!!
WE HAVE TO GET BACK QUICK AND HAVE HECATE LOOK AT—
DON
(THUMP)

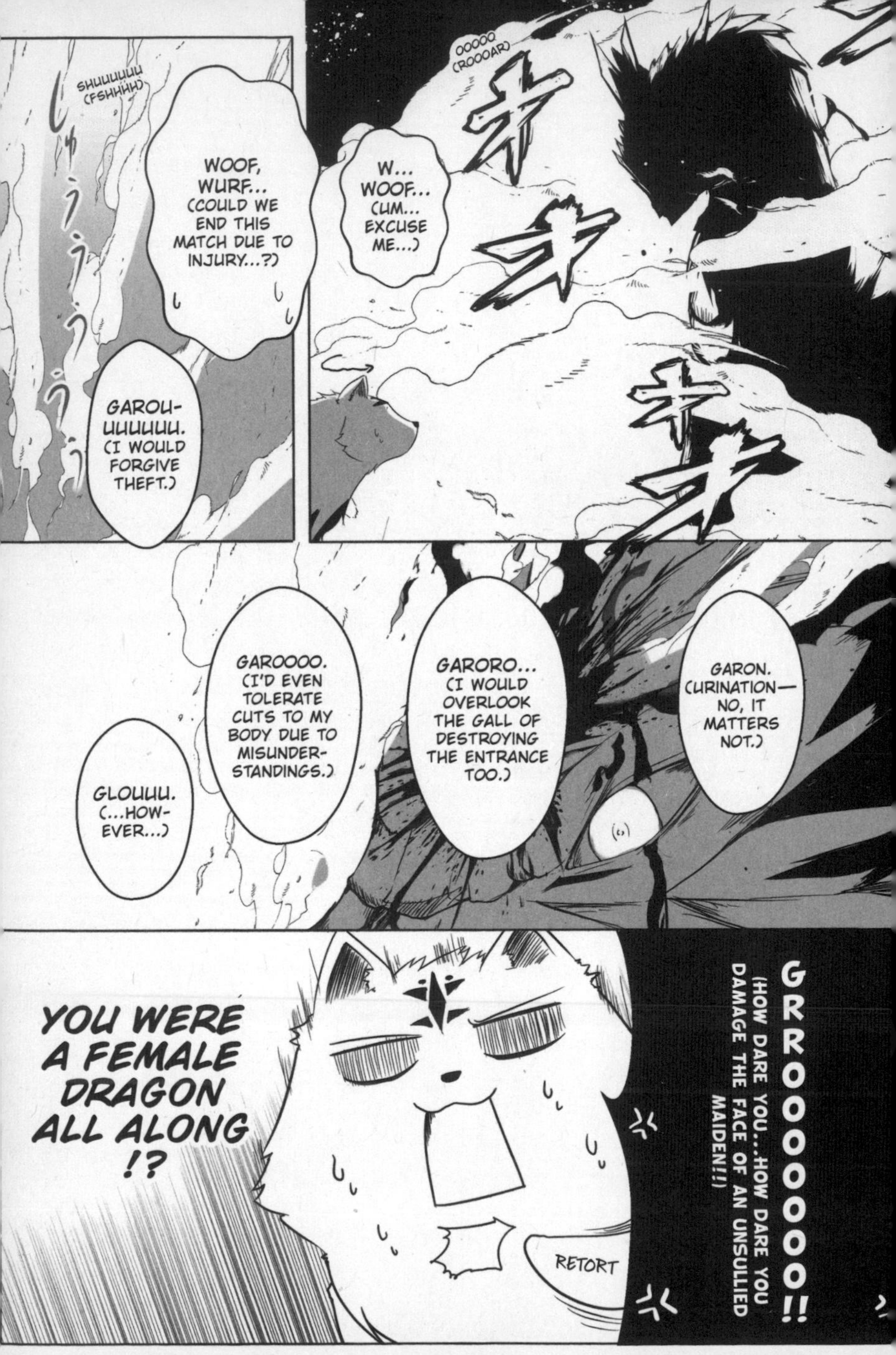
OOOOO (ROOOAR)
W... WOOF... (UM... EXCUSE ME...)
SHUUUUUU (FSHHHH)
WOOF, WURF... (COULD WE END THIS MATCH DUE TO INJURY...?)
GAROU-UUUUUU. (I WOULD FORGIVE THEFT.)
GARON. (URINATION—NO, IT MATTERS NOT.)
GARORO... (I WOULD OVERLOOK THE GALL OF DESTROYING THE ENTRANCE TOO.)
GAROOOO. (I'D EVEN TOLERATE CUTS TO MY BODY DUE TO MISUNDER-STANDINGS.)
GLOUUU. (...HOW-EVER...)
GRROOOOOOO!! (HOW DARE YOU...HOW DARE YOU DAMAGE THE FACE OF AN UNSULLIED MAIDEN!!)
RETORT
YOU WERE A FEMALE DRAGON ALL ALONG!?

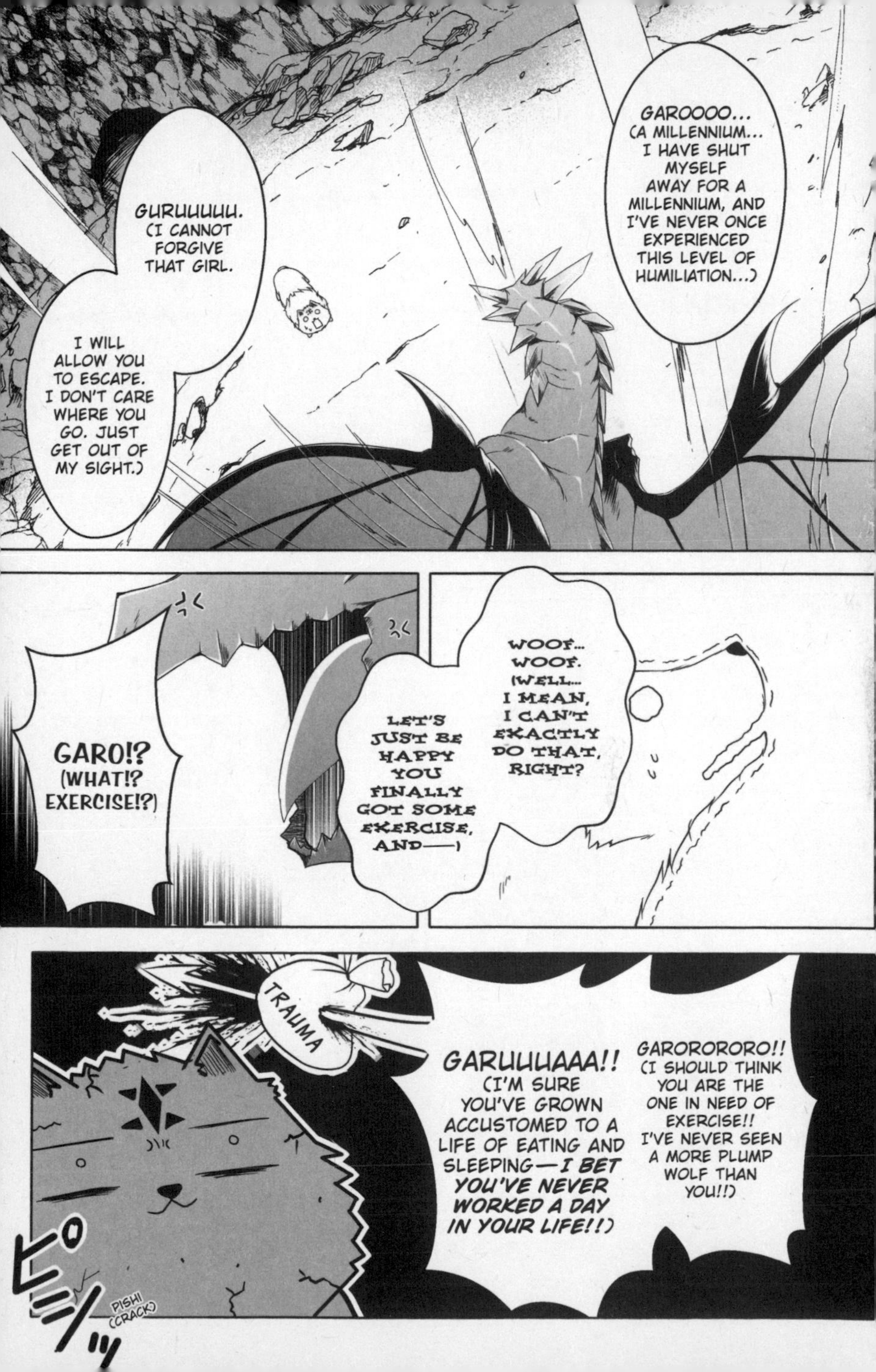
GAROOOO... (A MILLENNIUM... I HAVE SHUT MYSELF AWAY FOR A MILLENNIUM, AND I'VE NEVER ONCE EXPERIENCED THIS LEVEL OF HUMILIATION...)
GURUUUUU. (I CANNOT FORGIVE THAT GIRL.
I WILL ALLOW YOU TO ESCAPE. I DON'T CARE WHERE YOU GO. JUST GET OUT OF MY SIGHT.)
WOOF... WOOF. (WELL... I MEAN, I CAN'T EXACTLY DO THAT, RIGHT?
LET'S JUST BE HAPPY YOU FINALLY GOT SOME EXERCISE, AND—)
GARO!? (WHAT!? EXERCISE!?)
GARORORORO!! (I SHOULD THINK YOU ARE THE ONE IN NEED OF EXERCISE!! I'VE NEVER SEEN A MORE PLUMP WOLF THAN YOU!!)
GARUUUAAA!! (I'M SURE YOU'VE GROWN ACCUSTOMED TO A LIFE OF EATING AND SLEEPING—*I BET YOU'VE NEVER WORKED A DAY IN YOUR LIFE!!*)
TRAUMA
PISHI (CRACK)

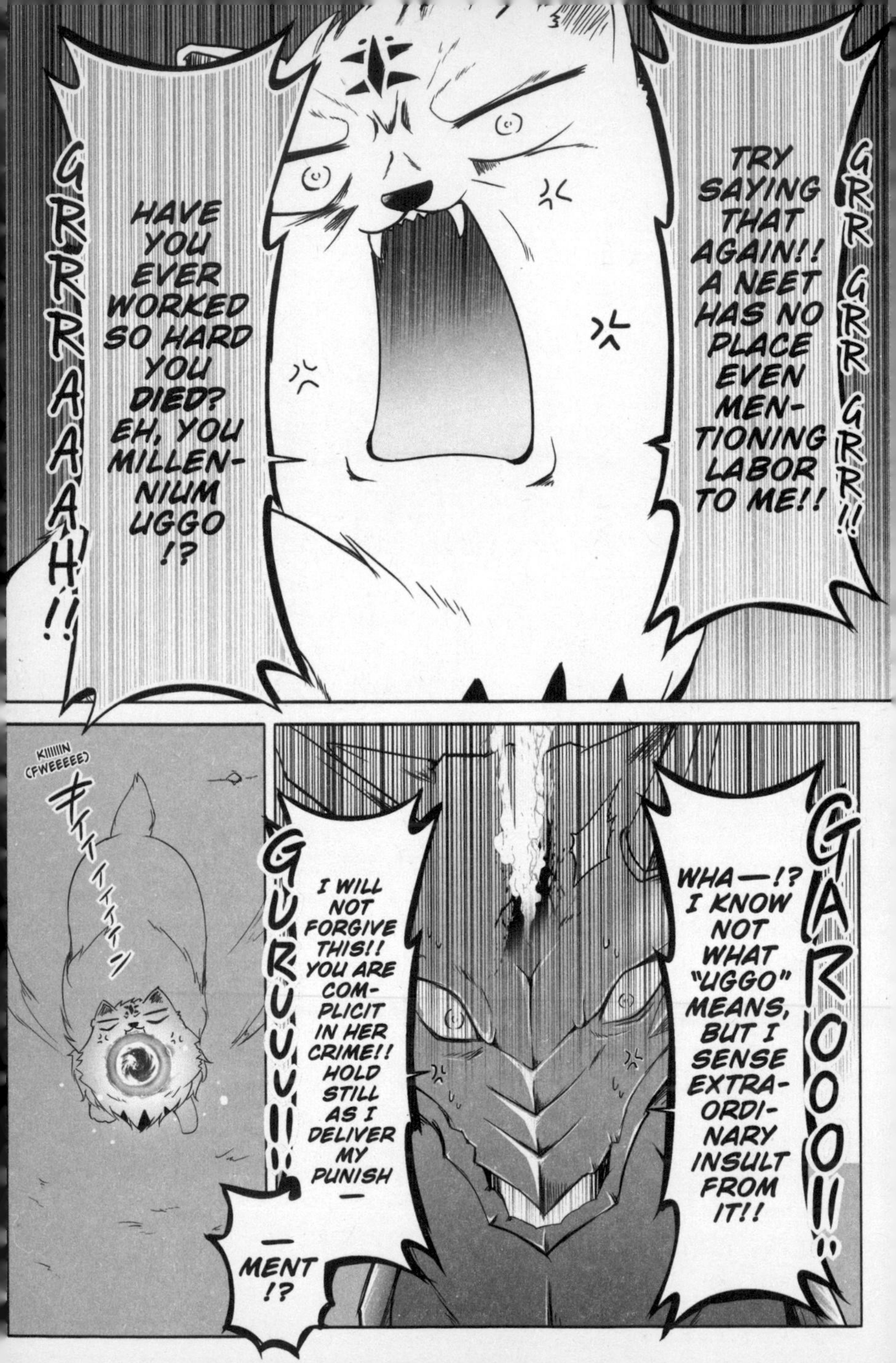
TRY SAYING THAT AGAIN!! A NEET HAS NO PLACE EVEN MEN-TIONING LABOR TO ME!!
GRR GRR GRR GRR!!
HAVE YOU EVER WORKED SO HARD YOU DIED? EH, YOU MILLEN-NIUM UGGO!?
GRRRAAAAH!!
WHA—!? I KNOW NOT WHAT "UGGO" MEANS, BUT I SENSE EXTRA-ORDI-NARY INSULT FROM IT!!
GAROOO!!
I WILL NOT FORGIVE THIS!! YOU ARE COM-PLICIT IN HER CRIME!! HOLD STILL AS I DELIVER MY PUNISH—
GURUUU!!
—MENT!?
KIIIIIN (FWEEEEE)
キイイイイイン

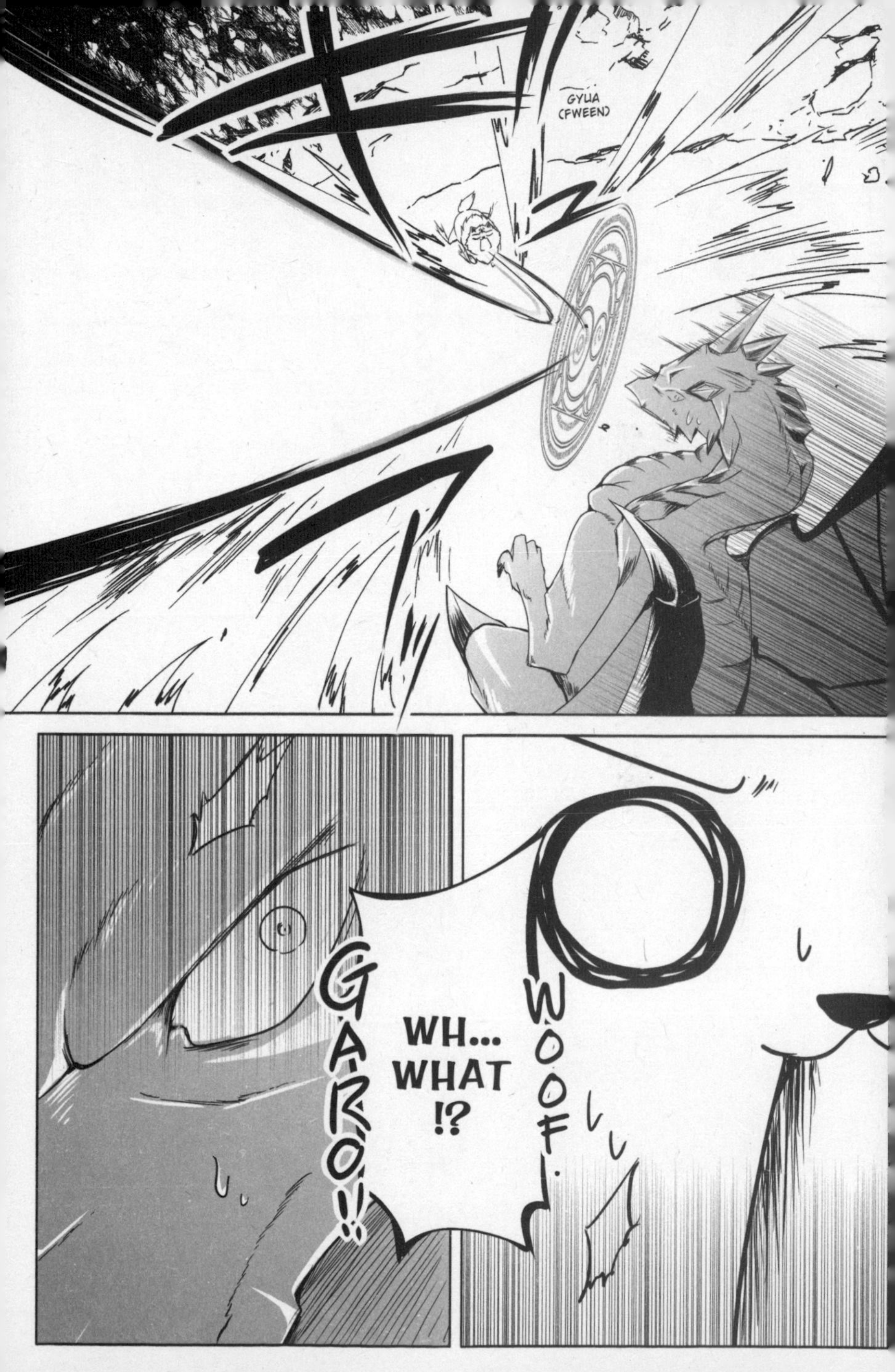
GYUA
(FWEEN)
WOOF.
WH... WHAT!?
GARO!!

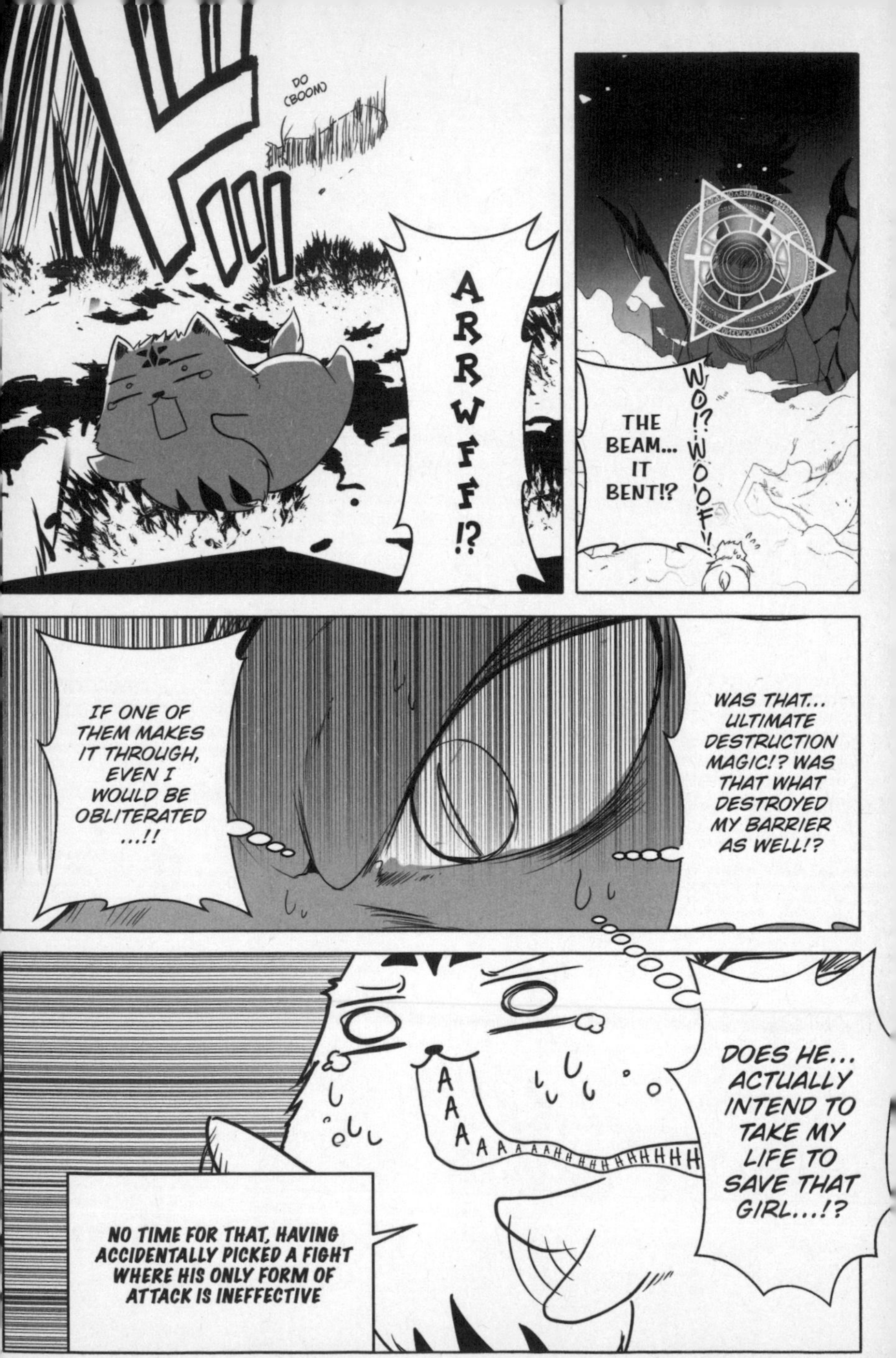
THE BEAM... IT BENT!?
WO!? WOOOF!!
DO (BOOM)
ARRWFF!?
WAS THAT... ULTIMATE DESTRUCTION MAGIC!? WAS THAT WHAT DESTROYED MY BARRIER AS WELL!?
IF ONE OF THEM MAKES IT THROUGH, EVEN I WOULD BE OBLITERATED...!!
DOES HE... ACTUALLY INTEND TO TAKE MY LIFE TO SAVE THAT GIRL...!?
AAAAAAAAHHHHHHHHHHHH
NO TIME FOR THAT, HAVING ACCIDENTALLY PICKED A FIGHT WHERE HIS ONLY FORM OF ATTACK IS INEFFECTIVE

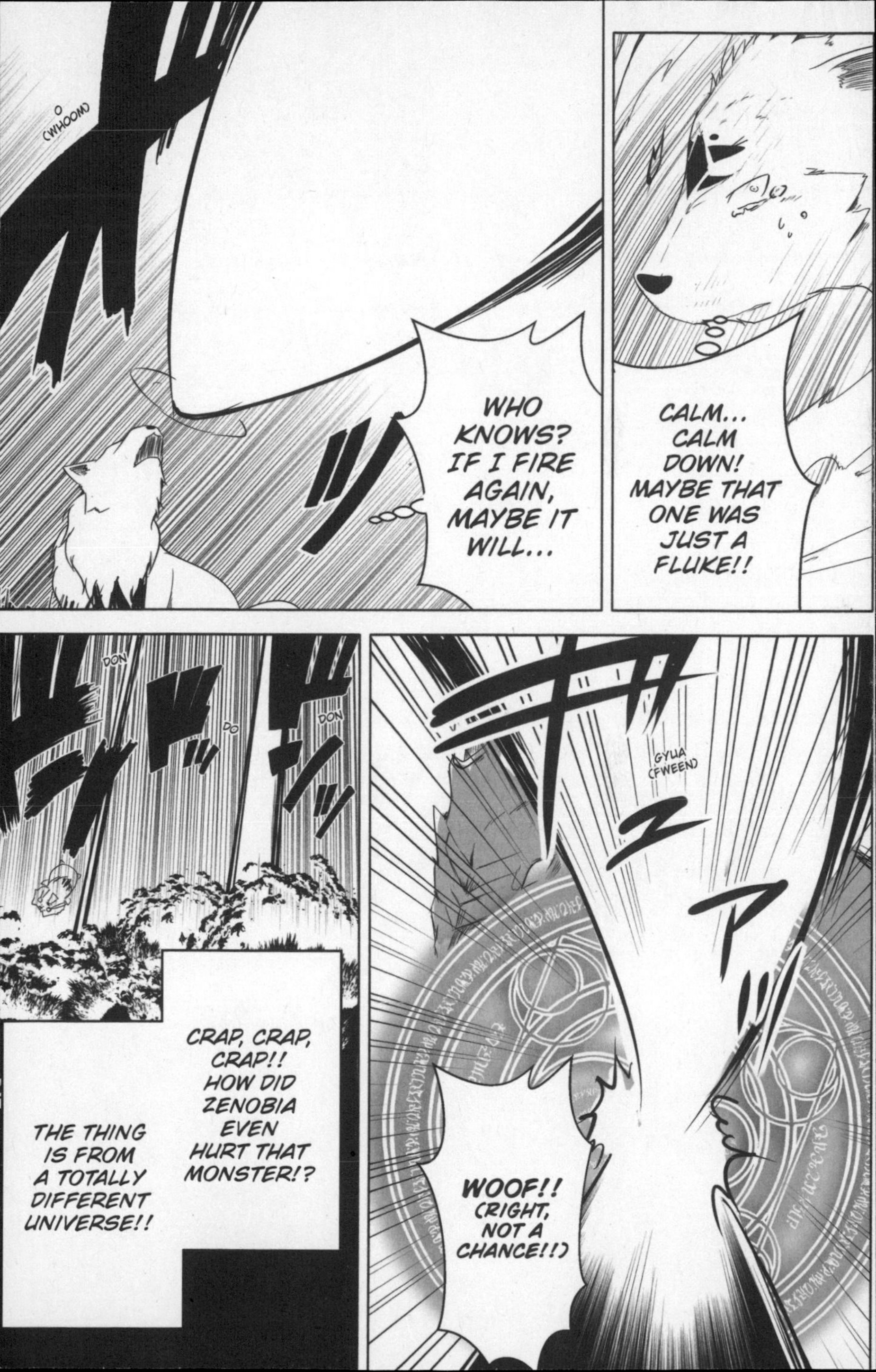
CALM... CALM DOWN! MAYBE THAT ONE WAS JUST A FLUKE!!
WHO KNOWS? IF I FIRE AGAIN, MAYBE IT WILL...
O (WHOOM)
GYUA (FWEEN)
WOOF!! (RIGHT, NOT A CHANCE!!)
DON
DO
DON
CRAP, CRAP, CRAP!! HOW DID ZENOBIA EVEN HURT THAT MONSTER!?
THE THING IS FROM A TOTALLY DIFFERENT UNIVERSE!!

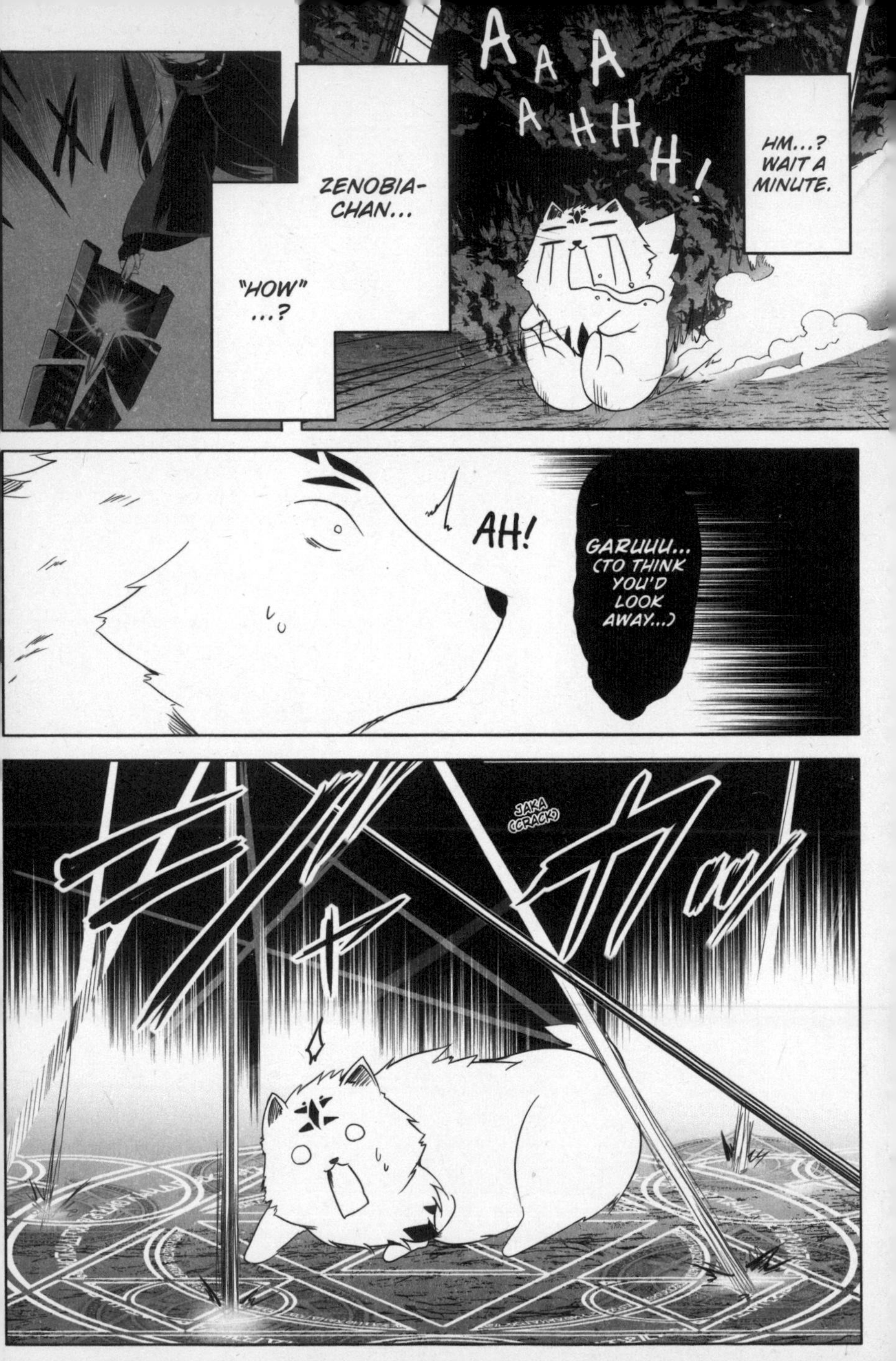
HM...? WAIT A MINUTE.
AAAAHHHH!
ZENOBIA-CHAN...
"HOW" ...?
GARUUU... (TO THINK YOU'D LOOK AWAY...)
AH!
JAKA (CRACK)

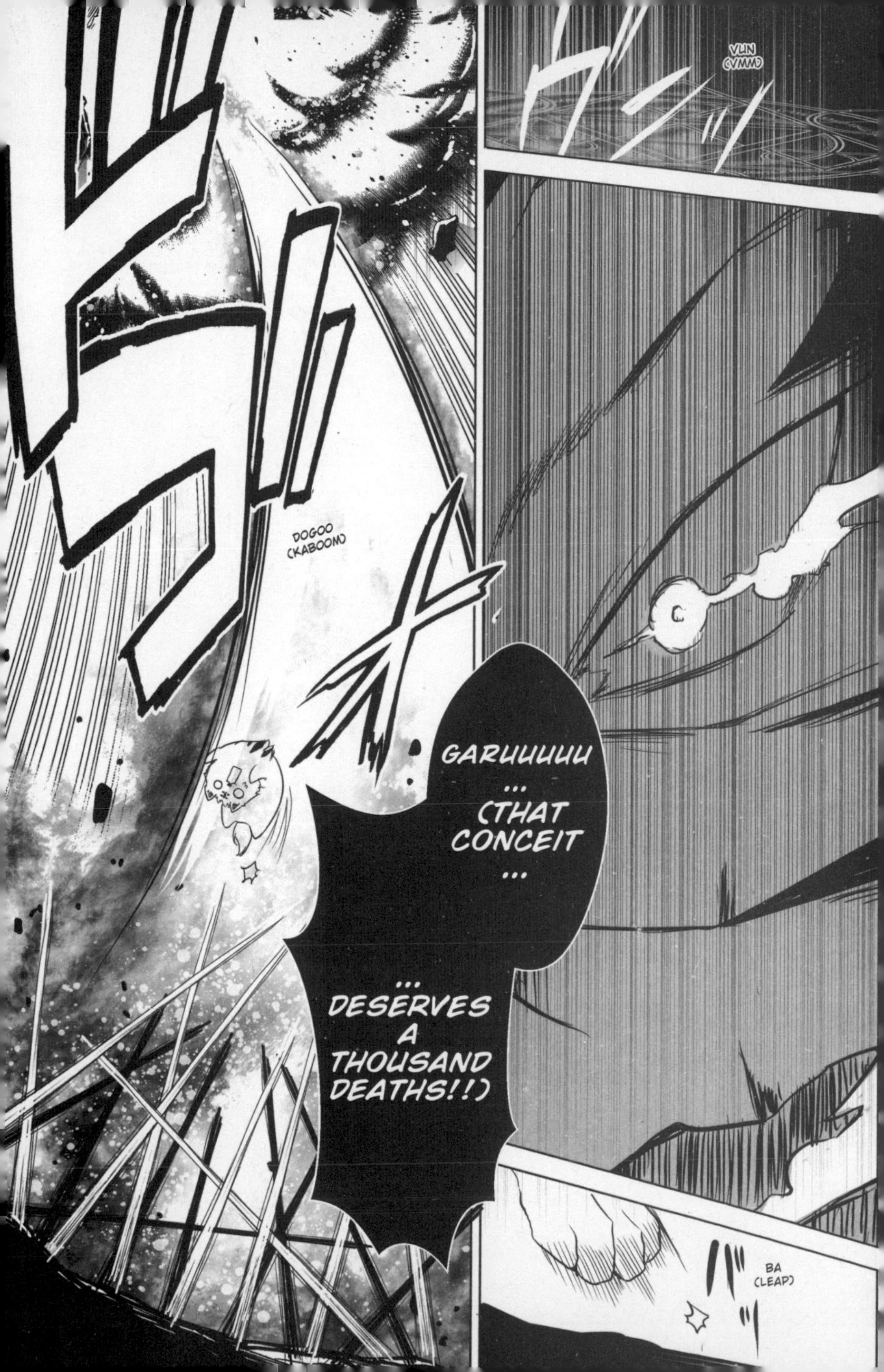
VUN (VMM)
GARUUUUU ... (THAT CONCEIT ... ... DESERVES A THOUSAND DEATHS!!)
BA (LEAP)
DOGOO (KABOOM)

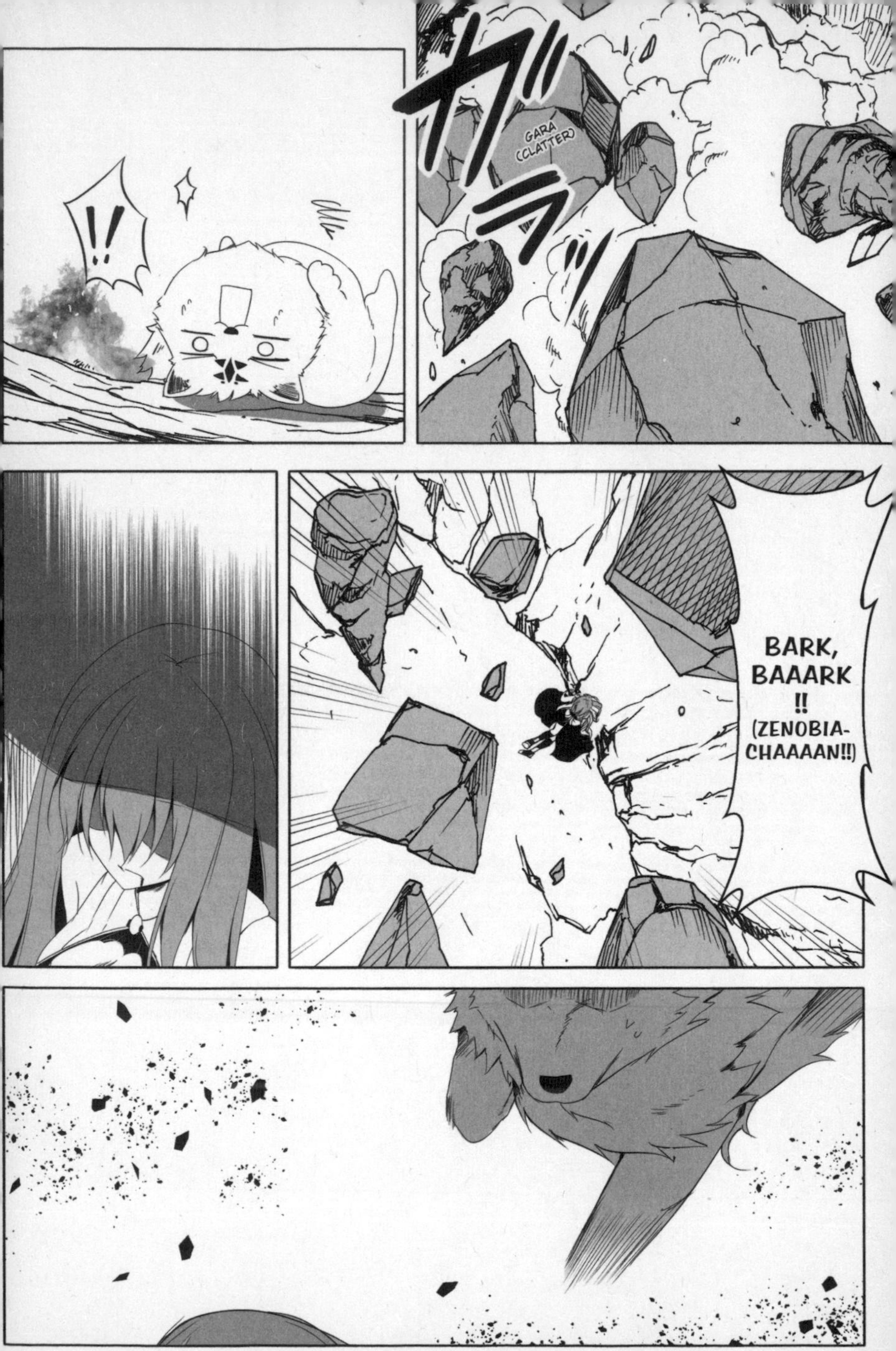
GARA (CLATTER)
!!
BARK, BAAARK!! (ZENOBIA-CHAAAAN!!)

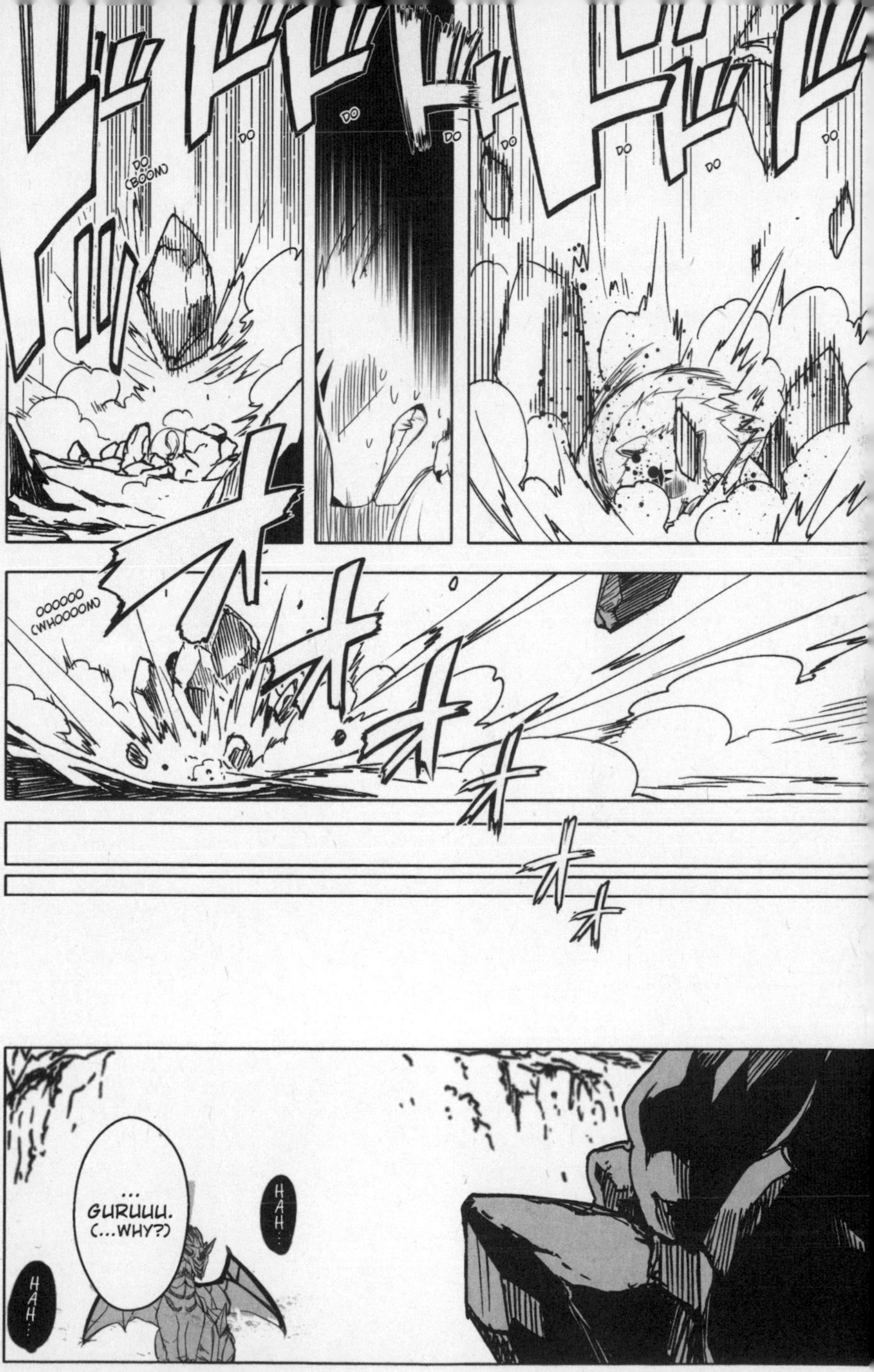
DO
DO
DO
DO
DO
DO
DO
DO
(BOOM)
OOOOOO
(WHOOOOM)
HAH...
...
GURUUU.
(...WHY?)
HAH...

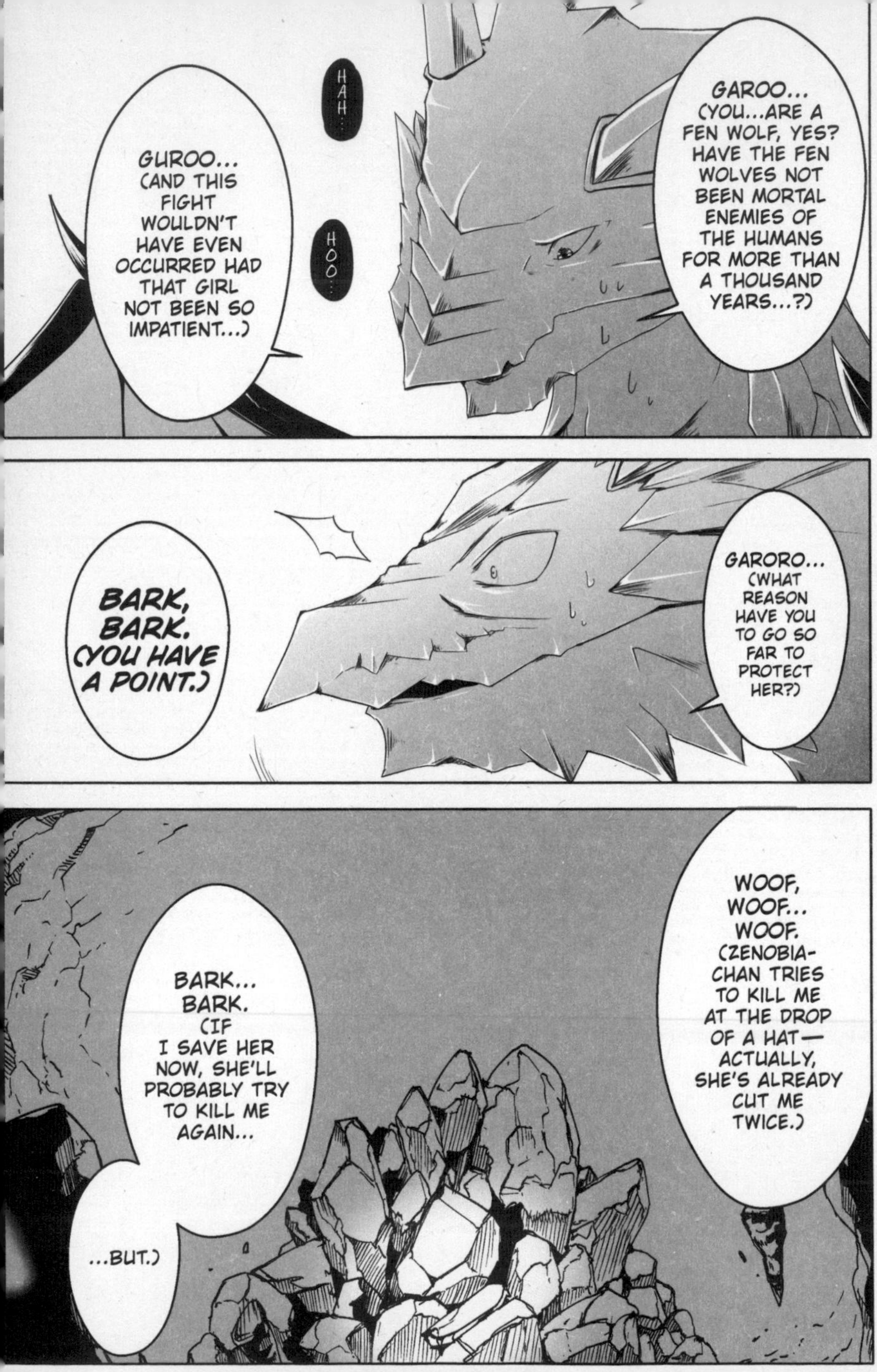
GAROO... (YOU...ARE A FEN WOLF, YES? HAVE THE FEN WOLVES NOT BEEN MORTAL ENEMIES OF THE HUMANS FOR MORE THAN A THOUSAND YEARS...?)
HAH...
HOO...
GUROO... (AND THIS FIGHT WOULDN'T HAVE EVEN OCCURRED HAD THAT GIRL NOT BEEN SO IMPATIENT...)
GARORO... (WHAT REASON HAVE YOU TO GO SO FAR TO PROTECT HER?)
BARK, BARK. (YOU HAVE A POINT.)
WOOF, WOOF... WOOF. (ZENOBIA-CHAN TRIES TO KILL ME AT THE DROP OF A HAT—ACTUALLY, SHE'S ALREADY CUT ME TWICE.)
BARK... BARK. (IF I SAVE HER NOW, SHE'LL PROBABLY TRY TO KILL ME AGAIN...
...BUT.)

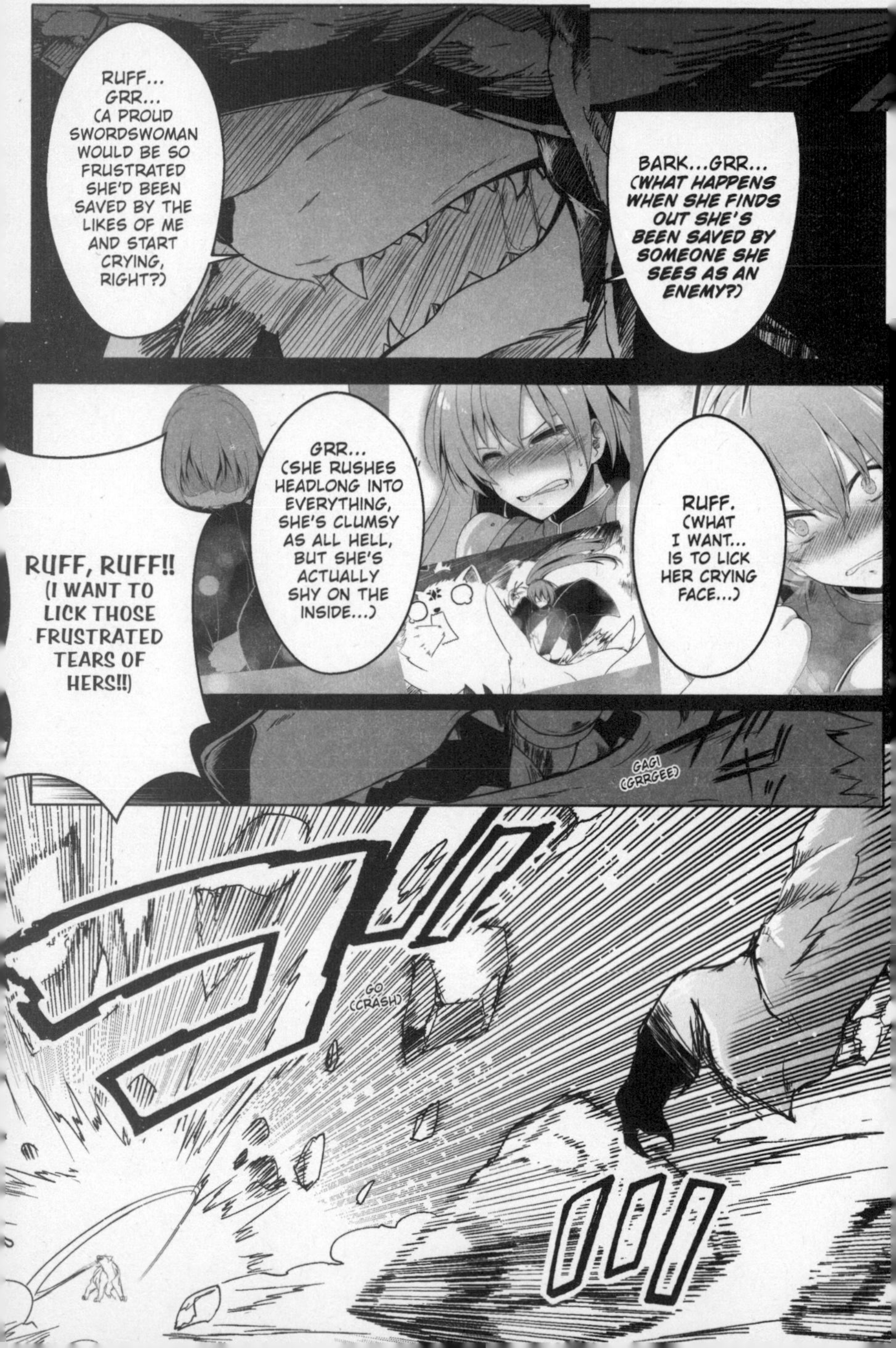
BARK...GRR... (WHAT HAPPENS WHEN SHE FINDS OUT SHE'S BEEN SAVED BY SOMEONE SHE SEES AS AN ENEMY?)
RUFF... GRR... (A PROUD SWORDSWOMAN WOULD BE SO FRUSTRATED SHE'D BEEN SAVED BY THE LIKES OF ME AND START CRYING, RIGHT?)
RUFF. (WHAT I WANT... IS TO LICK HER CRYING FACE...)
GRR... (SHE RUSHES HEADLONG INTO EVERYTHING, SHE'S CLUMSY AS ALL HELL, BUT SHE'S ACTUALLY SHY ON THE INSIDE...)
RUFF, RUFF!! (I WANT TO LICK THOSE FRUSTRATED TEARS OF HERS!!)
GAGI (GRRGEE)
GO (CRASH)

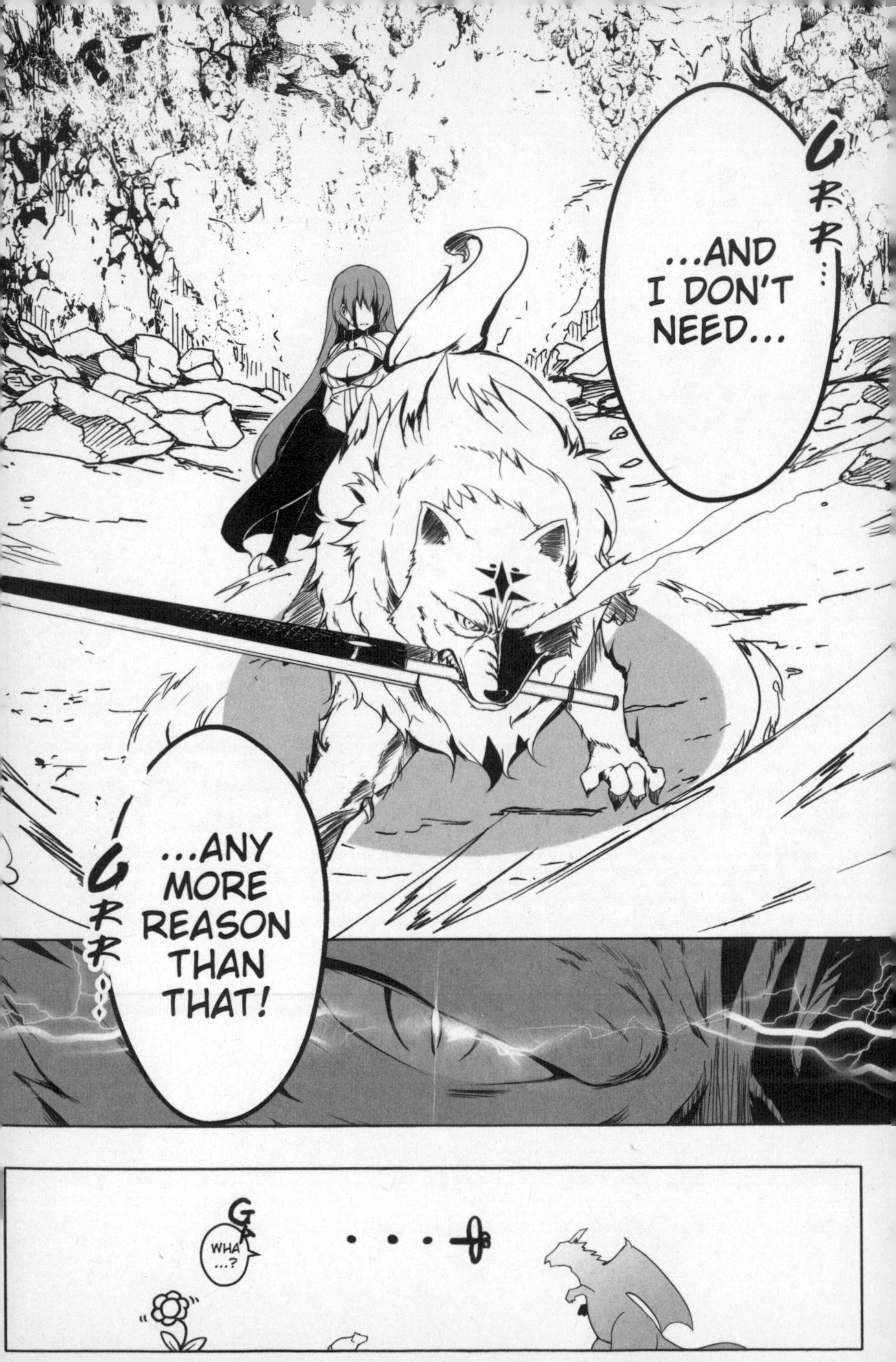
GRR...
...AND I DON'T NEED...
GRR...
...ANY MORE REASON THAN THAT!
GR
WHA...?

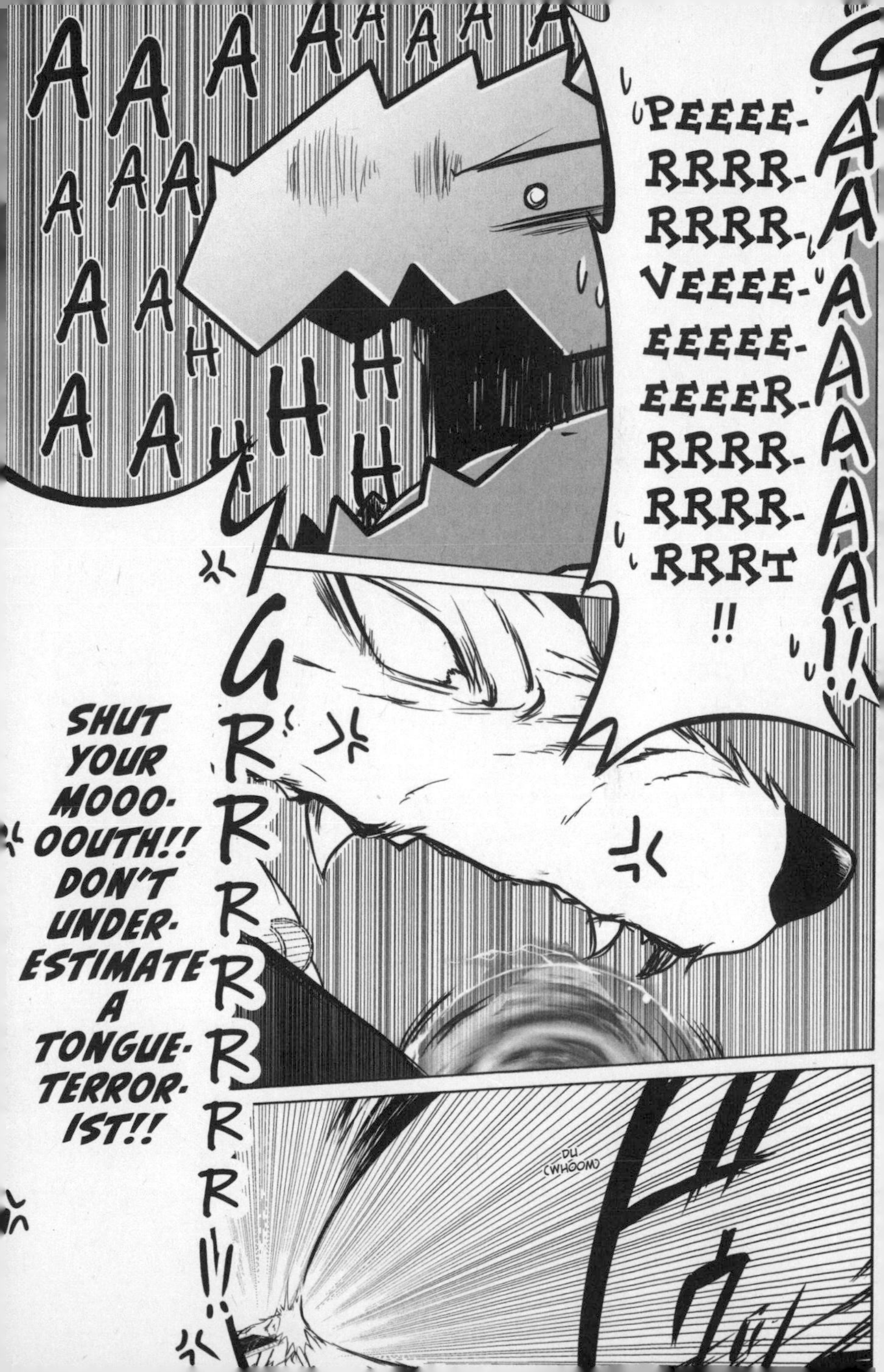
GAAAAAAAAA!!
PEEEE-RRRR-RRRR-VEEEE-EEEEE-EEEER-RRRR-RRRR-RRRT!!
AAAAAAAAAAAAAAAAAHHHHH
SHUT YOUR MOOO-OOUTH!! DON'T UNDER-ESTIMATE A TONGUE-TERROR-IST!!
GURRRRRRRRR!!
DU (WHOOM)

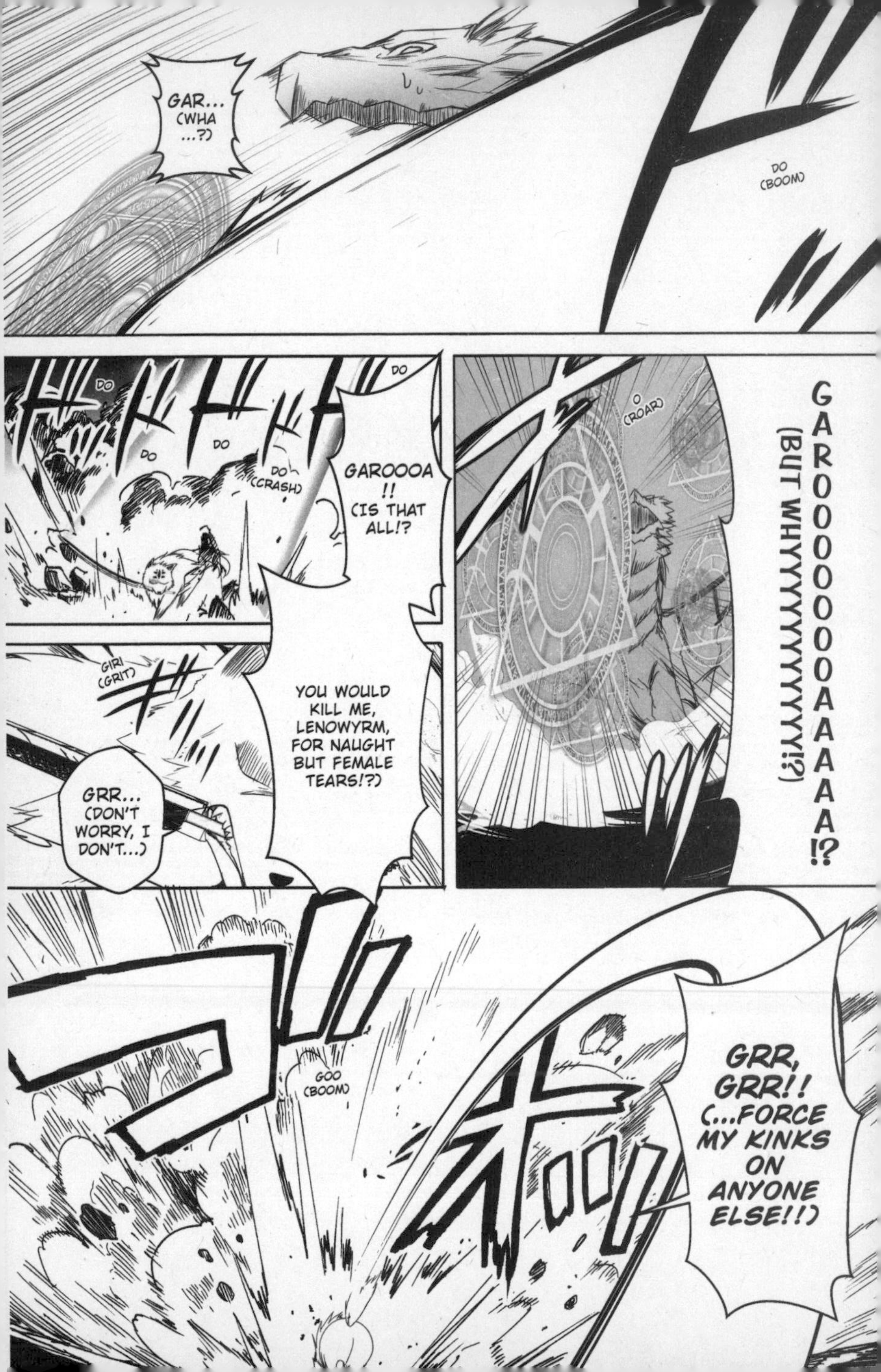
DO (BOOM)
GAR... (WHA ...?)
GAROOOOOOOOAAAAAA!?
(BUT WHYYYYYYYY!?)
O (ROAR)
DO
GAROOOA!! (IS THAT ALL!?)
DO
DO
DO
DO (CRASH)
YOU WOULD KILL ME, LENOWYRM, FOR NAUGHT BUT FEMALE TEARS!?)
GIRI (GRIT)
GRR... (DON'T WORRY, I DON'T...)
GRR, GRR!! (...FORCE MY KINKS ON ANYONE ELSE!!)
GOO (BOOM)

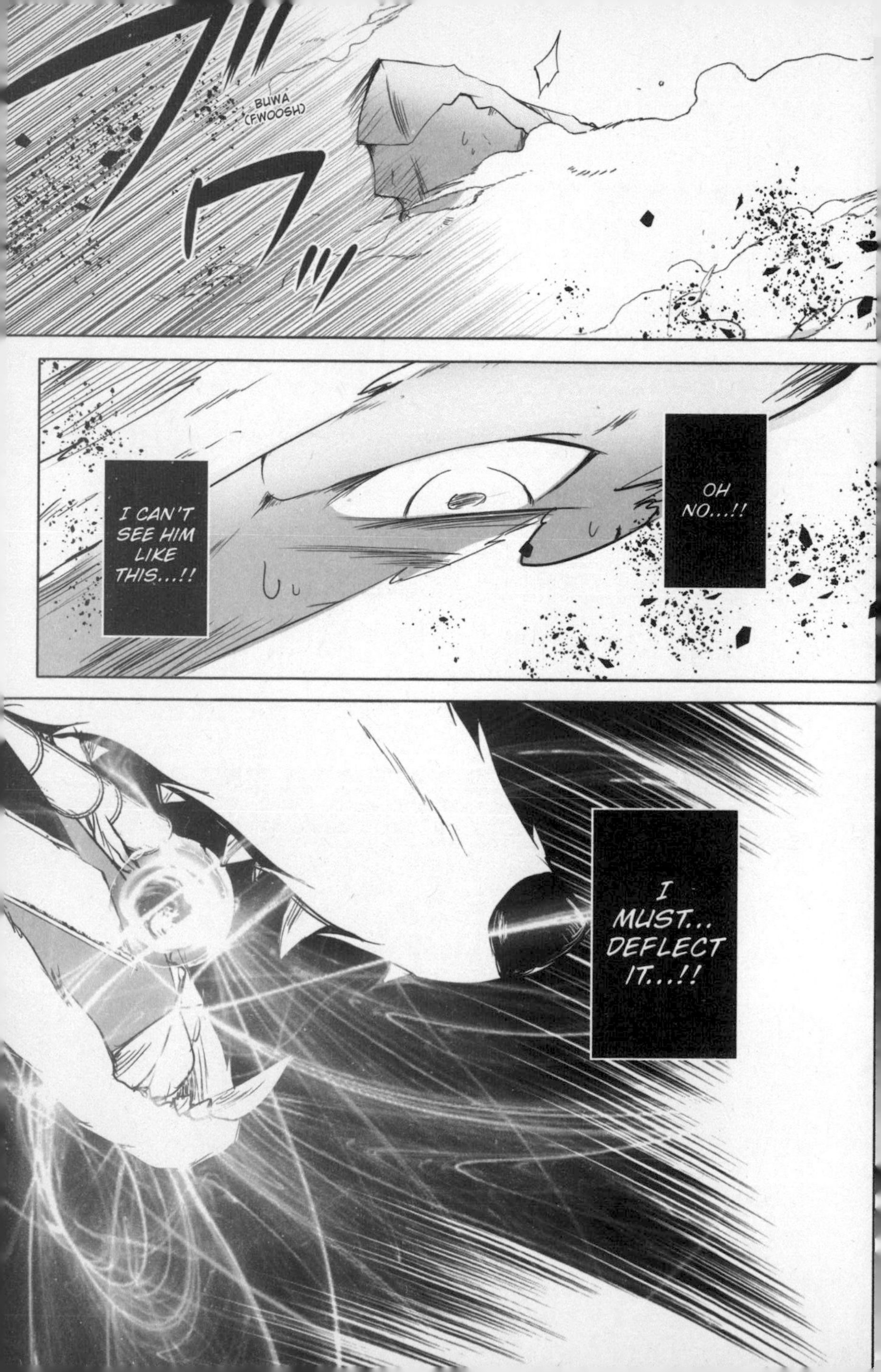
BUWA
(FWOOSH)
OH NO...!!
I CAN'T SEE HIM LIKE THIS...!!
I MUST... DEFLECT IT...!!

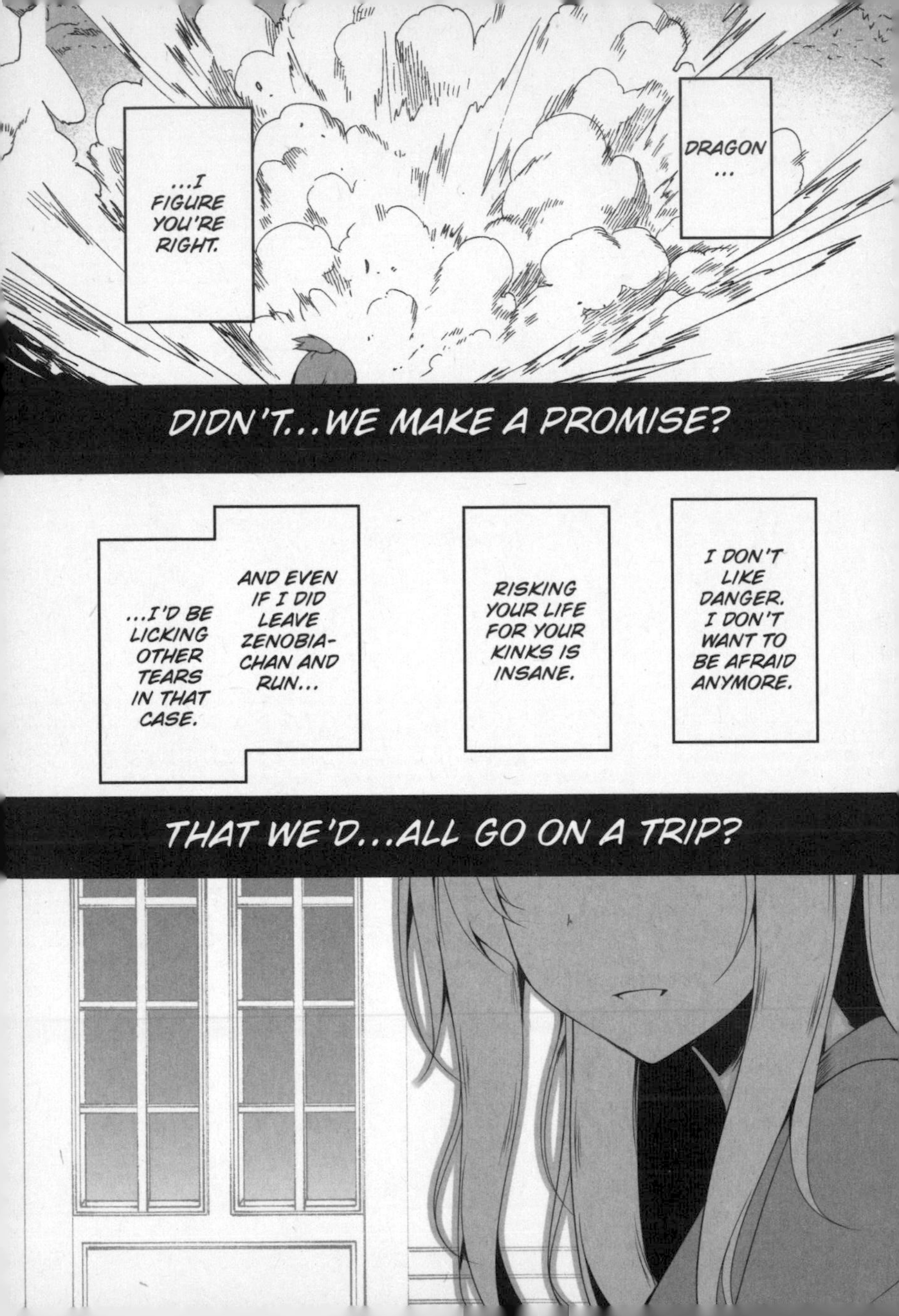
DRAGON...
...I FIGURE YOU'RE RIGHT.
DIDN'T...WE MAKE A PROMISE?
I DON'T LIKE DANGER. I DON'T WANT TO BE AFRAID ANYMORE.
RISKING YOUR LIFE FOR YOUR KINKS IS INSANE.
AND EVEN IF I DID LEAVE ZENOBIA-CHAN AND RUN...
...I'D BE LICKING OTHER TEARS IN THAT CASE.
THAT WE'D...ALL GO ON A TRIP?

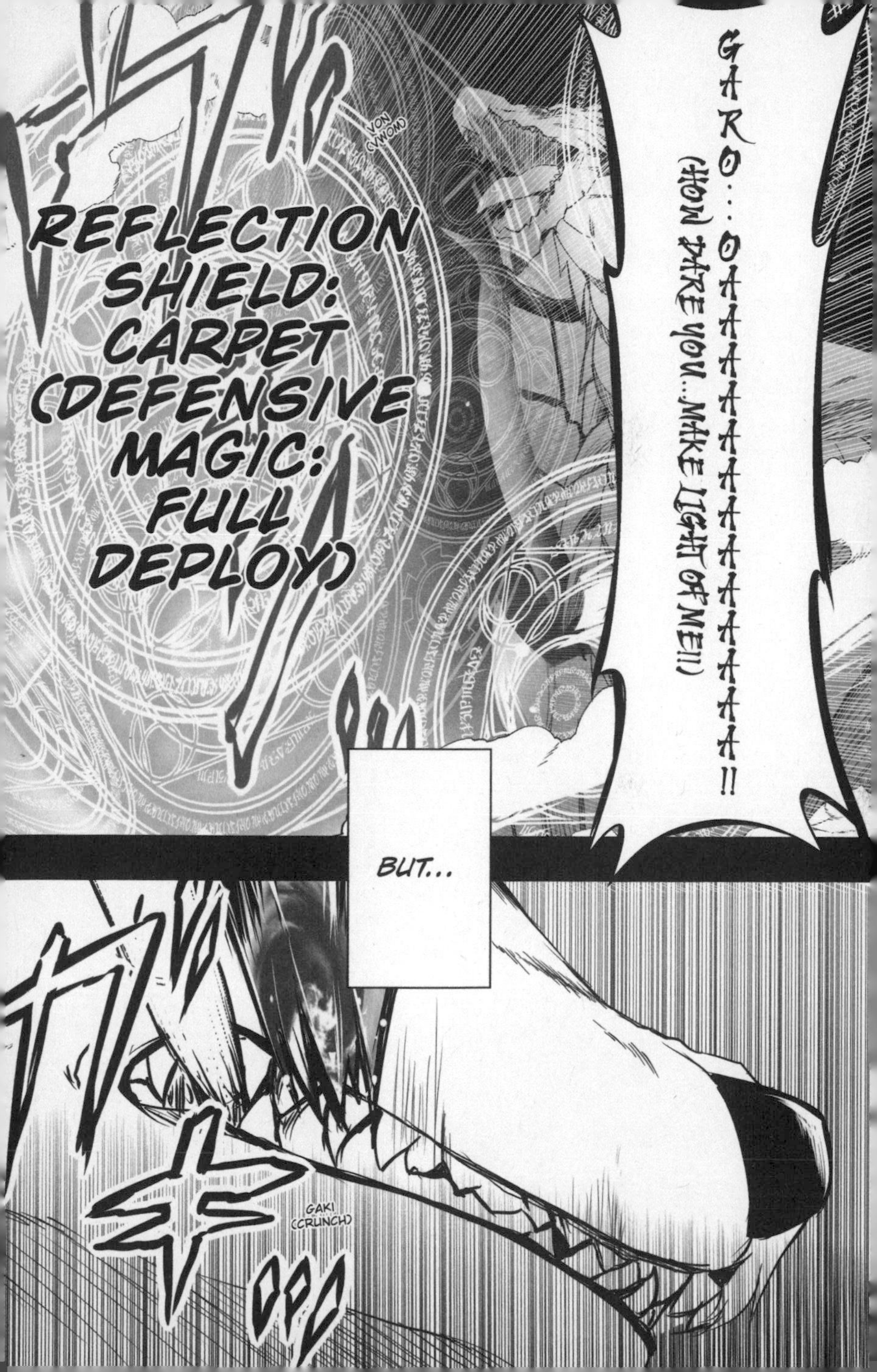
GARO...OAAAAAAAAAAAAAAAA!!
(HOW DARE YOU...MAKE LIGHT OF ME!!)
VON (VWON)
REFLECTION SHIELD: CARPET (DEFENSIVE MAGIC: FULL DEPLOY)
BUT...
GAKI (CRUNCH)

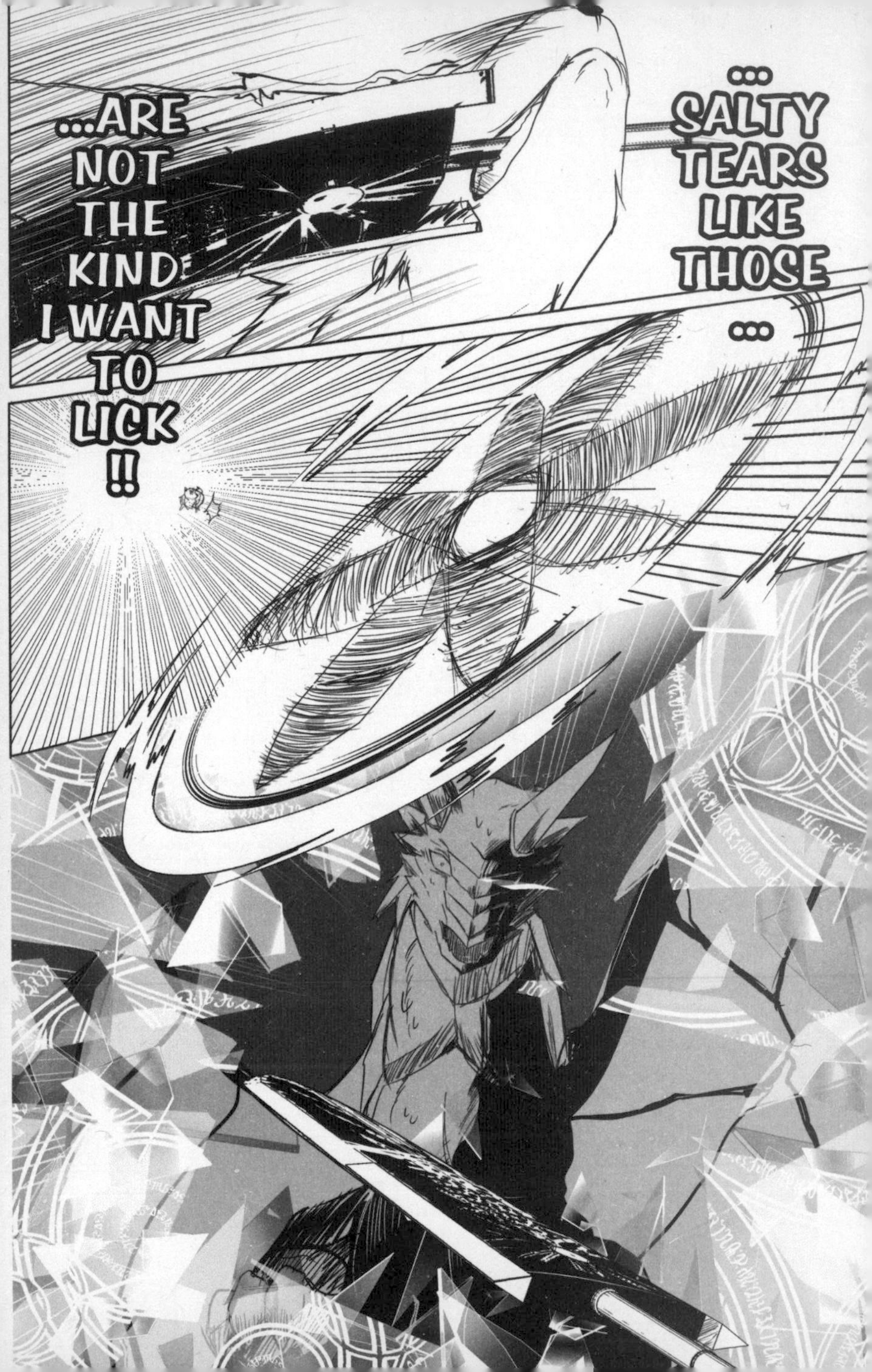
...SALTY TEARS LIKE THOSE ...
...ARE NOT THE KIND I WANT TO LICK !!

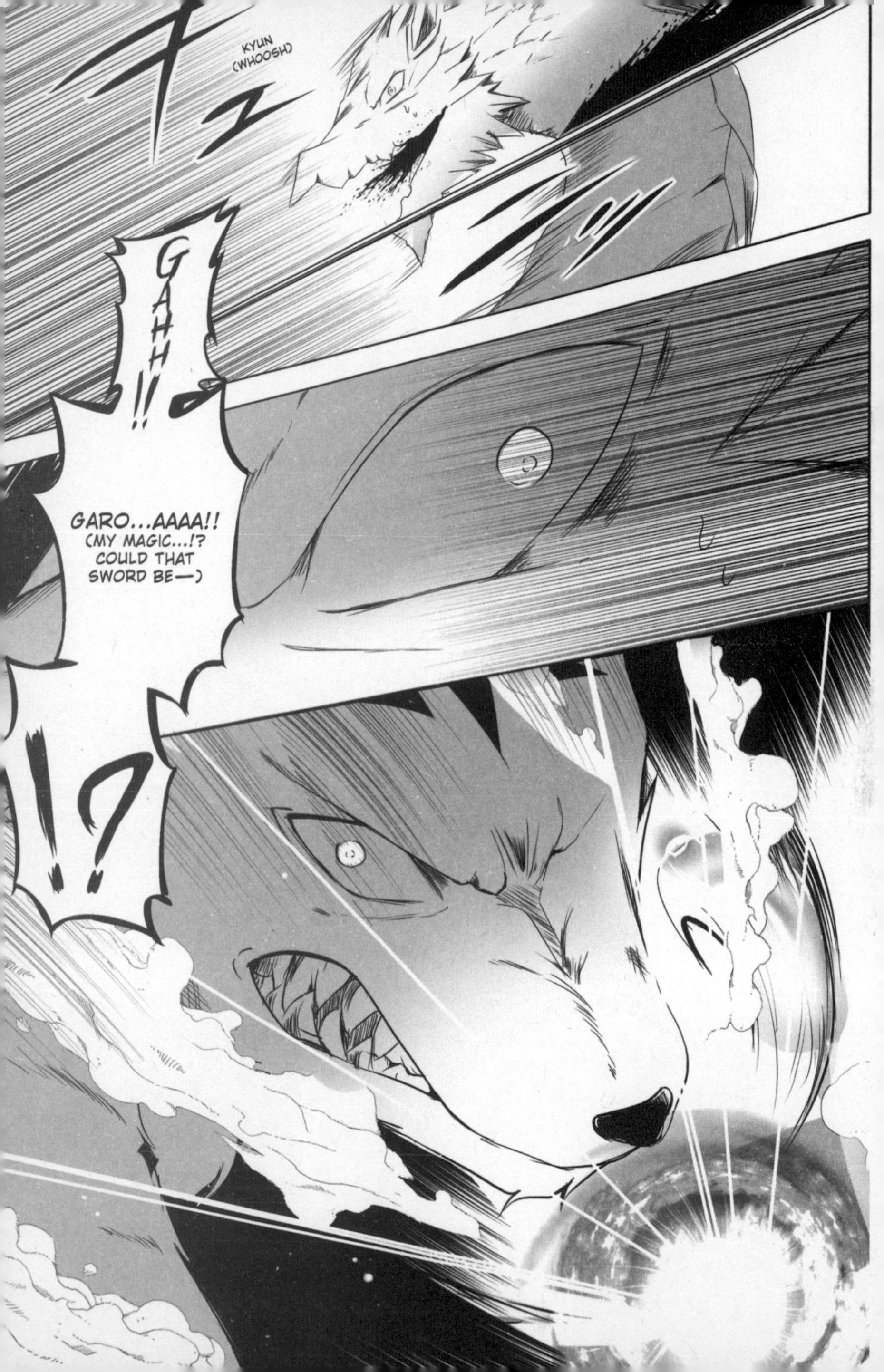
KYUN
(WHOOSH)
GAHH!!
GARO...AAAA!!
(MY MAGIC...!? COULD THAT SWORD BE—)
!?

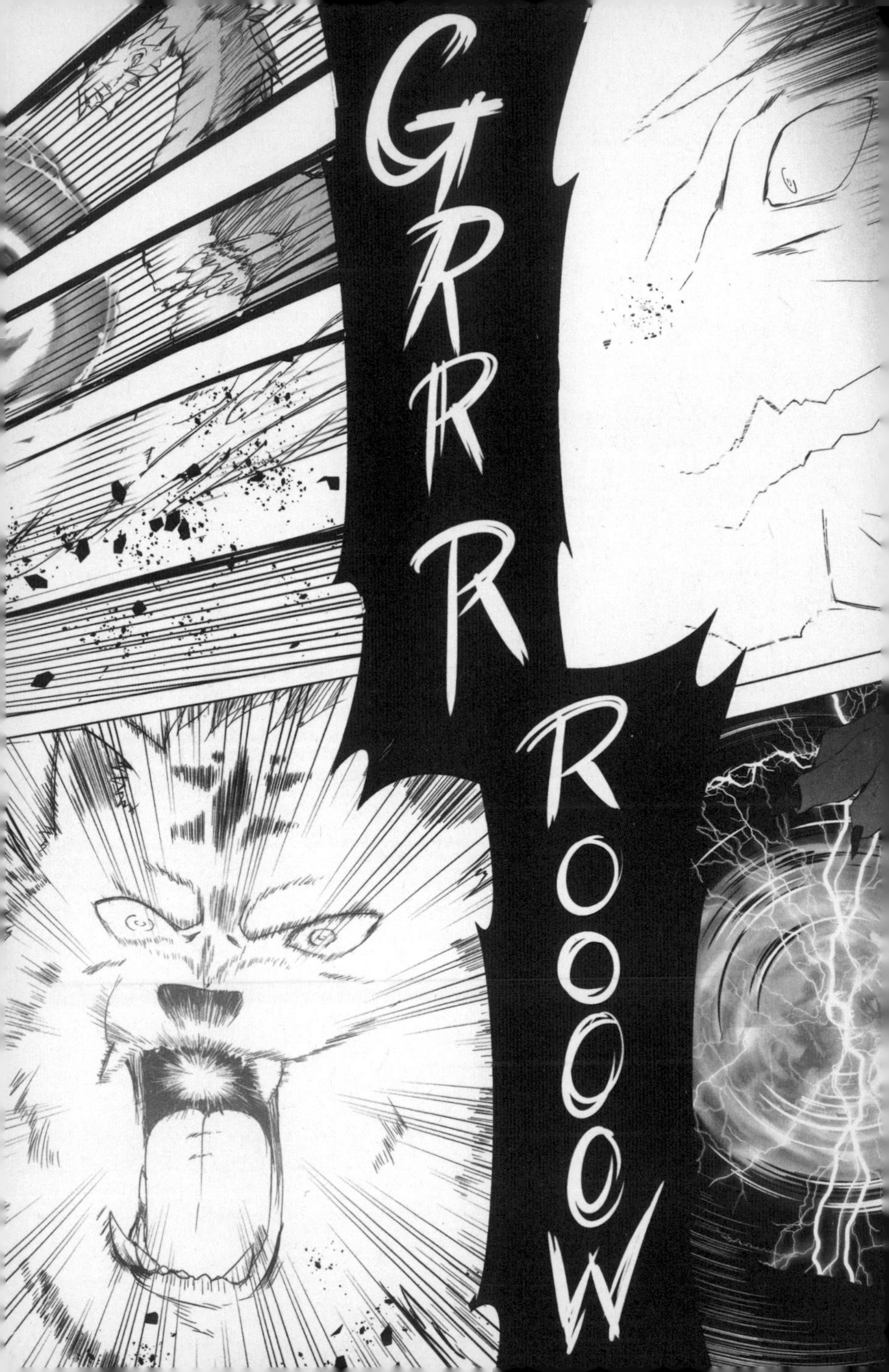
GRRRROOOOOW

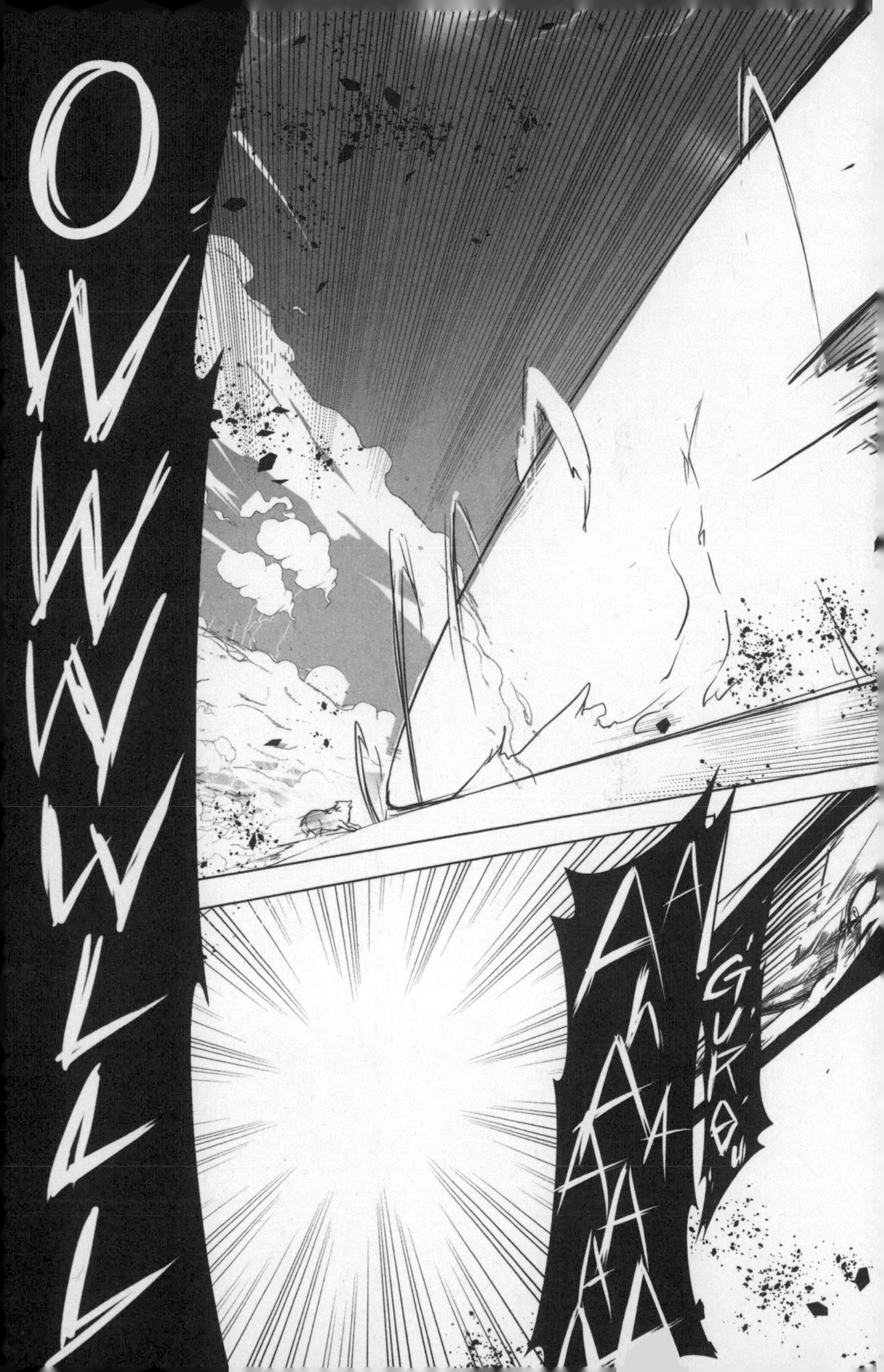
GURO...
AAhAAAAAA
OWWWWLLL

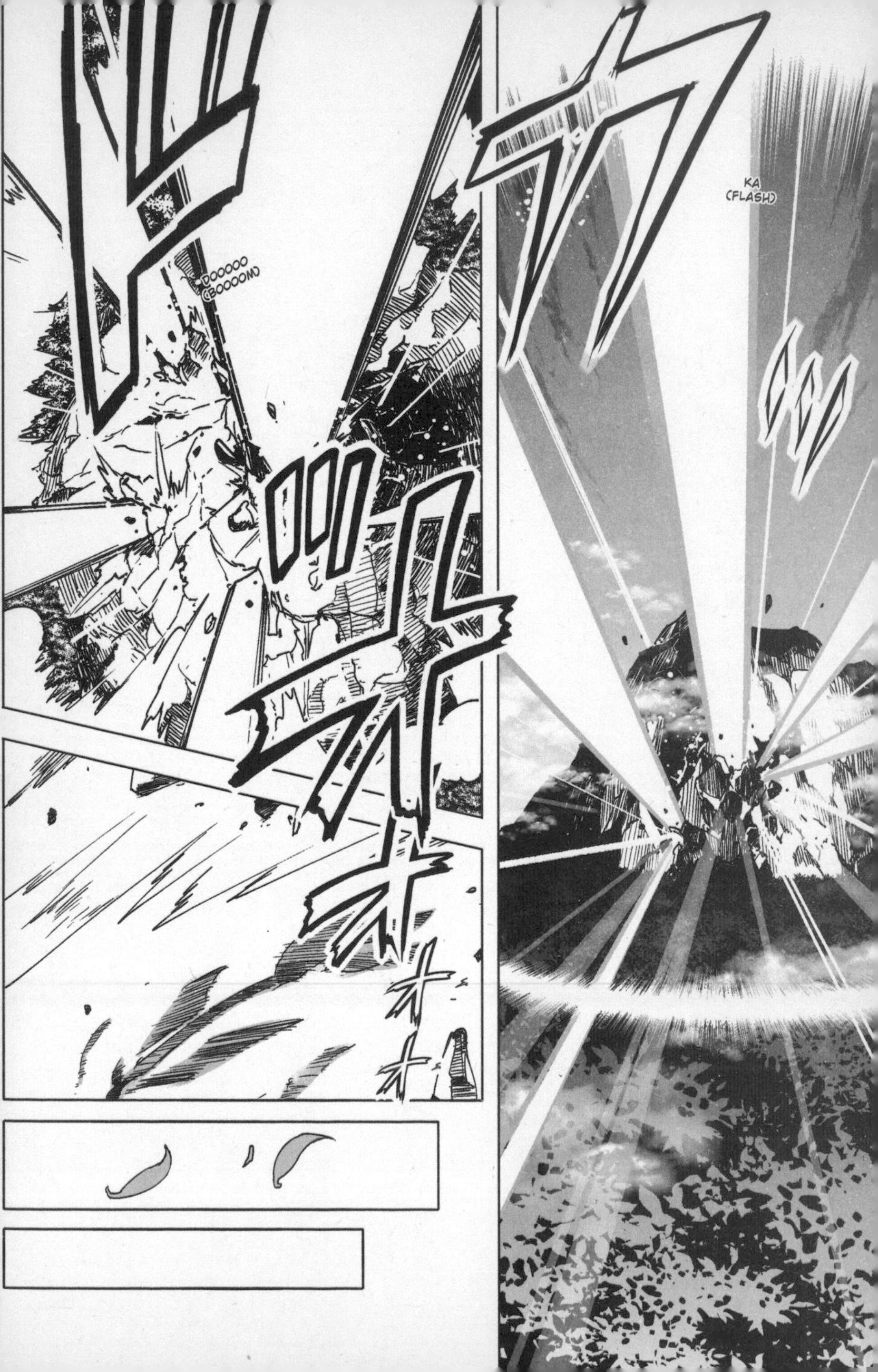
KA
(FLASH)
DOOOOO
(BOOOOM)

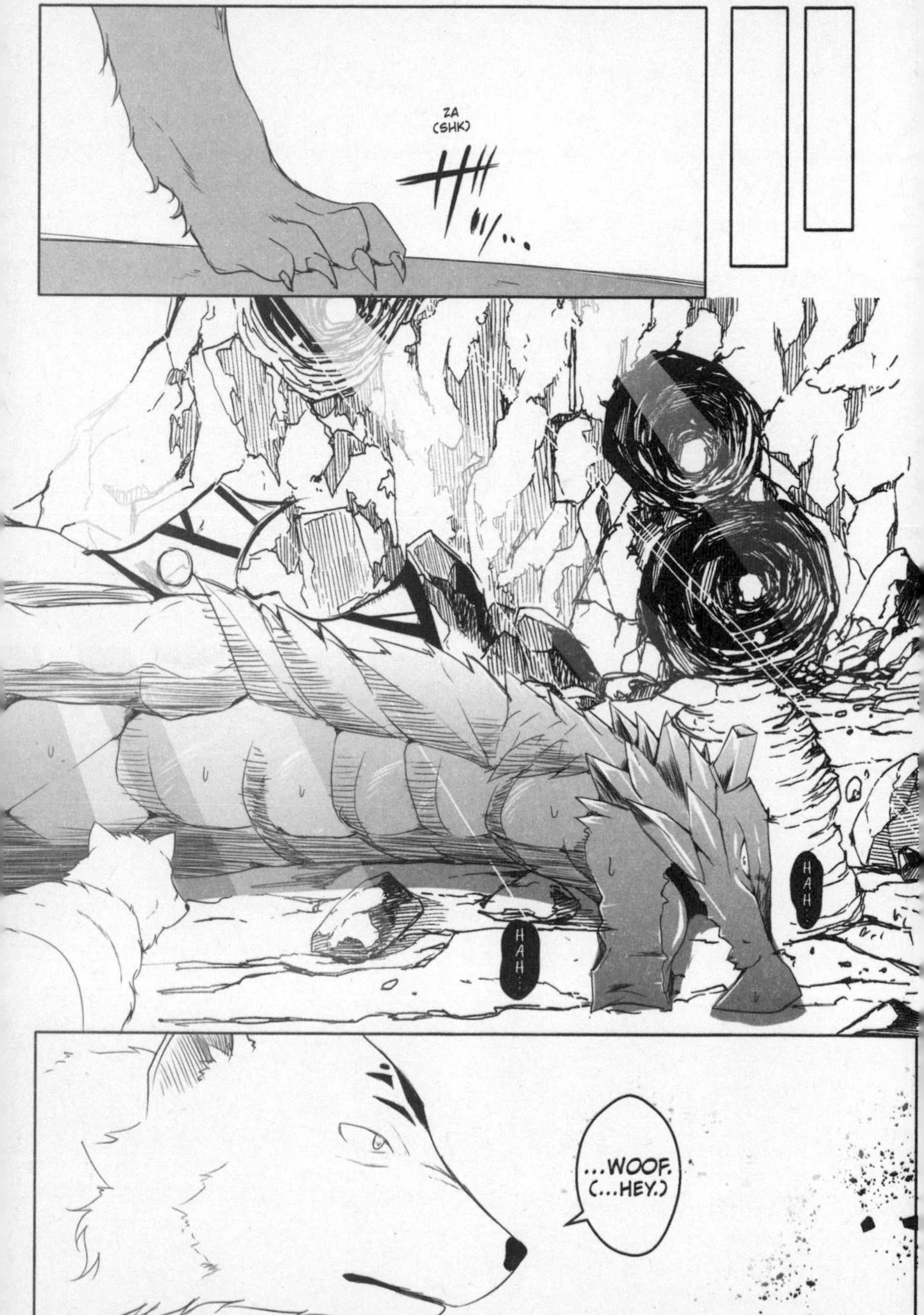
ZA
(SHK)
HAH...
HAH...
...WOOF.
(...HEY.)

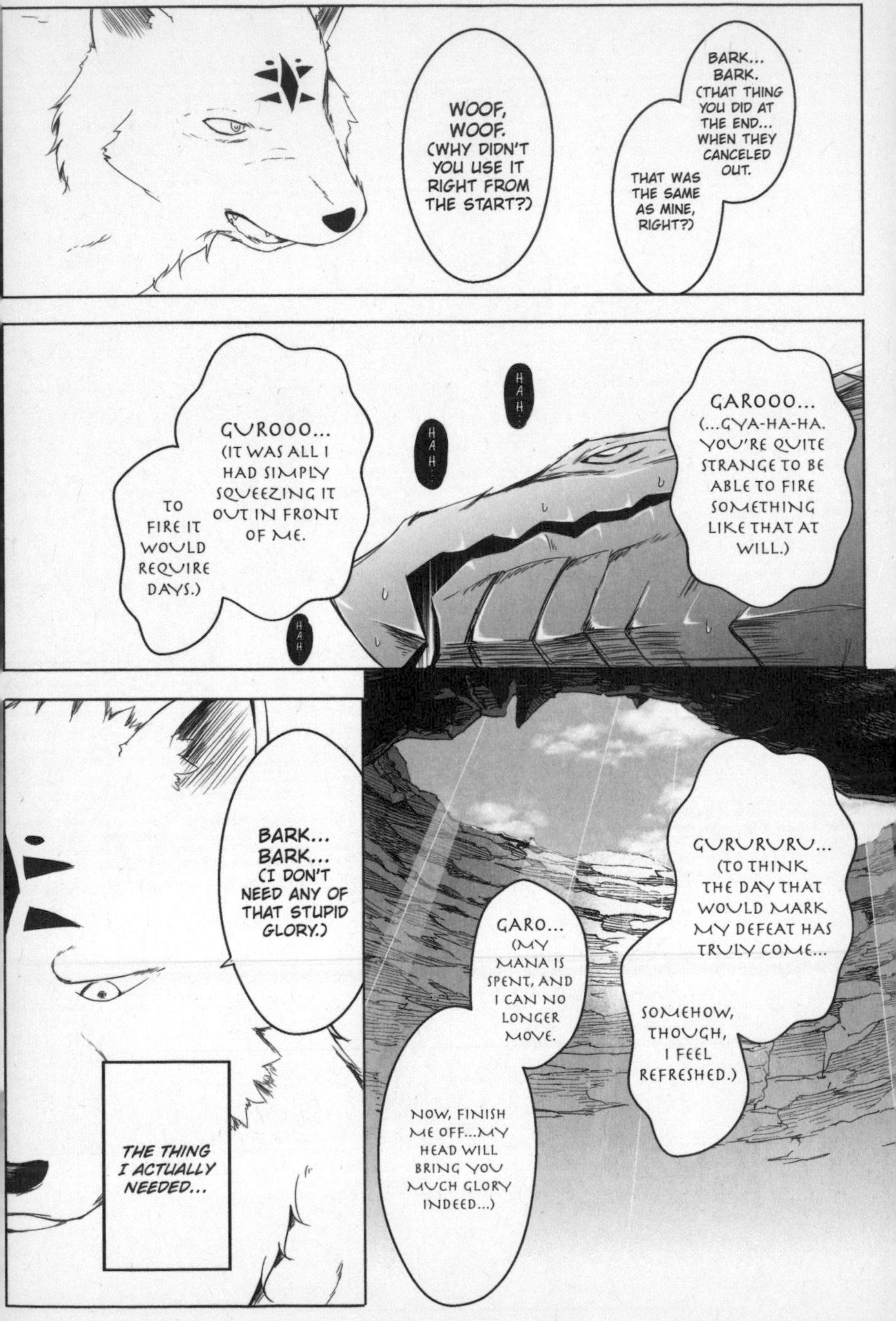
BARK... BARK. (THAT THING YOU DID AT THE END... WHEN THEY CANCELED OUT.
THAT WAS THE SAME AS MINE, RIGHT?)
WOOF, WOOF. (WHY DIDN'T YOU USE IT RIGHT FROM THE START?)
GAROOO... (...GYA-HA-HA. YOU'RE QUITE STRANGE TO BE ABLE TO FIRE SOMETHING LIKE THAT AT WILL.)
HAH...
HAH...
GUROOO... (IT WAS ALL I HAD SIMPLY SQUEEZING IT OUT IN FRONT OF ME.
TO FIRE IT WOULD REQUIRE DAYS.)
HAH
GURURURU... (TO THINK THE DAY THAT WOULD MARK MY DEFEAT HAS TRULY COME...
SOMEHOW, THOUGH, I FEEL REFRESHED.)
GARO... (MY MANA IS SPENT, AND I CAN NO LONGER MOVE.
NOW, FINISH ME OFF...MY HEAD WILL BRING YOU MUCH GLORY INDEED...)
BARK... BARK... (I DON'T NEED ANY OF THAT STUPID GLORY.)
THE THING I ACTUALLY NEEDED...

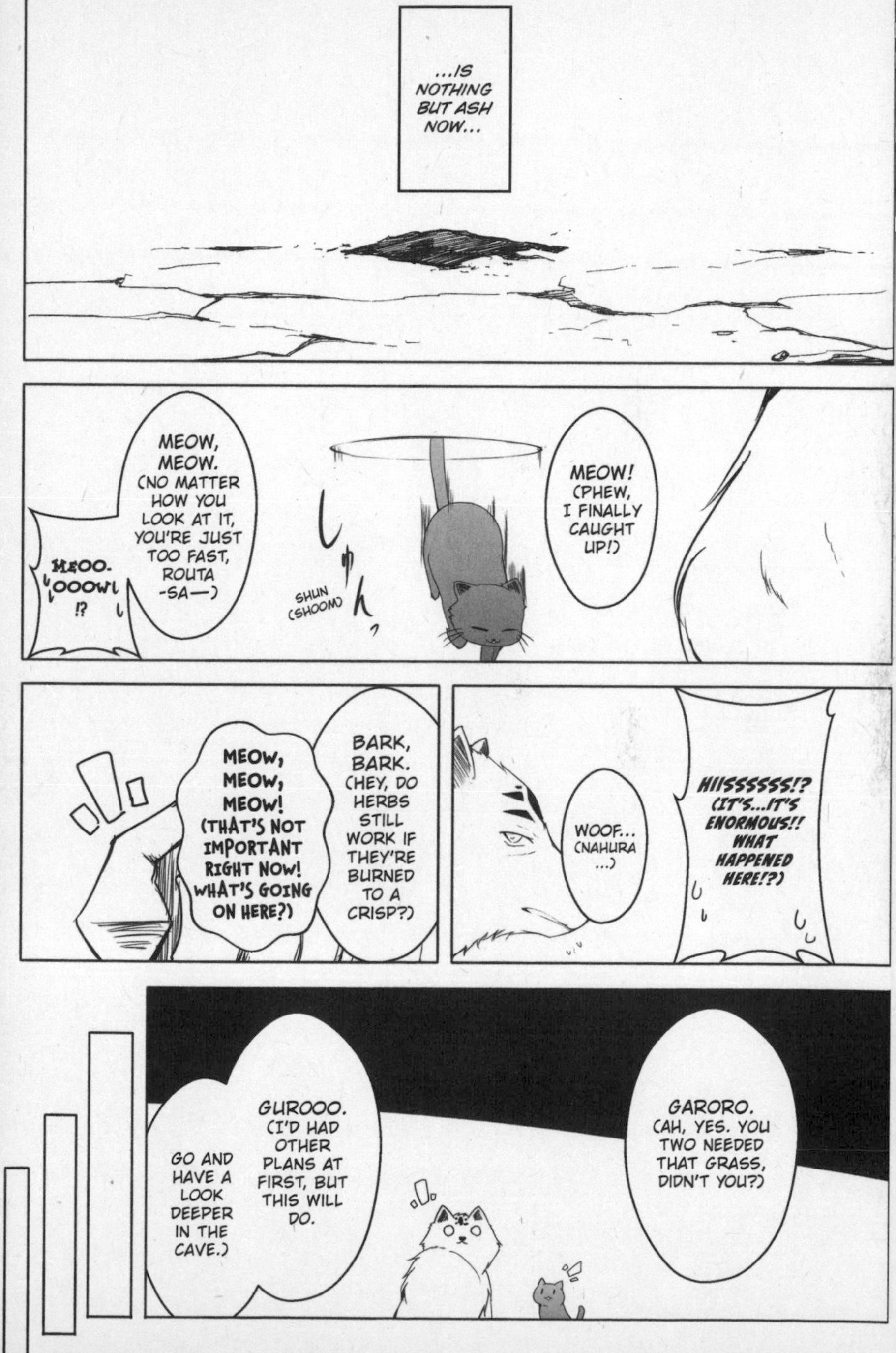
...IS NOTHING BUT ASH NOW...
MEOW! (PHEW, I FINALLY CAUGHT UP!)
SHUN (SHOOM)
MEOW, MEOW. (NO MATTER HOW YOU LOOK AT IT, YOU'RE JUST TOO FAST, ROUTA-SA—)
MEOO-OOOW!?
HIISSSSSS!? (IT'S...IT'S ENORMOUS!! WHAT HAPPENED HERE!?)
WOOF... (NAHURA...)
BARK, BARK. (HEY, DO HERBS STILL WORK IF THEY'RE BURNED TO A CRISP?)
MEOW, MEOW, MEOW! (THAT'S NOT IMPORTANT RIGHT NOW! WHAT'S GOING ON HERE?)
GARORO. (AH, YES. YOU TWO NEEDED THAT GRASS, DIDN'T YOU?)
GUROOO. (I'D HAD OTHER PLANS AT FIRST, BUT THIS WILL DO. GO AND HAVE A LOOK DEEPER IN THE CAVE.)

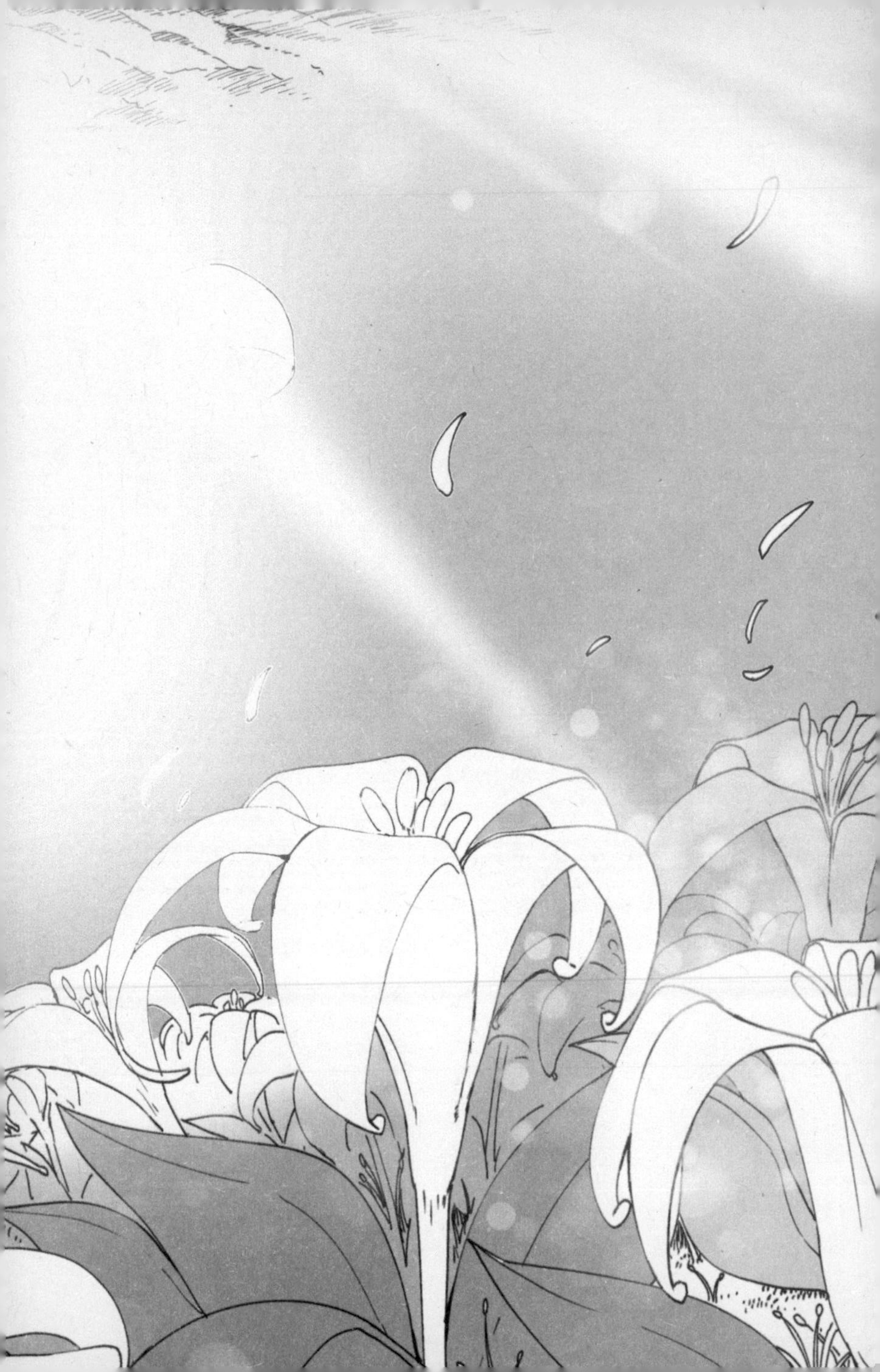

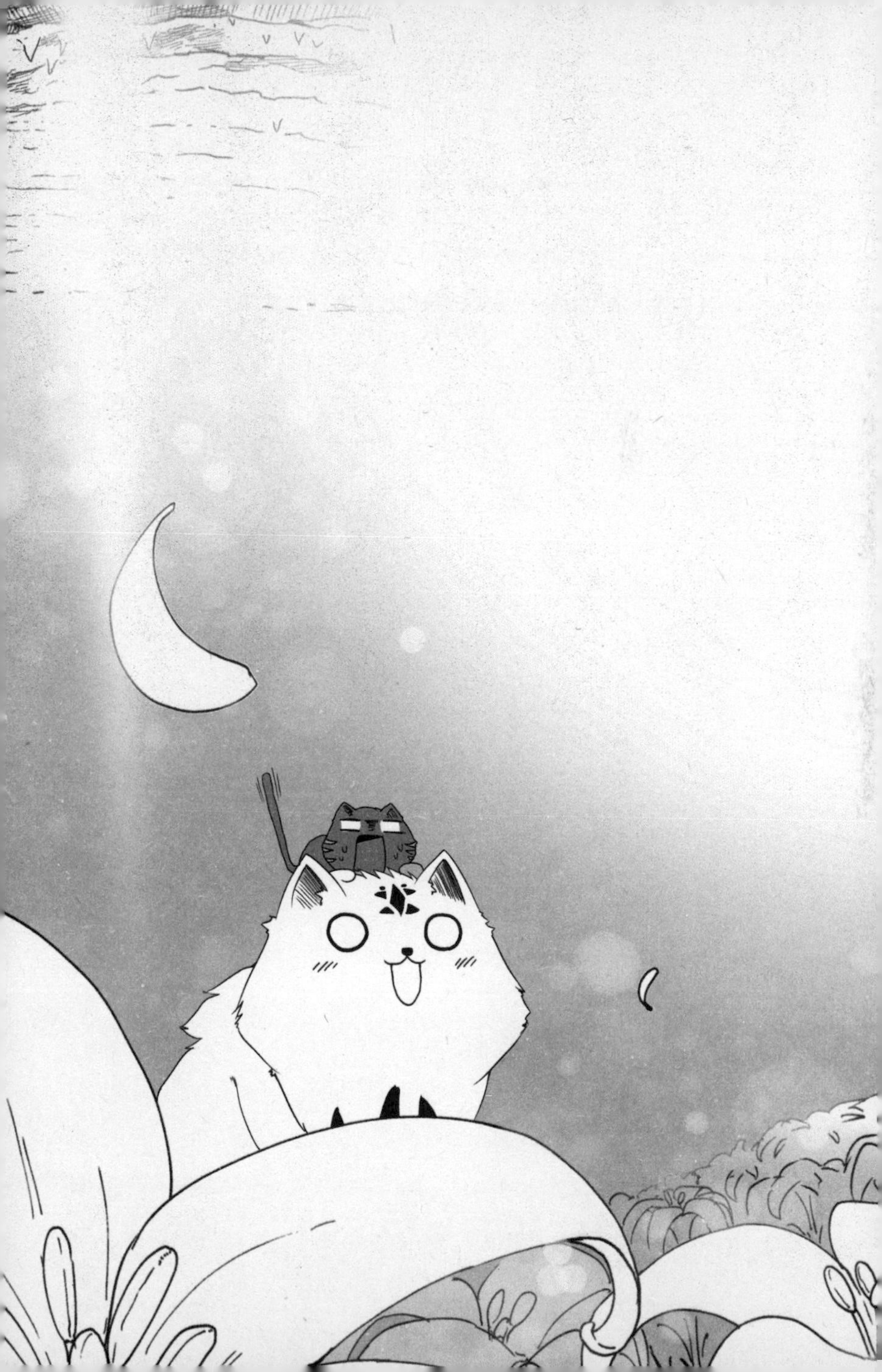

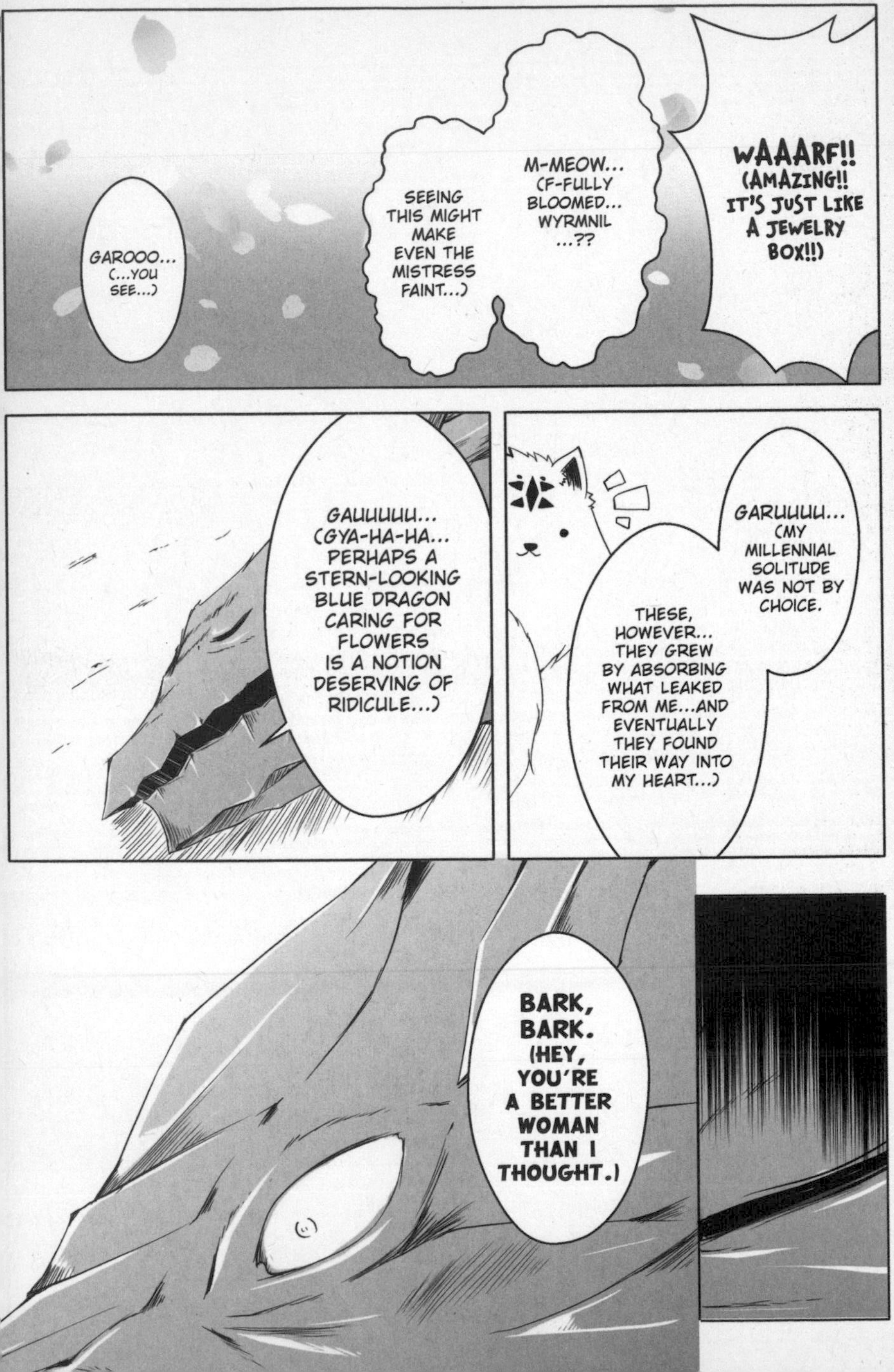
WAAARF!! (AMAZING!! IT'S JUST LIKE A JEWELRY BOX!!)
M-MEOW... (F-FULLY BLOOMED... WYRMNIL ...??
SEEING THIS MIGHT MAKE EVEN THE MISTRESS FAINT...)
GAROOO... (...YOU SEE...)
GARUUUU... (MY MILLENNIAL SOLITUDE WAS NOT BY CHOICE.
THESE, HOWEVER... THEY GREW BY ABSORBING WHAT LEAKED FROM ME...AND EVENTUALLY THEY FOUND THEIR WAY INTO MY HEART...)
GAUUUUU... (GYA-HA-HA... PERHAPS A STERN-LOOKING BLUE DRAGON CARING FOR FLOWERS IS A NOTION DESERVING OF RIDICULE...)
BARK, BARK. (HEY, YOU'RE A BETTER WOMAN THAN I THOUGHT.)

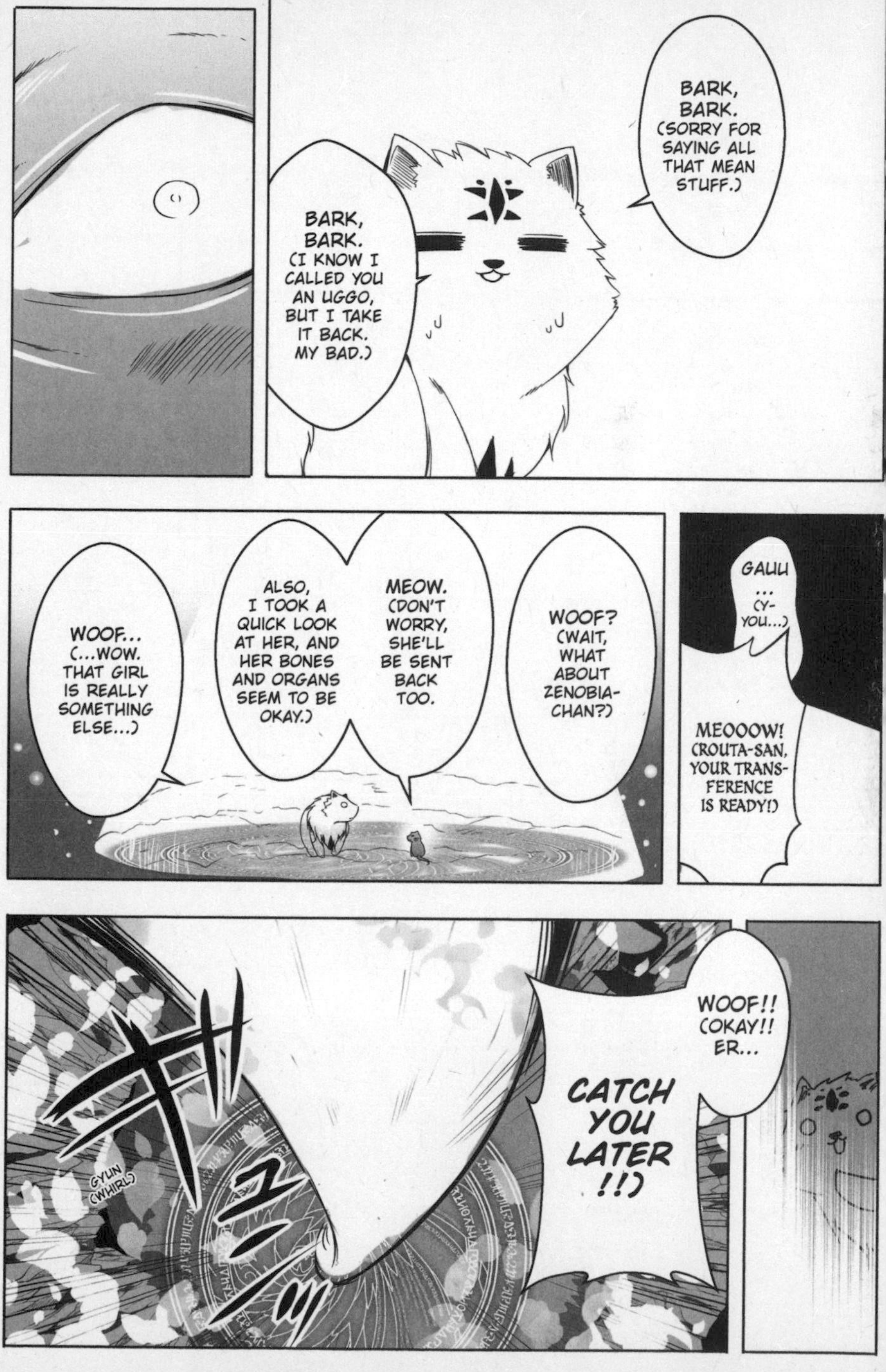
BARK, BARK. (SORRY FOR SAYING ALL THAT MEAN STUFF.)
BARK, BARK. (I KNOW I CALLED YOU AN UGGO, BUT I TAKE IT BACK. MY BAD.)
GAUU... (Y-YOU...)
MEOOOW! (ROUTA-SAN, YOUR TRANSFERENCE IS READY!)
WOOF? (WAIT, WHAT ABOUT ZENOBIA-CHAN?)
MEOW. (DON'T WORRY, SHE'LL BE SENT BACK TOO.
ALSO, I TOOK A QUICK LOOK AT HER, AND HER BONES AND ORGANS SEEM TO BE OKAY.)
WOOF... (...WOW. THAT GIRL IS REALLY SOMETHING ELSE...)
WOOF!! (OKAY!! ER...
CATCH YOU LATER!!)
GYUN (WHIRL)

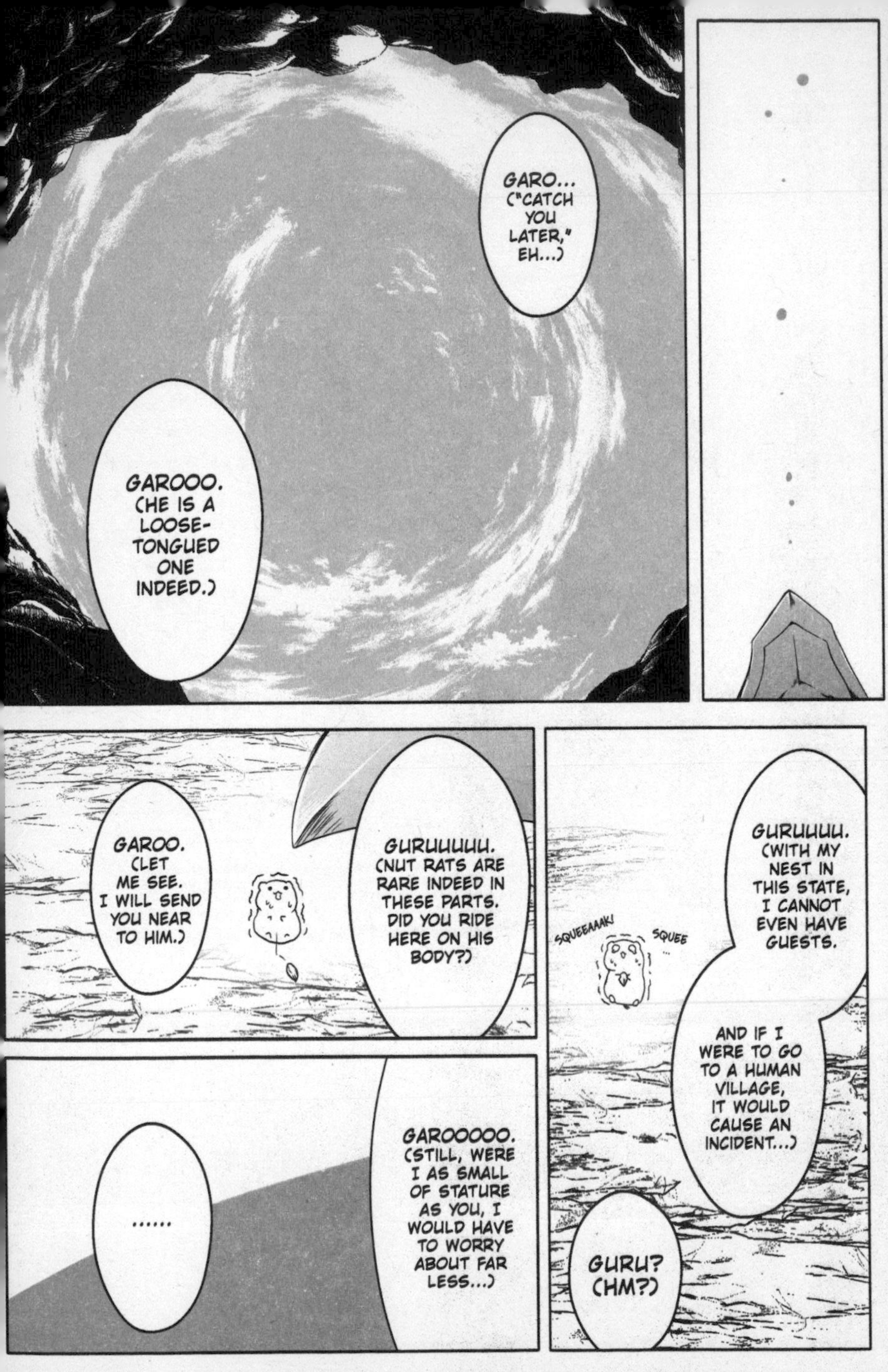
GARO... ("CATCH YOU LATER," EH...)
GAROOO. (HE IS A LOOSE-TONGUED ONE INDEED.)
GURUUUU. (WITH MY NEST IN THIS STATE, I CANNOT EVEN HAVE GUESTS.
SQUEEAAAK!
SQUEE...
AND IF I WERE TO GO TO A HUMAN VILLAGE, IT WOULD CAUSE AN INCIDENT...)
GURU? (HM?)
GURUUUUU. (NUT RATS ARE RARE INDEED IN THESE PARTS. DID YOU RIDE HERE ON HIS BODY?)
GAROO. (LET ME SEE. I WILL SEND YOU NEAR TO HIM.)
GAROOOOO. (STILL, WERE I AS SMALL OF STATURE AS YOU, I WOULD HAVE TO WORRY ABOUT FAR LESS...)
......

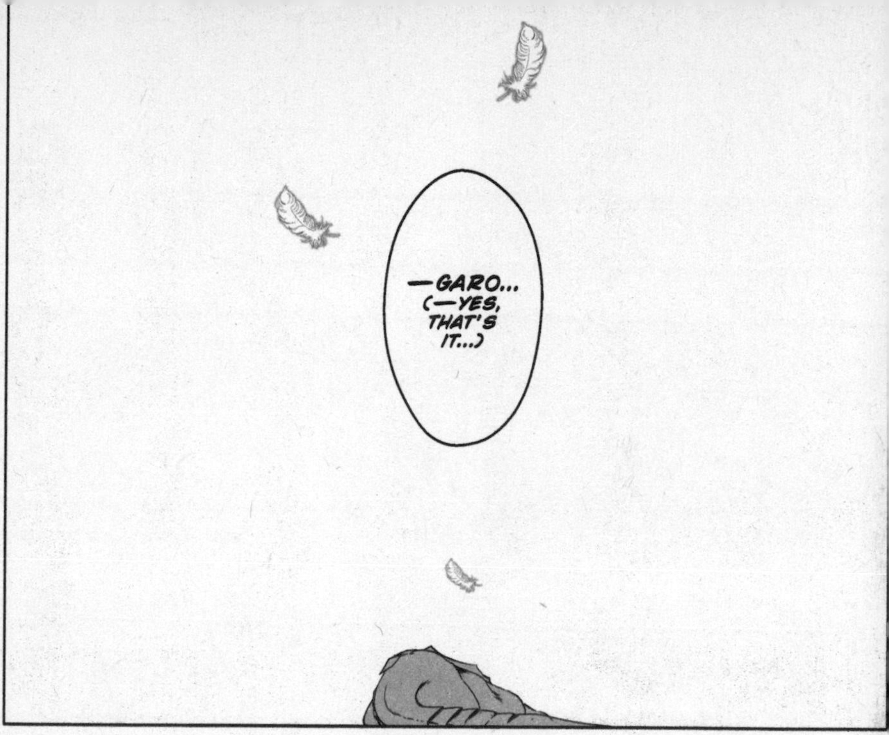
—GARO... (—YES, THAT'S IT...)

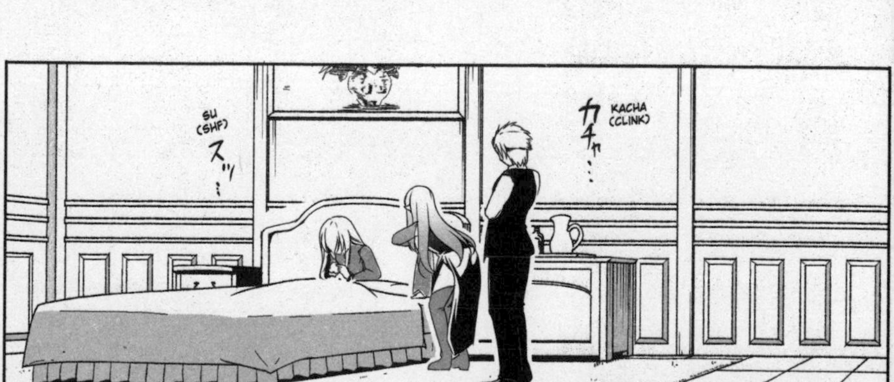
カチャ
KACHA (CLINK)
スッ
SU (SHF)

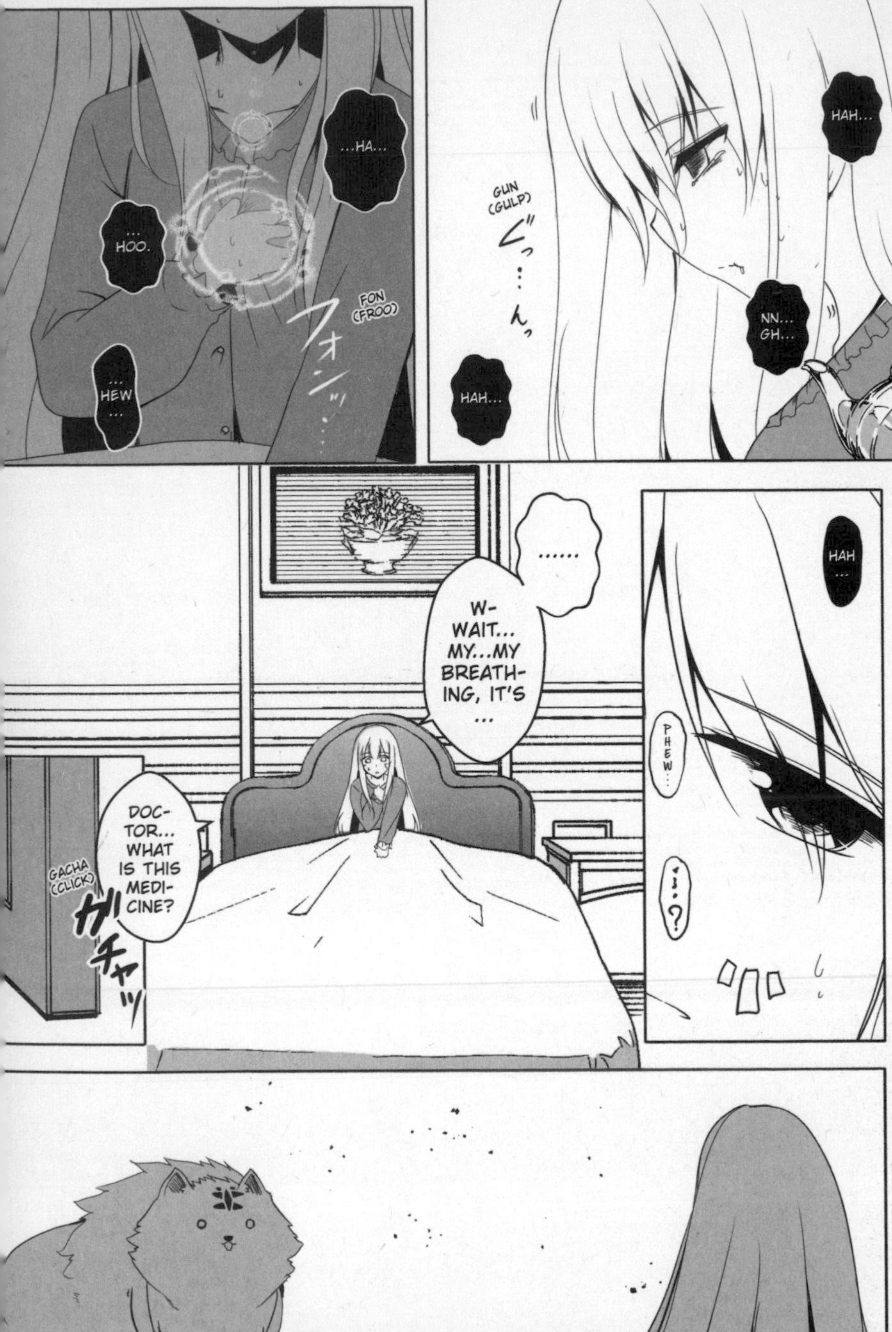
HAH...
GUN (GULP)
ぐっ…んっ
NN... GH...
HAH...
...HA...
... HOO.
FON (FROO)
フォンッ
... HEW ...
HAH ...
PHEW...
?
......
W-WAIT... MY...MY BREATHING, IT'S ...
DOCTOR... WHAT IS THIS MEDICINE?
GACHA (CLICK)
ガチャッ

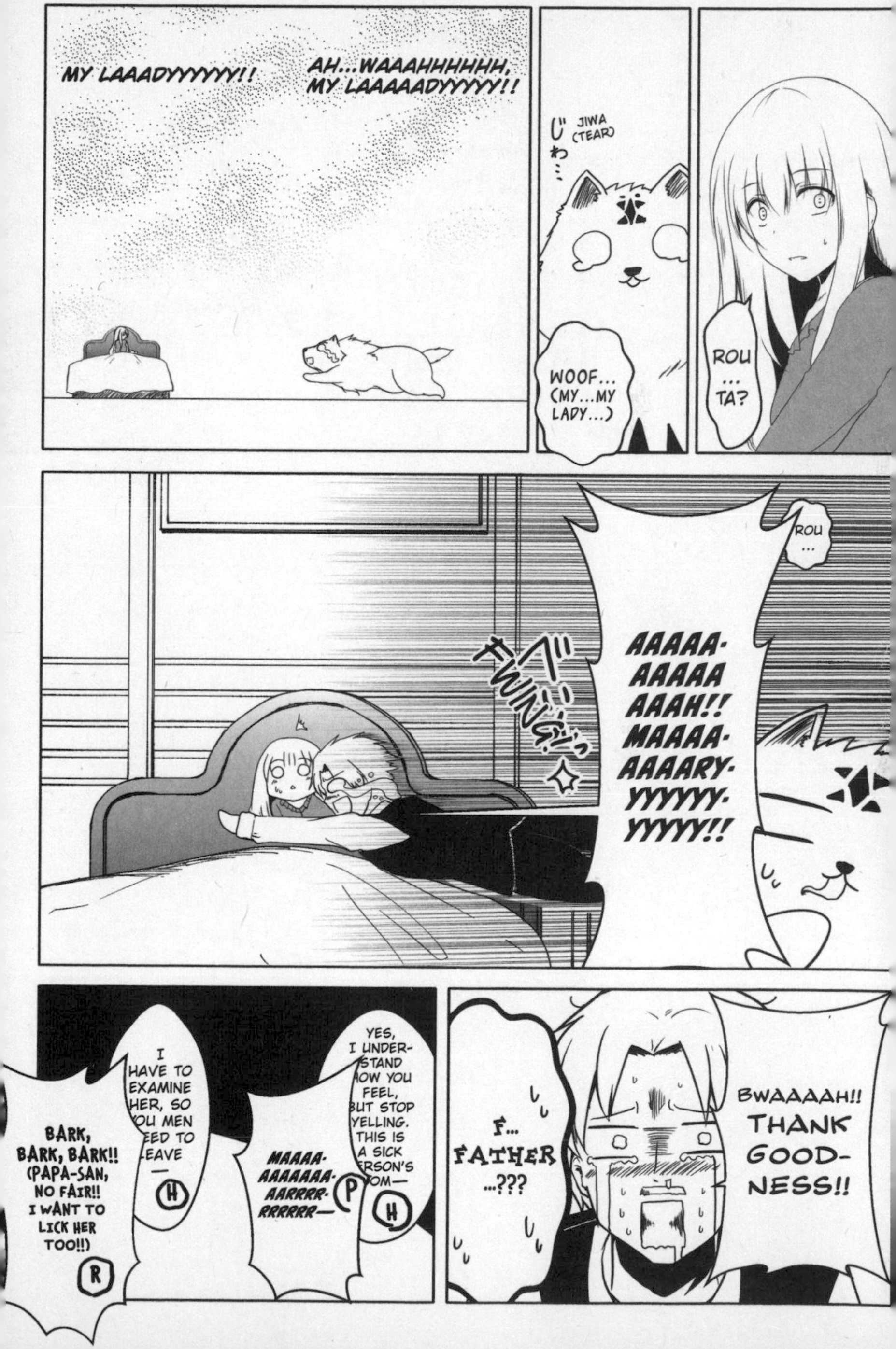
ROU ... TA?
JIWA (TEAR)
じわ…
WOOF... (MY...MY LADY...)
AH...WAAAHHHHHH, MY LAAAAADYYYYY!!
MY LAAADYYYYYY!!
ROU ...
AAAAA-AAAAA AAAH!! MAAAA-AAAARY-YYYYYY-YYYYY!!
FWING!!
BWAAAAH!! THANK GOOD-NESS!!
F... FATHER ...???
YES, I UNDER-STAND OW YOU FEEL, BUT STOP YELLING. THIS IS A SICK ERSON'S OM—
H
MAAAA-AAAAAAA-AARRRRR-RRRRRR—
P
I HAVE TO EXAMINE HER, SO OU MEN EED TO EAVE —
H
BARK, BARK, BARK!! (PAPA-SAN, NO FAIR!! I WANT TO LICK HER TOO!!)
R

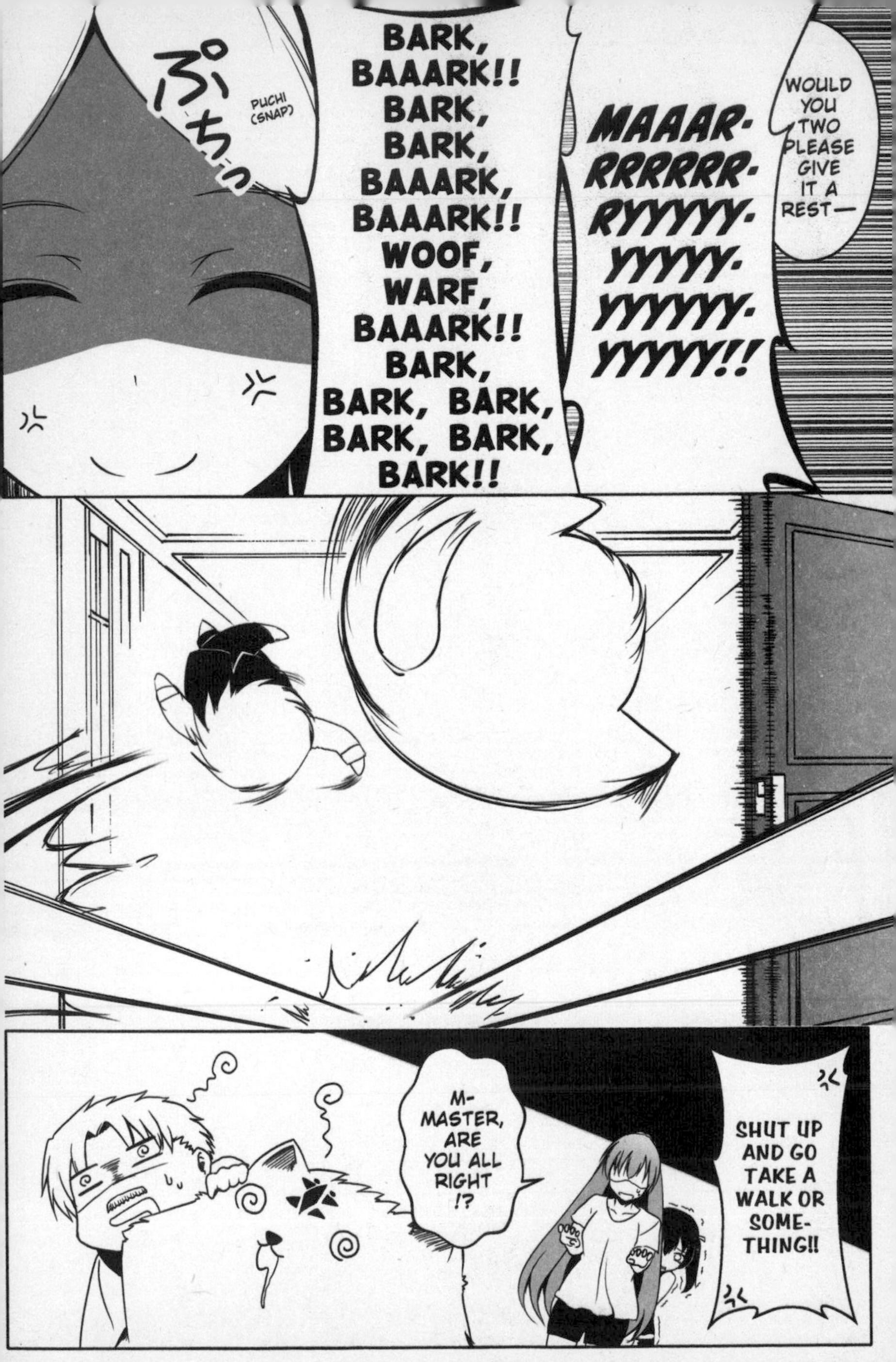
WOULD YOU TWO PLEASE GIVE IT A REST—
MAAARRRRRRRYYYYYYYYYYYYYYYYYY!!
BARK, BAAARK!! BARK, BARK, BAAARK, BAAARK!! WOOF, WARF, BAAARK!! BARK, BARK, BARK, BARK, BARK, BARK!!
ぷちっ
PUCHI (SNAP)
SHUT UP AND GO TAKE A WALK OR SOMETHING!!
M-MASTER, ARE YOU ALL RIGHT!?

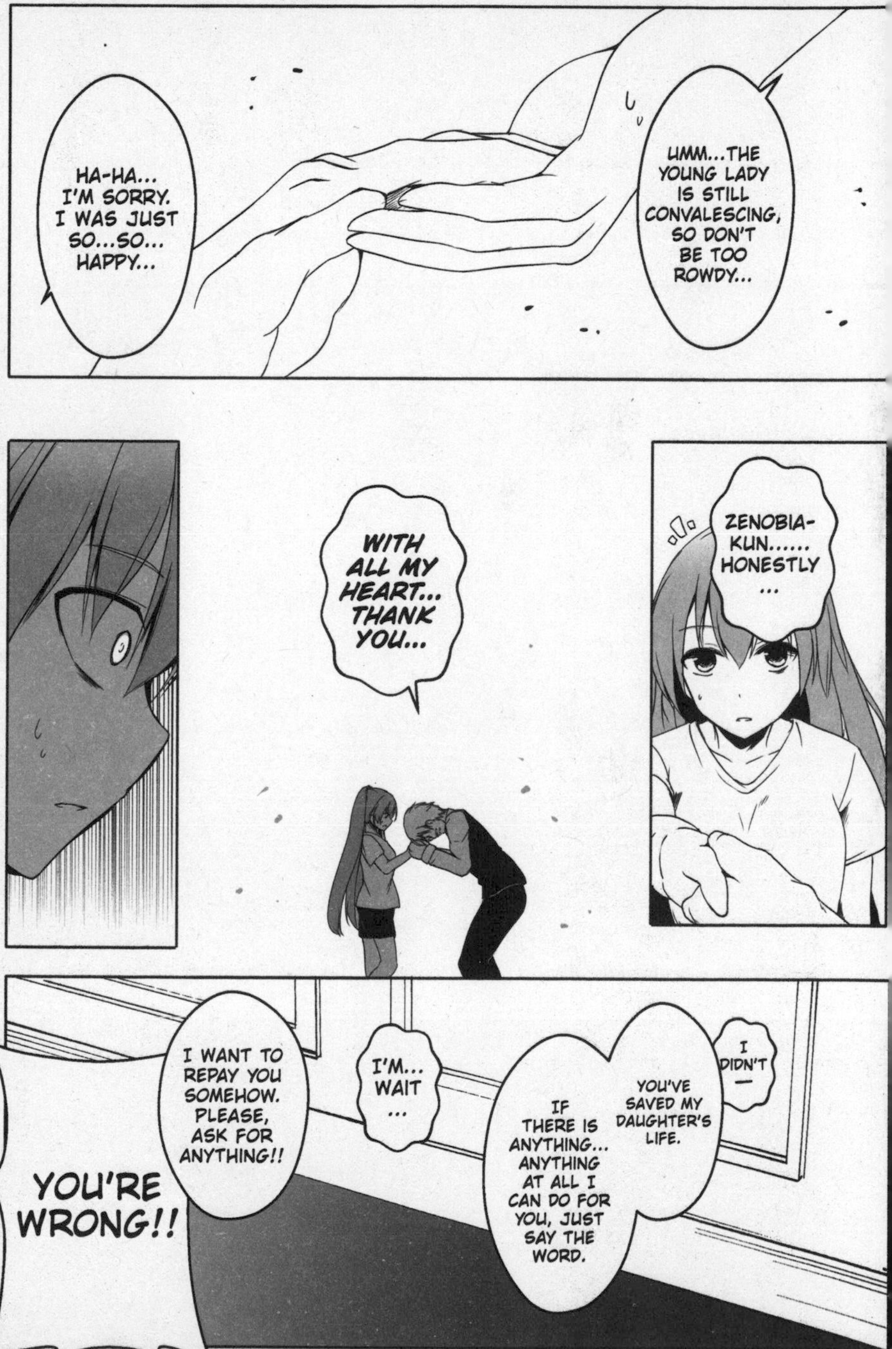
UMM...THE YOUNG LADY IS STILL CONVALESCING, SO DON'T BE TOO ROWDY...
HA-HA... I'M SORRY. I WAS JUST SO...SO... HAPPY...
ZENOBIA-KUN...... HONESTLY ...
WITH ALL MY HEART... THANK YOU...
I DIDN'T —
YOU'VE SAVED MY DAUGHTER'S LIFE.
IF THERE IS ANYTHING... ANYTHING AT ALL I CAN DO FOR YOU, JUST SAY THE WORD.
I'M... WAIT ...
I WANT TO REPAY YOU SOMEHOW. PLEASE, ASK FOR ANYTHING!!
YOU'RE WRONG!!

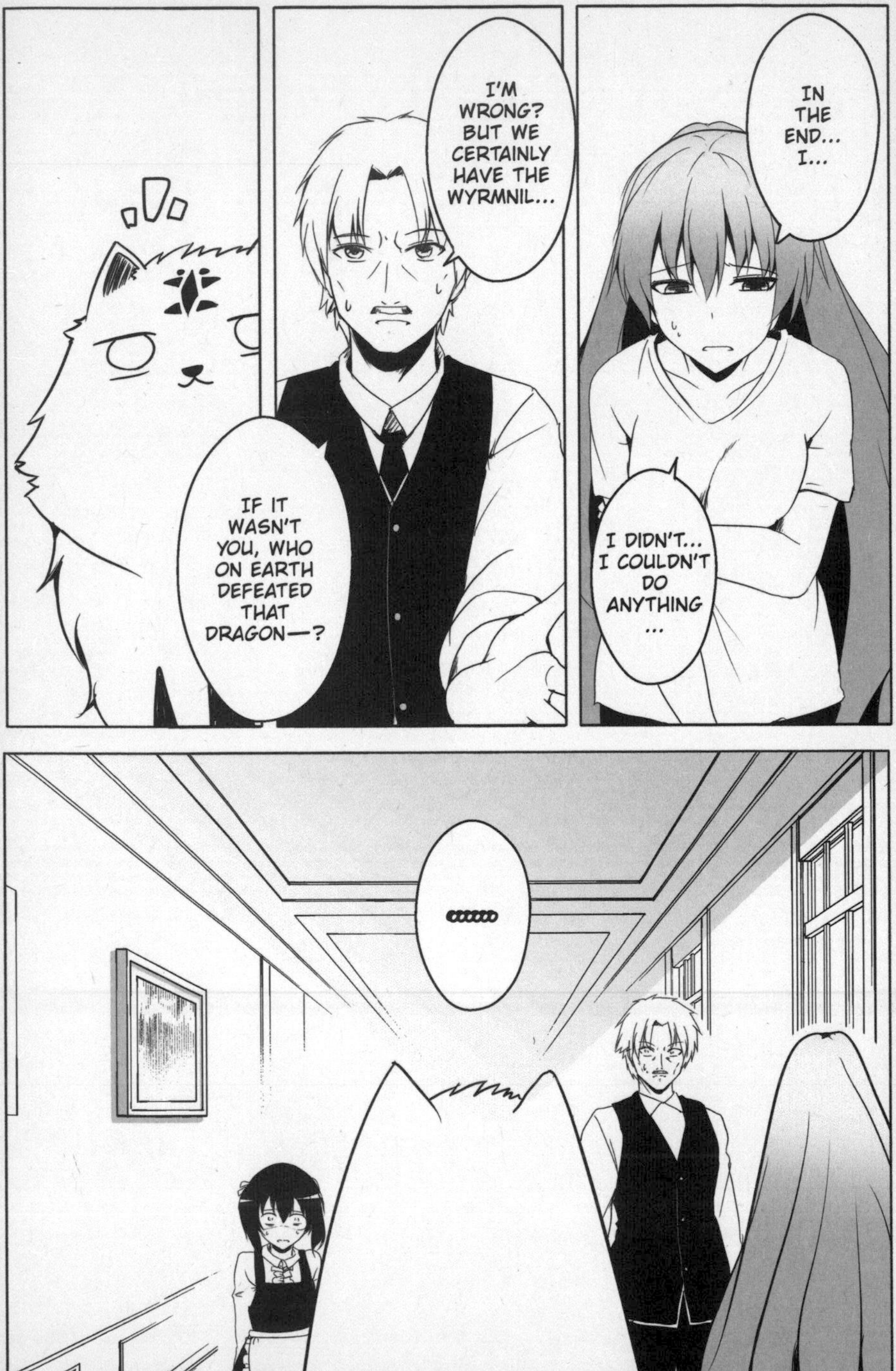
IN THE END... I...
I DIDN'T... I COULDN'T DO ANYTHING...
I'M WRONG? BUT WE CERTAINLY HAVE THE WYRMNIL...
IF IT WASN'T YOU, WHO ON EARTH DEFEATED THAT DRAGON—?
......

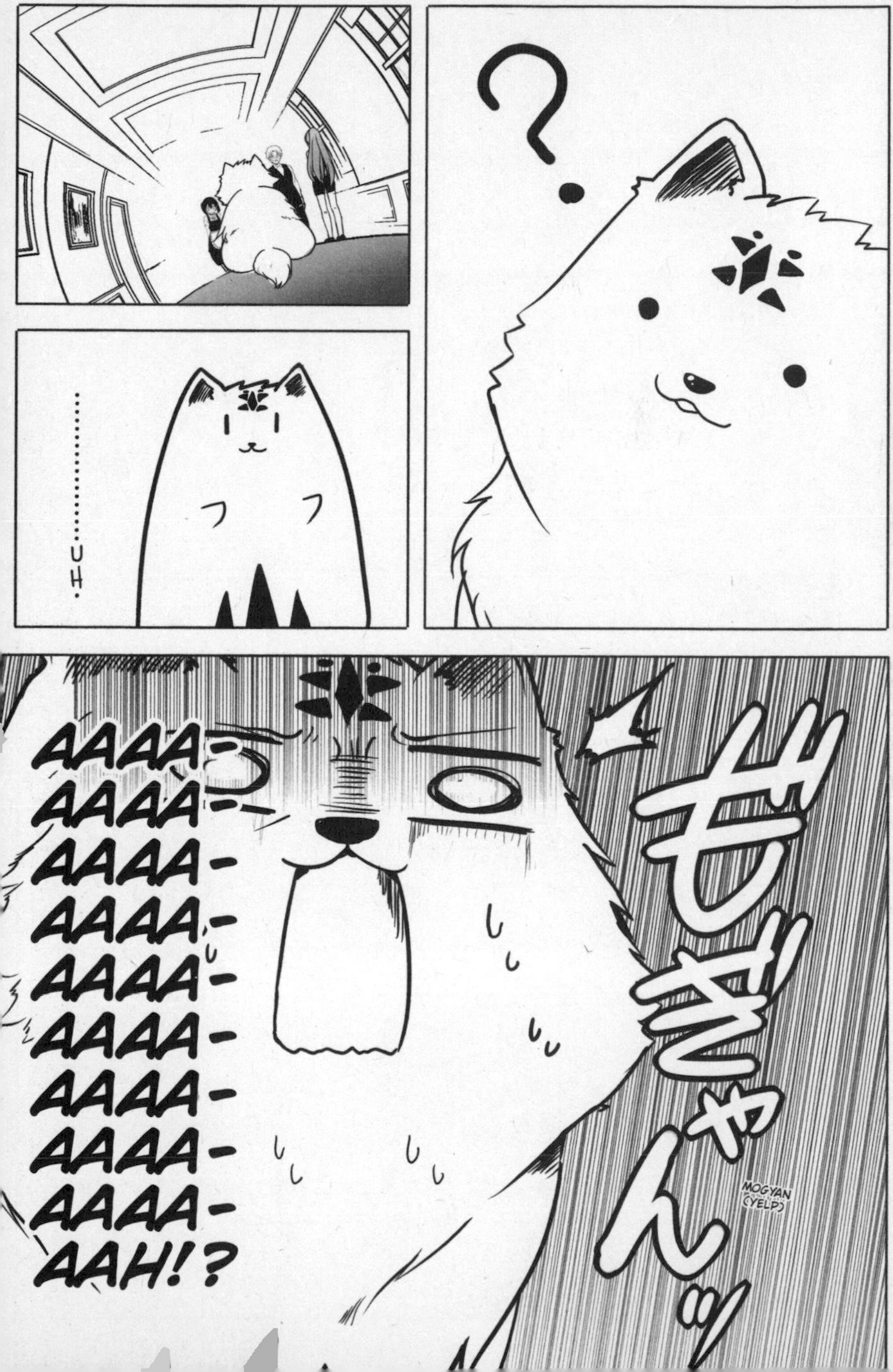
?
......UH.
もぎゃんっ
MOGYAN (YELP)
AAAA-AAAA-AAAA-AAAA-AAAA-AAAA-AAAA-AAAA-AAAA-AAH!?

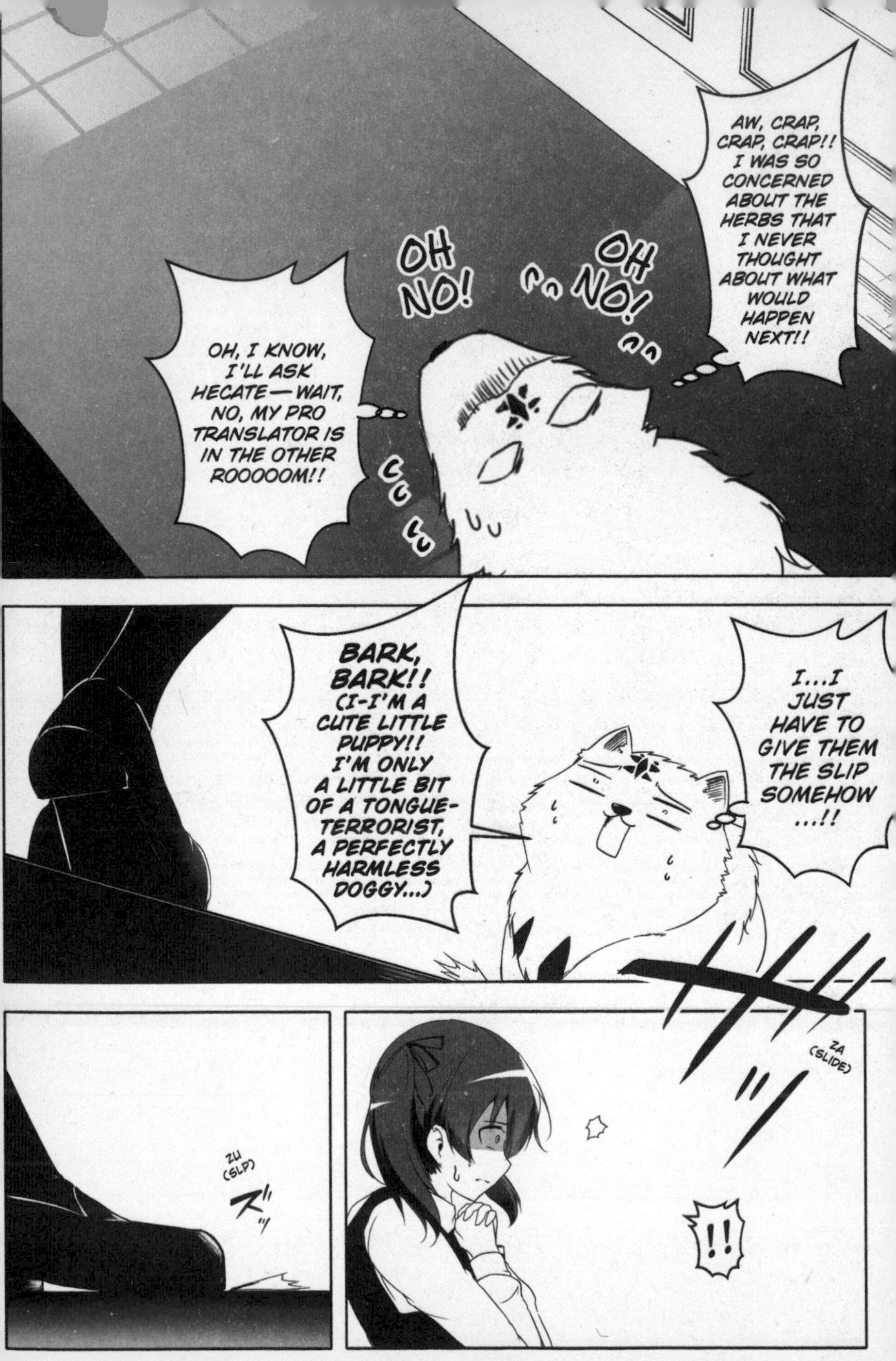
AW, CRAP, CRAP, CRAP!! I WAS SO CONCERNED ABOUT THE HERBS THAT I NEVER THOUGHT ABOUT WHAT WOULD HAPPEN NEXT!!
OH NO!
OH NO!
OH, I KNOW, I'LL ASK HECATE—WAIT, NO, MY PRO TRANSLATOR IS IN THE OTHER ROOOOOM!!
I...I JUST HAVE TO GIVE THEM THE SLIP SOMEHOW ...!!
BARK, BARK!! (I-I'M A CUTE LITTLE PUPPY!! I'M ONLY A LITTLE BIT OF A TONGUE-TERRORIST, A PERFECTLY HARMLESS DOGGY...)
ZA (SLIDE)
!!
ZU (SLP)

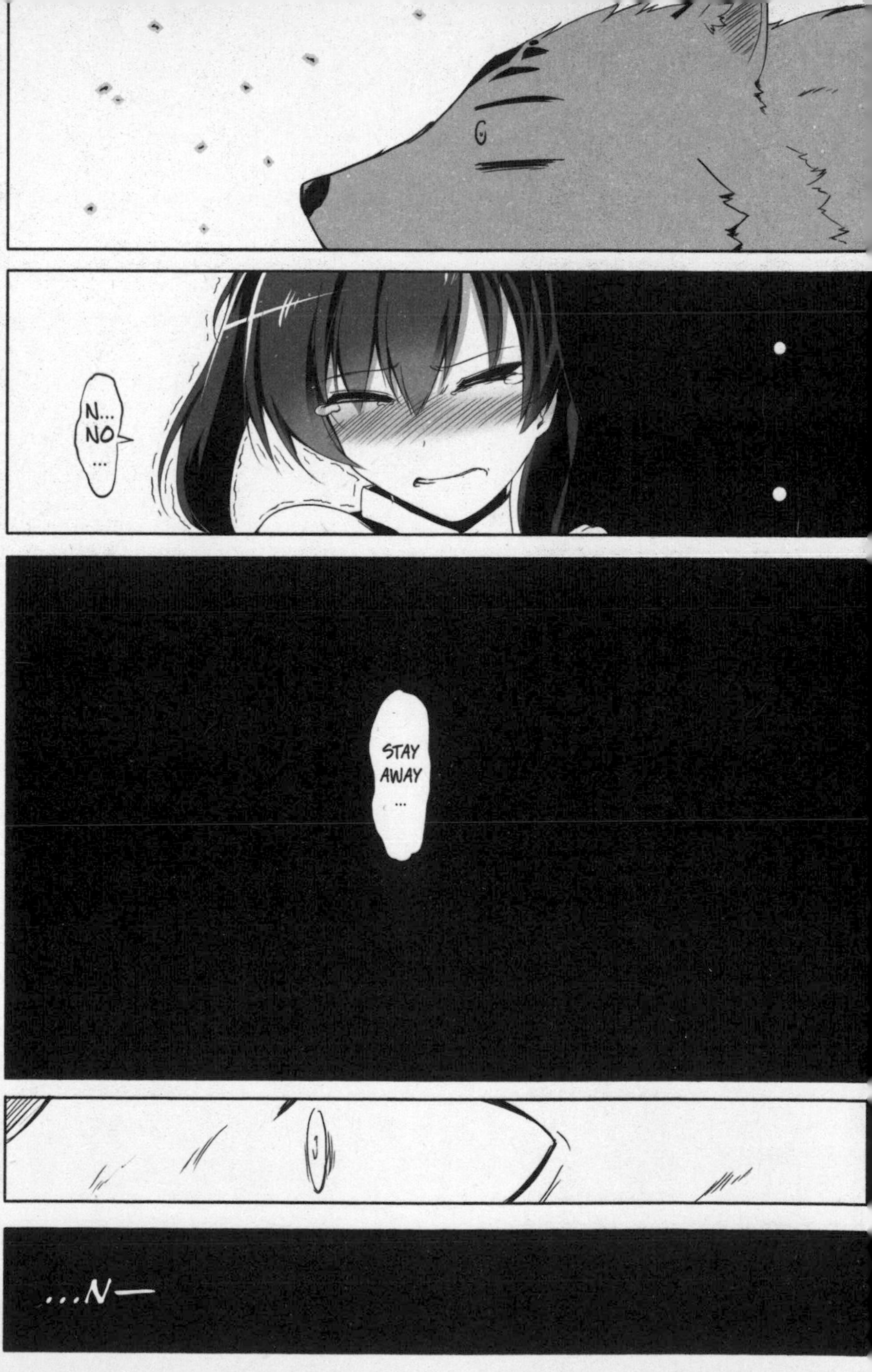
N... NO ...
STAY AWAY ...
...N—

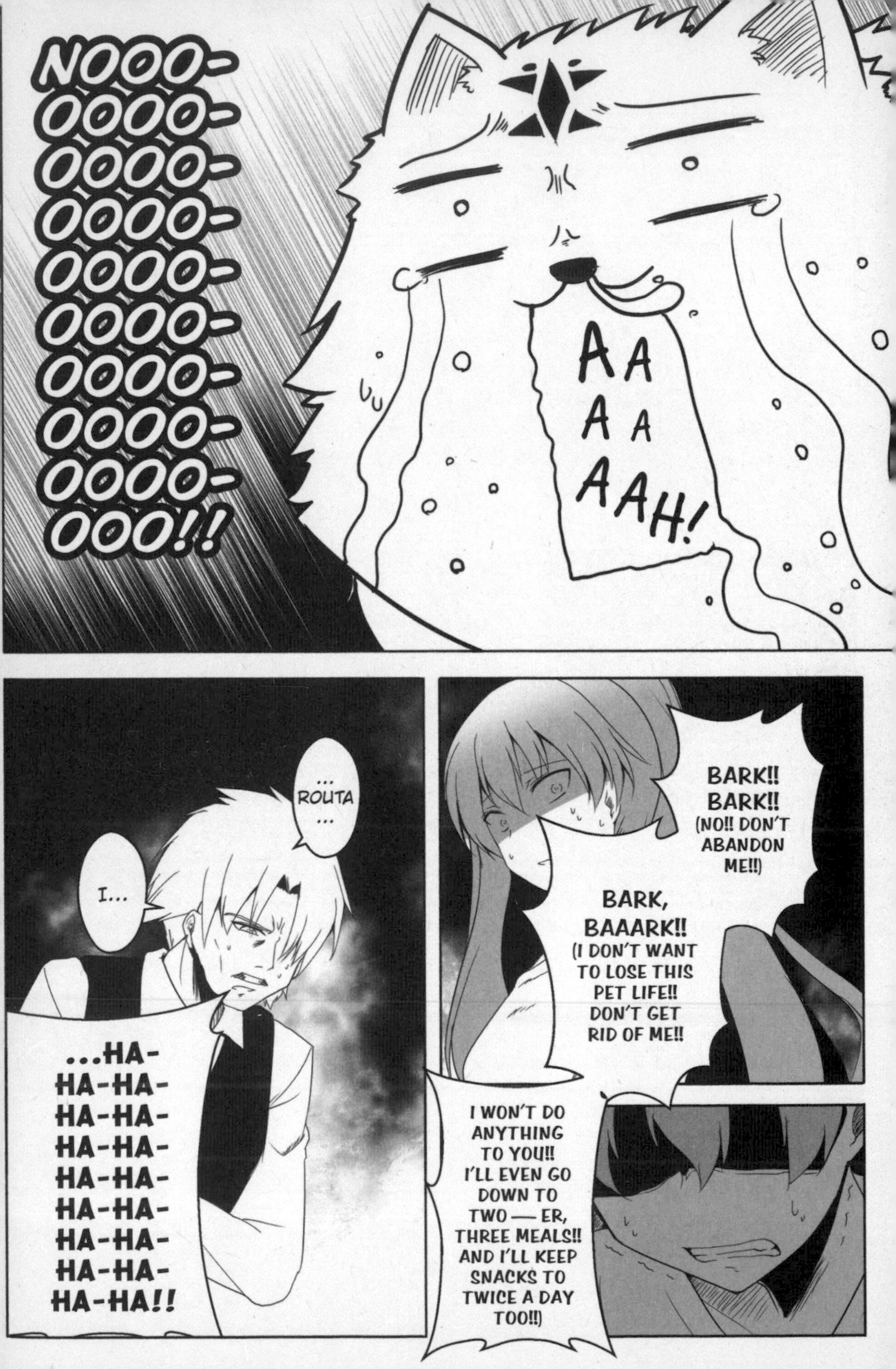
AAAAAAH!
NOOO-OOOO-OOOO-OOOO-OOOO-OOOO-OOOO-OOOO-OOOO-OOO!!
BARK!! BARK!! (NO!! DON'T ABANDON ME!!)
BARK, BAAARK!! (I DON'T WANT TO LOSE THIS PET LIFE!! DON'T GET RID OF ME!!
I WON'T DO ANYTHING TO YOU!! I'LL EVEN GO DOWN TO TWO — ER, THREE MEALS!! AND I'LL KEEP SNACKS TO TWICE A DAY TOO!!)
...ROUTA...
I...
...HA-HA-HA-HA-HA-HA-HA-HA-HA-HA-HA-HA-HA-HA-HA-HA-HA-HA!!

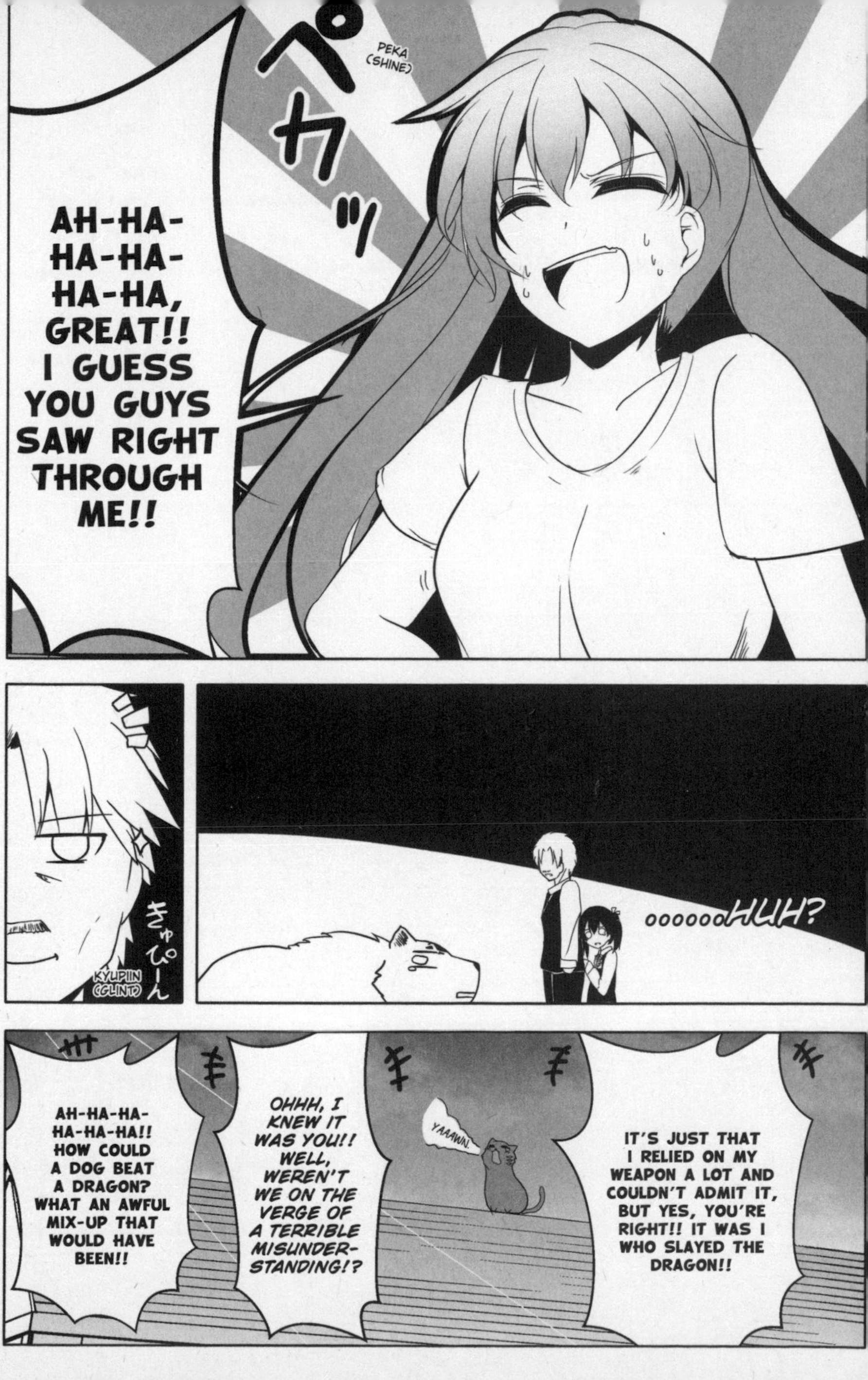
ペカッ
PEKA (SHINE)
AH-HA-HA-HA-HA-HA-HA, GREAT!! I GUESS YOU GUYS SAW RIGHT THROUGH ME!!
OOOOOOHUH?
きゅぴーん
KYUPIIN (GLINT)
IT'S JUST THAT I RELIED ON MY WEAPON A LOT AND COULDN'T ADMIT IT, BUT YES, YOU'RE RIGHT!! IT WAS I WHO SLAYED THE DRAGON!!
YAAAWN.
OHHH, I KNEW IT WAS YOU!! WELL, WEREN'T WE ON THE VERGE OF A TERRIBLE MISUNDERSTANDING!?
AH-HA-HA-HA-HA-HA!! HOW COULD A DOG BEAT A DRAGON? WHAT AN AWFUL MIX-UP THAT WOULD HAVE BEEN!!

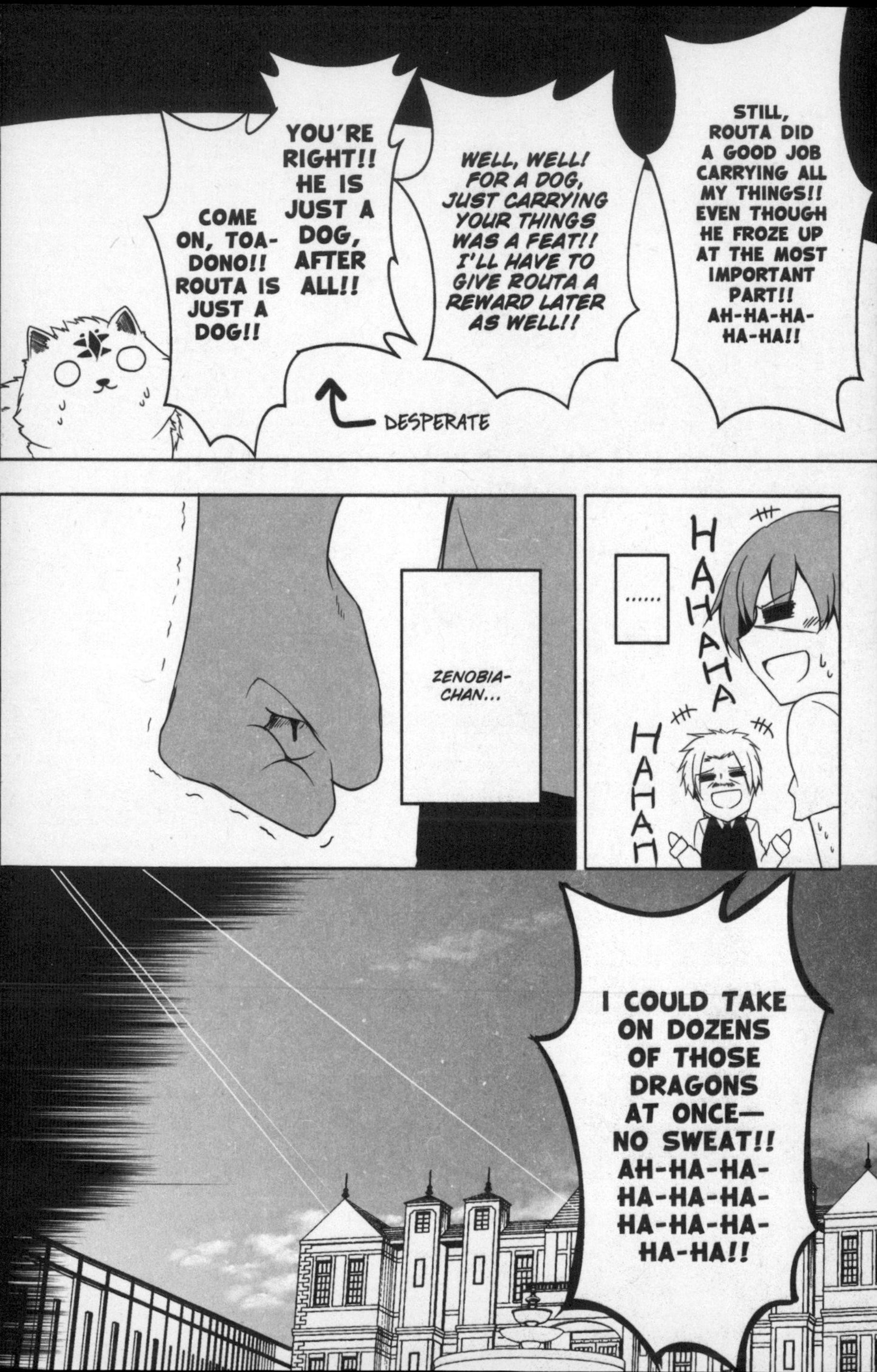
STILL, ROUTA DID A GOOD JOB CARRYING ALL MY THINGS!! EVEN THOUGH HE FROZE UP AT THE MOST IMPORTANT PART!! AH-HA-HA-HA-HA!!
WELL, WELL! FOR A DOG, JUST CARRYING YOUR THINGS WAS A FEAT!! I'LL HAVE TO GIVE ROUTA A REWARD LATER AS WELL!!
YOU'RE RIGHT!! HE IS JUST A DOG, AFTER ALL!!
COME ON, TOA-DONO!! ROUTA IS JUST A DOG!!
DESPERATE
......
HAHAHAHA
HAHAH
ZENOBIA-CHAN...
I COULD TAKE ON DOZENS OF THOSE DRAGONS AT ONCE—NO SWEAT!! AH-HA-HA-HA-HA-HA-HA-HA-HA-HA-HA!!

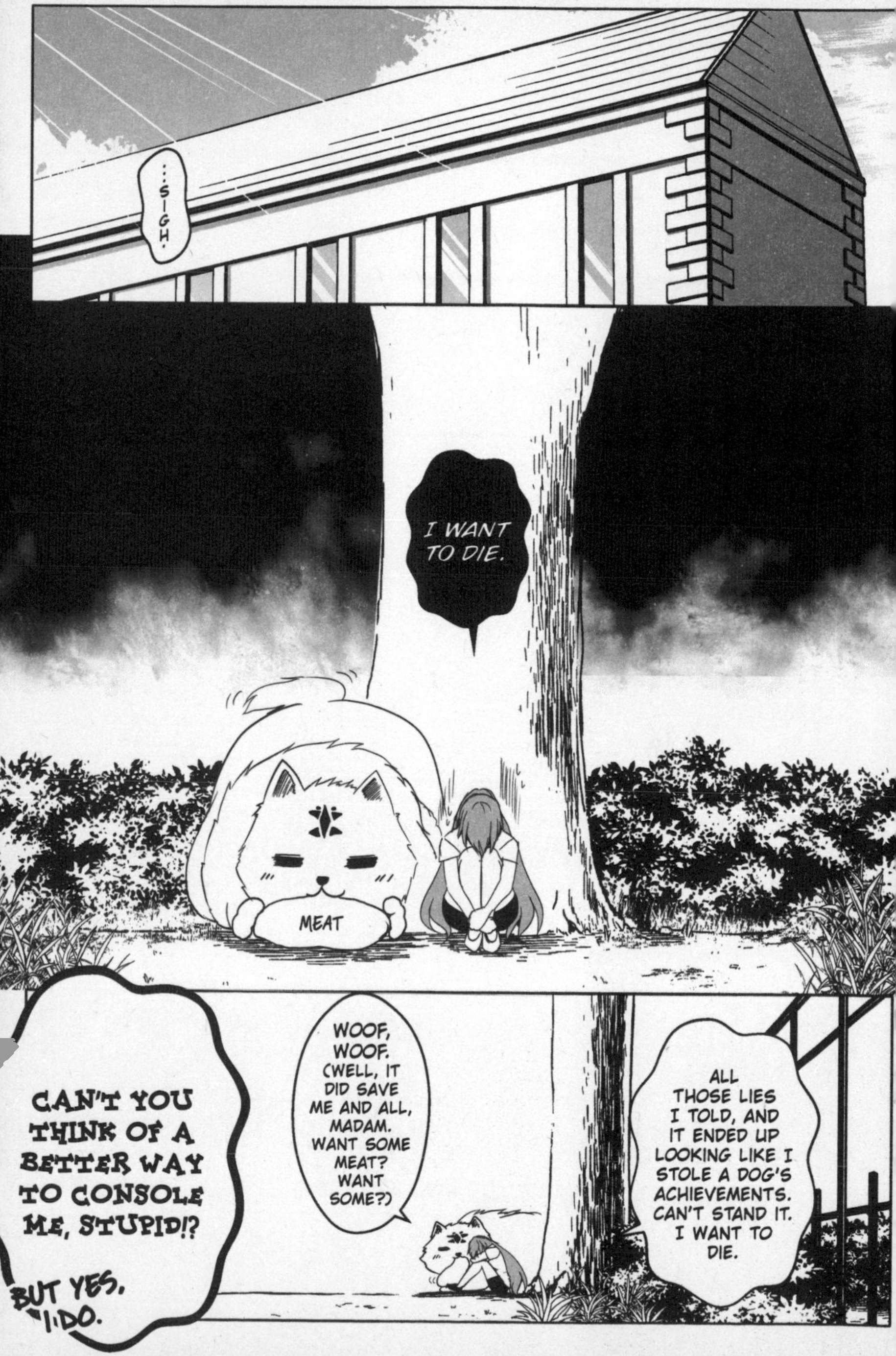
...SIGH.
I WANT TO DIE.
MEAT
ALL THOSE LIES I TOLD, AND IT ENDED UP LOOKING LIKE I STOLE A DOG'S ACHIEVEMENTS. CAN'T STAND IT. I WANT TO DIE.
WOOF, WOOF. (WELL, IT DID SAVE ME AND ALL, MADAM. WANT SOME MEAT? WANT SOME?)
CAN'T YOU THINK OF A BETTER WAY TO CONSOLE ME, STUPID!?
BUT YES. I DO.

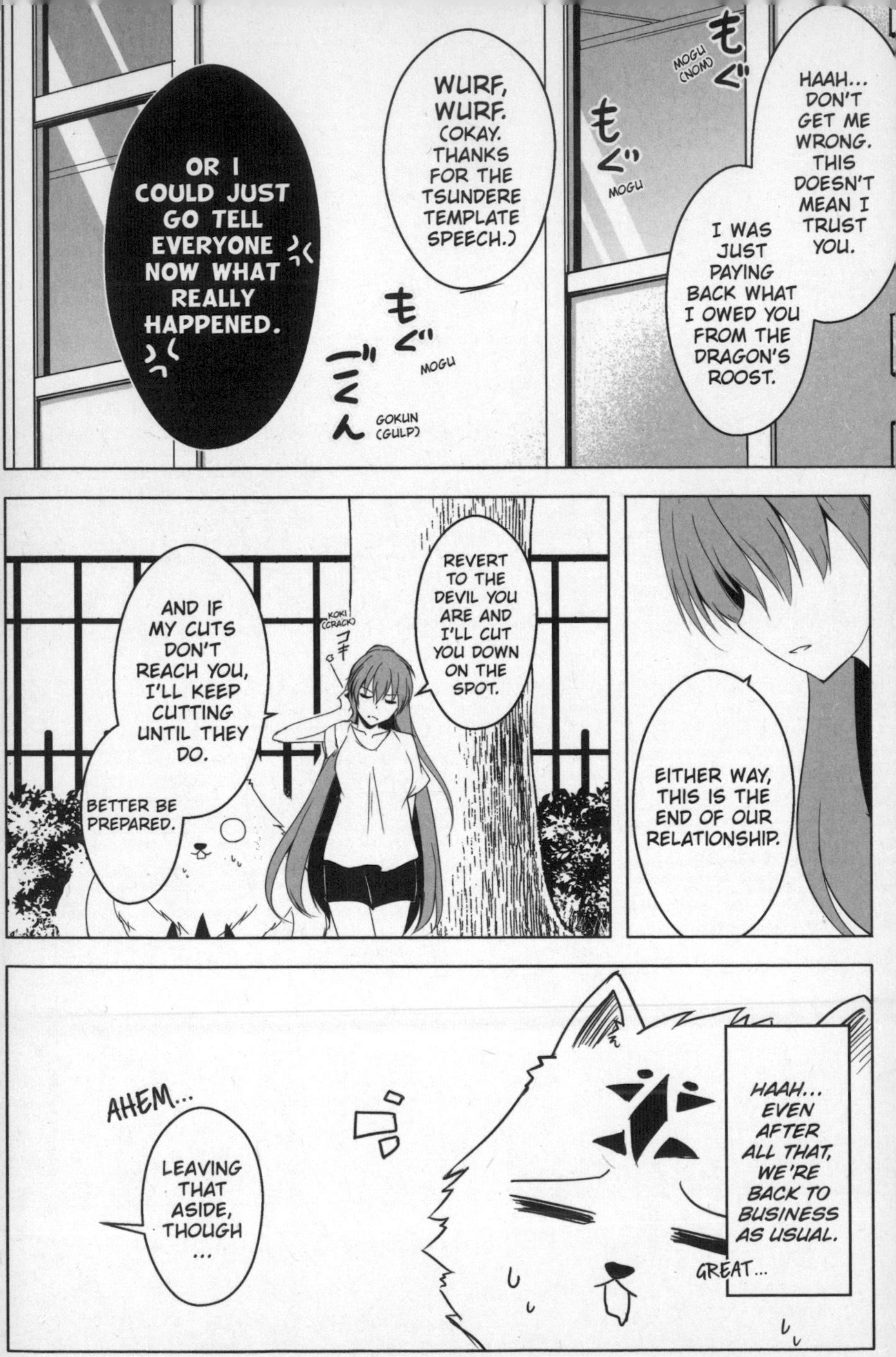
HAAH... DON'T GET ME WRONG. THIS DOESN'T MEAN I TRUST YOU.
I WAS JUST PAYING BACK WHAT I OWED YOU FROM THE DRAGON'S ROOST.
もぐ
MOGU (NOM)
もぐ
MOGU
WURF, WURF. (OKAY. THANKS FOR THE TSUNDERE TEMPLATE SPEECH.)
もぐ
MOGU
ごくん
GOKUN (GULP)
OR I COULD JUST GO TELL EVERYONE NOW WHAT REALLY HAPPENED.
EITHER WAY, THIS IS THE END OF OUR RELATIONSHIP.
REVERT TO THE DEVIL YOU ARE AND I'LL CUT YOU DOWN ON THE SPOT.
コキ
KOKI (CRACK)
AND IF MY CUTS DON'T REACH YOU, I'LL KEEP CUTTING UNTIL THEY DO.
BETTER BE PREPARED.
HAAH... EVEN AFTER ALL THAT, WE'RE BACK TO BUSINESS AS USUAL.
GREAT...
AHEM...
LEAVING THAT ASIDE, THOUGH...

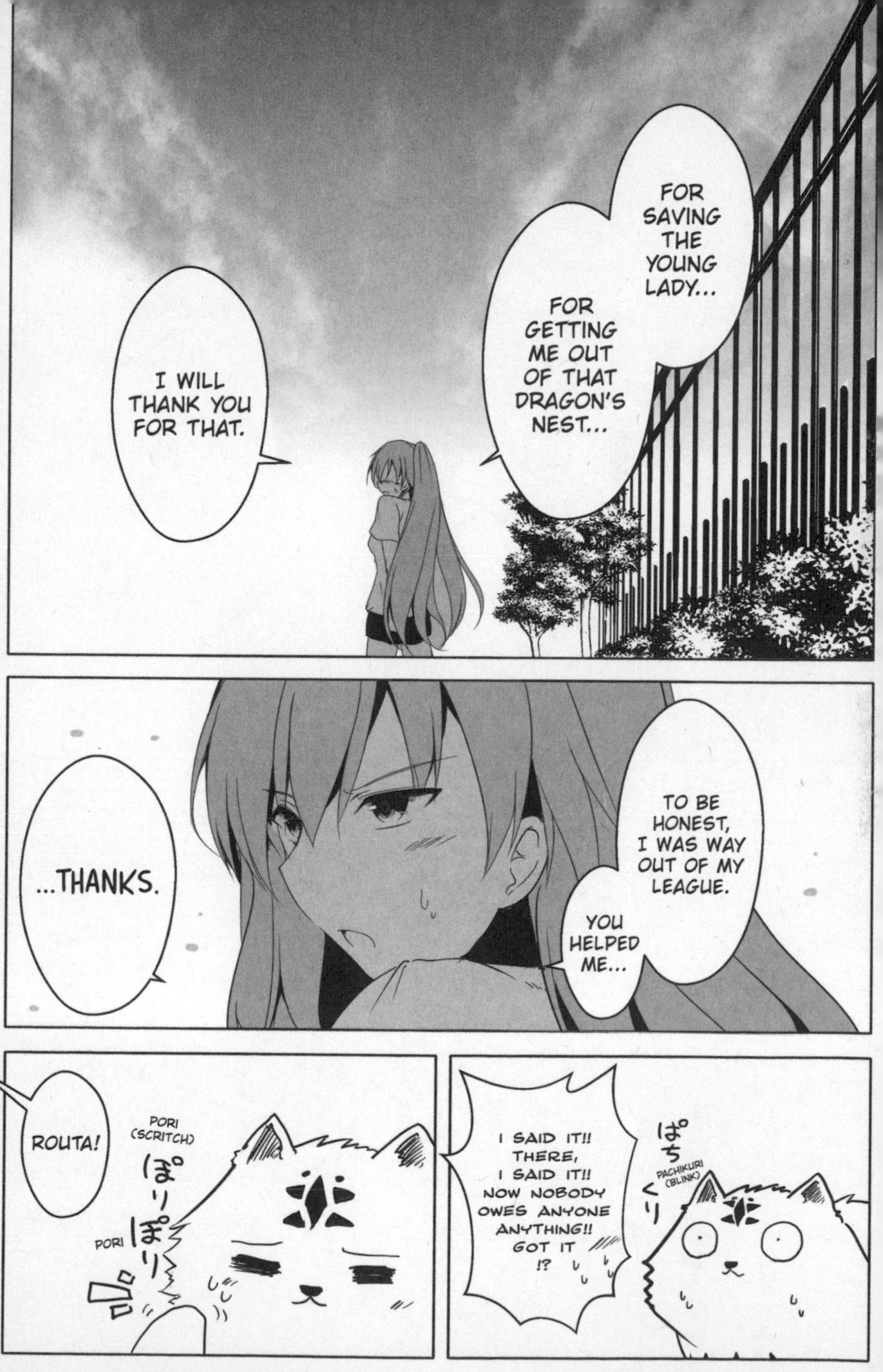
FOR SAVING THE YOUNG LADY...
FOR GETTING ME OUT OF THAT DRAGON'S NEST...
I WILL THANK YOU FOR THAT.
TO BE HONEST, I WAS WAY OUT OF MY LEAGUE.
YOU HELPED ME...
...THANKS.
ぱちくり
PACHIKURI (BLINK)
I SAID IT!! THERE, I SAID IT!! NOW NOBODY OWES ANYONE ANYTHING!! GOT IT !?
PORI (SCRITCH)
ぽりぽり
PORI
ROUTA!

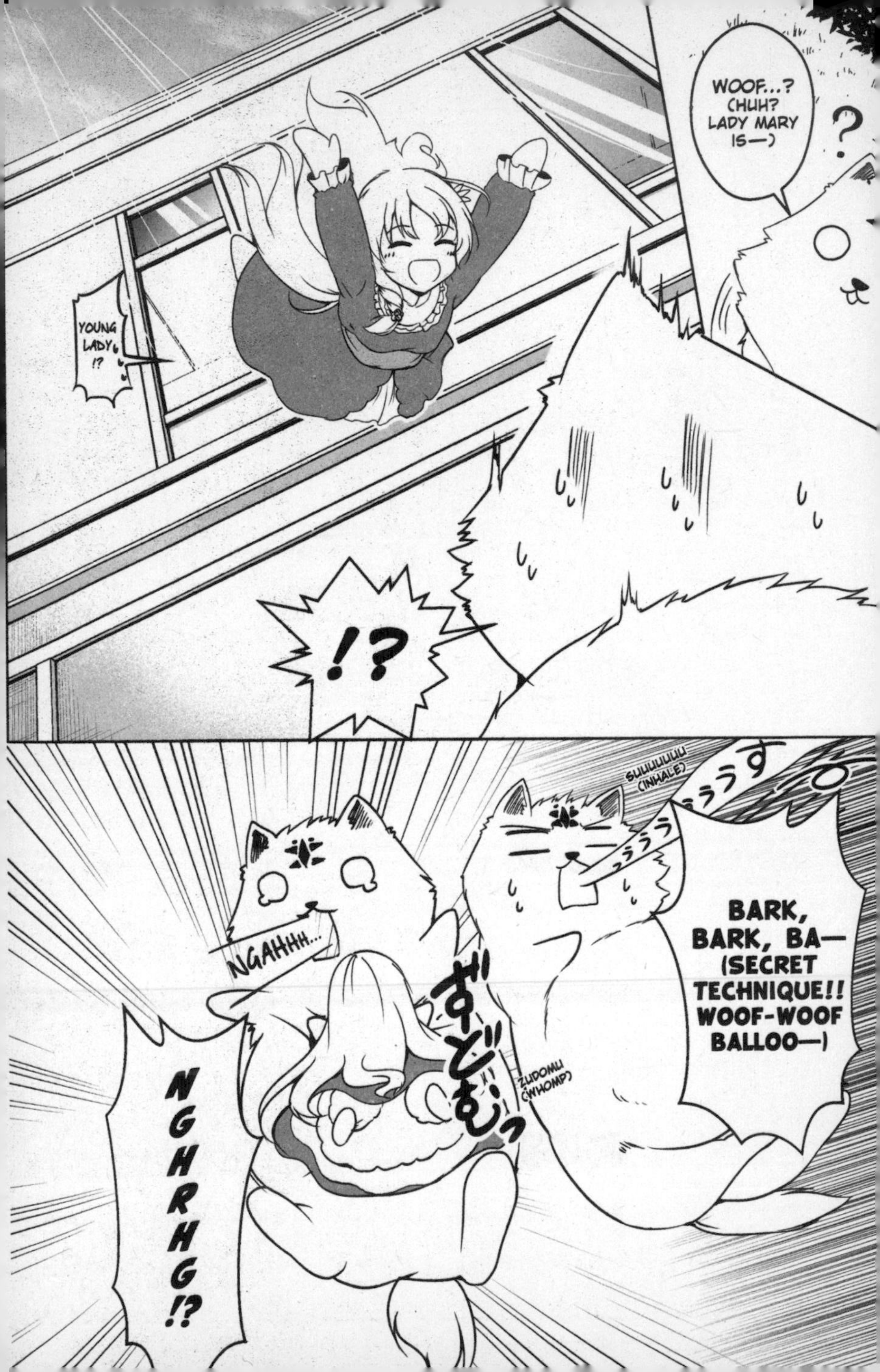

WOOF...? (HUH? LADY MARY IS—)
?
YOUNG LADY!?
!?
SUUUUUUU (INHALE)
BARK, BARK, BA— (SECRET TECHNIQUE!! WOOF-WOOF BALLOO—)
ずどむっ
ZUDOMU (WHOMP)
NGAHHH...
NGHRHG!?

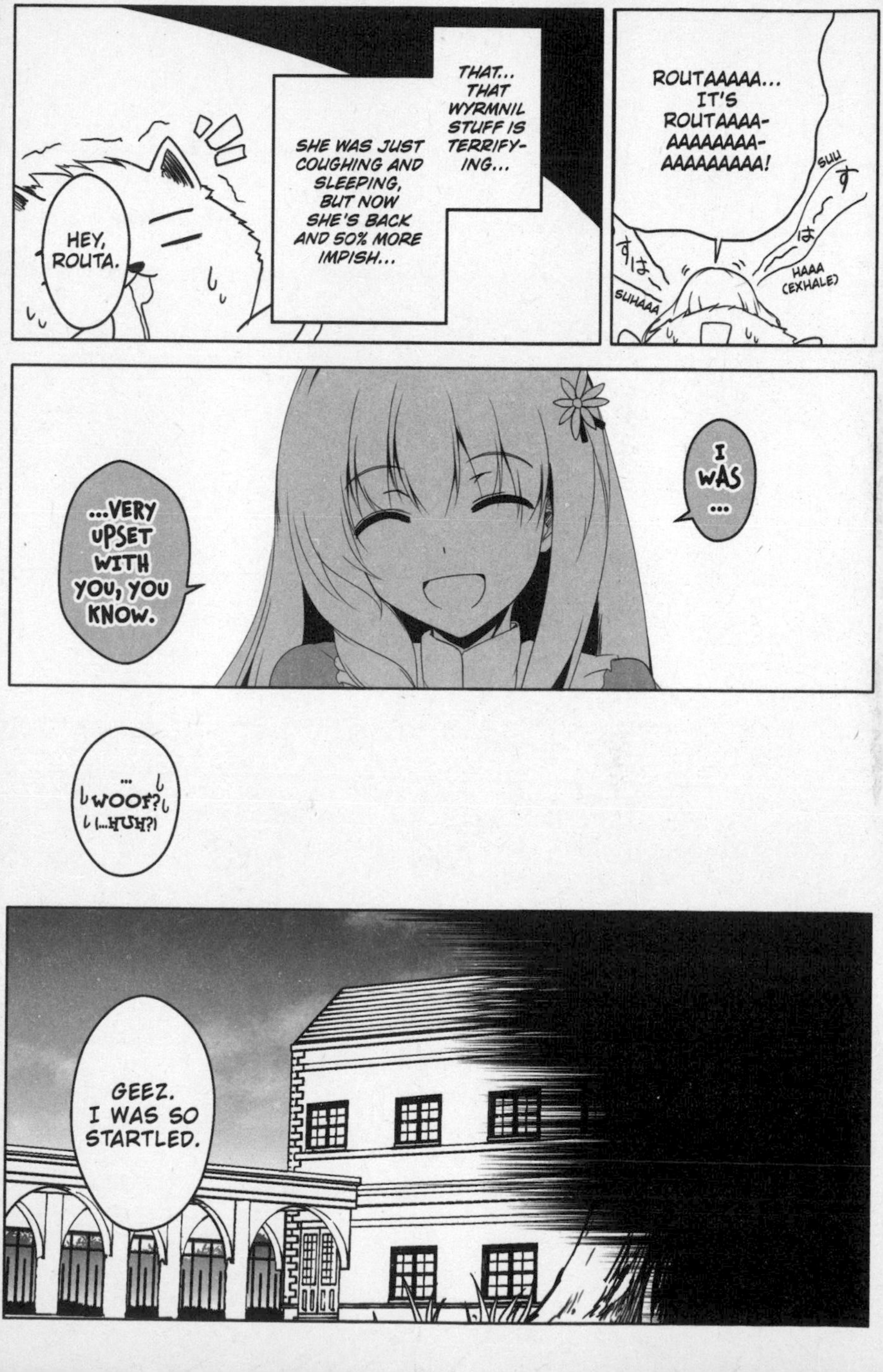
ROUTAAAAA... IT'S ROUTAAAA-AAAAAAAAA-AAAAAAAAAA!
すー SUU
は〜 HAAA (EXHALE)
すは SUHAAA
THAT... THAT WYRMNIL STUFF IS TERRIFY-ING...
SHE WAS JUST COUGHING AND SLEEPING, BUT NOW SHE'S BACK AND 50% MORE IMPISH...
HEY, ROUTA.
I WAS...
...VERY UPSET WITH YOU, YOU KNOW.
...WOOF?
(...HUH?)
GEEZ. I WAS SO STARTLED.

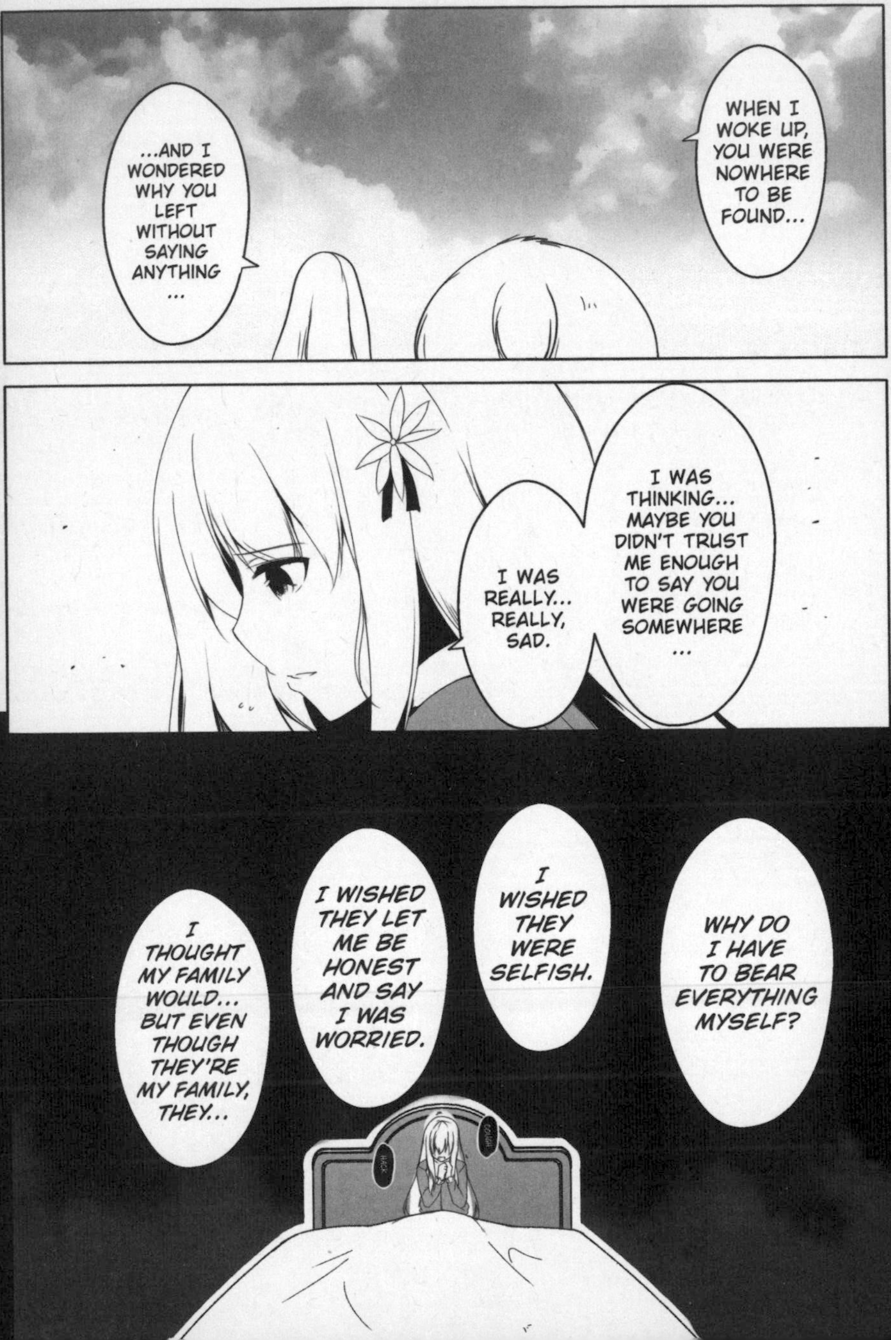
WHEN I WOKE UP, YOU WERE NOWHERE TO BE FOUND...
...AND I WONDERED WHY YOU LEFT WITHOUT SAYING ANYTHING...
I WAS THINKING... MAYBE YOU DIDN'T TRUST ME ENOUGH TO SAY YOU WERE GOING SOMEWHERE...
I WAS REALLY... REALLY, SAD.
WHY DO I HAVE TO BEAR EVERYTHING MYSELF?
I WISHED THEY WERE SELFISH.
I WISHED THEY LET ME BE HONEST AND SAY I WAS WORRIED.
I THOUGHT MY FAMILY WOULD... BUT EVEN THOUGH THEY'RE MY FAMILY, THEY...
COUGH
HACK

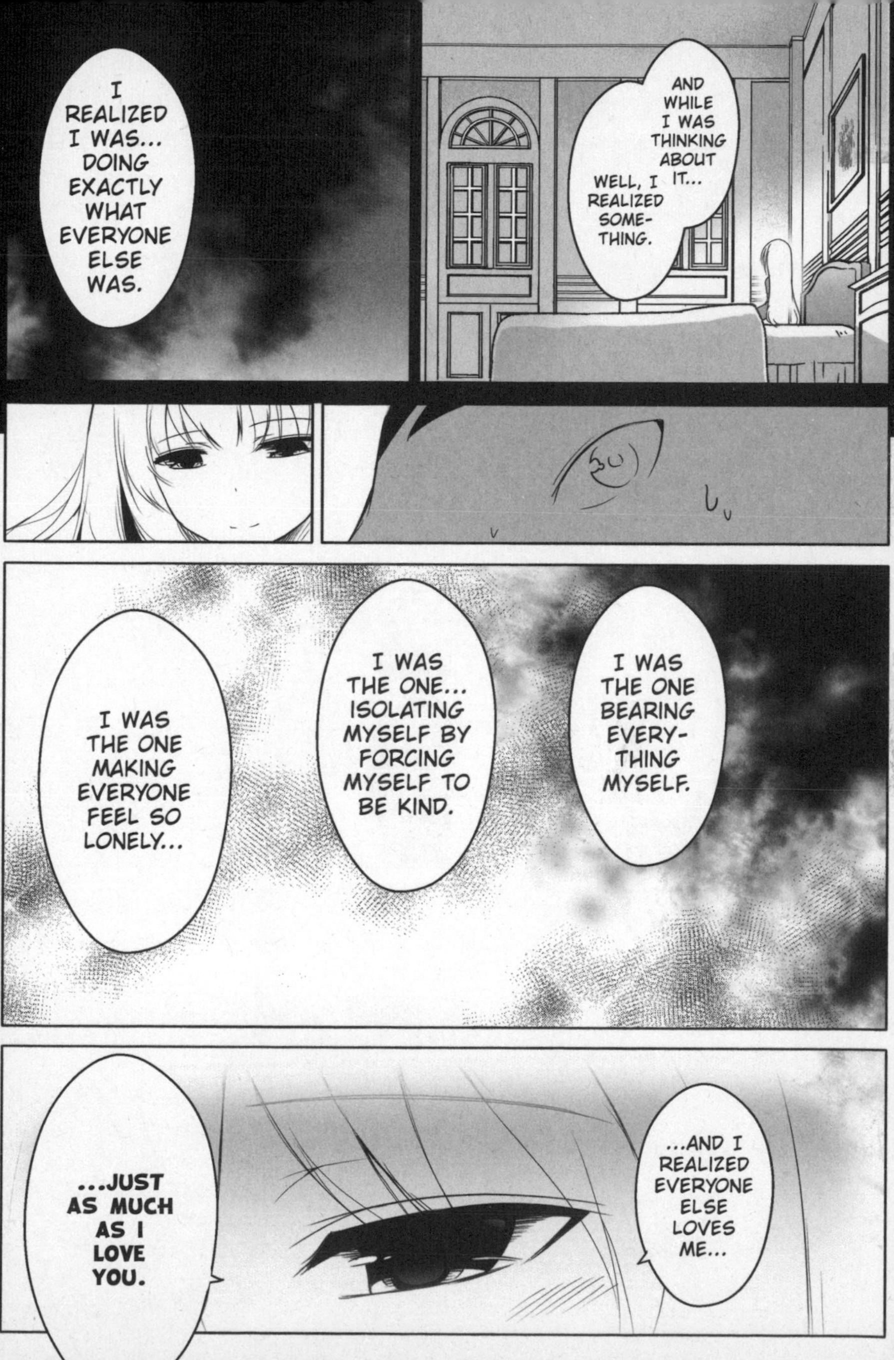
AND WHILE I WAS THINKING ABOUT IT...
WELL, I REALIZED SOME-THING.
I REALIZED I WAS... DOING EXACTLY WHAT EVERYONE ELSE WAS.
I WAS THE ONE BEARING EVERY-THING MYSELF.
I WAS THE ONE... ISOLATING MYSELF BY FORCING MYSELF TO BE KIND.
I WAS THE ONE MAKING EVERYONE FEEL SO LONELY...
...AND I REALIZED EVERYONE ELSE LOVES ME...
...JUST AS MUCH AS I LOVE YOU.

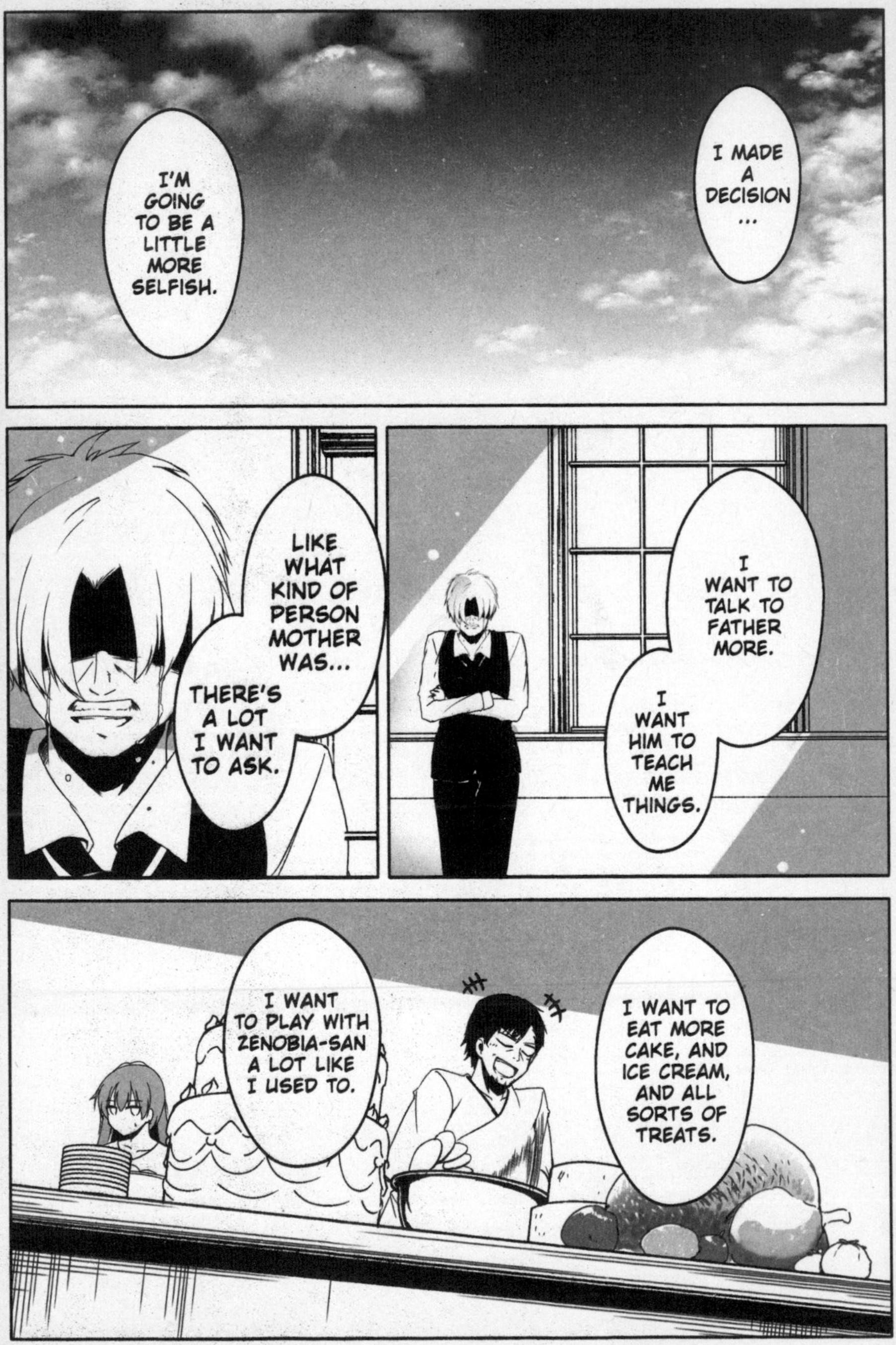
I MADE A DECISION ...
I'M GOING TO BE A LITTLE MORE SELFISH.
I WANT TO TALK TO FATHER MORE.
I WANT HIM TO TEACH ME THINGS.
LIKE WHAT KIND OF PERSON MOTHER WAS...
THERE'S A LOT I WANT TO ASK.
I WANT TO EAT MORE CAKE, AND ICE CREAM, AND ALL SORTS OF TREATS.
I WANT TO PLAY WITH ZENOBIA-SAN A LOT LIKE I USED TO.

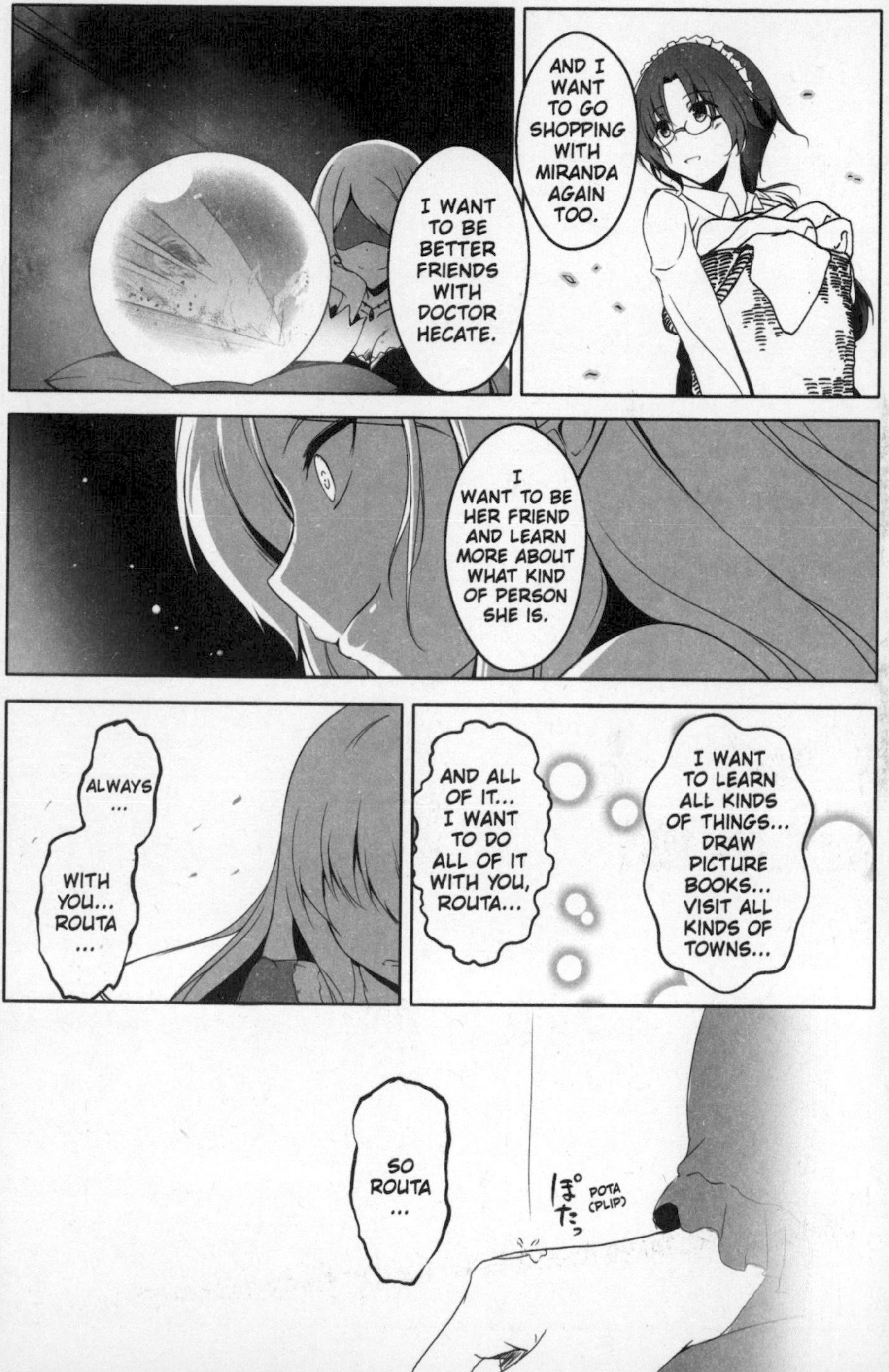
AND I WANT TO GO SHOPPING WITH MIRANDA AGAIN TOO.
I WANT TO BE BETTER FRIENDS WITH DOCTOR HECATE.
I WANT TO BE HER FRIEND AND LEARN MORE ABOUT WHAT KIND OF PERSON SHE IS.
I WANT TO LEARN ALL KINDS OF THINGS... DRAW PICTURE BOOKS... VISIT ALL KINDS OF TOWNS...
AND ALL OF IT... I WANT TO DO ALL OF IT WITH YOU, ROUTA...
ALWAYS...
WITH YOU... ROUTA...
ぽたっ
POTA (PLIP)
SO ROUTA...

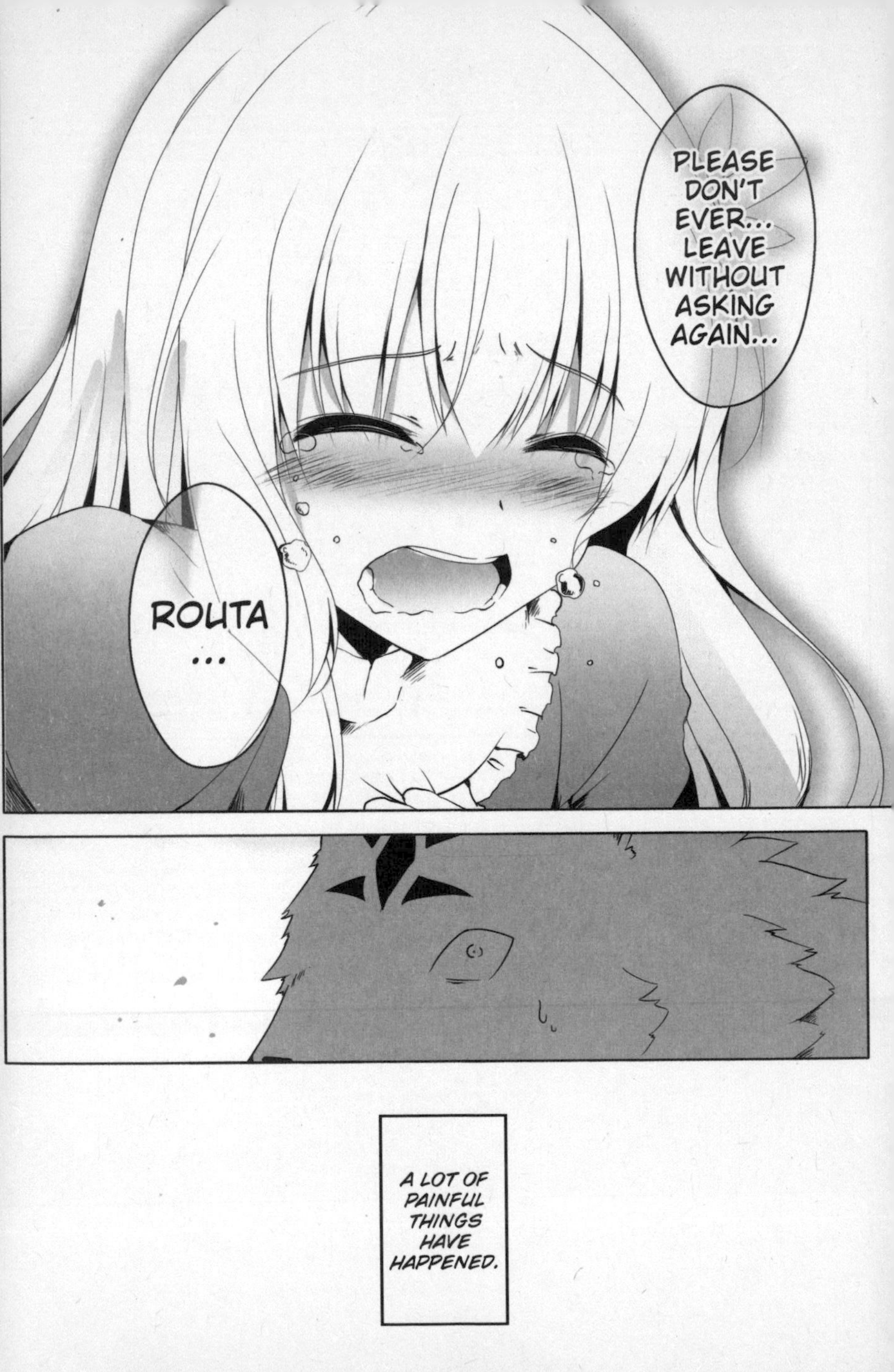
PLEASE DON'T EVER... LEAVE WITHOUT ASKING AGAIN...
ROUTA ...
A LOT OF PAINFUL THINGS HAVE HAPPENED.

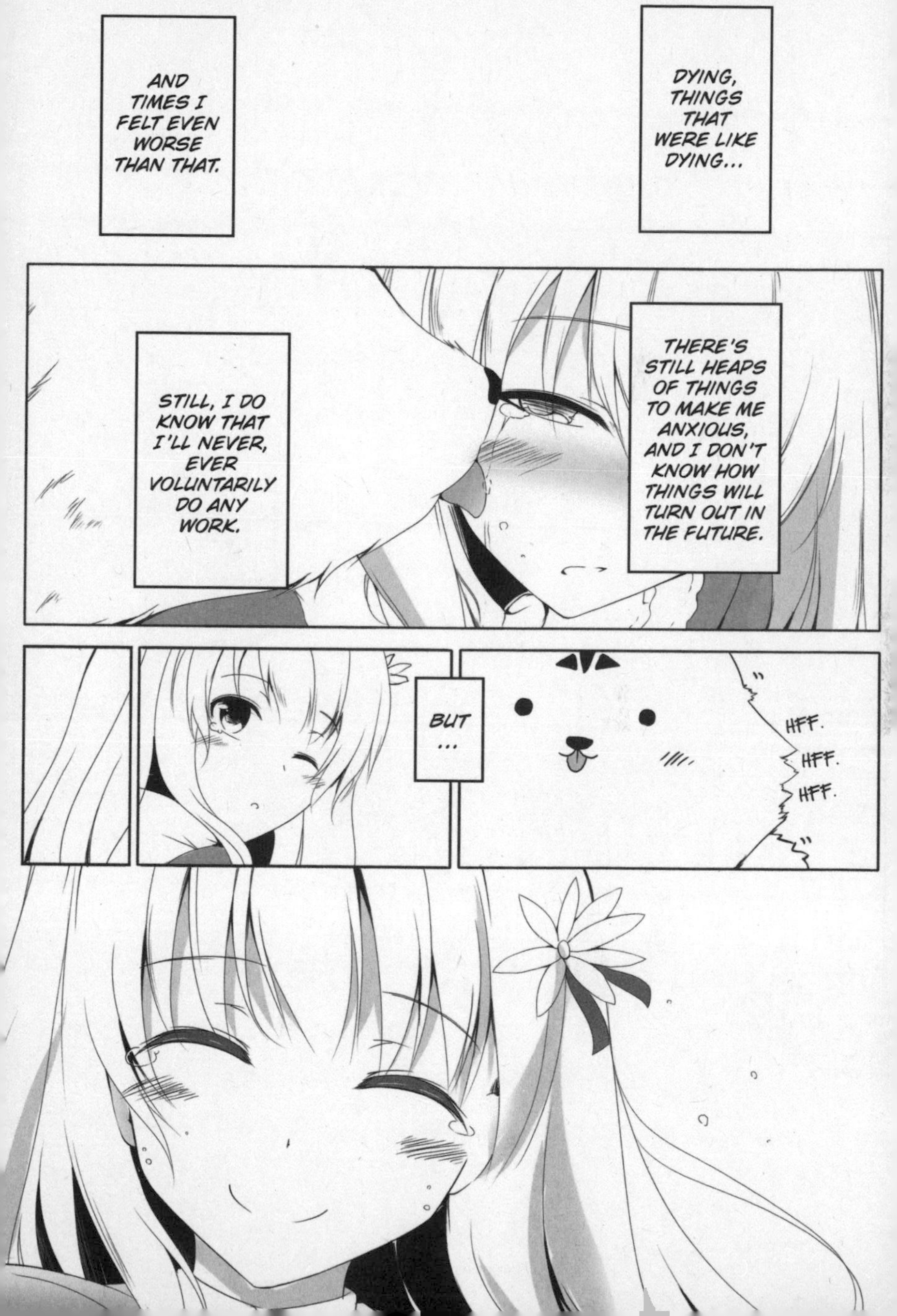
DYING, THINGS THAT WERE LIKE DYING...
AND TIMES I FELT EVEN WORSE THAN THAT.
THERE'S STILL HEAPS OF THINGS TO MAKE ME ANXIOUS, AND I DON'T KNOW HOW THINGS WILL TURN OUT IN THE FUTURE.
STILL, I DO KNOW THAT I'LL NEVER, EVER VOLUNTARILY DO ANY WORK.
HFF.
HFF.
HFF.
BUT ...

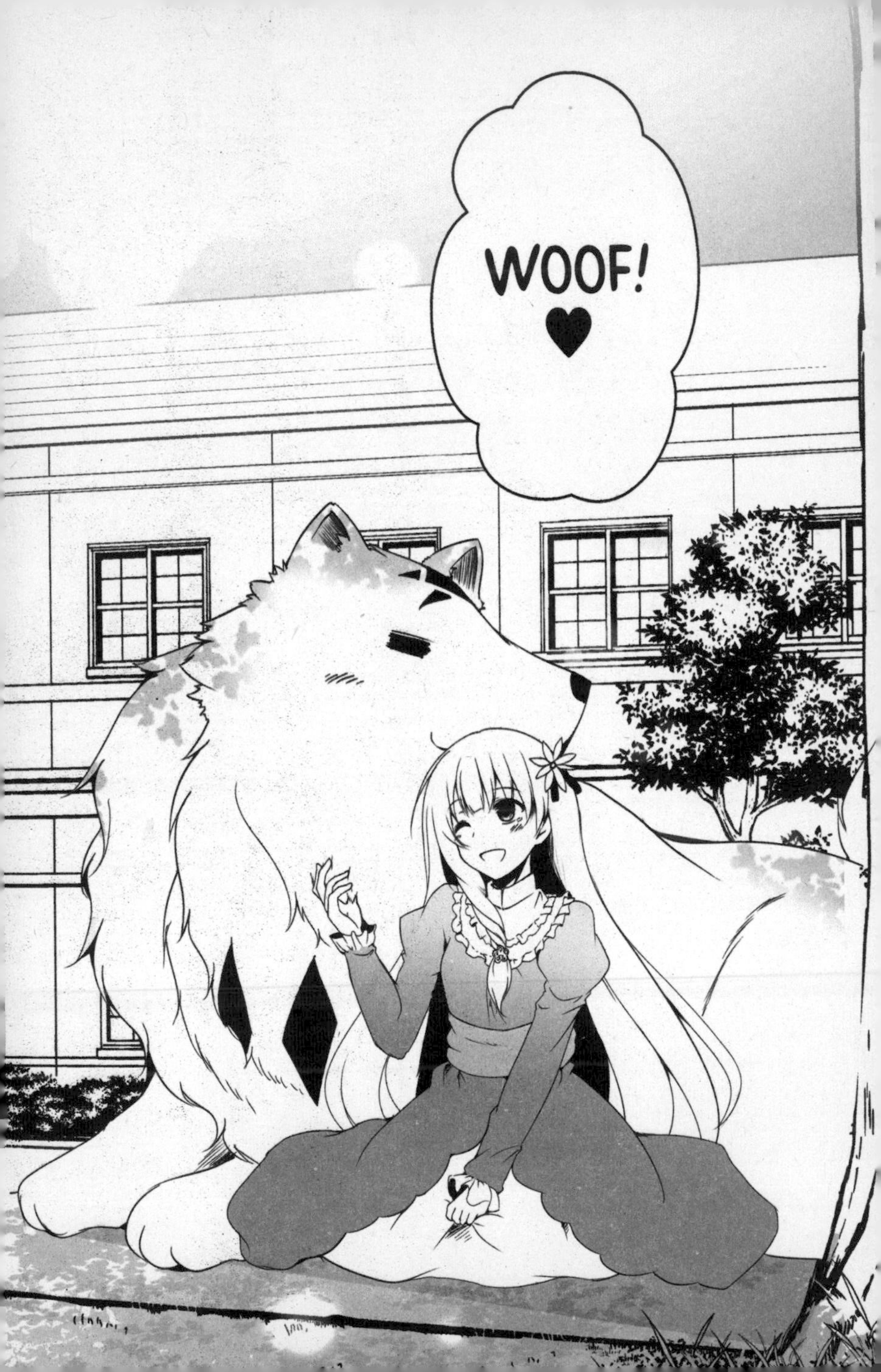
WOOF! ♥

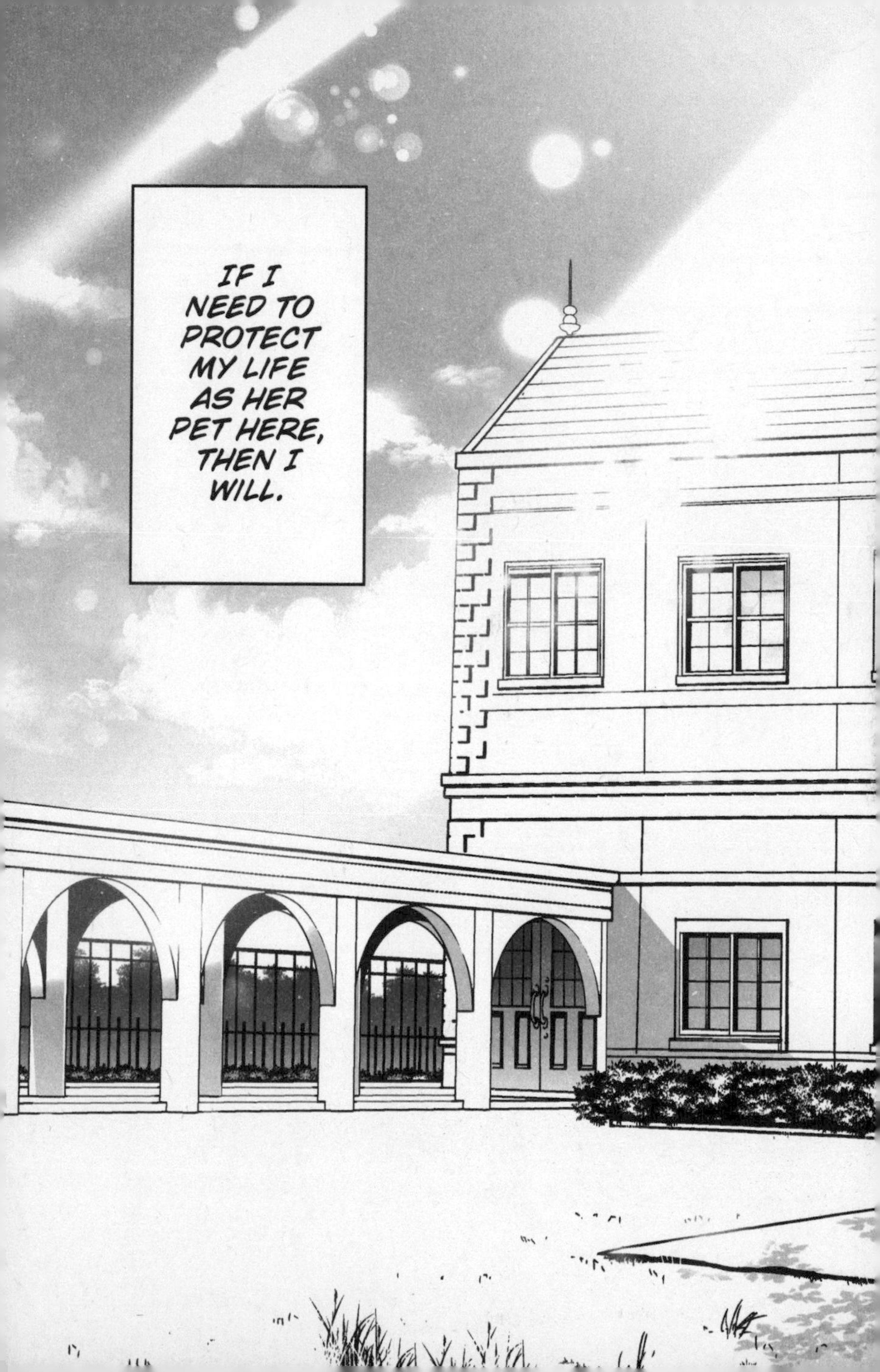
IF I NEED TO PROTECT MY LIFE AS HER PET HERE, THEN I WILL.

AFTERWORD (SCENES DEPICTING THE COMIC ADAPTATION PROCESS)

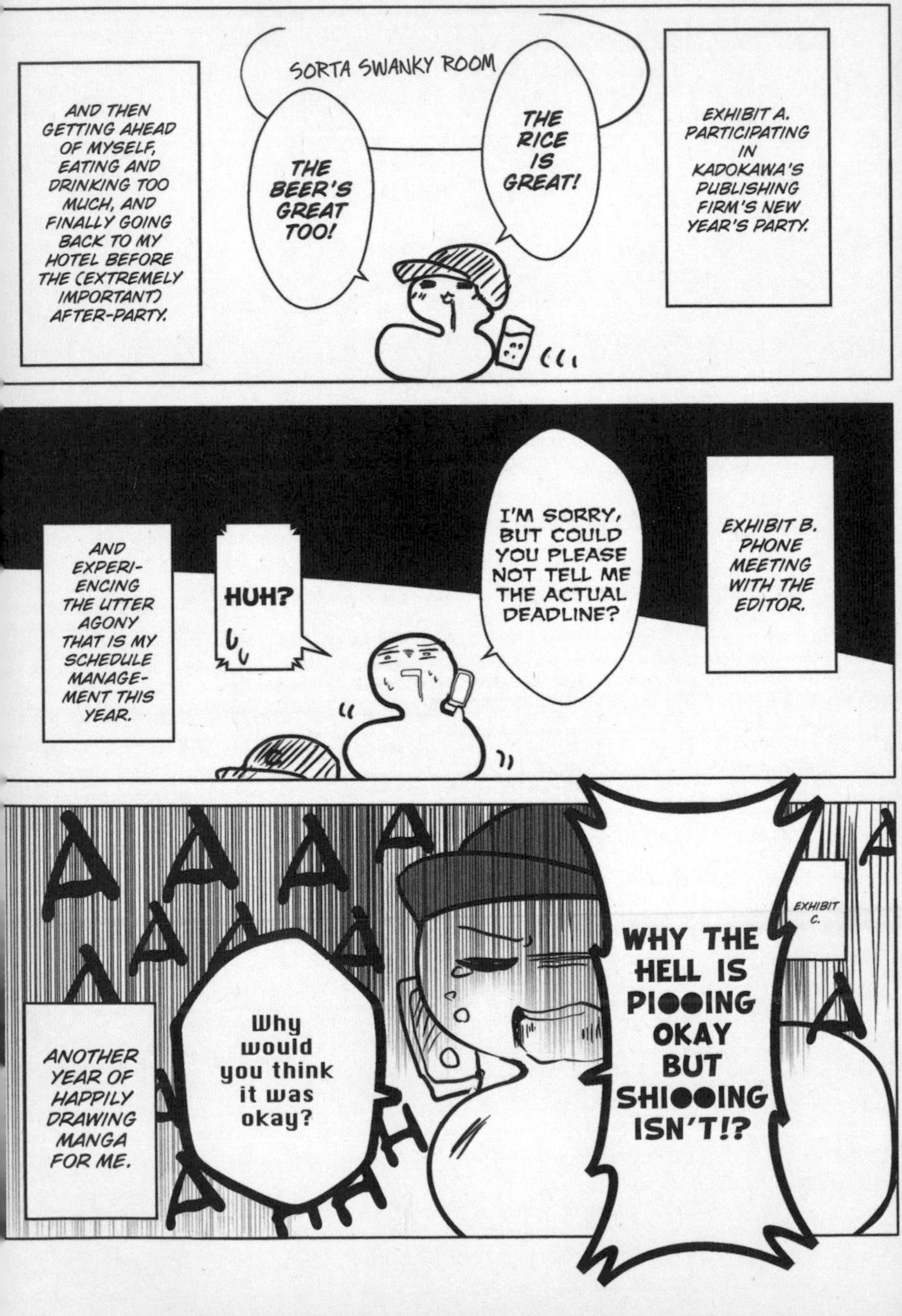
EXHIBIT A. PARTICIPATING IN KADOKAWA'S PUBLISHING FIRM'S NEW YEAR'S PARTY.
SORTA SWANKY ROOM
THE RICE IS GREAT!
THE BEER'S GREAT TOO!
AND THEN GETTING AHEAD OF MYSELF, EATING AND DRINKING TOO MUCH, AND FINALLY GOING BACK TO MY HOTEL BEFORE THE (EXTREMELY IMPORTANT) AFTER-PARTY.
EXHIBIT B. PHONE MEETING WITH THE EDITOR.
I'M SORRY, BUT COULD YOU PLEASE NOT TELL ME THE ACTUAL DEADLINE?
HUH?
AND EXPERIENCING THE UTTER AGONY THAT IS MY SCHEDULE MANAGEMENT THIS YEAR.
EXHIBIT C.
WHY THE HELL IS PI●●ING OKAY BUT SHI●●ING ISN'T!?
Why would you think it was okay?
ANOTHER YEAR OF HAPPILY DRAWING MANGA FOR ME.

Translation Notes

Page 9
The health bar and evolution dialogue box here are a nod to the **Pokémon** series of games.

Page 47–48
Routa is referencing Nobita from **Doraemon**, one of Japan's biggest media franchises. Nobita regularly asks Doraemon, a robot cat from the future, to help with his problems.

Page 52
A **rolling sobat** (sometimes "rolling savate") is a kind of jumping spin kick frequently used in Japanese professional wrestling.

Page 62
Instead of Garo being embarrassed by the phrase **"weenie up,"** in the Japanese edition, she's blushing over the word *chinchin*—which can mean both "begging" and "penis."

Pages 70–72
"What lies even further beyond speed" is a line from the motorcycle manga **Kaze Densetsu Bukkomi no Taku**. Routa's drifting skills, Eurobeat soundtrack, and T-shirt parodying a tofu shop are all shout-outs to the street-racing anime **Initial D**. **Plumber carts** refers to the Super Mario Kart video game franchise.

Page 73
"Souls weighed down by gravity" is a phrase taken from a speech by the character Char Aznable in the anime *Mobile Suit Zeta Gundam*. Similarly, the image of Routa seemingly entering Earth's atmosphere is reminiscent of similar scenes from throughout the Gundam franchise.

Page 78
"Che-Che-Kule" is a Ghanaian children's song. It has been adapted into other languages, including Japanese.

Pages 80–81
These two pages feature mutiple references to the anime **Heidi, Girl of the Alps**, which is based on the book *Heidi* by Johanna Spyri. The melted cheese on bread (first seen in Episode 2) is considered a kind of "only in anime" food, hence Routa's joy in getting to eat it for the first time. The character **Clara** is a wheelchair-bound girl who the main character Heidi befriends. In the final episode, after much hardship, Clara discovers she is able to stand on her own again.

Page 160
Tongue-terrorist in Japanese is *perorisuto*, a combination of *pero* ("licking") and "terrorist." The term has its origins in the fandom of *K-ON!* character Azusa Nakano.

Woof Woof Story

I TOLD YOU TO TURN ME INTO A *Pampered Pooch,* NOT FENRIR!

2

Koikuchi Kiki Inumajin Kochimo

Translation: Wesley O'Donnell ✦ Lettering: DK

WANWAN MONOGATARI ⸢KANEMOCHI NO INU NI SHITETOHAITTAGA, FENRIR NI SHIROTOHA ITTENE!⸥ Vol. 2
©Koikuchi Kiki 2019
©Inumajin, Kochimo 2019
First published in Japan in 2019 by KADOKAWA CORPORATION, Tokyo. English translation rights arranged with KADOKAWA CORPORATION, Tokyo through TUTTLE-MORI AGENCY, INC., Tokyo.

English translation © 2020 by Yen Press, LLC.

Yen Press
150 West 30th Street, 19th Floor
New York, NY 10001

Visit us at yenpress.com

facebook.com/yenpress
twitter.com/yenpress

yenpress.tumblr.com
instagram.com/yenpress

Yen Press is an imprint of Yen Press, LLC.
The Yen Press name and logo are trademarks of Yen Press, LLC.

The publisher is not responsible for websites (or their content) that are not owned by the publisher.

First Yen Press Edition: May 2020

Library of Congress Control Number: 2019939096

ISBNs: 978-1-9753-0856-8 (paperback)
978-1-9753-0857-5 (ebook)

10 9 8 7 6 5 4 3 2 1

WOR

Printed in the United States of America